romancing the workplace series

Bookish with Benefits

alia smith

BAL
KON
media

BOOKISH WITH BENEFITS

Published by Balkon Media

Paperback edition ISBN: 978-1-916970-09-0
Also available as an E-book

A CIP catalogue record for this title is available from the British Library.

Edited by Hanna Elizabeth

Cover Illustrations & Design: graphichouse123

www.balkon.media

ALSO BY ALIA SMITH

ROMANCING THE WORKPLACE SERIES

The Plus-One Clause (Novella)

Bookish with Benefits

The Maine Event

The Midnight Meet-Up

*To those who prove that sometimes the best matches are
the ones that don't quite match at all.*

ONE

Happily-ever-afters are my job. Believing in them is optional. Which is probably why I have no patience for romance that doesn't add up on the page.

I circle yet another clunky sentence, the margins already drowning in corrections. It's chapter ten—or maybe eleven—of *Lovers in the Cotswolds*, and I'm knee-deep in untangling a subplot that makes no sense. A grand romantic gesture from a character who's been emotionally unavailable throughout the entire book? Bold choice, Melissa. Bold. My red pen hovers over the printed pages spread across my desk, poised for another surgical strike.

"Show, don't tell..." I mutter, crossing out yet another paragraph where the heroine spends three sentences describing how much she *loves* sunsets. "We get it. The sky is orange. Move on."

There's a rhythm to this work, soothing in its predictability. Problems present themselves; I fix them. Stories have shapes, rules, and I wield omnipotent power over errant commas, adverb abuse, and obscure metaphors. Order and precision. Satisfaction hums in my chest when the prose sharpens under my hand.

I adjust my glasses—third time in five minutes—and reach for my coffee. It's cold. Of course, it's cold. I grimace but take a sip anyway, distracted by the next note forming in my head.

Melissa, I write in the margin on page ninety-five, *Consider introducing emotional stakes here instead of more interior monologue. Readers need something to root for.*

And then, just as I'm hitting my stride, my phone buzzes. Fiona's name lights up my screen like an ominous flare.

"Great." When Fiona chooses to call rather than email, it's never good news. Usually, those calls are accompanied by a tone that suggests I should already be halfway through solving whatever disaster she's about to unload.

"Hi Fiona," I answer, balancing the phone between my shoulder and ear as I keep writing corrections. Multitasking: the lifeblood of publishing.

"Drop what you're doing," Fiona snaps, crisp and efficient as ever. I can practically hear her manicured nails tapping against her desk. "Meeting room. Now."

"Is this about the new cover concept?" I ask, my eyes continue scrolling through the manuscript as though finishing this sentence might save me. "Because if it's another water-colour design, I swear—"

"Not the cover. Bigger problem. Just come."

"How big are we talking—" But the line goes dead. Classic Fiona.

I sigh, snapping my laptop shut and grabbing my notebook. Whatever this is, it's serious enough to interrupt my carefully curated workflow, which means it's bound to ruin my day. As I make my way toward the meeting room, I mentally brace myself. Fiona's emergencies usually involve bestselling authors with god complexes or last-minute requests that defy both logic and the laws of time.

When I push open the door, Fiona is already pacing, a clear sign she's in full battle mode. She doesn't even glance up as I enter.

"Rachel's pregnant," she announces, as though this is somehow my fault.

"Uh... congratulations to Rachel?"

"She's going on maternity leave. Effective immediately."

"Wow." I blink. "That's... sudden. Did she just find out?"

"Don't be ridiculous, Lara. She's known for months, just somehow failed to inform me. Apparently, she 'didn't want to make a fuss.'" Fiona's air quotes could slice through steel. "What she also didn't want to do was inform me that Rory Keane is *months* behind on his manuscript. Months."

Ah. There it is. The penny drops so hard that I feel the reverberation in my spine. Rory Keane. The golden boy of Scott & Drake Publishing House. Bestselling author. Romance darling. The incredibly good-looking, chronic deadline dodger... is behind schedule.

"Let me guess," I say dryly, sinking into a chair. "It's not just late; it's nowhere near finished."

"Nowhere," Fiona confirms, stopping mid-pace to level me with a look. Her eyes are fierce, unyielding. "Rachel's been covering for him, stringing me along with vague updates. And now she's gone, leaving us with a mess to clean up."

"Sounds like a Rachel problem," I offer, though I know exactly where this is heading.

"Not anymore. Now, it's your problem."

"Of course it is."

"Pre-orders for *Fully, Forever* are in the tens of thousands," Fiona announces, her voice slicing through the sterile air of the meeting room like a guillotine. "Marketing has been building buzz for months. The publication date is locked. We've got daytime TV spots arranged. This book *has* to launch on time, Lara."

I cross my arms and lean back in the too-stiff chair, trying not to bristle under her pinpoint gaze. The smell of burnt coffee lingers from some forgotten cup left nearby, mingling with the faint hint of Fiona's crisp, lemony perfume. She's immaculately composed as always, but there's a tension simmering beneath her usual poise. It's like staring at an elegant swan that you know could bite your finger off if provoked.

"Let me get this straight," I say slowly, keeping my tone level. "Rachel's been babysitting Rory Keane for months while he... what? Channels his inner tortured artist? And now, because she decided to ghost us in favour of baby booties and Lamaze classes, I'm supposed to swoop in and save the day?"

"Pretty much," Fiona replies without missing a beat. Her expression doesn't so much as twitch. Impressive.

"Right." I let out a slow breath. "And by 'save the day,' you mean, whip a manuscript into shape that I'm assuming is less novel and more... existential crisis in Word document form?"

"Exactly," she says, folding her hands neatly on the polished table. "You've got six weeks."

"Six weeks?" My voice pitches higher than I'd like, and I clear my throat, forcing it back down. "Fiona, six weeks isn't enough time to line edit one of Rory Keane's novels, let alone fix any major plot issues. Assuming he's even written anything at all."

"That's why I need you," she says, her tone unflinching, like this is all perfectly reasonable. Like she hasn't just handed me a flaming bag of chaos tied up with a neat little bow. "You're the best editor we have, Lara. You'll make it work."

"Flattery's cute, but it doesn't change the fact that this is impossible." I gesture vaguely toward the ceiling, where Rory Keane's name might as well be emblazoned in gold letters. "The man is infamously allergic to deadlines. And structure. And, dare I say, accountability."

"Which is why I trust *you* to handle him." Fiona leans forward, her eyes narrowing in that way that makes me feel like prey. "Think about what's at stake here. We're looking at a PR nightmare. Cancelled pre-orders. No point-of-sale displays. A very public black eye for Scott & Drake. Not to mention, our competitors would love nothing more than to see our star author crash and burn. Both Colleen and Emily have books coming out in the autumn, so we'd have to push back until next spring. Total nightmare."

"Sounds fun."

"Fun or not, it's happening," she snaps, her voice cracking like a whip. "Unless you'd prefer I hand this off to someone else? Perhaps someone who isn't as capable as you? Someone who might let this entire project implode and take our reputation along with it?"

Ah. There it is. The velvet threat wrapped in a compliment. Classic Fiona. I narrow my eyes at her, my mind racing. Somewhere deep down, I know she's right. The stakes are astronomical, and if anyone can pull this off, it's probably me. But that doesn't make the prospect any less maddening.

"Fine," I say tightly, sitting up straighter. "But let me be clear: Rory Keane and I are going to have words. Many of them. Possibly loud ones."

"Good." Fiona smiles faintly, the kind of smile that doesn't reach her eyes. "Quite frankly, he deserves a good kick in the bollocks. You'll be meeting with him here tomorrow."

Fiona's voice drones on, crisp and commanding, but I only catch every third word. Something about how publishing would be so much more enjoyable if we didn't have to deal with authors. My focus keeps snagging on the edge of the table where my fingers tap against the polished wood in a nervous staccato. I force them to stop, curling my hand into a fist instead. Professional. Composed. That's who I'm supposed to be right now.

"Are you even listening, Lara?" Fiona's tone snaps me back into the room like a rubber band against bare skin.

"Of course," I reply, straightening in my chair and adjusting my glasses with one deliberate finger. "Save Rory Keane. Save the book. Save Scott & Drake from public humiliation. Did I miss anything?"

"Yes, the part where you stop acting like this is optional." She levels me with that laser-focused stare, and I reluctantly nod my acceptance.

My stomach twists, not at her words but at what they imply. Rory Keane. The *Rory Keane*. The golden boy of romance, whose last eight books have made our company millions, who charms interviewers and readers alike with that easy grin of his, as if he's never known a day of struggle in his enviable life. Charming, talented, unreliable. A trifecta of everything I avoid in both authors and human beings.

As I leave the room, I feel a strange mix of dread and determination settling over me. This is going to be a disaster. A disaster I'm somehow responsible for averting. But if anyone can handle Rory Keane and his unfinished masterpiece, it's me. Probably.

TWO

I have to re-read one of Rory Keane's sentences three times just to make sure they are indeed the words that are written on the page; a line so saccharine it makes my teeth ache.

"'Love poured from his soul like sunlight spilling through an open window.'" I read the line aloud under my breath, and if sarcasm had a tone-setting, I'd just nailed it. My face twists involuntarily—half grimace, half smirk. Sunlight spilling? His soul? I scribble a note in the margin: *Overwrought. Too abstract. Where is the emotional anchor?*

My fingers drum faster now, glancing at the clock for what must be the third time in five minutes. Late. Of course, he's late. Rory Keane, *The Sunday Times* #1 bestselling darling and literary sensation, can't possibly be expected to arrive on schedule like the rest of us mere mortals. No, punctuality would probably clash with his carefully cultivated image of effortless brilliance.

I lean back, crossing my arms, and try not to picture him breezing in here with that trademark grin—the one that sells millions of paperbacks, breaks thousands of hearts, and somehow manages to say both *Trust me* and *Good luck figuring me out.* It's infuriating how someone can look so put-together on his back cover author photo, and yet write sentences like *Her love was a lighthouse guiding his ship-wrecked heart.*

Another note: The nautical metaphors need to stop.

Just as I'm debating whether I have time to pour another coffee before he decides to grace me with his presence, the door creaks open. And there he is. The man of the hour, in all his casually dishevelled glory, sauntering into the room as if he owns, not just this meeting, but time itself.

"Hi, Rory. I'm Lara Yates. I'll be taking over from Rachel." I offer a hand and he shakes it.

"Afternoon," he says, his voice warm and unhurried, like we're old friends catching up over lunch rather than two professionals with a looming deadline. His dark hair is mussed, as though he's spent the morning running his hands through it in deep creative thought—or maybe he just rolled out of bed. The sleeves of his creased white shirt are shoved up to his elbows, revealing forearms that no doubt inspire fanfiction somewhere, and his jeans are just this side of inappropriate for a business meeting.

"Nice of you to join me," I reply, my tone clipped. I don't bother masking the irritation in my voice; he doesn't deserve that courtesy.

He flashes me a wide, unapologetic smile, one dimple appearing like punctuation at the end of his charm offensive.

"Wouldn't miss it," he says, dropping into the chair across from me with a lazy grace that makes me want to roll my eyes so hard they might never come back down. His bag slouches onto the floor, the very picture of carelessness.

I glance at the manuscript in front of me, then back at him. The contrast between us couldn't be starker. My jacket is immaculate, my notes colour-coded and neatly stacked. Rory looks like he's wandered in from some bohemian artist loft, where he's just finished a spirited debate about the meaning of life over cigars and cognac.

"Let's get started," I say crisply, ignoring the way his grin deepens, as though he finds my no-nonsense demeanour endlessly entertaining. God help me, I already regret agreeing to this meeting.

"Your heroine, Sophie," I begin, flipping to the first flagged page in the manuscript, "is about as emotionally available as a plank of wood." I tap a manicured nail on the edge of the table for emphasis. My voice is flat, my words precise, and I don't so much as glance up at Rory. Eye contact feels like conceding ground, and I'm not in a generous mood today.

Across from me, I can feel him stretch out in his chair, every movement deliberate, unhurried. When I finally do look up, the corner of his mouth quirks, an expression that screams *amused, not alarmed.*

"Go on," he says, his tone light, inviting even. Like I'm telling some engaging yarn over drinks and not systematically dismantling his life's work.

"Right," I snap, flipping to another tabbed section with the precision of someone tearing through a legal brief. "This scene here? Page fifty-eight? Where they're supposed to be connecting over their shared childhood trauma but instead just... flirt awkwardly? It doesn't work. You've got dialogue standing in for substance, and it's not even good dialogue. A lot of it reads like filler, or notes to yourself that you meant to replace later."

"Filler?" he repeats, drawing out the word like it's a new flavour of ice cream he's sampling. The grin widens into something toothier, and I swear it takes everything in me not to hurl the manuscript across the table. "Interesting choice of critique."

"Is it?" I arch a brow, refusing to let him bait me. "Because what I'm seeing here are two characters who are presumably falling in love but sound more like they're reading cue cards for a health and safety in the workplace video."

His forefinger brushes the faint stubble shadowing his jawline, a casual gesture that makes it clear he's not taking any of this seriously.

"I'll admit, that's a new one. Do I get points for originality?"

"Do you want points, or do you want a functional manuscript?"

"Why not both?" he counters smoothly, leaning forward, resting his elbows on the table like we're conspirators in some grand scheme rather than editor and client locked in battle. His eyes crinkle slightly at the corners, betraying genuine amusement. "I mean, isn't that the dream?"

"Not mine," I fire back. "My dream involves authors turning in manuscripts that don't require me to perform emergency surgery on every single chapter."

"Ah, right, and here I thought we were doing some kind of creative tango. You know, pushing artistic boundaries together, making magic happen."

"Magic doesn't happen when your characters spend seventy percent of their time bickering about pizza toppings."

"Hey, now just a minute," he interjects, raising a finger as if I've crossed some sacred line. "That was a metaphorical argument about compromise."

"Sure," I say, "and metaphors are great when they actually land. Yours? Crash and burn."

His grin doesn't falter, but I catch the faintest flicker of something else beneath it. If I didn't know better, I'd think I'd managed to land a blow. But then he shifts in his seat, rolling his shoulders like he's shaking off the weight of the moment, and the smirk returns in full force.

"Remind me to never invite you to my birthday party," he

quips, his voice laced with mock injury. "You'd probably critique the cake."

"Only if it's half-baked," I reply without missing a beat. "Page one-eighty-seven. Oliver confesses his love during a... drumroll please... a car chase. A *car chase*, Rory. Because nothing says 'soulmate' like dodging articulated lorries on the motorway."

"High stakes," he offers, shrugging one shoulder as if this is some kind of brilliant defence. "Adrenaline. Passion. Tyres squealing—it's all very cinematic."

"Sure, if you're trying to write *Fast & Furious: Valentine Edition*," I snap, flipping the page with more force than necessary. My voice starts to rise, but I rein it in, aiming for cool and professional. Failing spectacularly. "But romance? Real romance? It's about connection. Vulnerability. Not... horsepower."

"Don't forget the nitrous oxide," he says, his grin widening as though he knows exactly how much he's getting under my skin.

"Rory." My hands flatten against the desk, palms pressing hard enough that I can feel the grain of the wood biting into my skin. "Some parts of this book are truly beautiful. The descriptive prose is assured, the sense of place is outstanding. Chapter four made me cry. I'm there with them on the rolling hills, tasting the same air, hoping that Oliver will just take her hand in his."

"But?" He cocks his head.

"But... most of the dialogue is shockingly bad. Corny, cheap puns, it feels lazy and I *know* you can do better. You've written entire chapters where your characters are literally running from explosions. How is the reader supposed to believe they're falling in love when they don't spend five consecutive minutes actually talking to each other?"

"Talking isn't their love language," he counters. "They

communicate through action. And dodging shrapnel together builds trust. That's science."

"No, Rory. Science is me keeping my blood pressure below stroke levels every time I read another one of these implausible, over-the-top scenes. Look at this—" I jab at the page again, its edges crinkling under my nail. "The big romantic moment takes place while they're defusing a bomb. A literal bomb. What even *is* this?"

"Symbolic," he says smoothly, tilting his head. "Love is the ultimate ticking time bomb, after all."

"That is not symbolic," I shoot back, glaring at him. "That is you watching too many action movies and trying to pass it off as emotional depth."

"Would you rather I have them fall in love over coffee dates and awkward silences, then?" His tone is breezy, teasing, but there's an edge to it now—a faint ripple beneath the calm surface. "Because that's been done to death. I'm innovating here, Lara. Breaking the mould."

"You're breaking something, alright," I reply, "And it's not the mould. It's my will to live."

He laughs, loud and unrestrained, and despite myself, I feel a prickle of something dangerously close to amusement. Damn him. Damn that stupid, boyish laugh that somehow softens the harsh angles of his arrogance.

"Come on," he says, his voice dropping into something warmer, coaxing. "Don't tell me you didn't at least enjoy the scene in the burning warehouse. That was gold."

"If by gold, you mean completely ridiculous, then sure. Gold."

"Ridiculous can be charming, look at us."

"Us?" I repeat, and the word feels absurd on my tongue. Like trying on a pair of shoes two sizes too small. "There is no 'us,' Rory. There's you, me, and this manuscript that's nowhere near ready for publication. And I think you know it. You must do."

"Harsh," he says, clutching his chest in mock pain. "But I think there's a little chemistry here. Don't you?"

"The only chemistry I feel right now is the urge to throw hydrochloric acid on this excuse for a plot."

"See?" He grins again, wide and maddening. "That fire. That passion. It's inspiring."

"Do *not* use me as inspiration," I warn him, pointing a finger in his direction. "Whatever this is"—I gesture vaguely between us, mostly out of frustration—"it stays out of your book."

"Noted," he says, though the glint in his eyes tells me he's lying through his teeth. "But for the record, I think we'd make a great subplot."

"Then it's a good thing this is strictly a professional relationship," I say, my voice cutting like a knife. Still, there's heat crawling up my neck, and I hate that he can see it. Worse, I hate that he seems to be enjoying it.

"Strictly professional," he repeats, his tone light and teasing.

"Rory," I say, my patience thinning. "You can't just smirk your way out of your publication date. This—" I jab my finger at the manuscript spread between us. "This isn't working, it bears absolutely no resemblance to your previous books. It's... not good enough."

His grin falters, just a flicker, but I catch it. His fingers stop drumming against the armrest of his chair, and for the first time since he sauntered in late with that devil-may-care charm, he looks... still. Like the weight of my words has landed somewhere soft.

"Not good enough?" he repeats, quieter than I expected. There's something raw in his expression—something unpolished, unguarded. His voice drops into a register I've never heard from him before. "You think I don't know that?"

I blink, thrown off balance by the sudden honesty. The Rory Keane I've come to expect—the one who deflects with a joke and a flash of teeth—is nowhere to be found. Instead, there's this version of him: sombre, exposed, and unsettlingly human.

"You have a winning formula. Why are you trying to do something different?" My voice carries more accusation than curiosity. I hate how defensive I sound, as if his vulnerability is some kind of ambush I wasn't prepared for.

"Because I don't have it anymore," he admits, running a hand through his dark hair. It sticks up slightly afterward, messy and imperfect, and somehow that detail makes him feel more real than ever. "The spark, the... whatever it was that made me good at writing this stuff. It's gone." He gestures vaguely, as if trying to grab hold of something invisible just out of reach. "I thought maybe I could fake it—ride on what worked before—but clearly, you see right through that."

"Clearly," I echo faintly, though the usual satisfaction I get from uncovering flaws is absent. Instead, there's an ache in my chest, unwelcome and persistent, like the sting of a paper cut.

"Look," he continues, his gaze fixed on the pile of pages between us instead of on me. "I'm not proud of it, okay? But it's hard to write about love when..." He hesitates, his mouth pressing into a tight line. "When you haven't felt it in a long time."

Something twists deep inside me at that confession. It feels too personal, too intimate for this sterile conference room with its fluorescent lighting and corporate furniture. I should pivot, steer us back to safe ground. But I don't.

Instead, I study him—the tension in his jaw, the way his hands lay motionless on the table, so unlike their usual restless energy. There's no trace of the confident playboy author here, just a man who's quietly admitting that he's lost.

"Rory..." I'm unsure where I'm even going with this. Sympathy isn't part of my job description. Empathy certainly isn't. And yet, here I am, feeling both in spades.

He meets my eyes, and for once, there's no teasing glint, no smirk—just sincerity, raw and disarming.

"You wanted serious, Lara. Well, here it is. I don't know how to fix this because I don't know how to feel it anymore."

My throat tightens, and I force myself to look away, focusing instead on the red ink scrawled across his manuscript. The clean lines of my edits blur slightly, and I realise with alarm that this moment—this stupid, vulnerable moment—is testing every boundary I've carefully erected between us.

"That's not my problem," I say briskly. I shuffle the pages unnecessarily, needing something—anything—to keep my hands busy. "My job is to help you write a better book, not play therapist to your existential crisis."

"Fair enough," he says softly, leaning back in his chair again. But the vulnerability doesn't vanish entirely; it lingers in his eyes, a shadow refusing to retreat.

I tell myself to focus on the work, on the deadline looming over us like a guillotine. But his words stick, stubborn and intrusive, as if they've wedged themselves into some hidden corner of my brain. Because the truth is, I know what it's like to lose that spark—to stare at a blank page and wonder if you'll ever be able to fill it with something meaningful again. I know it too well.

"Let's just stick to the manuscript," I say finally, my tone clipped but wavering at the edges.

If he notices, he doesn't comment. Instead, he gives a small nod, subdued and strangely respectful.

"Whatever you say, Captain Critique," he says, but there's no bite to the moniker. Just resignation.

It should feel like a victory. Instead, it feels like a truce.

"Maybe that's the problem," Rory says, his voice smooth as honey, but with a deliberate edge that makes me glance up from my notes. His fingers are interlocked like he's about to deliver some groundbreaking revelation. "I'm trying to write about love without... you know, actually feeling it."

I narrow my eyes at him, unsure where this is going, but already annoyed.

"And whose fault is that?"

"Touché." He grins, unrepentant. "But hear me out. Maybe what I need isn't another lecture on emotional stakes or narrative arcs." His gaze flickers—no, lingers—on me, and something shifts in the air between us, subtle but unmistakable. "Maybe I need to experience romance firsthand. You know, for research purposes."

Oh, no. Absolutely not. I set my pen down with deliberate precision. "Please tell me you're joking."

"Not entirely," he says. "Think about it. How can I write something authentic if I don't feel it? And who better to help me than my esteemed editor, who clearly has all the answers about what love should look like?"

"Stop." I hold up a hand, cutting him off before he can dig himself any deeper into this absurdity. "First of all, your job is to create fiction, not live it. If every author needed firsthand experience to write convincingly, half the fantasy genre wouldn't exist. Second"—I push my glasses up the bridge of my nose, a gesture that buys me half a second to reassemble my composure—"what you're suggesting is wildly unprofessional, not to mention ridiculous."

"Ridiculous?" His eyebrows lift, mock-offended. "I think it's innovative. Immersive storytelling. Method writing."

"Method writing isn't a thing," I snap, "and even if it were, I am not going to... to *date* you for the sake of a manuscript."

"Who said anything about dating?" His smirk deepens,

and I instantly regret my choice of words. "You've got quite the imagination, Lara. No wonder you're such a good editor."

"Rory." My tone is pure ice, my expression carefully neutral despite the heat creeping up my neck. "Focus. On. The. Manuscript."

"Fine, fine," he concedes, raising his hands in surrender but looking far too pleased with himself. "It was just an idea. A good one, if you ask me."

"Which I didn't," I say, flipping through the pages in front of me. My pulse is annoyingly quick, and I hate that he knows exactly how to rankle me, how to pull reactions out of me I'd rather keep hidden. "Now, if we're done brainstorming your extracurricular activities, can we please get back to fixing your female protagonist's complete lack of emotional growth?"

He doesn't respond immediately, and when I glance up, he's watching me with an unreadable expression. The teasing smile is still there, faint but present, yet his eyes... they're softer now, quieter.

"Sure," he says finally, his voice lower, almost thoughtful. "Back to the manuscript."

"Good." I nod briskly, pretending I didn't just lose some invisible battle. Pretending his earlier comment hasn't lodged itself somewhere in my chest, stubborn and unwelcome.

"Rory, I need you to understand something." I set my pen down with a deliberate click against the glass tabletop, meeting his eyes head-on. "The deadline isn't some arbitrary date. This manuscript is scheduled for the summer release slot to catch all the *Best Beach Reads* lists. The marketing team already has their campaign working overtime. Preorders are rolling in and we've booked and paid for point-of-sale displays in hundreds of bookstores. If this doesn't come together—" I take a breath, forcing myself not to sound like I'm lecturing a wayward teenager, though the temptation is strong. "It's not just your reputation on the line. It's the publisher's. And, frankly, mine."

"Yours?" He arches an eyebrow. "I didn't realise you were personally invested in my success, Lara."

"This is my job. My name is attached to this project as much as yours is. If it tanks because you've decided to blag this one, we both lose."

"Blag? Ouch."

I push the manuscript toward him, keen to crack on, my finger tapping on one of the many highlighted sections. "Page seventy-three. Your protagonist confesses his love for the heroine after three dates. Three. It's rushed, it's shallow, and it reads like... like..."

"Like someone who hasn't been in love in a while?" he offers, deadpan, and I freeze mid-tap.

"That's not what I was going to say," I reply, but the heat rising in my cheeks betrays me.

"Uh-huh."

"Let me make one thing clear." I stand, gathering the papers strewn across the table, each motion precise and measured. "This isn't a game, Rory. You might enjoy playing the charming rogue, but if this book doesn't meet expectations, no amount of winking and smirking will save you. Or me."

I snap my notebook shut with a decisive thud, the sound punctuating the end of this maddeningly unproductive meeting. The pages are now filled with messy notes and asterisks, each one a reminder of Rory Keane's inability—or refusal—to approach his manuscript with anything resembling focus.

"You've got plenty to be getting on with." My voice is clipped, all business, even as my mind is already spinning with more potential fixes for the train wreck he handed in disguised as a manuscript.

"Plenty is an understatement," Rory replies.

"You need to get started on these edits, like, today. Only then might we stand a chance of salvaging this before the deadline." I adjust my glasses for good measure.

"Salvage. What a glowing vote of confidence. You know, for someone who spends so much time dissecting romance, you're surprisingly ruthless about it."

"Ruthless gets results," I counter, standing and slipping my bag over my shoulder. "And last I checked, results are what you need right now."

I walk towards the door, but he doesn't move to leave.

"Was there something else?" I ask, arching an eyebrow. My patience is thinning, but my curiosity—it seems—isn't. A dangerous combination.

"You're kind of fascinating when you're in editor mode. Terrifying, sure. But fascinating."

I take a step toward the door. "If that's all, I have actual work to do."

"You know, for someone who claims this isn't a game, you're playing your role awfully well."

"And what role would that be?"

"The untouchable perfectionist," he says easily, but there's a weight behind the words that catches me off guard. "All harsh edges and no room for mistakes. Makes me wonder if you ever let yourself slip. Even just a little."

The air between us stretches taut, and I hate that my pulse quickens. "My personal habits are none of your concern," I reply coolly, pulling the door open. "Focus on fixing your manuscript. That's the only thing that matters here."

"Right," he says, standing at last. As I step through the doorway, his voice follows me, low and warm, tinged with something I can't quite pin down. "But maybe... if you ever want to talk about what *does* matter, you know where to find me."

I don't look back. I don't trust myself to.

THREE

I've been sitting here for fifteen minutes just staring at the screen. My laptop is open, my inbox overflowing, and the manuscript I'm supposed to be reviewing is right in front of me. But instead of making notes, I'm just... stuck. Paralysed.

The logical part of my brain knows I'm working from home today, knows the deadline looms, knows I should be doing something—*anything*—productive. But the rest of me? The part still reeling from Rory's ridiculous suggestion? That part refuses to cooperate.

Method writing... the gall of the man.

Like he's some tortured artist in need of a muse, rather than a bestselling author who's quite literally *made a career* out of fabricating romance. Like this—*whatever this is*—is just another plot device to be tested, tweaked, and perfected.

"Focus," I say under my breath, gripping the arms of my chair as though sheer willpower alone might tether my thoughts to the task at hand. But no amount of glaring at the screen changes the fact that my mind is anything but here.

Instead, it's spinning—no, spiralling—with the memory of his voice: smooth, warm, and casual, like he hadn't just unleashed a hurricane into my meticulously compartmentalised life.

Like he hadn't just proposed the most ridiculous, unprofessional, entirely inappropriate arrangement with the kind of straight-faced ease one might use to suggest grabbing coffee.

Like I was the unreasonable one for being completely floored by it.

I shove back from the desk, the wheels of my chair skittering against the floor with a groan.

"The audacity," I say aloud, pressing my palms to my temples as though I can physically massage the irritation out of my skull. "Who *does* that?"

It wasn't just what he'd said—it was the way he said it, with that half-smile that made it impossible to tell if he was serious or just messing with me for fun. A proposition, he'd called it. Like we were negotiating some kind of business deal.

"'Work together more closely, Lara,'" I mimic his voice, low and velvety, dripping in charm. My stomach twists, heat creeping up my neck at how easily the timbre of it settles in my ears, even now. "'*Explore new creative possibilities*,'" I add, punctuating the air with sarcastic finger quotes.

Maybe you'd like me to express my editorial suggestions through the medium of dance. Is that creative enough for you?

I pinch the bridge of my nose, forcing myself to take a deep breath. This isn't about him. Not really. This is about me, about maintaining control, about—what had he called it? Oh, right. *Loosening up.* As if I'm some uptight spinster who needs to pop open a bottle of wine and throw caution to the wind.

But beneath my irritation, there's something else. Something unwelcome. A flicker of intrigue, maybe. Or curiosity. Or the faintest whisper of temptation.

No. Nope. Absolutely not. Whatever Rory Keane thinks he's offering with that insufferable grin and those maddeningly expressive eyes, I am not buying it.

I'm pacing now. My arms are crossed tightly over my chest, fingers digging into my sleeves as if holding myself together physically will somehow stop me from unravelling mentally. Spoiler alert: it's not working.

My feet carry me to the living room window, almost unbidden, and I press my palms lightly against the cool glass. Outside, the city stretches wide and glittering in the early evening light, a mosaic of buildings and bustling streets that hum with life. From here, everyone looks so purposeful. So certain.

"How long has it been?"

The question slips out before I can stop it, soft and unfamiliar, like testing the weight of something fragile in my hands. How long since someone looked at me the way Rory had in that moment? Not just saw me, but *wanted* me. Me, not the polished editor in her sensible heels and tailored jackets, but the person underneath all of that.

It's unsettling, that thought. Intriguing too, but mostly, if I'm being honest, it's flattering.

I trace a small circle on my now-stone-cold cup of tea with my fingertip. It's not that I feel unattractive. Not exactly. But there's a difference between being appreciated for your work— or even admired—and being truly *desired*. Desired in a way that feels electric, magnetic, reckless.

Reckless, now there's a word that feels like it doesn't belong in my vocabulary. Because it doesn't. At least, not anymore.

I shake my head and step back from the window, ignoring the faint pull in my chest as I turn away from the view. Whatever Rory thinks he sees when he looks at me—whatever spark of madness made him think this was a good idea—it's better left unexplored. Safer. Cleaner. Controlled. Boundaries exist for a reason.

Rory, with that annoying way he tilts his head when he's

trying to make a point, doesn't seem to understand this. Or maybe he does, and he just enjoys watching me squirm. Either way, I'm not about to let him bulldoze through the lines I've carefully drawn—no matter how attractive he might be—lines that have been securely constructed for some time now and that keep things predictable, orderly. Safe.

My gaze snags on the framed photo on the wall above my desk. It's an old picture, slightly faded around the edges, but the subjects are still clear: my parents, seated side by side on the couch in our living room. My mother wears her usual polite teacher smile; my father stares straight ahead, expressionless, almost shell-shocked. They look more like coworkers from different departments posing for a company social media post than two people who once exchanged vows.

I pick up the frame and run my thumb along the edge, the cool glass grounding me as memories bubble uninvited to the surface. Their marriage was—and remains—functional, I suppose. Efficient, like a well-oiled machine. They shared the logistics—finances, schedules, shopping lists—but passion? Affection? Desire? Those were foreign concepts, dismissed as frivolities.

"Love isn't practical, Lara," my mother used to say whenever I asked why they didn't laugh much, or touch much, or... *feel* much. "And practicality is what keeps a house running."

Practicality. The cornerstone of their relationship. And the slow, silent poison that drained it of colour. I'd scoff, but for the fact that I'm self-aware enough to know that a little bit of that pragmatism has rubbed off on me.

I look away from the photo of my parents. I don't want that life. I never have. But the alternative—the messiness, the uncertainty, the heartbreak—terrifies me just as much. Maybe more.

This is exactly why emotions can't be trusted. They cloud judgment. They lead to bad decisions. They...

I trail off from the thought as Rory's voice echoes in my mind, low and teasing. *"You're too buttoned-up, Yates. Loosen the top button once in a while."*

"Dickhead," I hiss. But even as I wiggle my mouse to wake up my screen, my fingers tremble. Because part of me knows the truth—the kind of truth I wouldn't dare admit out loud.

The problem isn't just Rory. It's that, for the first time in years, someone made me wonder what it might feel like to loosen the top button. Even just once. Better yet, they might actually loosen it for me.

The last person I loved didn't have Rory's reckless grin or his maddening confidence. Another face swims into view. A steadier one. Softer. Predictable.

"James," I whisper. And just like that, the memory pulls me under.

The air smells like fresh-cut grass and sunscreen, a summer barbecue humming around us as James flips burgers with the same precision he brings to every task. His shirt is tucked into his khakis—khakis!—and his expression is one of deep concentration, brow furrowed just slightly as he adjusts the spatula in his hand.

"Relax, Gordon Ramsay," I tease, nudging him playfully with my hip. He glances at me, startled for half a second, before his mouth softens into that familiar smile. Warm. Comfortable. Safe.

"Someone has to make sure these don't burn," he says, his tone amused but measured. Always measured. James was nothing if not predictable. The kind of man who never left a text unanswered, never forgot your coffee order, never raised his voice even when he was angry. A man you could build a life with because you always knew exactly where you stood.

And yet... as I watch him carefully flip another burger, I remember the hollow ache that had started growing in those last few months. Like I'd been living in a house with perfectly painted walls, but no furniture. No warmth. Just... space.

"Do you ever want more than this?" I'd asked him once, the question spilling out before I could stop it. We were sitting on his pristine grey couch—of course it was grey—watching reruns of some sitcom neither of us really cared about. He glanced at me then, confused.

"More than what?"

"More than comfort. More than... predictability."

He frowned, clearly trying to understand. "Comfort's not a bad thing, Lara. Comfort lasts. Passion burns out." He paused, then added, almost shyly, "Isn't this enough?"

I shake my head, like I'm trying to dislodge the memories clinging to me. James's lopsided smile dissolves into Rory's wolfish grin, and suddenly I feel like I've been caught in some kind of emotional tug-of-war that I never agreed to play.

Messy.

My monitor's screensaver continues looping, the manuscript I should be editing, untouched. But it's not the keyboard catching my eye—it's my phone. Sitting there, mocking me, daring me.

I pick up the phone without thinking, the smooth weight of it grounding me for half a second, before finding Rory in my contacts. His profile photo—just his initials because I refuse to assign him anything more personal—stares back at me. My thumb hovers over his name, inches away from opening the message or, God forbid, calling him.

"Don't do it, Lara," I whisper, my voice barely audible but firm. "Nothing good comes from impulsive decisions. You know this."

And yet, I feel the pull. The same magnetic draw I felt when he smirked across the conference room table today and said, *"You're too wound up, Yates. When's the last time you did something just for fun?"*

"Editing is fun," I'd shot back, defensive, before I could stop myself. He'd only laughed, low and rich and entirely too self-assured, as though he already knew how this story ended.

Now here I am, holding my phone like it's a grenade with the pin half-pulled. My thumb dips closer to the screen, brushing the edge of his name. One tap, and I could hear that lazy, teasing drawl again. One tap, and...

"Nope." I drop the phone onto the desk like it burned me, rolling my chair back from the desk for good measure. "Not happening."

It takes a full minute for my pulse to settle, though I'm still acutely aware of the phone sitting there, still glowing faintly. I know I won't delete his number—I'm not *that* dramatic—but I also know I'm not ready to open that door. Not today. Maybe never.

My gaze flickers to the framed photo of my parents again. Their stiff and unconvincing smiles, a reminder of everything I promised myself I wouldn't settle for. Or risk.

I don't do complicated.

Rory's name lingers in the air, unspoken but impossible to ignore.

And I hate the part of me that is already wondering what he'll say next.

"Tea," I announce to the empty room, because apparently saying it aloud makes it official. "Tea fixes everything." Lies, obviously, but at least it gives me something to do with my hands that doesn't involve picking up that damn phone again.

I focus on the mundane motions—the weight of the kettle, the steady stream filling it to just the right level, the satisfying roar as I turn it on. Rituals are good. Practical. Rational. Not at all like the ridiculous proposition I keep replaying in my mind, no matter how hard I've tried to drown it out.

While the kettle begins its slow climb to a boil, I lean back against the counter. My gaze lands on the chipped mug sitting next to the sink, the one I never got around to replacing. A secret Santa gift received during my first Christmas at Scott & Drake. It reads *Keep Calm and Edit On*, the lettering faded from years of overuse. Fitting, really. If only calming down were as easy as slapping the words on ceramic.

"Letting loose," I scoff under my breath. Letting loose is what people like Rory do effortlessly—he probably came out of the womb with that twinkle in his eye and a perfectly tousled head of hair. Meanwhile, I've spent my entire adult life building walls taller than any fairytale castle, complete with a moat and dragon for good measure.

The kettle clicks off, snapping me out of my thoughts. I lunge for it like it's a lifeline, pouring the steaming water over the tea bag waiting in my mug. The scent of chamomile rises, soft and familiar, grounding me and helping to clarify why this is wrong on so many levels.

Point one: Rory Keane is a client.

Point two: His proposition—that ludicrous, audacious *proposition*—would require spending *even* more time with him beyond what is contractually required to get his book completed.

Point three: He has a face that looks like it belongs on a movie poster for some brooding indie film. That face alone spells trouble. No doubt he'd use that mouth to toss out lines about "creative synergy" while I resist the urge to throttle him with his own scarf. Does he even wear scarves? Cravats proba-bly. He seems like the type.

Point four: Casual arrangements—I don't *do* casual. Not well, anyway. Not without getting caught in the weeds of feel-ings and expectations and all the things I've spent half my life avoiding.

And point five: This isn't about feelings. This is about control. And if there's one thing I hate, it's losing control.

But as much as I try to convince myself, there's a niggling little whisper at the back of my mind—a suggestion, barely audible but persistent. *What if letting go doesn't mean losing control? What if it means... freedom?*

God help me, despite all the evidence to the contrary, there's something about the idea that's tempting. Just for a moment. Just to see what it's like to stop thinking, to stop second-guessing, to stop dissecting every interaction for hidden subtext and ulterior motives. To feel wanted—not for my ability to fix plot holes and tighten dialogue, but for *me*.

"Brilliant," I groan, sinking back into my chair. "I'm arguing with myself now. Fantastic. This is fine. Totally fine."

The mug of tea is still sitting on the desk, untouched and lukewarm. I pick it up anyway, cradling it in my hands as if it might help me navigate tonight. It doesn't, of course. Chamomile has its limits.

Tomorrow.

I tell myself firmly, though the word tastes bitter on my tongue. "I'll deal with it tomorrow."

FOUR

Tomorrow, however, arrives faster than I would have liked and I am back in the office to find the publishing gods have conspired to ensure that there will be no gentle easing into the day. The email sits on my screen, a glowing harbinger of doom. Subject: *Fully, Forever/R. Keane—Critical Revenue Stream.* Subtle.

I skim the lines for the third time, but they don't get any gentler with rereading. Phrases like "key fiscal quarter" and "projected profit margin" jump out and tighten around my chest like a vice. The numbers are staggering—high six figures, veering dangerously close to seven. It's not even about Rory's ego anymore; it's the company's bottom line. Fiona might as well have written, "No pressure, Lara, but if this book tanks, we're all screwed. Have a nice day!"

This is what I signed up for, right? Fixing broken stories. Holding trembling authorial hands. Saving the publishing day, one misplaced subplot at a time. But Rory Keane? Bestselling, award-winning Rory Keane? He's supposed to be untouchable. The man practically breathes success. And now it's on me to ensure his latest manuscript doesn't send Scott & Drake spiralling into financial ruin. No big deal.

My gaze flickers to the framed print on my desk—a simple black-and-white quote from Dorothy Parker: *I hate writing, I love having written.*

Same, Dorothy. Same. Only, I haven't written anything in years unless you count scathing margin notes, which no one does.

When I enter the meeting room, I'm hit with a blast of air conditioning. It feels colder than usual, or maybe that's just my nerves catching up with me. I find Rory Keane, the man who is single-handedly keeping our lights on, seated at the far end of the table.

"Wow," I say before I can stop myself. "You're here on time?"

Rory looks up, startled, and I immediately notice two things: one, his hair is dishevelled—more so than usual—like he's been running his hands through it all morning; and two, he's fidgeting with a pen, flipping it between his fingers. Rory Keane doesn't fidget. He lounges. He smirks. He charms. This... nervous energy? Completely off-brand.

"Don't sound so shocked," he says, flashing a quick grin. "It's almost insulting."

"Almost?" There's something off—something raw beneath his usual polished exterior. The pen slips from his fingers, clattering against the table, and he swears under his breath, scooping it up like it holds the meaning of life.

"Rough morning?" I ask lightly, sliding into my seat. My tone is casual, professional even, but my editor brain is already cataloguing every detail: the tension in his shoulders, the faint crease between his brows, the way his knee bounces under the table like he's trying to outrun a thought he doesn't want to catch.

"Something like that," he says, spinning the pen again.

"Well," I say briskly, "let's see if we can salvage this thing before your existential crisis gets any worse."

"Lead the way, Yates," he says, his voice smooth again. Polished. Back to brand.

"It's Lara." I remind him.

"I prefer Yates. Strong literary name. Suits you."

I've got too much I want to say about his manuscript to fight him on this. If he heeds my advice and gets his revisions back to me quickly, he can call me anything he likes.

"Alright, let's get to it. We've got a lot of ground to cover if we want this to resemble something publishable."

His eyes flick back to me, but there's something off about the way they focus. Like he's here in body, but not entirely in spirit.

"Rory," I prompt, keeping my voice pointedly professional, though my curiosity itches at the edges. "Any reason you're looking at me like you've just remembered where you left your car keys?"

"Just thinking," he says lightly, still spinning the pen. It's an answer designed to be harmless, but the weight in his tone doesn't match. Before I can decide whether to push or let it go, he adds, almost offhandedly, "You know, it's funny. All of the changes you're suggesting I make to Sophie's character— remind me of you."

The shift is so abrupt I blink. "Oh?" His tone is too casual, too calculated.

"Yeah." His gaze zeros in on me with unnerving precision. "You want me to make Sophie so... sceptical about romance. Almost like she doesn't believe in it at all."

And there it is. The trap, perfectly baited. I feel my irritation bubble up before I can tamp it down.

"Are you seriously psychoanalysing your own character right now?" I shoot him a pointed look over the rim of my glasses. "Because if you are, I'd suggest saving it for therapy and focusing on fixing her motivation instead."

"If anything, I'm psychoanalysing you," he counters smoothly, one brow arching. "More to the point, you didn't deny it."

"That's because it's absurd," I reply, my voice flinty, but amused despite myself. "Sophie's scepticism is perfectly grounded in her backstory. It means she's got further to travel on her emotional journey. It's called *character development.* You might want to try it sometime."

"I shall. Promise."

"Good. Right. I have some more notes on the midpoint conflict. As it stands, there's not enough tension driving the characters' decisions. We need a stronger emotional catalyst— something that feels inevitable but still surprising."

"You really know how to kill the mood, don't you?"

"Someone has to," I reply, jotting down a quick note before glancing up at him again. "And since you seem determined to avoid doing any actual work today, that someone is me."

"Harsh," he says, "but fair."

"Glad we're on the same page... finally," I retort, flipping another page in the manuscript with a deliberate flourish. I keep my focus trained on the words in front of me, even as I feel his eyes lingering on me, studying me. Let him look. Let him think whatever he wants. I have a job to do, and I refuse to let him—or his maddening grin—distract me from it.

"If you're not ready for the midpoint. Let's at least tackle the opening scene."

"You love it, don't you?"

"I hate it."

"Oh."

"After three exquisite descriptive paragraphs, Sophie literally starts her morning by arguing with her cat over a burnt piece of toast. It's not exactly the stuff of bestselling romance."

"Hey, my readers love cats," he counters, "and burnt toast is relatable. I'm going for authenticity here."

"Authenticity is great," I reply, scribbling a quick note in the margin of his manuscript. "But your readers aren't picking up this book for flowery descriptive prose. They want conflict, stakes, something that grabs them by the throat and doesn't let go. Right now, it's more like a polite handshake."

"Wait," he interrupts, holding up a hand. "What if—and hear me out—the cat isn't just there for comic relief? Maybe I put it in because it's... a metaphor?"

I blink at him. "A metaphor for what?"

"Loneliness," he says seriously. "Think about it. The cat represents her fear of connection. It's her safe, predictable companion because she's too scared to let anyone else in."

"Or, it's just a cat. And instead of shoehorning in an unnecessary metaphor, we could use the space to actually establish her emotional wound. You know, the thing driving her arc?"

"Tell me something, Yates," he says, his voice low and conspiratorial, like we're sharing some grand secret instead of sitting under the fluorescent lights of a soulless conference room. "Do you even believe in love?"

I blink at him, once, twice, letting the question hang in the air like a particularly bad smell.

"What?"

"Just curious," he says smoothly, leaning closer, his gaze fixed on mine with unnerving intensity. Those stupid dark eyes of his are sparkling, and I hate that I notice. "You spend so much time breaking love stories into narrative beats that must be hit at a certain moment, I'm starting to wonder if you even think it's real, or just manufactured."

"Don't," I warn, holding up a hand like I'm warding off a bad idea.

But it's too late. Rory Keane thinks he's dug up a meaty bone, and he's not about to let it go.

"I think it's you who's fallen out of love with love, and consciously or subconsciously, it's guiding how you imagine Sophie's character. Every single note urges caution, care, distrust... and fear. I think you see her in you... and you in her." The grin tugging at his mouth is the kind that makes me want to throw something small, hard, and unbreakable at him. Preferably at his head.

"Love is very real," I reply crisply. "It's also subjective, highly marketable, and prone to cliché. That's why it's my job to make sure *your* version of it doesn't send readers into diabetic shock. You're welcome, by the way."

"Ah, and there it is." He points the pen at me like he's just cracked some ancient code. "The clinical detachment. 'Love is subjective.' 'Love is marketable.' 'Love is a trope.' You could put that on a coffee mug. Do you hear yourself? It's no wonder you think Sophie is allergic to emotional vulnerability."

"I didn't say she's *allergic*," I retort, scribbling something nonsensical in my notes just to avoid looking directly at him. "I said she needs to be more cautious. Realistic. And frankly, that's what's missing from your entire manuscript, realism."

"Realism," he repeats, dragging out the word. His expression shifts—less teasing now, more thoughtful. "Okay, then. Let's test your realism, shall we?"

"Let's not," I say quickly, looking at him over the edge of my glasses. This feels like a setup, and I don't like where it's heading.

"Just hypothetically," he presses, undeterred. "What if I could prove to you that love isn't just some... construct or plot point to be analysed and edited into submission? What if I could show you it's real? Tangible. Even for someone as... 'cautious' as you."

"Prove it?" I repeat, incredulous. A laugh escapes before I

can stop it—short and entirely dismissive. "What exactly are you suggesting? A field study? Should I expect a slide deck with stats and bar charts by the end of the week?"

"Maybe," he shoots back without missing a beat, his grin returning full force. "Or maybe something a little more... experiential."

"Experiential," I echo flatly, because apparently, I've been reduced to parroting his nonsense now. "And what does that entail, exactly? Romantic scavenger hunts? Candlelit dinners? Long walks on the beach where you regale me with poetry about moonlight and destiny?"

"Could be fun," he says. "But no. I was thinking something simpler. A deal, of sorts."

"Absolutely not," I say instantly, slapping the cap back onto my pen with finality. Whatever this is, it needs to end before it gets any more ridiculous.

"Come on, Yates." His tone is light, almost playful, but there's something lurking beneath it—a challenge, barely veiled. "Humour me. If I win, you have to admit you're wrong about love. Just once. Out loud. To me."

"And if I win?" I ask, mostly to humour *him*.

"Then I'll rewrite Sophie's entire character arc however you want. No arguments."

I narrow my eyes, searching his face for cracks in his armour, but all I find is confidence. Too much confidence. It's maddening.

"This hypothetical deal of yours has no basis in logic or professionalism," I point out, already reaching for my notes. "So naturally, I'm rejecting it."

"Naturally," he echoes, as if he's already won something. And somehow, that's more aggravating than anything he's said so far.

"You're ridiculous," I say flatly.

A deal. He wants me to make a *deal*. As if this manuscript

—this project that's dangling precariously between disaster and redemption—isn't already enough pressure without adding personal stakes.

My mind races, unspooling every possible consequence. If I say yes, I'm indulging him, giving him permission to derail us further—and for what? To prove some abstract point about love? And yet... if I say no, will he dig his heels in even harder? Will Sophie's character arc remain the same flimsy mess because I refused to play along?

"You're thinking about it," he says.

"Absolutely not." I snap the words out instinctively, but they feel hollow, even to me.

"Sure you're not," he says, voice smooth as silk. "That furrow in your brow? Totally unrelated. Probably just thinking about... comma placement."

"Comma placement *matters*," I retort, because it's easier than addressing the truth hanging between us. I'm hesitating. God help me, I'm actually hesitating.

I tell myself it's because of the deadline. That's all this is—the story needs fixing, and if playing along with Rory gets him to cooperate, maybe it's worth considering. But somewhere, deep in the quiet corner of my brain I try not to visit too often another thought flickers: *What if he's right? About me. About love. About everything I've spent years cynically dissecting and dismissing.*

"Okay," I say finally, dragging the word out as I force myself to meet his gaze. "Here's the thing, *Keane*—I don't have time for whatever romantic comedy subplot you think we're living in. I'm here to fix your book, not entertain your whims."

"Noted," he says, but his grin doesn't falter. If anything, it grows wider, more insufferable. "But you didn't say no."

"Because it's beneath me to dignify this nonsense with an actual answer," I shoot back. "Now, let's get back to the part where I save your career from its inevitable nosedive, shall we?"

"Deflection," he muses, tapping a finger against his chin like he's solving a puzzle. "Interesting strategy, Yates."

"Observation," I counter. "Not your strong suit, apparently."

He laughs—a low, genuine sound that lightens the mood immediately. "You're good at this, you know. The whole icy-editor thing. Very convincing. Almost had me fooled there for a second."

"Glad to see you're finally catching on."

"Fine, you win," he says at last. "Let's talk about the manuscript. For now."

"Thank you," I reply, already scribbling notes in the margins of the page in front of me. My voice is steady, professional, exactly what it needs to be. But in the back of my mind, his words linger, unsettling as they are undeniable: *You didn't say no.* He knows. Somehow, he knows he's gotten under my skin, and worse, he's enjoying it. Smug bastard.

FIVE

The café smells like roasted coffee beans and freshly baked croissants, but the noise level is just short of deafening—hissing milk steamers, clinking mugs, someone punctuating their conversation with aggressive taps of a spoon on a saucer, and the hum of too many conversations stacked on top of each other. I push through the crowd, dodging a guy with a laptop screen so large it might double as a home entertainment system. My eyes scan the room until they land on Danny at our usual corner table, already grinning like he knows something I don't.

And, of course, he does.

"Lara," he calls out, raising his mug like he's at Oktoberfest. "Looking delightfully... unhinged this morning."

"Charming," I say, weaving through a maze of chairs and elbows to reach him.

"Don't take this the wrong way," he says, leaning forward as I drop into the chair across from him, "but you look like you've just gone twelve rounds with a malfunctioning printer and lost. Badly."

"Wow. That's... inspiring." I shrug off my jacket and toss it over the back of my chair. "So nice to know my best friend moonlights as a walking insult generator."

"Just doing my civic duty," he quips, gesturing dramatically with his coffee cup. "But seriously—" His gaze flicks to my slightly crooked glasses and the frazzled bun perched precariously on top of my head. "Rory Keane, huh? The man, the myth, the... migraine?"

"Don't." I hold up a hand, but Danny's grin only widens.

"How does it feel to be working with the literary equivalent of a human golden retriever?" His voice is teasing, but there's that trademark sparkle in his eye—the one that says he's about to go all in.

"Exhausting," I reply flatly, though I can't stop the smile from forming. "And for your information, Rory Keane is more of a... hyperactive border collie than a golden retriever. But thanks for the analysis."

"Anytime," Danny fires back, folding his hands under his chin like he's about to offer sage wisdom. "I mean, let's face it, Lara. You've got this whole..." He gestures vaguely at me, taking in everything from my wrinkled blouse to the faint ink smudge on my left wrist. "*Overworked editor chic* thing going on. It's honestly impressive. A little tragic, but impressive."

"Remind me why I keep you around?" I ask, reaching for the menu even though I already know I'm ordering the same black coffee as always.

"Because I'm your not-gay-best friend," he says without missing a beat. "And one day I'm hoping when you decide you're ready to settle down, you'll pick me."

"Ewww. No."

"I'd settle for a casual fling."

"Double-Ewww."

"Okay, fine, because deep down, you love it when someone tells you the truth instead of feeding you polite lies. Admit it— I'm your emotional support cynic."

"More like my emotional support headache," I retort, but my smile gives me away. Danny knows exactly how far to push, toeing the line between infuriating and oddly comforting with the precision of someone who's been doing this for years.

"So? Out with it. How bad is Mr. Border Collie?"

I sigh like I'm expelling a decade of frustration in one breath, slumping against the backrest of my chair.

"Catastrophic is putting it lightly. He's nowhere near finished. Bar a few chapters of genius, what he's written is not good enough to even call derivative crap, and I don't think there's a hope in hell we're going to meet the deadline. No pressure at all, right?"

"None," he says brightly, picking up his mug and taking a sip. "Sounds like your usual Tuesday to me."

"Except this isn't just any Tuesday," I counter, leaning forward as if proximity might somehow make him understand the absurdity of my predicament. "This is... Rory Keane Tuesday, which, by the way, is now officially a category of stress in my life. He breezes in with that stupid smile—"

"Charming smile," Danny interrupts.

"Stupid," I insist, glaring at him as he smirks into his coffee. "And he's all smooth lines and effortless confidence. Meanwhile, everyone upstairs is treating him like he personally invented human emotion or something. And here I am, supposed to, what? Magically fix whatever creative crisis he's having, while not combusting under the weight of the expectations they've dumped on me? Sure. Totally fine. I'll just casually save the day like some editorial superhero."

"You'll manage, you always do."

"Danny, I'm serious. The guy's a bestselling author. His books have movie deals. There are fan accounts dedicated to his characters. Tonight he's up for a Rose Award. And his latest work is... awful."

"Are we really going to pretend you don't secretly enjoy

the chaos of fixing other people's messes? Because I seem to recall you getting downright giddy about tearing apart that last thriller."

"That was different." I shake my head. "That was for a midlist author who, to be fair, had the foundations in place. This is Rory fucking Keane. He's practically publishing royalty. And apparently, I'm the lucky peasant who gets to polish the turd he's submitted so he can keep wearing his crown."

"Lara, darling," Danny says, setting his mug down with a theatrical flourish, "you're looking at this all wrong."

"Am I?" I ask, raising an eyebrow.

"Yes," he says firmly. "Look, I get it. Big name, big stakes, blah blah blah. But this? This is your moment. Your *spotlight*. You get to take *Rory Keane*, Mr. International Romance King, and remind the world why Lara Yates is the editor everyone wants in their corner." He taps the table for emphasis. "You don't just polish turds—you build thrones. This is the project that will send your career to the stratosphere."

"Wow." I blink at him, caught somewhere between amusement and disbelief. "That might be the most dramatic pep talk you've ever given me."

"Thank you," he says, grinning. "But seriously, stop selling yourself short. If anyone can handle Rory Keane and his turds, it's you. Use this. Show them what you're made of. Hell, show *him* what you're made of."

"That," I say, waving him off, "was almost inspiring."

"Almost?" His eyebrows shoot up dramatically. "Darling, I don't do *almost*. My pep talks are TED Talk worthy. Admit it —you feel empowered already."

"Empowered to run and hide? Sure." I retreat with a sip of my coffee, letting its bitter warmth distract me. "Look, I appreciate the whole 'rah-rah Lara' routine, but let's be real. I'm not some creative genius. I don't have a vision or a voice. I'm just an editor—a glorified spellchecker who occasionally tells people their plot twists suck."

"Ah, yes, the modesty act." Danny rolls his eyes. "First of all, you're not 'just' anything. And second"—he leans in, lowering his voice like we're conspiring on something illegal—"you've got more vision than half the writers you babysit. Don't think I haven't forgotten those story ideas you spout after one too many glasses of prosecco."

"Those aren't... They're nothing. Just... ideas. Word doodles, really. Not enough to sustain a novel."

"Suuure," he says, dragging the word out like he doesn't believe a single syllable coming out of my mouth.

"Stop," I snap, though there's no real bite behind it. Mostly because he's hit too close to home.

"Fine, fine," he says, holding the menu up like a shield. "But one day, mark my words, you're going to stop editing other people's happily-ever-afters and start writing your own."

"Not likely," I say, though my voice wavers enough to make me cringe.

I glance at my phone and sigh. "I should head back to the office. I've got a few things to finish before the RNA Awards tonight. Not that I want to go."

Danny perks up. "No? Free wine and overenthusiastic romance authors aren't enough of a draw?"

I shake my head. "I'd rather be working. We're running out of time. And Rory should be buried in his manuscript, not parading around Bookstagrammers."

Danny hums thoughtfully and then grins. "Funny. You keep talking about focus, and yet, somehow, he's all you're thinking about."

I huff, standing up and grabbing my coat. "Goodbye, Danny."

He throws his hands up in surrender, laughing. "Enjoy your evening! Or at least pretend to."

SIX

♥

The champagne is warm, the lighting is aggressively atmospheric, and I'm currently contemplating whether it would be frowned upon to down the entire contents of my flute in one go.

Because I'm at the RNA Awards, the industry's glitziest exercise in mutual back-patting, where romance authors, editors, and PR teams gather to celebrate the best of the best at the Grosvenor House Hotel. And by "celebrate," I mean drinking heavily while pretending not to care about who wins.

Scott & Drake has a prime table near the stage, which means we're *technically* important. The marketing team is buzzing with anticipation, half watching the other tables to see who's here, half mentally drafting tomorrow's "Congratulations to our very own Rory Keane!" social media posts. Because, let's be honest, he's going to win.

And speaking of the man himself—

"Oh, look at you." Rory slides into the seat next to mine, expression bright with amusement. "Miss Yates, you're positively glowing tonight."

I glance up from my menu—an utterly pointless document, as we all know these events are ninety percent canapés and ten percent crushed dreams.

"You scrub up pretty well yourself," I reply. "An actual tux. I'm impressed. Did someone wrestle you into that, or did you just lose a bet?"

He smirks, raking a hand through his unruly mop of hair. The mood lighting catches on the sharp angles of his jaw, and for a brief, horrifying second, I realise that if I weren't so deeply familiar with his maddening personality, I might—objectively speaking—find him attractive. Very attractive.

Fortunately, I *am* familiar.

"I managed to dress all by myself, even the bowtie. A real one, I'll have you know." He grins.

I fold my arms, surveying him with mock admiration. "Incredible. Truly ground-breaking. Have they called to revoke your 'hopelessly dishevelled writer' badge yet, or are they letting you keep it for sentimental reasons?"

"Lifetime member, and they do give out a badge. I have it here somewhere." Rory pats his pockets, trying to locate it...

"Very good." I set my glass down and glance around the ballroom. "Do you enjoy these things?"

"Only when I win," he says easily. "Nothing says *objective artistic merit* quite like a thousand people in black tie clapping for whichever book made the most money this year."

I huff a laugh. "Bet you've prepared a speech and everything."

"Well," he leans in, voice warm with mischief, "we don't want to let down the fans, do we?"

I roll my eyes, but there's something about the way he's looking at me—light amusement mixed with something else I can't quite place.

Before I can figure it out, Rory straightens, glancing toward the entrance. "Going to do the rounds before things kick off," he announces, pushing back his chair. "Try not to miss me too much."

I tilt my head. "I'll do my best."

And with that, he vanishes into the crowd.

The second he's gone, I return my attention to my champagne and attempt to be a normal, functioning adult, exchanging pleasantries with the PR team—all of whom are new to the company, and by the looks of it, about fourteen years old.

Until my gaze snags on him across the ballroom.

More specifically, on who he's talking to.

At first glance, it's nothing unusual—just Rory, all charm and ease, making conversation with a young woman at one of the rival publisher tables.

But then—

Then I see her laugh, all hand-on-arm contact and wide-eyed admiration.

Ah.

I know exactly who she is.

Alice Morgan. The debut dark romance author. A viral sensation. Her book—a filthy, angsty, TikTok darling—is up for Debut Novel of the Year. Every industry exec wants a piece of her. Including, it seems, Rory Keane.

I look away. Because, this? This is none of my business.

He's a bestselling author. He can flirt with whomever he likes.

And yet—

There's a small, annoying flicker in my stomach.

It's not jealousy. Obviously. It's just... it's unprofessional. That's all.

He should be here, at his own publisher's table. Not over there, flashing dimples at the competition.

I pointedly turn my attention back to my table. The Scott

& Drake PR team are chatting about sales figures, completely oblivious to my sudden and *completely unjustified* annoyance.

The lights dim, signalling the start of the ceremony. I glance back one last time.

Rory is still over there.

And when the host welcomes us to the Romantic Novelists' Association Awards, when everyone settles in to watch, when he could have come back to sit next to me—

He doesn't.

He stays.

Sitting right next to her.

I sip my champagne and pretend not to care.

The moment Rory's name is announced as the winner of Romance of the Year, the room erupts into applause.

I clap, of course—because, well, that's what you do, and this is good for Scott & Drake—but my expression is perfectly neutral.

Rory, meanwhile, flashes his signature grin as he rises from his chair. And wouldn't you know it? The debut author beside him practically sparkles with admiration, giving him an enthusiastic, lingering hug before he makes his way to the stage.

Of course she does.

I sip my champagne. Not irritated at all.

The speech is classic Rory—charming, self-effacing, and just the right amount of heartfelt. He thanks his readers, his agent, his editors (plural, of course, which I pointedly do not overthink), and then ends with some grand remark about how love stories bring us together.

The audience eats it up.

Then, award in hand, he finally makes his way back to our table.

To me.

The team showers him in congratulations as he reaches us, everyone keen to bask in the glow of a win. I don't move from my seat, arms loosely folded, my glass of champagne still half-full.

"Multi-award-winning author Rory Keane," he says, tipping his trophy slightly towards me, voice laced with something teasing. "It's fair to say I am a fan of these events."

"Of course you are," I deadpan.

He grins like he's expecting me to fawn or fuss or—God forbid—look impressed.

Instead, I raise an eyebrow.

"Nice of you to rejoin us," I say smoothly, gesturing vaguely toward the table he'd occupied for most of the ceremony. "Didn't realise Scott & Drake was just a pit stop on your social calendar."

The warmth in his eyes flickers.

Ah. He clocked that. Good.

He recovers quickly, of course—he's Rory Keane, professional charmer, after all—but I know the difference between his genuine and performative smiles.

This one? A little forced.

"Come on, Yates," he says lightly, adjusting the trophy in his grip. "I didn't have you down as the jealous type."

I blink. "Jealous?"

He leans in slightly, voice dropping just enough that only I can hear. "Because if you are, that's very interesting."

I scoff. Because scoffing is dignified.

"Rory," I say, tone clipped. "I don't care where you sit."

"Right," he nods slowly. "Which is why you're bringing it up."

"I'm bringing it up," I say, "because it's a bad look for an author to ignore his own publisher on the biggest industry night of the year. Not a great PR move."

He watches me, green eyes unreadable.

Then, just as I think I've won whatever battle this is, his lips curve into a knowing smirk.

"You think she was flirting with me," he says.

I stiffen. The bastard is enjoying this.

"She was flirting with you," I reply flatly.

He tilts his head. "Was she?"

I shoot him a glare. "Oh, don't play dumb, Rory. The hand on the arm, the breathy laughter, the doe-eyed lingering looks—textbook."

His smirk deepens. "And you noticed all of that?"

My jaw tightens. He's impossible.

"Relax," he says finally, amusement still thick in his voice. "She's not into me."

"Oh, please."

"She's married."

That stops me short.

"To a lovely woman named Jessica, who is, coincidentally, a quantity surveyor."

I blink.

He leans in again, voice softer now, without the teasing edge. "She's one of my writers. I started an online romance writing group four years ago, and she was one of my first students. I just wanted to support her tonight."

Something in my chest tightens.

For a brief, fleeting second, I feel—

Oh, no. Absolutely not.

I refuse to acknowledge whatever unwelcome feeling is creeping in.

Instead, I force out a casual shrug. "Well. Good for her."

He watches me for a second longer—like he's deciding whether or not to press the issue—but then he lets it go, suddenly changing gears.

"You know what this event doesn't have?" he says, lifting his award slightly. "Decent food."

I huff. "Agreed. It's a three-hour ceremony and all they've

fed us is a sad wafer-thin slice of beef, two roast potatoes the size of radishes and a spoonful of gravy."

His smirk returns, but this time, it's softer. "Let's get something to eat."

I arch a brow. "Are you asking me out again, Keane?"

"No." He grins. "Not a date. Just two colleagues, mutually suffering from canape-induced starvation, grabbing a meal."

I hesitate.

Then, before I can think about it too much, I nod. "Fine."

Because it's not a date.

It's just food.

And I am ravenous.

Rory picks a late-night cafe two streets over, the kind of place that stays open past midnight for cabbies and jetlagged tourists. It's all fluorescent lights, Formica countertops, and the faint din of house music playing somewhere in the background.

I tell myself the location's not important.

Because it's *not* a date.

The waitress leads us to a quiet booth in the corner, and the moment I sit down, I feel it—the *tiniest* shift in the air between us. Maybe it's just the contrast between the noisy, champagne-fuelled chaos of the RNA Awards and the relative calm of the restaurant. Maybe it's that I'm finally sitting down after hours in too-high heels. Maybe it's nothing.

But Rory watches me as I pick up my menu, his gaze lingering in a way I can't quite ignore.

I clear my throat, needing something—*anything*—to cut the strange tension creeping in. "If you so much as *hint* at ordering something that contains less than one thousand calories, I'm walking out."

He huffs a quiet laugh, scanning the menu. "Wouldn't dream of it. I'm thinking steak. Fries. Possibly a side order of onion rings. Something that actually *qualifies* as a meal."

I nod, approving. "Good choice."

The waitress comes back, takes our order, and leaves a jug of water and two glasses on the table. I pour for us both, just for something to do.

"So," Rory says, leaning back against the leather booth. "You're really not going to admit it?"

I glance up. "Admit *what?*"

"That you were a tiny bit jealous."

I make a noise in the back of my throat—somewhere between a scoff and a groan. "Rory."

"What? It's a simple question."

"And a *ridiculous* one."

He grins. "You were irritated."

I sip my water slowly. "I was *bored.*"

"You were *glaring.*"

"I was *waiting* for the ceremony to start."

He hums, clearly not convinced, but lets it drop.

The waitress brings our food—mercifully fast—and for a while we eat in relative silence. It's... *nice*, actually. I hadn't realised how hungry I was until I took the first bite of my steak, and I don't bother pretending otherwise.

Rory notices.

"You look *very* serious about that meal," he observes, amused.

I point my knife at him. "I've just endured three hours of forced industry small talk, whilst our star author was flirting with our biggest competitor. I *deserve* this meal."

He chuckles, cutting into his own steak. "Not flirting."

"So you *keep* saying."

His gaze flicks to me again, softer now. "I'd rather talk to you, anyway."

It's such a simple statement. Almost *casual*. But it *lands* somewhere it shouldn't, sending a ripple of warmth through me.

I shift slightly in my seat, willing my pulse to slow. "Well. Consider yourself privileged, multi-award-winning author Rory Keane."

"Oh, I do," he says easily.

And just like that, the conversation flows.

We talk about the event, about the industry, about the latest publishing gossip. He tells me about the first time he was ever invited, years ago, and how *terrified* he was to walk into a room full of authors he admired. I share a particularly cringeworthy anecdote about the time I accidentally introduced a *debut* author to someone as a *deceased* author.

"In my defence," I say, "his name *sounded* very similar to a poet from the 1800s."

Rory laughs—*really* laughs—so much that he has to set his fork down, and I find myself *smiling* before I even realise I'm doing it.

It's easy.

It's *too* easy.

Which is exactly why, when the plates are cleared and the bill arrives, I suddenly feel an *itch* at the back of my mind. A *warning* bell, faint but insistent.

Rory leans forward slightly, elbows on the table. "So?"

I blink. "So... what?"

"You going to say it?"

I frown. "Say *what*?"

"That this *felt* like a date."

I wag my finger. "It *wasn't* a date."

"But it *felt* like one," he presses.

I roll my eyes. "You're insufferable."

He grins. "And yet, you're still here."

Not a date, I remind myself. *Just food. Just a meal between colleagues.*

And yet—

I can't quite shake the feeling that *something* has shifted.

The night air is crisp as we step outside the restaurant, a welcome relief after the warmth of the brasserie. The streets are quieter now, save for the occasional cab zipping past and the faint hum of late-night conversation from nearby bars. I wrap my coat tighter around myself, willing the fresh air to clear my head.

Rory shoves his hands into his pockets, walking beside me at a relaxed pace. For once, he's not filling the silence with teasing remarks or smug observations, and I don't know if that makes this moment better or worse.

I steal a glance at him. He's got that look again—the one that suggests he's *thinking* about something. Rory Keane, *thinking*, is dangerous.

I keep my voice even. "You're being suspiciously quiet."

He exhales a soft laugh. "Just enjoying the moment."

I narrow my eyes. "Liar."

"Alright." He tilts his head, considering. "I was thinking about something you said earlier."

"Oh God," I groan. "What now?"

He stops walking, turning slightly to face me. "Back at the table, when you said you *deserved* that meal."

I frown, caught off guard. "What about it?"

"You said you'd spent the night watching me flirt my way across the room." He pauses, eyes searching mine. "Did it really *bother* you?"

"I told you, it gives the wrong message to the industry.

"That's not what I'm talking about."

I shift on my feet, my pulse suddenly *too* loud in my ears. "I wasn't *bothered*, exactly. It was..." I wave a hand vaguely, stalling. "Others might have seen it as a message you're not happy with your current publisher. Don't be surprised if you receive a call from your agent tomorrow with a couple of offers from interested parties."

He hums, unconvinced. "Right. *Interested parties*."

I sigh, exasperated. "Rory."

His lips twitch. "You *were* annoyed."

I fold my arms. "You *ditched* your team to sit with someone else."

"For five minutes," he counters, stepping closer. "And let's be honest—this isn't about Scott & Drake, is it?"

I don't answer.

Because I *can't*.

Because I *don't know*.

He watches me, waiting.

And suddenly, I *hate* him for this. For always reading between the lines. For always pushing, needling, irritating me until I don't know which way is up.

I look away, forcing my voice into something breezy, detached. "It doesn't matter."

But deep down, it does.

This isn't *just* casual banter. It isn't *just* friendly teasing.

It's a slow, dangerous slide into something else entirely.

And suddenly, I'm worried. If he asks me on an actual date... I'm not sure how I'll answer.

SEVEN

I'd like a strong word with the sadist who thought organising an awards ceremony on a school night was a good idea.

By the time I reach the conference room, I've managed to convince myself that last night was just two colleagues enjoying each other's company. Or, at least, agreed with myself to shove any thoughts to the contrary into a neat little box labelled *Do Not Open Until After Publication*.

The thumping hangover headache, however, is proving particularly reluctant to be boxed up, and instead plonks itself down on the comfy chair just above my left eye socket, making it clear that it's in for the long haul, and it would be better for all concerned to just bloody well get used to the idea.

I adjust my glasses, smooth down my jacket, and take a deep breath before stepping inside.

And there he is. Rory Keane. Romance of the Year Award Winner. The man who writes love stories that make grown women weep. If confidence were currency, he'd be a billionaire.

"Good morning," I say, forcing my tone into something resembling professional neutrality.

"Morning," Rory replies, his voice warm and smooth, like he's auditioning for a coffee commercial. "Wasn't completely sure you'd come back."

"Well," I say, setting my laptop on the table and keeping my movements brisk, "truth is, I'm only here because someone's paying me to be."

His grin widens, completely unbothered by the jab. Of course he isn't. Rory Keane probably hasn't encountered a situation in his life where charm didn't immediately neutralise any tension.

"Let me guess," he says, "you've already condensed all of yesterday's notes into a bullet-point list of everything I need to fix, haven't you?"

I nod.

"And that's what you want us to focus on today, but a little part of you can't quite stop thinking about our deal."

"You're so very wrong. Well, not about the bullet points. I have lots of them," I reply, matching his gaze with a steady one of my own. "So, if we're done with the chit-chat, I suggest we get straight to it."

"Can't wait," he says, his eyes sparkling with amusement.

I sit down, determined to hold on to whatever shred of authority I can muster. This is just another meeting, I tell myself. Another project. Another client. It doesn't matter that he's practically oozing charisma, or that more than a little part of me thought *what if...* It really doesn't help that Danny's words about thrones and kings, and to be honest, polished turds, are still rattling around in my head. What matters is maintaining professionalism. Control. Distance.

"Shall we get started?" I ask, opening my laptop and pointedly not looking at his annoyingly perfect smile.

"Absolutely," Rory says, his tone as irreverent as ever. "Here's the thing, Lara. I have a proposal."

The way he says "proposal" makes me want to roll my eyes

so far back that I would be able to see my own brain. Instead, I adjust my glasses and give him the kind of blank stare that has sent lesser authors scrambling to rewrite entire chapters.

"A proposal," I repeat flatly. "How ominous."

"Not ominous. Inspired." He sits up, drumming his fingers lightly on the table. "I need your help with some research."

"For what? A new book? Or are you planning to pivot into investigative journalism now?"

"Funny," he says, flashing me another megawatt smile. "No, it's for *this* book. The one you're currently editing with all the enthusiasm of someone being forced to assemble IKEA furniture without instructions."

"Editing is my job," I reply coolly, ignoring the jab. "And I happen to be very good at it."

"Of course you are," he says, "but this isn't about editing. It's about authenticity. About elevating the story. The characters. The romance."

"Right, because God knows what this book is currently lacking is authenticity."

"Exactly!" He snaps his fingers. "Which is why I need you to go on a date with me."

I blink. "Excuse me?"

"A date," he repeats, as though this is the most reasonable suggestion in the world. "You know—for research."

"Research?"

"Yes. Research." He leans forward again, so close I catch the faint scent of his cologne—something warm, woodsy, and maddeningly distracting. "If I'm going to write convincingly about falling in love, I need to experience it. Or at least... fake it. And who better to fake it with than my brilliant, brutally honest editor? You'll keep me grounded, tell me when I'm being ridiculous, and—bonus—you already know how to pick apart every single one of my flaws. It's perfect."

"Perfect," I repeat, my voice laced with scepticism. "Except for the part where it's not happening."

"Why not?" he asks, utterly unfazed by my response. "You don't even have to call it a date if that makes you feel better. We can call it... a field trip."

"Rory," I say, pinching the bridge of my nose. "This is ridiculous, even for you."

"Is it?" he counters, his expression suddenly serious in a way that catches me off guard. "Think about it, Lara. How can I write about love—real, messy, complicated love—if I don't immerse myself in it? If I don't take risks? Isn't that what we're always telling writers? Write what you know?"

"Yes, but generally speaking, we don't mean, 'Go harass your editor into role-playing date night for fun and profit.'"

"Come on," he presses, his grin returning as he senses the tiniest crack in my resolve. "It'll be a professional outing. Just like last night. Nothing more. Just two colleagues having dinner—or coffee, or whatever you want—and talking about love. For research purposes only."

"Are you listening to yourself right now? Do you even hear how absurd this sounds?"

"Maybe. But so is love, don't you think? And isn't that exactly what we're trying to capture? The absurdity. The unpredictability. The... chemistry."

"Chemistry," I scoff, though the word lingers somewhere in the back of my mind longer than it should.

"Exactly," he says, lowering his voice just enough to make it feel like a secret meant only for me. "So, what do you say?"

"I say you need to rethink your approach to creative inspiration," I reply. My answers feel oddly flimsy under the weight of his gaze, and I hate it. I hate the way he somehow manages to make even the most ludicrous ideas sound almost plausible. Almost.

"Just think about it," he says. "No pressure. No expectations. Just an experiment. For the sake of great storytelling."

"Fine. One drink," I say, the words leaving my mouth before I've fully processed the betrayal of my own voice. "But purely professional. For the sake of the book and that's all. It's most certainly not a date, so no funny business."

Rory's grin spreads, slow and smug, like he's just won a bet no one else knew about. "Funny business? Me?"

"I mean it, Rory," I snap, jabbing a finger in his direction for emphasis. "This is for research. *Your* research. Don't think for a second that this—whatever this is—means anything beyond that."

"Strictly professional. Like two colleagues sharing... an immersive creative experience."

"You sound like a pretentious art school brochure."

"Hey, I don't make the rules," he says with a shrug, grabbing his coat from the back of the chair. "I just follow where inspiration leads. Come on, it's Friday night. We start immediately."

The bar he picks is maddeningly charming, all warm lighting and vintage wood accents. It's the kind of place that feels both intimate and casual, with jazz humming softly in the background and candles flickering on every table. Of course, Rory would choose a setting ripped straight out of a Nicholas Sparks adaptation.

"Let me guess," I say as we slide into a corner booth, "you bring all your 'research projects' here?"

"Only the special ones," he replies smoothly.

"How lucky for me," I say flatly, picking up the menu. I

scan it, focusing on the tiny font as if it holds the key to surviving this night with my dignity intact.

"Don't worry," he says. "I promise not to bite. Unless, of course, it's for authenticity."

I lower the menu just enough to glare at him over the top of it. "Do you always talk like this, or is it just when you're trying to irritate me?"

"Wouldn't dream of irritating you," he says, his tone dripping with faux sincerity. "You're my editor. My creative partner. My muse."

"Stop," I groan, setting the menu down entirely now because clearly, reading is impossible with him sitting there, looking so damn pleased with himself. "If you call me your 'muse' one more time, I'm walking out of here, and you'll be writing your book without any editorial support."

"Alright, no more 'muse.' How about collaborator? Co-conspirator? Partner in crime?"

"How about, 'person who regrets being here already'?" I shoot back, folding my arms across my chest.

"Now, now," he says, holding up his glass of whiskey—the one he somehow managed to order while I was busy fuming. "Let's toast to new experiences. To great storytelling. And to you, Lara Yates, for taking a chance on a crazy idea."

"Don't push your luck," I warn, though I reluctantly lift my water glass to meet his. Our glasses clink softly, and for a moment, there's something almost... sincere in the way he looks at me. Almost.

"To us," he says, his voice lower now, softer, like he's peeling back a layer of that charm just enough to reveal something more genuine underneath.

"To the book," I correct quickly, breaking whatever strange spell has settled between us. I take another sip of water, ignoring the warmth creeping up my neck as I remind myself—again—that this is strictly business.

"Right, the book."

"Exactly," I reply firmly, forcing my focus back to the task at hand. "And since this is for the book, let's cut to the chase. What exactly are you hoping to accomplish with this little experiment?"

"I told you. Authenticity," he answers immediately. "I want to write characters who feel real. Who speak to people right here"—he taps his chest—"and not just here"—he taps his temple.

"That's great," I say, nodding slowly. "But you realise I'm an editor, not a method actor, right? You don't need me for this."

"Ah, but that's where you're wrong," he says. "Because you, Lara, are the most honest person I know. Brutally so, in fact. If I can convince you, I can convince anyone."

"Convince me of what?" I ask, raising an eyebrow.

"That love, in all its absurdity, is worth believing in."

For a moment, I don't answer. Because for all his bravado and clever wordplay, there's something startlingly earnest in his expression. Something that makes it hard to dismiss him outright.

"Good luck with that," I say finally, refusing to let my guard down any further. "You've got a lot of convincing to do."

"Challenge accepted," he replies, his grin returning full force. "Now, tell me, are you a fan of live music? Because I hear they have a pretty fantastic band starting up soon..."

And just like that, the moment shifts again—back to banter, back to the safety of our usual dynamic.

The band is louder than I expected. Not overwhelmingly so, but just enough to make it harder to focus. The cosy bar Rory chose—*perfect ambience for research*, as he described it— has all the hallmarks of a place that prides itself on charm: exposed brick walls, dim lighting, and the faint aroma of vanilla wafting from candles scattered on every table. It's designed to disarm, to seduce, and I'm starting to think Rory knew exactly what he was doing when he picked it.

"Okay, we've been here for two hours, and I still don't understand how this qualifies as 'research.'"

"You're having fun. Admit it."

"Fun isn't exactly the word I'd use."

"What *would* you call this? Pure agony? Mild irritation? Or"—that grin deepens—"a reluctant good time?"

"Somewhere between mild irritation and a reluctant good time," I say dryly. "Heavy on the irritation."

He raises his glass. "To being mildly irritating, then."

I roll my eyes but lift my glass—gin and tonic now, because I need something crisp and distracting—to clink lightly against his. "To your unparalleled ability to test my patience."

"*Sláinte,*" he says with a laugh, his gaze lingering a beat too long before he takes another sip.

And there it is again—that shift. Subtle but undeniable, like the moment you realise the tide has turned and you're no longer standing on solid ground. I glance away, pretending to be fascinated by the candle flickering between us, but my thoughts are suddenly tangled, uncooperative.

The band begins a new song, a slow, soulful melody that fills the space between us. For a moment, neither of us speaks. Rory shifts slightly closer, his arm brushing against mine as he props his elbow on the edge of the table.

"Can I tell you something?" he asks, his voice low enough that it feels like it's meant only for me.

"Depends," I say, trying to keep my tone casual. "Is it going to involve another sales pitch for why I should believe in love?"

"Maybe," he says, his lips curving into that maddening half-smile. "Or maybe it's just an observation."

"Go on, then," I say, even though I'm not entirely sure I want him to.

"You underestimate yourself," he says simply.

The words catch me off guard—not because they're particularly profound, but because of the way he says them, like they're an indisputable fact.

"Rory…" I start, but whatever deflection I was about to throw his way dies on my tongue.

"Just something to think about," he says, his gaze steady and unflinching.

The distance between us feels impossibly small now, the lines between professional and personal blurring in ways that leave me breathless. I should pull back, reestablish the boundaries I've worked so hard to maintain, but for some reason, I don't.

"Careful," I say, forcing a smirk to mask the sudden vulnerability threatening to surface. "You're starting to sound sincere."

"Who says I'm not?" His smile softens, and for once, there's no trace of teasing in his expression. Just quiet, unguarded intensity.

The song shifts to something livelier, breaking the spell, and I seize the opportunity to lean back, creating a sliver of space between us.

"Well," I say, clearing my throat. "If this is what you consider research, I think you might need to reevaluate your methods."

"Only if you promise to help me," he says, his tone light again, though his eyes haven't lost that unsettling focus.

"Let's not get ahead of ourselves," I reply, refusing to let my guard slip any further. But even as I redirect the conversation back to safer topics, I can't quite shake the feeling that something unspoken has shifted between us—something I'm not ready to face just yet.

EIGHT

♥

The cool night air hits me as we step out of the bar, a sharp contrast to the warmth inside. The street is alive—headlights reflecting off wet pavement, the low hum of conversation blending with the occasional beep of a car horn. My heels click against the pavement, a steady rhythm that keeps my focus forward and away from the man at my side.

"Careful!" Rory's voice cuts through the din just as his hand wraps around my wrist, firm and startling.

The jolt—both his touch and the sudden yank—sends my heart skittering as I stumble back a step, barely processing the blur of motion in front of me. A cyclist shoots past, tyres hissing on the damp pavement, close enough that I catch a flash of fluorescent yellow.

"Are you trying to get run over, or is this some sort of dramatic exit strategy?"

"Let go," I snap, more out of reflex than actual indignation. Except he doesn't. Not immediately, anyway.

His fingers stay locked around my wrist, warm and solid, holding me in place as if I might dart into traffic again without supervision. I'm far too aware of the pulse in my wrist thudding rapidly under his grip.

"Relax," he says, his thumb brushing lightly against my skin in a way that feels... deliberate. "I'm not about to let you get run over. You're far too valuable to the publishing world."

"Valuable?" I arch a brow, yanking my arm back with more force than necessary. His hand falls away, but the ghost of his touch lingers like static electricity. "You've clearly had too much to drink if you're throwing compliments around now."

"Just calling it like I see it," he says.

"Well, next time, try doing it without grabbing me,"

I take a step back, but the moment clings to me—his touch, his voice, that damn smirk. My arm feels bare, exposed without his hand there. It's ridiculous. I've shaken hands with authors before, hugged colleagues at office parties, even endured the occasional awkward cheek kisses from overzealous freelancers. And yet, Rory Keane grabs my wrist for half a second, and suddenly my brain decides it's hosting its own fireworks display.

"Hey." His voice is softer now, pulling my attention back to him whether I want it or not. He's watching me, his head tilted slightly, amused but... waiting. For what? My spontaneous combustion? An apology?

His gaze is steady, too steady, and I hate how aware of it I am. Aware of him. The way his dark hair has fallen just slightly out of place, as if he's been running his hands through it all night. The way another button on his shirt has opened, giving him this careless, end-of-the-day charm that's entirely too easy on the eyes. And those eyes—piercing, intent, like he can see every thought I'm trying so hard to suppress.

"Thanks for saving me. I wasn't paying attention."

He doesn't say anything. He just keeps looking at me, unhurried, like he's letting the silence do the talking. It's unnerving. No—it's *dangerous*.

Because here's the thing: I know better. I *know* better than to let myself get caught up in this moment that should mean nothing, that *has* to mean nothing. Rory Keane is a client. A bestselling, untouchable, pain-in-my-arse client, whose current draft is riddled with plot holes and he doesn't seem to be in any great rush to fix it. We need to deliver a completed manuscript in a matter of weeks, and nothing, nothing whatsoever, can get in the way. Certainly not a complication of my own making.

I should be annoyed. I *am* annoyed. And yet... Part of me is screaming, *what if?* Why does this have to mean nothing? Can I not wrangle a publishable novel out of the man and explore... *this*, if I want? Are the two things really mutually exclusive?

Just as empathically, the other part of me—the sensible, safe, risk-averse Lara— is pleading not to go there. Not again. Not in thought, and certainly not in action, unless I want a repeat of James all over again.

The street noise fades, muffled under the thrum of my pulse as I catch the faintest flicker of something behind his expression. Something careful, expectant. Like he's daring me to close the distance between us, but won't make the first move. My throat tightens, heat pooling low in my stomach as my mind scrambles to find solid ground.

This isn't happening. This *can't* be happening. Except it is, because I'm standing here, rooted to the spot, staring at him like an idiot, ignoring my own cautionary tale, while the air between us grows thicker, heavier, electric. My heart hammers louder than it should, drowning out every rational thought I've ever had about boundaries and professionalism and common sense.

"Rory—" I start, but my voice catches. His name comes out softer than intended, brushing between us like an admission.

And then, before I can talk myself out of it—or maybe because I can't—I move.

It's not calculated or graceful or anything remotely resembling good judgment. It's pure impulse, driven by a cocktail of frustration, adrenaline, and something I don't have the courage to name. I lean in, closing the gap in one swift, reckless motion, and press my lips to his.

His lips are warm and softer than I expect, but the kiss is anything but gentle. It's fast, reckless—like a match striking against flint—and for one dizzying second, all I can focus on is the way he tastes. A mix of whiskey and something inherently *him*, something that makes my stomach freefall in a way I'm not ready to deal with.

The world tips sideways. My fingers curl instinctively into the front of his jacket, anchoring me as heat crashes through my body like a wave. Rory doesn't hesitate—not even for a heartbeat. His hand slides up, firm and sure, until his palm cradles my jaw, his thumb brushing just below my cheekbone. The sensation sends sparks skittering down my spine, and I swear my knees threaten mutiny.

He angles closer, deepening the kiss, and I feel it everywhere—radiating through my chest, coiling low in my belly, making the rest of the bustling street dissolve into static. His grip tightens just enough to keep me grounded, to keep me from floating away entirely, and for a fleeting, maddening moment, I forget why this is a terrible idea.

The city blurs at the edges, dimming under the sheer intensity of him. There's no traffic noise, no faint chatter from passersby—just the rush of blood in my ears and the pressure of his mouth moving against mine. Every nerve feels alive, hyper-aware of where we're connected, where his fingers skim the edge of my jawline or dip slightly into my hair.

I don't know when I stopped breathing—maybe somewhere between the first stolen second and now—but every part of me aches with the need to pull him closer, to chase the spark before reality catches up.

I pull back, abruptly, like I've just remembered how to breathe and it's the most urgent thing in the world. My lips tingle with the ghost of his, my pulse hammering away as if I've just sprinted up twenty flights of stairs. What the hell did I just do?

"Okay," I blurt, though I have no idea what I'm trying to convey with that single, useless word. My voice sounds breathless—traitorous—and I hate how it hangs between us, exposed and raw.

Rory doesn't move right away. His hand lingers near my face for a fraction longer, as though he hasn't fully caught up with the fact that I ended things. Slowly, his fingers drop, brushing against my shoulder before they retreat entirely. And then he grins.

Not a small grin. Not polite or bashful. No, this is the full Rory Keane Special: wide, wolfish, and so unbearably smug I want to smack it off his face. Or kiss it again. God, no. Not that.

"Okay," he mirrors, his voice low and maddeningly smooth. "That was unexpected."

"Don't." The word shoots out, sharp and defensive, my last-ditch effort to salvage some semblance of dignity. I take a step back, putting precious inches of space between us, but it doesn't help. He's still looking at me like I've just become his favourite plot twist.

"Don't... what?" he drawls, his head tilting like he genuinely wants clarification, but the sparkle in his eyes says different. He knows *exactly* what I mean.

"Don't make this a thing." My hands are restless now, smoothing down the front of my jacket, adjusting my glasses— anything to avoid meeting his gaze directly. "It's not a thing."

"Right. Not a thing," he echoes, clearly amused. He

crosses his arms over his chest, his weight shifting to one leg in that effortless way he has, all casual confidence. "Just a totally spontaneous, completely unprovoked kiss in the middle of the street. Happens all the time."

"Exactly." I nod once, curt and decisive, as if agreeing with him will somehow make this less mortifying. "A momentary lapse in judgment. Nothing more."

"Momentary, huh?" He lets the word hang there, rolling it around like it's delicious on his tongue. Then, because he can't help himself, he adds, "You sure about that?"

"Rory." I finally meet his eyes, and it's a mistake. They're soft now—still teasing, yes, but there's something else there too. Warmth. Curiosity. A quiet sort of delight that makes me feel like I'm standing under a spotlight.

"Relax, Lara," he says gently. "I'm not complaining."

"Right. Well. I should—" My voice comes out strangled, the syllables tripping over each other like they're trying to flee the scene before I can. Relatable.

I gesture vaguely behind me, as if the direction of my escape is a foregone conclusion and not something I'm currently inventing on the spot. "I just remembered—emails. Agent submissions. Publishing emergencies." My mouth keeps moving, but none of it makes sense, even to me. "You know how it is."

"Emails," Rory echoes. His eyebrows lift slightly, but he doesn't move, doesn't step back, doesn't do anything helpful like make this easier for me. Instead, he stays exactly where he is, arms still crossed, looking far too entertained for someone who just got ambushed by a kiss in public.

"Yes. Emails." I nod quickly, as though that single word explains everything: my sudden lack of composure, the way my heart is hammering against my ribs, the fact that I just kissed Rory Keane. And oh God, I *kissed* Rory Keane.

"Urgent, life-altering emails," I add, because apparently digging holes is my new hobby. "And probably a fire to put out somewhere. Metaphorically speaking."

"Suuure," he replies, dragging the word out, letting it drip with amusement.

"Okay, great talk." I spin on my heel so fast I nearly twist my ankle, but momentum is key here. If I slow down, I'll start thinking again, and thinking leads to feeling, and no good can come from that. Not when the feeling in question involves the heat of his hand still ghosting on my wrist, or the way his lips were— Nope. Not going there.

I start to put one foot in front of the other. Each step is a declaration: I am *leaving this situation.* My jacket flaps slightly in the breeze, and I yank it tighter around me, as if I can shield myself from the lingering awareness prickling along my skin.

"Emails," I say under my breath, half a mantra, half an alibi. The streetlights blur at the edges of my vision, and I deliberately focus on them, letting their soft glow ground me. Focusing on literally anything but the electricity still buzzing in my veins or the stupid, self-satisfied tilt of Rory's grin now permanently etched into my memory. Why does he have to look like that all the time? Like he's perpetually five seconds away from ruining your entire day—and somehow making you grateful for it?

I don't look back. I don't dare. Because if I see him now—if I catch even a glimpse of those knowing eyes—I might actually combust. Or worse, I might stop walking. And stopping would be catastrophic. Stopping would mean staying, and staying would mean facing what just happened. What *I* just did.

So I keep moving. Quick, deliberate steps, each one distancing me from the moment I let my guard slip and everything changed.

A black cab splashes through a puddle, a car horn blasts

somewhere down the road, and everything around me feels too loud, too bright, *too much*. But it's fine. It's all fine. All I have to do is get home without looking back.

Naturally, I look back.

It's a glance, barely half a second, but it lands with the force of a meteor strike. Rory's standing where I left him, hands shoved casually into his coat pockets like he doesn't have a care in the world. And that grin—that slow, devastating curve of his mouth—is spreading across his face. His dark eyes catch mine, locking me in place for one traitorous moment too long.

Oh, come on. Who *looks* like that after being ambushed by a kiss? Content, amused, like he's already filing this away as some kind of victory. He tilts his head slightly, eyebrow quirking in an unspoken challenge, and I know—just *know*— he's waiting for me to turn around and go back to him. Or maybe trip over my own feet again. Either option would probably make his night.

What was I thinking? Seriously, what part of me thought kissing Rory Keane—a man who thrives on chaos and charm like plants thrive on sunlight—was even remotely a good idea?

Spoiler alert: none of me thought it was a good idea. Not my brain, not my heart, and certainly not the tiny, rational editor voice in my head that usually keeps me from doing reckless, career-ending things like this. No, this was pure, unfiltered impulse. The kind of impulse that gets people turned into cautionary tales at office happy hours.

"God, you're an idiot," I whisper, my voice swallowed by the city din. My pace picks up, as if I can outrun the memory of Rory's eyes boring into me. But it doesn't work. Of course, it doesn't work. Because the truth is, I'm not running from Rory.

I'm running from the fact that—for one insane, gravity-defying moment—I wanted to kiss him again.

And that scares me more than anything. Because this isn't just complicated—it's catastrophic. Rory isn't just some random guy at a bar. He's *Rory Keane*, my client and my company's biggest asset. This isn't a fling or a flirtation or whatever other word people use to justify bad decisions. This is work. This is my job. My carefully structured life. And now, thanks to one impulsive kiss, it's all teetering on the edge of ruin.

NINE

I close the door to my flat and immediately sag against it, hyperventilating like I've just sprinted up ten flights of stairs instead of making the five-minute walk from the tube station. My fingers hover over the lock for a beat before I twist it, like that extra barrier will somehow keep the reality of the last few hours from creeping in after me, making me sit on the naughty chair, and asking me to have a think about my behaviour.

Because, that kiss? That *ridiculous*, reckless, completely unprofessional kiss?

I don't know what the hell I was thinking.

I toe off my shoes, crossing the room on autopilot, ignoring the mess of half-read manuscripts and stray red pens littering my coffee table. My laptop sits open, screen glowing, a blinking cursor waiting for me to get back to work. Instead, I grab a glass from the kitchen shelf and fill it from the tap, gulping down water like it might flush out the heat still simmering under my skin.

But nothing washes away the feeling of his hands on me, the way he kissed me back like he meant it, like I was something he wanted.

I shake my head, setting the glass down too hard. *Get a grip.*

It was just a kiss. A moment of... what? Weakness? Impulse? Poor decision-making?

I press my palms against the cool edge of the counter, forcing myself to breathe, to be rational—but the problem is, I wasn't rational back there. I was reckless, and I don't *do* reckless. I don't get swept up in the moment. I don't initiate *anything* without thinking it through. And yet, there I was, tangling my fingers in Rory Keane's hair and pulling him closer like some romance heroine in a third-act confession scene.

I squeeze my eyes shut. This is a disaster.

I should never have let myself be alone with him like that. Should never have let my guard down—not even for a second, not even for a kiss. Because now? Now I'm in trouble.

My phone buzzes on the table, and my stomach lurches as I glance at the screen. Not Rory. Just Danny.

Relief floods through me, which is stupid—why would Rory be texting me? He probably hasn't given that kiss half the thought I have.

And that's the real problem, isn't it?

Because if I say something now—if I bring it up, if I admit that it *meant* something to me—I'll be the fool. The *hopeless* one. And I refuse to be the one who confuses a moment of attraction for something more.

Not again. Not after James. Not after standing in a kitchen three years ago, holding a wedding invitation and wondering how the hell I let myself believe in something that never existed.

I let out a breath, slow and controlled. Whatever this is— whatever *that* was—it doesn't matter.

Because Rory Keane is just a job, and I am a professional.

I pick up my phone and text Danny back:

> Hey, just off to bed. Catch up over the weekend. All good xx

I'm not ready to share details. I haven't fully processed the implications, and the last thing I need is *I told you so* vibes from Danny, even via text message. To ensure a communications blackout, I shove my phone deep into the sofa cushions and collapse on top of it all.

But it's impossible to relax. I replay the evening over and over again, hoping I can both alter the outcome and feel the sensations all over again.

It's just lust. That's all it ever is. That's all it ever remains.

Because, love? Love is something else entirely. Something that promises forever but always finds a way to fall apart.

I learned that lesson the hard way.

The last time I let myself believe in forever, I was in a flat just like this one, an engagement ring on my finger, my voice raw from words that changed nothing.

Standing in the kitchen, James just across from me, arms crossed, jaw tight, eyes fixed on the floor like he was already halfway out the door.

And maybe he was. Maybe he had been leaving for months. Maybe I just wasn't paying attention.

"I don't know what you want me to say," he says finally, voice clipped.

I grip the counter to keep from shaking. "You could start with the truth."

He lets out a hollow laugh, running a hand through his hair. "The truth? The truth is, you've already decided how this conversation ends, Lara."

I flinch—not at his words, but at how right they sound. Like he knows me better than I know myself.

"I just don't understand how we got here," I say, hating the way my voice wavers. Hating that I'm *pleading*.

James exhales pointedly, stepping back like he's trying to physically remove himself from the weight of this conversation. "Lara, we've been here for a while."

The words land like a slap.

"No, *you've* been here," I snap. "You've been pulling away, making excuses, treating me like I'm just— just *here*—"

"You *are* just here!" he cuts in, frustration spilling over. "You're always here. Sitting at your desk, buried in your work, fixing everyone else's words but never saying a damn thing about what you actually *want*."

I stagger back, his words hitting a little too close, a little too true.

"That's not fair."

"Isn't it?" His voice softens, but not in a way that soothes. In a way that makes me realise this moment—this *end*—has already been decided.

I press my lips together, swallowing the lump in my throat.

"James," I say, quietly now. "If you don't want to be here, just say so."

He looks at me then, really looks at me, and I know—I know—what's coming.

"Lara, I think we're done."

I nod, even though it feels like the floor has been yanked from beneath me.

"Right." My voice is even, cool, like I knew this was inevitable. "So, that's it?"

James hesitates. "I didn't want it to end like this."

"Then why did it?"

He doesn't answer. Maybe he doesn't have one.

Maybe he does, and I just don't want to hear it.

The silence stretches between us. It's the most honest conversation we've had in months.

Finally, James sighs. He grabs his coat from the chair, slings it over his arm, and lingers for half a second too long. Like he's waiting for me to change my mind. Like he's waiting for me to stop him.

I don't.

Because love is not enough.

Because no matter how much you want someone to stay, sometimes... they don't.

Sometimes, they never planned to in the first place.

The door closes behind him, and I let out a breath.

And just like that, I stop believing in love.

Because it's not real. Not in the way books make it out to be.

It's lust, attraction, chemistry—whatever you want to call it. But real love? The kind that lasts? The kind that doesn't just fizzle out or fall apart the moment life gets inconvenient?

That's fiction.

And I, for one, prefer to keep my expectations *realistic*.

The memory still lingers like the smell of burnt toast in a kitchen long after the charred remains have been tossed in the wheelie bin outside.

I'm curled up on my sofa, glass of wine in one hand, trying not to recover my phone from under the cushion, resisting the ridiculous temptation to text Rory. *Not to say anything meaningful, of course. Just something flippant. Casual.*

Something that wouldn't make it obvious I've spent the last hour replaying the way he kissed me.

What the hell am I doing?

I tip my head back against the cushions and groan. I can't believe I let that happen. *I kissed him.* I started it. It wasn't some moment of romantic serendipity where we were swept up by forces beyond our control. *No. I knew exactly what I was doing.* And I did it anyway.

I bring my knees up to my chest, trying to fold myself into something smaller, something that takes up less space. As if I can physically shrink my feelings into something manageable.

Because, this? This isn't manageable. This is a problem.

I know how this story ends.

I learned it with James. I saw it with my parents, who still orbit each other like housemates rather than partners. Love—real love—*doesn't last.* It starts with passion, with chemistry, with an unbearable *need* to be around each other, and then... it fades. It cools. It turns into something stale, or worse, something bitter.

And the idea of letting that happen again—of letting someone get close enough to hurt me like that again? No. Absolutely not.

I bet Rory isn't sitting around analysing our kiss, questioning what it means. That he's perfectly fine, typing away at his manuscript, *not thinking about me at all.*

And why should he be?

This isn't that kind of thing, I remind myself. *He's not that kind of guy.* Rory Keane is fun. He's a flirt. He's *temporary.*

And that's perfect. That's exactly what I need.

Not the complicated, falling-too-hard-too-fast kind of thing I swore I'd never do again.

I take another sip of wine and push the memory of James—of that final conversation, of the years I spent convincing myself we were forever—out of my mind.

This time, I won't make the same mistake.

This time, I'll be *smarter.*

I won't let feelings get involved.

I *can't.*

I set my wineglass down with more force than necessary, the sound of it meeting the coffee table with a loud clink.

Enough.

This spiral ends now.

I stand, stretching out my limbs as if shaking off the weight of memory. The room is dimly lit, the hum of the city outside a constant, steady presence. I exhale, slow and controlled, and head straight for my desk. If my brain insists on obsessing over Rory, then I'll channel that energy into something productive.

The manuscript. The thing I should have been focusing on in the first place.

I flip through my notes, scanning the latest pages Rory sent over, ignoring the way my stomach clenches slightly at the thought of him.

Because that's all this is. A physical response. A fleeting attraction.

And I know how to compartmentalise.

I pause at a passage—a romantic confession from Oliver to Sophie.

"I don't know when it happened, but it did. One day, you were just there. And now I can't imagine a life where you're not."

I swallow, pressing my lips together. Too sentimental. The kind of thing that makes people believe love is inevitable.

I replace it with something safer, something more logical.

"I like being around you. That's enough for me."

Much better.

I keep going, pushing aside the thoughts clawing at the edges of my mind. This is what I do. I fix things. I make them cleaner, smoother, less dangerous.

And that's exactly how I'm going to handle Rory Keane.

We kissed. That's all it was. It doesn't need to mean anything.

Tomorrow, I'll see him. We'll talk about the book.

I'll draw a line between us and make damn sure neither of us crosses it again.

I close the manuscript's folder, stacking it neatly on my desk. Everything is in its place. The book. My thoughts. My resolve.

And yet...

My fingers hover over the file, hesitating. My heartbeat is steady, controlled—but there's something underneath it. A flicker of something I don't want to name.

Because when I kissed Rory, it felt *different*.

Not just reckless, not just heat or attraction or a moment of bad judgment.

Something deeper. Something dangerous.

And that makes it ten times more terrifying.

I need to go to bed, to put today, and especially tonight, behind me. I won't go down that road again. I can't.

I get up off the sofa and reach for the light switch, flipping it off with more force than necessary.

This isn't love. It's lust.

And as long as I remember that, I'll be fine.

Saturday afternoon and the rhythmic hum of my keyboard is the only sound in my living room, save for the occasional annoyed sigh I let escape when a sentence refuses to cooperate. My fingers hover over the keys, motionless now, as I stare at the blinking cursor on the new chapters Rory has sent through.

"Just work," I grumble under my breath, trying to convince myself. My glasses slide down my nose, and I push them back up, a ritual that seems to happen more often when I'm editing his material. Coincidence? Unlikely.

I scroll through the document again, scanning the scene he'd been so insistent on "researching" together. The fictional couple—thinly veiled versions of us, much to my mortification —are mid-banter, their dialogue crackling with flirtation framed as rivalry. It's annoyingly good. Worse, it's dizzyingly familiar. I can hear Rory's voice in every line, see the way his eyes crinkle at the corners when he's particularly pleased with himself. The memory of his lopsided grin from last tonight nudges at me like an elbow in the ribs.

"Stop it," I command myself, shaking my head hard enough to make my ponytail swish. "This isn't about him. It's about the work."

But the problem is, it's not just the work. Not anymore. We kissed. We actually kissed, and I was the one who'd initiated it. Rory Keane has managed to wedge himself into my brain like a splinter that I can't seem to tweeze out. And maybe I don't want to.

The thought shocks me so much I nearly knock my coffee mug off the desk. I grab it just in time, my fingers curling around the ceramic as if holding onto it will stabilise me. Coffee is safe. Predictable. Rory is neither.

"Focus," I whisper, staring hard at the screen. The cursor blinks back at me, unhelpful as ever.

My phone buzzes next to the keyboard, jolting me. I glance at the notification. A text from Danny:

> How's the border collie's manuscript coming along? Still resisting his obvious charms, or should I start planning your wedding hashtag?

"Ugh," I groan, but I can't help the laughter that bubbles up. Of course, Danny would feel *a disturbance in the force*. I'm still not ready to tell him anything and I type back quickly:

> It's fine. Everything is fine. Zero charm resistance required.

A blatant lie, but one day he'll forgive me.

As soon as I hit send, another message pops up. This one isn't from Danny. It's from Rory:

> Still thinking about last night? Don't worry—I'll start planning our next research outing. You're welcome in advance. 😌

I stare at the screen, heat creeping up my neck. The audacity of this man. But also... the absolute nerve of my stupid heart to skip a beat at the sight of his name lighting up my phone.

I should ignore him. Pretend I didn't see it. Better yet, respond with some scathing remark that makes it clear that what happened yesterday was most certainly a one-off. But instead, my thumb hovers over the keyboard, indecisive.

"Don't engage," I tell myself firmly. "Do *not* engage."

And yet, against my better judgment—or perhaps because of it—I find myself typing back.

> Professional curiosity. That's all it was. Don't flatter yourself, Keane.

I hit send before I can second-guess it, instantly regretting how flirty it sounds. Flirting wasn't the goal. Professional boundaries were the goal. Right?

The dots indicating he's typing appear immediately. I set the phone facedown on the desk, determined not to let him get any more space in my head today. Except, of course, I pick it back up thirty seconds later.

> Flattered anyway

Enjoy the new chapters, Lara. Your research methodology really helped.

"Damn you." Though, I catch myself smiling. *Damn him.*

I close the laptop with a decisive snap, leaning back in my chair and staring at the ceiling. This was supposed to be simple. Edit the book. Keep things professional. Ignore the magnetic pull of Rory Keane's ridiculous charisma.

I'm failing spectacularly on every single point.

"Just work," I say aloud one last time, but the words ring hollow now. Because deep down, I know the truth. Nothing about this feels like *just work* anymore. That kiss wasn't just a mistake. It was a shift—a tectonic one—and now there's no going back.

I vow that all future editorial meetings will be conducted online; there's absolutely no need for us to be in the same room. This is all totally manageable remotely.

TEN

The gravel crunches underfoot as I wrestle my suitcase up the narrow garden path, my laptop bag bouncing against my hip with every awkward step. The cottage looms ahead—quaint, picturesque, and thoroughly irritating. Of course Fiona would think this was a good idea. Nothing says "professional collaboration" like isolating two people in a countryside retreat with questionable Wi-Fi and a history of bad decisions.

Obviously, Fiona doesn't know about last week's kiss.

Obviously, I couldn't tell her the real reason I didn't want to go to Somerset.

So, now I'm here. Obviously.

"Charming, isn't it?" Rory's voice floats over my shoulder, far too amused for my liking. He's trailing behind me, his suitcase rolling effortlessly along, because of course it is.

"Charming," I echo flatly, gripping the handle of my bag like it might sprout wings and fly off if I let go. "If you're into twee aesthetics and forced proximity."

"Forced proximity can be fun," he says, breezing past me up the steps to the front door. "Depends on the company."

I swallow the scathing reply bubbling at the back of my

throat and follow him inside, determined not to engage. The air smells faintly of lavender and aged wood, the kind of scent that belongs in overpriced candles marketed to women who've never experienced stress. It's annoyingly soothing, which only irritates me further.

Rory is already surveying the space, hands in his pockets, a relaxed confidence radiating off him like sunlight. I hate how comfortable he looks here, like he belongs, like this whole ridiculous setup is a big joke he intends to enjoy to its fullest. Meanwhile, I'm standing in the entryway clutching my things like a deranged pack mule, trying not to trip over the uneven flagstone floor.

"Cosy," he declares, turning toward me. "What do you think?"

"That I'll be billing Fiona for emotional damages," I grouse, brushing past him to claim the nearest available surface as my workspace. The dining table will do—solid, functional, and conveniently far from the fireplace where Rory has already draped himself across an armchair like some sort of literary lounge lizard.

As I pull out my laptop and arrange my notebooks with clinical precision, I can feel him watching me. There's a weight to his gaze, a heat that makes my skin prickle beneath my jacket. I keep my eyes fixed on the table, pretending not to notice.

"Need help setting up?" he offers, his tone light but laced with something that feels like a dare.

"I think I can manage plugging in a laptop without assistance, thanks," I reply, adjusting my glasses and keeping my focus firmly on my screen. My fingers hover over the keyboard, though I'm not typing anything yet. I just need to look busy. Distracted. Uninterested.

"Suit yourself." There's a rustling sound as he shifts in his seat, followed by a low chuckle that sets my teeth on edge.

"You always get this serious when you collaborate, or is this just for me?"

"Some of us take our jobs seriously," I say, finally glancing up just long enough to shoot him a pointed look.

"Ah, so I'm special."

"Special is one word for it," I mumble, focusing again on aligning the edges of my notebook with military precision. If I keep my hands busy, maybe I can distract myself from the memory of his lips on mine, from the way my heart had stumbled over itself in that split second before logic swooped in and ruined everything.

"Come on, Lara," he says after a beat, his voice softer now, almost coaxing. "This isn't so bad, is it? A little trip to the countryside, fresh air, some creative collaboration..."

"Let's just stick to the collaboration," I cut in. His eyebrows lift, but he doesn't push, and for that I'm grateful.

Rory ambles over and joins me at the dining table. He looks maddeningly unbothered, like we're here for a casual chat rather than surgery on his disaster of a second act.

"Okay," I say, finally breaking the silence. "Let's start with the obvious problem."

"By all means," he replies smoothly, gesturing with his free hand as if inviting me to destroy him. His confidence, I swear, is both exhausting and... No, it's just exhausting.

"Your protagonist, Oliver"—I emphasise the name like it's a personal affront—"spends half of Act Two, when he's not dealing with car chases and explosions, sulking about being dumped, but we're supposed to believe he's falling in love with someone new. It's emotionally inconsistent. You can't have depth if you're skimming the surface."

"Ah, yes," Rory says, nodding solemnly. "Depth. The sworn enemy of a good sulk."

"Rory," I snap, "I'm serious. You're avoiding the emotional work. Oliver needs to actually *feel* something beyond self-pity. Otherwise, your readers won't buy the romance."

"But what if Oliver's wallowing is part of the point? Maybe he's afraid to feel something real because it makes him vulnerable. Vulnerability is terrifying, Lara. Don't you agree?"

"Vulnerability is relatable," I counter evenly. "But only if it's earned. Right now, Oliver reads like a mopey teenager who doesn't know what he wants."

"Sounds familiar," Rory says under his breath, just loud enough for me to hear.

"Excuse me?"

"Nothing," he says innocently. "Seriously, though, you think the lack of emotional depth is the biggest issue?"

"One of them," I admit, keeping my eyes on the manuscript. "The pacing is also off, and some of the new dialogue feels... unnatural. Like you're trying too hard to be clever."

"I think I lost my way a little bit. It's been weird not meeting up face-to-face last week to work on the edit. I missed this, you know. Working with you."

"Working with me or arguing with me?" I ask, suspicious.

"Is there a difference?" he quips, but there's an undercurrent of sincerity in his tone.

"Let's get back to Oliver," I say briskly. "He needs a clear emotional arc. Start by asking yourself what he's afraid of. What's holding him back?"

"Fear of rejection, maybe." Rory's answer comes quickly, but his eyes linger on me a little too long, like he's testing the waters. "Or fear of getting hurt again. That's relatable, right?"

"Sure," I reply. "As long as it doesn't become an excuse for him to avoid growth. Readers want to see him evolve, not stagnate."

"Fine," he concedes. "What if he writes her a letter? Something raw, unpolished. Vulnerable."

"Finally," I say, exhaling like I've been waiting for him to arrive at this obvious conclusion all along. "Now we're getting somewhere. But it has to be earned. No clichés about sunsets or comparing her eyes to gemstones."

"Even sapphires?" he teases.

"Especially sapphires."

"Right, got it. Although, for the record, I think it's a killer line." He pulls out his laptop and starts writing, our earlier rhythm slowly reestablishing itself as we toss ideas back and forth. It's almost... fun, working like this. When he's not being insufferably smug, Rory actually listens. And when I'm not being hypercritical, I might even enjoy the way our minds click together. It's maddeningly productive. Almost dangerous, really.

With Rory deep into re-writing his end of Act One, I take the opportunity to have a nosey upstairs. My initial fears that Fiona didn't think to check there were two bedrooms were quickly put to rest. There are two and they're both beautiful. It's pure cottage-core and I'm an instant convert. I lay claim to the smaller of the two. Not because I'm feeling particularly magnanimous, but because it's the one with an en suite bath-room. Since I entered my thirties two years ago, I've found that my bladder likes to become hyperactive at night, and the last thing I need is being spotted in the early hours running back from the communal bathroom in my pyjamas.

It takes just minutes to unpack my case and the cottage immediately feels like a home away from home. I lay on top of the bedcovers to rest my eyes, and thanks to the ridiculously early start, and the long drive, I fall asleep.

When I wake, I'm energised and excited, and I bound down the stairs with a craving for herbal tea. Rory's deep into writing new material so I try not to disturb him, instead I browse through the small but eclectic selection of cookery books lined up next to the kettle.

With a tagine recipe committed to memory along with a solemn promise to try and cook it sometime this week, I sit at the kitchen table and stretch, willing some of the kinks out of my back.

Rory mirrors my movement, except instead of stretching, he tips his chair back on two legs, balancing precariously.

"Don't do that," I warn automatically. "You'll crack your skull open, and I'm not driving you to the hospital."

"Good to know where I stand with you." He lets the chair thud back onto all fours, then crosses his arms behind his head. "So... about that kiss."

The air between us shifts so suddenly, I swear I feel it. My spine stiffens. "*What* kiss?"

"Come on, you haven't forgotten."

"Of course not, but it's irrelevant."

"Is it? Because I don't think it is."

"Well, you'd be wrong. We're here to work, remember? Not rehash some—some lapse in judgment." My voice falters slightly on the last three words, and I hate myself for it.

"Interesting choice of words."

"Drop it, Rory,"

"Alright. If you insist. Back to work, then?"

"Back to work," I echo, forcing my focus back to the page. But the tension lingers, electric and unresolved, humming in the air between us.

"Chemistry," he says suddenly, breaking the silence like a pebble tossed into still water.

I glance up, frowning. "What about it?"

"In the book," he clarifies, though the way his gaze flicks

toward me suggests he's not *just* talking about the book. "You said earlier that the romance lacks chemistry. That it feels... flat."

"Yes, because it does," I reply, my editor voice kicking in automatically. "The interactions between your leads are still too surface-level. There's no real spark, none of the emotional depth of your other books. They're just—" I pause, searching for the right word. "Going through the motions."

"Then riddle me this. Do you think chemistry can be manufactured? Or is it something that has to already exist?"

"Are we really doing this?"

"Why not? It's relevant." He stands and begins to pace. "If the issue with Sophie and Oliver is a lack of believable chemistry, maybe we should examine what makes chemistry believable."

"Good luck with that. Chemistry, ironically, isn't a science experiment, Rory. You can't just"—I wave my pen vaguely—"engineer it."

"I agree, it's not science. It's human connection. Messy, complicated, unpredictable. Isn't that what you're saying I need to capture on the page?"

The second act of his manuscript *does* fall flat. The romance lacks life, it lacks spontaneity. It reads too practised, too rehearsed—as if the characters are playing their parts rather than living them. And if I'm being honest with myself (a big *if*), I've spent more nights than I care to admit staring at my ceiling, wondering why I care so much about fixing it. Wondering why his failure feels so personal.

"Stop doing that."

"Doing what?"

"Making sense."

Rory laughs, gets up, and pours his own drink.

I narrow my eyes. "You've got that look."

Rory leans against the counter opposite me, all lazy confidence, stirring sugar into his tea like he's not about to say something ridiculous. "What look?"

"The one that usually comes before a terrible idea."

He grins, lifting his mug to his lips. "What if it's a great idea?"

"Highly unlikely."

He studies me for a moment, like he's weighing his approach, then sets his mug down with a decisive clink. "There's obviously something here."

I arch a brow. "Something?"

"You know." He waves a hand between us, casual as anything. "Chemistry. Tension. The whole 'will-they-won't-they' thing we've been dancing around since we kissed the other night."

I scoff, ignoring the heat that pricks my skin at the memory. "I wasn't aware we were dancing around anything."

"Oh, we are." He tilts his head like he's enjoying this far too much. "And instead of fighting it, I propose we... lean in."

I exhale, pressing my fingers to my temples. "Lean in?"

He grins. "Friends with benefits."

I blink at him. "You're joking."

"Completely serious." He crosses his arms, mirroring my stance. "We're stuck with each other for the next four weeks, working on this book. You're my editor. I'm your reluctant manuscript disaster. There's attraction—we both know it. So why not have a little fun along the way? No commitment, no complications."

I stare at him, waiting for the punchline. It doesn't come.

"You think sleeping together will help you finish your book?"

He winces. "I wouldn't put it quite like that."

"How would you put it?"

"I'd say we both get something out of this arrangement."

I let out a dry laugh. "You're actually using writing as an excuse for sex?"

"Not an excuse," he says, smirking. "More of an incentive."

I shake my head, sipping the last dregs of my tea, needing to buy time before I do something ridiculous, like actually consider it.

"And when this inevitably blows up in our faces?" I ask.

He shrugs, entirely unbothered. "It won't. We're both adults. No expectations, no pressure. Just... an experiment in chemistry."

I roll my eyes. "You're an actual menace."

"You say that, but you're thinking about it."

Damn him, I am.

"Sorry," he says, not sounding sorry at all. "It's a bad habit. Comes with the territory, I guess." He gestures vaguely, as if his whole existence is one long exercise in effortless persuasion. "But seriously, what's holding you back? Afraid you'll lose control?"

"Control isn't the problem," I lie, folding my arms. "This is about professionalism. About boundaries."

"Boundaries can be flexible," he counters, voice low, smooth. "Especially when they lead to better art."

"Rory, you're unbelievable."

"Thank you," he says, grinning like I just paid him a compliment. "Look, I get it—you're cautious. Careful. But sometimes, Lara, taking risks is the only way to create something extraordinary."

"Risks," I echo, my mind flashing through the thousand ways this could go spectacularly wrong. My reputation tarnished, my emotions tangled in a mess, and one of us— *namely me*— left heartbroken, a mistake I swore I'd never make again after James. But then there's another thought, quieter, harder to ignore: *What if he's right?*

"Think about it," he says, his posture deceptively relaxed

while his gaze stays locked on mine. "You push me, I push you. We keep it professional during work hours, and after..." He trails off, letting the sentence dangle provocatively.

"And after, what?"

"After, we see what happens," he finishes, his grin widening. "No strings. Just— For the sake of the book, obviously."

"Obviously," I echo faintly, though nothing about this feels obvious. Or safe. Or sane.

"Come on, Yates." His voice softens, teasing, but not unkind. "You're the best editor I've ever worked with. Let me prove I can rise to the occasion. Literally." He smirks, and I groan, burying my face in my hands.

God help me, I think, though whether it's a prayer or a curse, I couldn't say.

"Fine," I say, the word scraped out of me like it's been pried loose with a crowbar. My arms are crossed so tightly across my chest that I'm surprised I haven't dislocated something. "I will *consider* it."

"Consider?" Rory repeats, his brows lifting in mock disbelief, his grin doing that thing where it makes him look both boyish and entirely too self-assured. "Lara Yates, did you just agree to be... mutually beneficial?"

"Don't push your luck." I shoot him a glare that would make most men flinch. Rory, of course, just looks more amused.

"Not luck. Just chemistry." His voice drops slightly, and there's something about the way he says it—soft, teasing, but also deliberate—that sends an unwelcome flutter through my chest.

"Boundaries," I announce, ignoring whatever that was. I snap my fingers for emphasis, like I'm calling this ridiculous meeting to order. "*If*—and this is hypothetical—if we do this, there will be rules."

"Rules." He nods solemnly, though the twitch at the corner of his mouth gives him away. "I love rules."

"Somehow, I doubt that." I adjust my glasses, mostly so I don't have to look directly into his eyes when I say the next part. "This stays separate from work. Completely. The manuscript comes first. If this"—I wave vaguely between us, as though gesturing to some invisible, idiotic agreement floating in the air—"gets in the way, it ends. Immediately."

"Understood." He sips his drink, watching me too intently now. It's unsettling, the way Rory has of looking at me like I'm not just a collection of editorial rules and professional boundaries, but an actual person. I prefer when people stick to the former.

"Also," I continue, clearing my throat, "no public displays. Discretion is non-negotiable."

"Discretion." Rory looks up, pretending to mull it over. "So no writing 'Rory + Lara' on any bathroom stalls? No shouting 'You complete me' from the rooftops?"

"Exactly." I level him with a pointed stare. "And if you call me babe or sweetheart even once, you and your book will be well and truly on your own."

"Noted." He smirks, but his expression softens, just barely. "Anything else, or am I officially allowed to consider this the best idea I've ever had?"

"Don't get ahead of yourself," I say, dropping my gaze to the notebook in front of me. I flip it open and start scribbling nonsense, anything to avoid looking at the man who's just managed to talk me into— What, exactly? An arrangement? A disaster waiting to happen? Both?

"Hey," Rory says after a beat, his tone quieter now, less playful. "Thanks for trusting me on this. I know it's... complicated."

Complicated doesn't begin to cover it, but I don't correct him. Instead, I glance up and catch an expression on his face that I don't recognise. Not the cocky grin, not the charming smirk. Something closer to sincerity, tinged with uncertainty. It throws me off balance enough that all I can manage is a curt nod before looking back down.

"Well then," he says, taking his seat at the dining table. "Time to get back to saving my literary masterpiece, yeah?"

"Finally, something sensible comes out of your mouth." I latch onto the shift in subject like a lifeline, flipping back to my notes with far more enthusiasm than anyone should ever feel toward structural edits. "Chapter twelve still needs a complete overhaul, by the way. That whole scene with Sophie accepting his apology so quickly? Incredibly cliché."

"Ah, yes. The make-up sex scene." He grins, reaching for his laptop. "What you fail to see, Yates, is that it's *romantic*. You know, like us."

ELEVEN

I lean against the kitchen counter, staring at the faint reflection of myself in the darkened window. I had forgotten just how quiet the countryside is. No traffic, no sirens, no raucous revellers on their way to, or from, the pub.

Rory's voice echoes from the living room, something about how bad movie dialogue is basically a crime against humanity. I half listen, nodding occasionally so he thinks I'm paying attention.

Because I can't. Not really.

This *agreement* between us— It's fine. It's casual. No strings. No messy feelings. Just two consenting adults who happen to have amazing chemistry.

I'm overthinking again.

The truth is, I've made rules for myself. Boundaries. I've drawn them with the precision of one of my editorial notes: clean lines, no ambiguity. Rory doesn't fit into my life in any way that goes beyond... this. He can't. I don't have the bandwidth for it, not when I still have so much to achieve, not when—

"Still brooding, Yates?" His voice snaps me out of my

spiral, and I glance up to find him leaning in the doorway, one shoulder propped against the frame. His white linen shirt has creases on the creases, and there's a lazy kind of confidence in the way he studies me, like he knows exactly what I'm thinking.

"Brooding is your department, Keane," I reply, keeping my tone light. It's easier that way—banter is safe. Banter doesn't come with consequences.

"Uh-huh." He takes a step closer, and my pulse trips over itself. "You keep telling yourself that."

"Someone has to." I grab my glass of water, pretending I need something to do with my hands.

"Funny," he says, closing the distance between us completely now. He's much taller than me, which is annoying because it gives him an unfair advantage. When he tilts his head, his eyes lock onto mine, and suddenly I feel like I want to just burrow into his chest.

"Rory," I start, aiming for a warning, but it comes out weaker than I'd intended.

"Relax," he whispers. "No overthinking tonight. Just... this."

And then he kisses me.

It's deliberate, like he's been planning it for hours, maybe days. His lips are warm, soft, but there's nothing tentative about the way they claim mine. His hand slides to the back of my neck, thumb brushing my jaw, and just like that, the world tilts.

I forget everything—the rules, the boundaries, the flimsy excuses I've clung to like a lifeline. All I can think about is him. The heat of his mouth, the subtle scrape of stubble against my skin, the way he tastes like camomile tea and something sweeter I can't name.

My breath hitches as he deepens the kiss, his other hand finding my waist, pulling me closer like he can't stand the idea of space between us. My water glass slips from my grip, landing somewhere on the counter with a dull thud, but I barely register the sound.

It's consuming. He's consuming. And for the first time, I wonder if maybe I've underestimated just how dangerous Rory Keane really is.

His kiss is a question I don't remember agreeing to answer.

My hands press against his chest—maybe to push him away, maybe to steady myself—but the second I feel the heat of him beneath my fingers, any thoughts of resistance scatter like loose papers in the wind. His mouth moves with a purpose that steals my breath and replaces it with something far more dangerous: need.

"Wait," I manage between kisses that leave me dizzy and untethered. "We shouldn't..."

"Shouldn't what?" Rory breathes against my lips, his voice low enough to make my knees weak. He doesn't stop kissing me, not really. His lips graze the corner of my mouth, then my jaw, then just under my ear, where he seems to know exactly how to unravel me.

"Think," I blurt out, though even as I say it, I can hear how unconvincing I sound. My brain is already mush, and the way his teeth scrape lightly against my earlobe isn't helping one bit.

"Thinking's overrated," he says, his words hot against my skin, and there's a damn smirk in his voice. Of course there is.

Instead of stepping back, I grip the fabric of his shirt, pulling him closer like some traitorous part of me wants to anchor myself to him. The logical part of my mind—the one screaming about boundaries and bad ideas—is rapidly losing ground. It's hard to argue with logic when your pulse is hammering and your body is enjoying every touch.

Abruptly, he stops and pulls away. "I know what we agreed on earlier. But I need to know. Is this what you want?"

"Rory," I say, his name coming out soft and breathless. "Yes. Yes, it is."

"Yeah?" His lips find mine again. This time, he kisses me slow and deep, a deliberate kind of torment that leaves no room for coherent thought.

I don't know who moves first, but suddenly we're stumbling backwards, or forwards, or sideways—I have no idea which direction because all I can focus on is him. His hands are on my waist, and mine are in his hair, and somehow we make it to the hallway and up the stairs without tripping over ourselves.

"Door," Rory says, his voice rough, and I realise he's waiting for me to lead the way.

"Right," I mumble, fumbling behind me for the handle of the nearest bedroom door. My heart is pounding so loud, I'm surprised neither of us comments on it. Finally, the door gives way, and we tumble inside his bedroom, our mouths never breaking contact.

The urgency between us is electric, sparking in every touch and every sound. My back hits the wall, and I gasp, but he's there, catching the sound with another kiss. His hands slide down to my hips, sending shivers racing across my skin even through the layers of fabric.

"Still thinking too much?" he teases, his voice thick with amusement and something darker that makes my stomach flip.

"Shut up," I snap, but it comes out more desperate than annoyed, especially when I tug him closer by the waistband of his jeans.

His laugh is low and wicked, and before I can think of a clever retort, his lips are on mine again, silencing everything except the wildfire spreading between us.

The bed finds us—or maybe we find it; I'm past caring about specifics. All I know is that the space between us disappears completely, and the world narrows to the heat of him and the way his hands seem to know exactly where to go.

"Trouble," I breathe against his mouth, though I'm not sure if I'm talking about him or me. Probably both.

"Good trouble," he counters, and I hate how much sense that makes right now.

His hands find my hips, firm yet maddeningly gentle, like he's coaxing something out of me I didn't know was there. Rory shifts us effortlessly, his movements confident but unhurried, and I realise with a mix of frustration and fascination that he's leading this—guiding me like we're in some kind of intricate dance where only one of us knows the steps.

"Relax," he whispers against my ear, his breath warm and annoyingly soothing.

"Who says I'm not relaxed?"

"Mm, you could've fooled me," he teases, pulling back just enough to look at me. It's unnerving and thrilling all at once. "But don't worry, Yates. I'm very good at distractions."

"Arrogant much?" I shoot back, trying to regain some semblance of control. But then his thumb brushes along my jawline, tipping my face toward him, and whatever pithy response I had dies on my tongue.

"Confident," he corrects, "there's a difference."

Before I can argue—not that I have any coherent arguments left—he kisses me again, slow and deliberate this time, as if daring me to keep thinking instead of feeling. And damn it, I feel everything—his mouth, firm yet soft, the way his hands slide up my hips, eliciting sparks beneath my skin, the heat building between us.

"Better," he whispers when we finally come up for air, his voice roughened by something primal and impossibly addictive. One of his hands tangles in my hair, tugging gently, while the other skims down my back, finding the curve of my waist and settling there like it belongs.

"Don't get cocky," I manage to say. My nails drag lightly down his chest, and I pretend not to notice the way his breath hitches, the way his pupils darken in response. At least I'm not the only one losing their shit here.

"Too late," he quips, but there's a softness beneath the bravado, an attentiveness that keeps catching me off guard. It's in the way he watches my face after every touch, every kiss, as if he's waiting for permission even while he takes charge. It's disarming, intoxicating.

I'm about to say something—what exactly, I have no idea— when he lifts me onto the bed, his movements fluid and assured. The mattress dips beneath my weight, and before I can process the shift, he's hovering over me, his eyes locking on mine with a focus that should be illegal.

"Still thinking too much?" he asks, echoing his earlier comment, but there's no humour in his tone now, just a quiet challenge. His fingers trail down my arm in a way that has goosebumps springing to life.

"Shut up," I breathe, pulling him down to me because words are officially useless now. The tension snaps, and suddenly there's no space, no hesitation, just us—completely in sync, like we've done this a thousand times before and still can't get enough.

Every touch feels both deliberate and instinctive, as if we're discovering and remembering each other all at once. His hands find bare skin beneath my blouse, and the contrast of cool air and his warm palms sends a shiver rippling through me. He notices, of course he does, and the satisfied smirk that follows is enough to make me want to smack him—or kiss him harder. I choose the latter.

"Trouble," I say again, my voice muffled against his shoulder.

"Good trouble," he repeats, his words a low vibration against my collarbone. His lips leave a trail there, igniting nerve endings I didn't know existed, and I have the distinct realisation that I'm utterly, completely outmatched.

But then he catches my gaze again, his smile softening into something almost reverent, and for a second—just a second—it feels less like a game and more like gravity, inevitable and undeniable.

His mouth moves like it knows me better than I know myself—intentional, consuming, devastating. Somewhere along the way, I lose track of where his hands are, of where mine are, frankly, because he's everywhere at once. There's a moment, fleeting but electric, when our movements falter, and then we laugh—low, breathless, the kind of laughter that only makes this more incendiary. His fingers trace patterns down my spine, pulling me closer.

"Testing limits, Keane?" I manage to say, though my voice shakes more than I'd like.

"Just making sure," he breathes against my ear, "that you're still okay with casual."

The sentence is a dare disguised as a question. My laugh catches in my throat, turning into something closer to a gasp as his lips find a spot just below my jaw that makes coherent thought a Herculean task.

"Shut up," I finally say, but there's no malice behind it, only surrender.

We're a tangle of limbs and breath and skin, each movement deliberate yet exploratory, like neither of us can quite believe we're allowed to do this. And oh, he's thorough—his hands, his lips, his body—a man who doesn't just skim a page; he reads every word, twice, looking for subtext. By the time we collapse together, the room feels different, as if the air itself has shifted to accommodate what just happened between us.

I stare at the ceiling, the jagged edge of my breathing gradually smoothing out. My hair sticks to my forehead, my legs feel like jelly, and somewhere in the back of my mind, I'm already editing this moment into something less... monumental. Something that won't make tomorrow impossible.

Okay, I think to myself, trying to wrangle my thoughts into submission. *This is fine. Normal people do this all the time. Casual. Fun. No strings. No problems.*

But the truth is, lying here with him—his arm pressed against mine, his rhythmically steady breathing both grounding and infuriating—I feel anything but casual. It's not just my body that's tired; it's my resolve, my carefully constructed barrier between logic and feeling. Because this wasn't supposed to be this... much.

I steal a glance at him out of the corner of my eye. He looks utterly unbothered, like someone who just successfully landed a plane they weren't even aware was crashing. My chest tightens, not from regret or shame, but from stark, terrifying clarity: I'm in over my head. And worse? I might actually like it.

The bed shifts as Rory moves beside me, disrupting the carefully fragile equilibrium I've been pretending to maintain. I keep my eyes fixed on the ceiling, like it's got all the answers written somewhere in the cracks of the plaster if I just squint hard enough.

"You're thinking," he says, his voice low and maddeningly amused. "I can actually hear the cogs turning from here."

"That's impossible," I reply deadpan, still staring upward. "Thinking isn't audible."

"Yours is," he counters smoothly, and I feel the mattress dip again as he props himself up on one elbow. He's closer now, and I can feel him looking at me, studying me with that unshakable confidence that makes me want to both kiss him again and throw something heavy at him.

"Go ahead, then," I reply. "Say whatever smug thing you're obviously dying to say."

"Oh, no," he says lightly. "I'm just basking in the moment. You know, taking notes... for research purposes."

That gets my attention. My head snaps toward him so fast I think I might have pulled something. "Research?"

"Mm-hmm," he hums, clearly enjoying himself far too much. "Not bad, by the way. For research."

"Are you kidding me?" I manage, though the words come out weak, half-breathless in a way that betrays how rattled I am. Which, of course, only makes his grin widen.

"Why would I joke about something so important?" he replies innocently, but there's a glint in his eye that tells me he knows *exactly* what he's doing. He's trying to get a rise out of me, and worse, he's succeeding.

"Unbelievable," I say. The nerve. The *audacity*.

"Relax," he says, his tone softening just enough to disarm me further. "I'm kidding. For what it's worth... I wasn't lying about it not being bad."

"Not bad," I echo flatly. A pillow connects with his face before I even realise I've swung it. It's a good hit too—solid, direct—though the satisfying *whump* is short-lived when Rory just laughs, low and unbothered, like he'd been expecting it.

"Really?" His voice is honeyed with amusement as he adjusts the pillow now sitting in his lap, casually leaning back against the headboard like I haven't just declared war. "That's your response? Resorting to violence?"

My fingers curl around the edge of another pillow, and I contemplate launching a second strike. "If you think *that* was violent, you clearly don't know me very well."

He raises his arms in a truce, and I lay back down, snuggling into his chest. His right arm wraps around my shoulder, and it feels unbelievably good to be held. To be wanted.

This was supposed to be simple. Casual. A bit of fun to blow off steam, nothing more. But as I lie here in his bed, staring at the ceiling, I can feel the weight of the truth pressing down on me: I'm in trouble. Big, messy, heart-shaped trouble.

The silence stretches, thick with everything unsaid. I can

feel him there, inches away, and it takes every ounce of willpower not to move my head. Not to look at him again and risk falling deeper into whatever this is.

"Night, Lara," he says finally.

"Night," I reply, barely above a whisper.

I lie there long after his breathing evens out, staring at the faint outlines of shadows dancing across the walls. This isn't supposed to feel like this. It isn't supposed to feel... *big*.

But it does.

And that terrifies me.

TWELVE

I wake to the kind of silence that feels too loud. The bright morning light filters through the blinds, harsh and unforgiving, illuminating the chaos in my head far more effectively than I'd like. My body stirs before my mind catches up—muscle memory pulling me upright, legs swinging over the side of the bed, feet searching for my slippers, which I'd thoughtfully left out next to my bed... in the room across the hall. Shit, I spent the night in his room.

He's there in the bed, fast asleep. I can smell him. Warm skin, cedar soap, and whatever reckless decision-making smells like. Casual, I remind myself. We agreed. Two adults making questionable choices but keeping it uncomplicated.

"Uncomplicated" is a lie I told myself at 10:37 PM when I kissed him in the kitchen and all the way up the stairs, and another I told myself when his hands slid down my back in a way that felt anything but casual.

I stand and locate my blouse draped over the back of a chair—thank God for small mercies. At least I'm not hunting for missing underwear or gathering up pieces of my dignity from the floor. Slipping into the crisp fabric, I straighten the collar and give myself a quick once-over in the mirror. Hair: messy but salvageable. Makeup: non-existent, but at least my glasses are where they should be, perched on the nightstand. Professional demeanour: intact, even if the person wearing it feels like she's been hit by emotional shrapnel.

"Keep it together," I say as I tug my hair into a low ponytail. It's a mantra now, as reliable as coffee or deadlines.

My phone buzzes on the bedside table, which is a welcome distraction. Grabbing it before it can wake sleeping beauty, I scroll through emails, news alerts, and a staff group text asking who's up for a mid-week drink tonight (spoiler: not me). Work is there too, waiting as always, steady and dependable in its demands. An email from marketing about Rory's book, subject line: *Urgent - Need Feedback ASAP*.

"Of course you do." I sigh, opening it. Feedback is my comfort zone. It's black-and-white, actionable, devoid of all things messy and grey—unlike whatever this thing is with Rory.

Casual. I repeat the word like it's a magic spell that'll keep my brain from short-circuiting. There's no room for complications here, no space for personal feelings to spill into professional waters. I've worked too hard, carved out too much of myself to build this career, to let it unravel because of one... okay, two nights of bad decisions wrapped in good intentions.

I try to focus, thumbing through the email. Marketing jargon, revised sales numbers, questions about appeal demographics—it's safe territory, blessedly impersonal. My chest loosens slightly, the familiar rhythm of work pushing everything else to the edges.

Work first, feelings later, I tell myself, even though I know damn well "later" isn't on my calendar. Not now, not ever.

I cross the room, skirt dangling from one hand, jacket draped over the other. My blouse buttoned— Well, mostly.

The last two buttons are still AWOL, but I'm not about to go crawling around looking for them. Casual hookups don't come with a lost-and-found.

I reach the door, hand hovering over the knob, and pause just long enough to take a breath. Inhale, exhale. Reset. This is fine. This *is* fine. Last night was... fun. Reckless, sure, but also contained. A neat little box of great sex tied up with a bow of mutual understanding: no strings, no complications, no messy emotions.

A one-time thing. No big deal.

Then, because this is my life, I hear his voice behind me.

"Leaving already? What, no coffee? No goodbye kiss?" Rory's tone is light, laced with amusement, like this is all some charming morning-after routine we've rehearsed a hundred times.

"That's presumptuous," I say, turning just enough to glance over my shoulder. He's leaning against the headboard, sheets pooled around his waist like he's starring in an ad campaign for "smug bastard." His hair is a mess, dark strands falling across his forehead in a way that should not look as good as it does at— What time is it? Seven in the morning? Nine? Who knows? Time loses meaning when you're trying to escape unnoticed.

"Presumptuous?" he repeats, raising an eyebrow. "Lara, you snuck out of bed like someone fleeing the scene of a crime. Forgive me if I thought offering you caffeine might be the neighbourly thing to do."

"I'm running late. Work, remember? That thing where people pay me to keep you on deadline?"

"Ah, yes. Work. Where we'll pretend you didn't just refer to last night as 'that thing.'"

"Last night was exactly what it needed to be," I say, keeping my voice even. "Nothing more, nothing less."

"Right." He tilts his head, studying me like I'm a particularly complicated plot twist he hasn't decided whether to love or hate. "And here I thought editors were supposed to be brutally honest."

"Brutal honesty doesn't require elaboration," I shoot back, hand back on the doorknob. "It's efficient. Like leaving before breakfast."

"If you say so."

I don't reply. Instead, I open the door and step through, letting it click shut behind me with a finality I don't quite feel.

My hand lingers on the knob for a second longer than it should, like my body hasn't quite caught up to my brain's carefully crafted exit plan.

But his voice—*And here I thought editors were supposed to be brutally honest*—sticks to me like a Post-it Note with half a sentence scribbled on it. Unfinished. Incomplete.

"Efficient" doesn't explain why my chest feels tight, or why I have to consciously unclench my jaw before heading to the sanctuary of my own room.

By the time I shower and make it downstairs to officially begin the day, the scent of coffee has already infiltrated the air, courtesy of Rory's foray into domesticity. The man can charm a crowd, draft a bestseller, and apparently brew a decent pot of coffee. Add that to the list of reasons I shouldn't let him get to me. Too much charm is dangerous; everyone knows that.

I sit down at the head of the table, where stacks of manuscript pages stare back at me like an accusation. Perfect. Something tangible. Something real. Not... last night. Or his teasing. Or the way he looked at me like I was both a puzzle and the solution. Just work.

Work is safe. Work is predictable. Work doesn't leave you—

"Good morning," he says, sliding into the seat across from me. He's holding two mugs, one of which he pushes in my direction. The coffee smells rich, dark, and entirely too tempting—sort of like its deliverer, if I were inclined to make that kind of comparison. Which, obviously, I'm not.

"Thanks," I say, my voice clipped, though my hand betrays me by reaching for the mug immediately. I take a sip and let the warmth seep through me, keeping my eyes locked on the manuscript in front of me. Don't engage. Don't encourage. Just... edit.

"Where should we begin?"

"I've got a list," I say, tapping my pen against the margin of page forty-seven.

"Why does that not surprise me?"

"Starting with this adjective cluster here. Did you really need three different ways to describe her smile? We get it. She's radiant, luminous, *and* dazzling."

"She's the love interest," he says, shrugging. "I thought you'd appreciate some variety."

"Variety is overrated," I shoot back, circling the offending words. "Pick one. Otherwise, it reads like you can't make up your mind."

"Okay. What else?"

"In the break into Act Three, Oliver's motivations still aren't clear," I explain, keeping my tone professional. Detached. "You've got all this buildup with his internal conflict, but then he just... forgives her? No hesitation? No fallout? It feels unearned."

"Alright, fair point," Rory says, nodding slowly. "So what if... What if we add a scene where he confronts her first? Like, really lays everything out before deciding whether or not to forgive her?"

"That could work," I admit, begrudgingly impressed by how quickly he pivots. "But it needs more than just confrontation. There has to be a moment where he questions himself too —whether he's ready to trust again. Make it messy."

"Got it."

"Also, lose the rooftop cliché," I add, pointing to the note I'd scrawled in red ink at the bottom of the page. "No one actually has heartfelt revelations while standing on a skyline at sunset. It's been done to death."

"Hey, I *like* rooftops," Rory protests, but there's a playful glint in his eye. "They're romantic."

"They're lazy," I counter. "And you're better than lazy."

"Wow," he nods. "A compliment and an insult in the same sentence. Ambassador, you really do spoil me."

"Don't get used to it,"

We dive deeper into Act Three, throwing ideas back and forth like a game of verbal ping-pong. And somewhere between debating the merits of a grand gesture versus a quiet reconciliation, I realise something strange. He's... listening. Really listening. And not in the performative, nod-and-smile way most authors do when I'm tearing apart their darlings. He's engaged, energised, feeding off the momentum of our conversation, like it's the act of collaboration itself that's sparking something in him. He genuinely wants *Fully, Forever* to be the best book it can be. He's willingly rewriting entire chapters if it improves the storytelling.

And, annoyingly, it's sparking something in me too.

"Wait," he says suddenly, snapping his fingers. "What if the big turning point isn't about her apologising to him? What if it's about him realising he doesn't need her apology to move on? Like, his closure comes from within, not from her."

I blink, caught off guard by the shift in perspective. It's... good. Really good. Better than anything I've suggested. My pen hovers over the manuscript as I try to process the unfamiliar sensation curling in my chest. Pride? Admiration? No. Definitely hunger.

"That... could work," I say carefully, not trusting myself to say more. Because the truth is, it doesn't just work—it's brilliant. And the fact that I might've played even a small role in helping him get there is equal parts exhilarating and terrifying.

"See?" Rory says, flashing me a triumphant grin. "Told you rooftops are romantic."

He flips open his laptop and wakes up the screen, scrolling to find the page in the document ready to write the scene. But then he stops and looks across.

"Hey, Lara?"

"Yes?"

"Thanks." His voice is quiet. When I finally look up, his smile is softer, less practised. More real.

"For what?" I ask, my own voice barely above a whisper.

"Helping me make it better," he says simply.

And damn it, the way he's looking at me right now—like I'm more than just his editor, more than just some fleeting distraction.

Rory's hand brushes against mine as he reaches for a pen that isn't even on *his* side of the table. The touch is fleeting, casual enough to be dismissible—except it feels anything but. I freeze mid-sentence, words evaporating like steam off of pavement.

"Stop that," I say, arching an eyebrow.

"Stop what?" His voice dips lower, smoother, the teasing edge softening into something warmer. More dangerous.

"You're supposed to be brainstorming, not... brooding at me."

"Brooding?" He chuckles, and the sound is rich, deeper than before. "I don't brood. I smoulder. There's a difference."

"Debatable," I say, but I want to laugh. Damn him.

"Admit it," he says, his grin widening. "You're smiling. You think I'm funny."

"Well, someone has to," I shoot back. Because the truth is, he *is* funny. And quick. And disarmingly good at making me forget why I'm supposed to keep my distance.

The silence stretches, taut and humming. I should look away, I don't. I look at him instead, and suddenly the table feels too small, the room too warm.

Before I fully realise what I'm doing, I'm standing. The chair scrapes against the floor, loud enough to jar me back to reality, except I don't stop. I step around the table, closing the space between us in three brisk strides.

"I'm testing a theory," I say shortly, my voice steadier than I feel.

"Which is?" His expression shifts, surprise flickering across his face, but there's no mistaking the anticipation in his eyes.

"Whether or not you smoulder," I reply, and then I'm kissing him.

It's not tentative or cautious or any of the other things I've spent years training myself to be. It's heat and friction and reckless abandon, and for once in my life, I don't care about consequences.

Rory reacts instantly, his hands gripping my waist as he pulls me closer, eliminating the last shred of space between us. The kiss deepens, his mouth moving against mine with a hunger that matches my own. One hand slides up my back, fingers tangling in my hair, while the other anchors me firmly in place.

I gasp against his lips, and he uses the opening to his advantage, his tongue sweeping into my mouth in a way that makes my knees threaten to give out. My hands clutch at his shirt.

"Still overthinking?" he says, his breath hot and uneven.

"Shut up," I manage, yanking him up off the seat to meet me.

The manuscript forgotten, the dining table becomes a battleground—a collision of need and frustration and unspoken truths. His lips trail down my jaw to the sensitive spot just below my ear, and I bite back a moan, my head falling back to give him better access.

"God, Lara," he whispers, his voice rough and wrecked, like I'm undoing him as much as he's undoing me. And maybe I am. Maybe we're both hurtling toward something we can't control, something that will inevitably shatter us.

But right now, I don't care. Right now, it's just him—his touch, his warmth, his everything—and for once, I let myself fall.

The cool air from the open window brushes against my bare shoulders, and I realise too late that I'm still standing in the middle of the kitchen, dishevelled and utterly undone. My gaze lands on the manuscript pages scattered across the table— forgotten casualties of our... detour—and a pang of guilt twists in my chest. I glance over at Rory.

"Don't," I say, holding up a hand before he can speak. "Whatever you're about to say, just don't."

"Say what?" He shrugs, far too pleased with himself. "That you look good when you're slightly unhinged? Because it's true."

"Rory."

"Alright, alright. Not going to say a word."

"Good." I snatch up my blouse from the back of a chair, for the second time this morning, and slip it on, buttoning it with more force than necessary. "Because we're not talking about this. Ever."

"Really? Not ever?" His tone is light, teasing. "Seems like kind of a shame. I mean, we were making some pretty solid progress on—"

"No," I cut him off, louder this time. "This doesn't change

anything. We're still here to work on your novel, and that's it. No complications. No distractions."

"Sure," he says easily, "if that's how you want to play it."

"That's exactly how I want to play it."

THIRTEEN

Day three. The novelty of countryside isolation has officially worn off, and routine has settled in—if you can call the delicate balance of writing, editing, and avoiding underlying sexual tension a routine.

We've talked through the major changes, agreed on the direction, and now Rory is buried in his manuscript, brow furrowed, fingers flying over the keyboard in that feverish, trance-like state that suggests he might actually be making progress. I'd revel in the victory, but I've learned the hard way not to celebrate too soon.

While he works, I take the opportunity to look at one of my other author's manuscripts that landed in my inbox. I don't generally like to switch between projects because it takes time to get in, and out, of the right headspace. I'm making an exception because I've been looking forward to reading Rebecca's latest book since Scott & Drake announced she'd signed a two-book deal, following her wonderful debut.

But it was a bad call. I've read the sentence three times now, and for the life of me, I can't tell if it's brilliant or insufferable.

"You're glaring at that screen like you want to ask it to go outside with you and have a fight in the car park," Rory's voice cuts through the silence, smooth and just a touch amused. He leans back against the opposite end of the table, arms crossed over his chest, one brow arched in mock concern.

"Maybe I do," I say. "If nothing else, I could do with stretching my legs."

"Ah, well, in that case..." He tilts his head toward the window, where the late afternoon sun is streaming through the curtains. "How about we call it quits for now? Go for a walk. Get some air before your eyes permanently cross."

"Quits?" I glance up, incredulous. "You're on a deadline, Keane. Deadlines don't take walks."

"True," he says, pushing off the table with a lazy grace that only someone annoyingly tall can manage. "But editors do. And writers. Or so I'm told." His grin is disarming, but I refuse to let it work on me. I've built an entire career on being immune to charm—especially his.

"Don't you have a chapter to rewrite?" I counter, crossing my arms and giving him my best you're-not-getting-out-of-this glare.

"All the experts say you shouldn't sit in front of a computer for longer than forty-five minutes at a time," he shoots back, already heading for the door. "Come on, it's lovely out."

I hesitate, glancing down at the same page on my screen and the half-empty mug of tea beside it. Fresh air sounds nice, sure, but fresh air with Rory? That's... complicated.

"Fine," I grumble, standing and smoothing the wrinkles out of my blouse. "But if this turns into some kind of inspirational nature walk where you start doing David Attenborough impressions, I'm leaving you in the woods."

"Deal," he says, holding the door open with an exaggerated flourish. "But only because I'd probably get lost without you."

The trail is soft beneath our feet, dappled sunlight filtering through the canopy of leaves overhead. Birds chirp somewhere in the distance, and the scent of pine hangs heavy in the air. It's idyllic. Picturesque. Like something out of one of his novels.

And yet, all I can focus on is the quiet between us. Not awkward, exactly—more like the kind of silence that feels full, loaded with something unspoken. Part of me wants to fill it, to say anything that will break the spell, while another part clings to the stillness like a lifeline.

Rory walks a step ahead of me, hands shoved casually into his pockets. There's an ease to him out here, his usual restless energy subdued by the rhythm of the trail. I wonder if he can feel it too—the strange weight of last night pressing down on us. The way everything shifted, almost imperceptibly, like a tectonic plate sliding beneath the surface.

Not that I'm thinking about last night. Much.

"You're fierce quiet," Rory says suddenly, glancing back at me with a teasing smile. "Should I be worried?"

"Just enjoying the peace," I reply, keeping my tone light. "It's rare for you to be this silent. I should savour it while I can."

"Right, but seriously, are you okay? You seem... different."

"Different how?"

"Not sure," he says, turning his gaze back to the trail ahead. "Guess I'll have to keep walking to figure it out."

There it is again—that shift, subtle but undeniable. I bite the inside of my cheek, resisting the urge to press him, to ask what he means. Instead, I let the silence stretch between us once more, each step carrying us deeper into the woods and further from whatever safe distance we'd managed to keep before.

"Careful," I say as Rory steps over a root with all the grace of a newborn deer. "Wouldn't want the great romance novelist to twist an ankle in the wilderness. Imagine the headlines."

"Imagine the book sales," he shoots back, glancing over his shoulder at me. "Writer survives harrowing ordeal in the woods. Finds inspiration. Pens masterpiece. Millions weep."

"I'd pay good money to see you try to survive out here. Pretty sure your idea of 'roughing it' involves lukewarm room service."

"Hey, I'll have you know I once camped for an entire weekend." He flexes his biceps. "No Wi-Fi. No minibar. Raw-dogging. Just me, the stars, and a very angry cow, who wasn't best pleased I'd decided to set up a tent in her 'hood.'"

"Truly heroic." His ridiculousness is almost endearing. Almost.

We walk a little farther, the sound of leaves crunching underfoot filling the spaces between us. The banter's familiar, easy—like slipping on an old sweater. Except this particular sweater has been stretched out of shape, tugged at by thoughts I can't quite wrangle into neat little boxes anymore.

"Your parents," Rory says suddenly, his tone shifting just enough to draw my attention. "What do they think about what you do?"

I hesitate, not because I don't know the answer, but because I've rehearsed it so many times before. "They're... practical people." I keep my voice even, measured. "Dad's an accountant at an engineering company, Mum's a history teacher. They like things they can quantify. Success in numbers, progress in clear steps. My career doesn't exactly come with a road map they understand."

"Hard to quantify editing genius?" he asks.

"Something like that," I say with a shrug, though the words

feel heavier than I intend. "I think they always thought I'd go into something more stable. Law, maybe. Finance. Definitely not publishing. But, well, here I am."

"Here you are," he echoes, his voice softer now. "And let me guess—they still ask when you're going to get a 'real job'?"

"Not in so many words," I admit, smiling faintly. "But yeah, there's always this undertone of... disappointment. Like I'm some kind of puzzle piece they can't make fit."

"That's ridiculous," Rory says, frowning. "If anything, they should be bragging about you at every dinner party. You're brilliant, Lara."

His words catch me off-guard, a strange warmth creeping up my neck. I deflect, because what else can I do? "You clearly haven't met them. Compliments are not their love language."

"Still," he persists, his expression earnest. "You're doing something you're passionate about. That's worth more than fitting into anyone's expectations."

"Spoken like a man who probably never had to worry about expectations."

"Ah, but that's where you're wrong," he says, sidestepping a low-hanging branch. "But I'll save that story for when we've finished the bottle of water and the packet of custard creams that I accidentally left in the hall when I was putting on my boots."

"You didn't?"

"I did. Sorry."

"You total knob."

"Yeah. Especially because I could murder a biscuit right now."

Rory shrugs and continues to walk, the cuffs of his jacket brushing against the denim of his jeans with each step. He's whistling—of course, he's whistling—and the tune is maddeningly cheerful, a stark contrast to the crunch of dead leaves underfoot and the occasional snap of a twig.

"Does it ever stop?" I call after him, half-jogging to keep up. "The charm offensive, I mean. Or are you just genetically programmed to be this insufferably upbeat?"

He glances back over his shoulder. "Insufferably? Ow. And here I thought I was being delightful."

"Delightful would involve letting me set the pace."

"Not my fault you've got legs like a leprechaun," he fires back, grinning.

"Charming *and* height-ist. What a catch," I reply, but I'm smiling now too. Against my better judgment. It's annoyingly hard not to when he looks at me like that—lopsided grin, eyes crinkled at the corners, like he's holding back an even better punchline.

"Fine, I'll slow down." He matches my stride, his arm brushing mine for the briefest second before falling away. It's nothing, really, but I feel it anyway, like a tiny electric shock.

"You're welcome," he says magnanimously, as if he's just gifted me the moon.

"Wow," I deadpan. "A gentleman and a scholar."

"Scholar?" He laughs, a low, rich sound that seems to ripple through the trees. "Haven't heard that one in a while."

"Don't try to deny it," I say, smirking. "Based on your cheeky grin alone, I'd bet good money you were your parents' favourite. Always getting away with murder while everyone else had to do the heavy lifting."

"Okay, first of all"—he holds up a finger—"it's called being resourceful, not getting away with murder. And second"—another finger joins the first—"I'll have you know being known for your beauty and not your brains takes its toll. So really, I'm the victim in all of this."

"Right," I say, unable to suppress a laugh. "Poor Rory. Must've been *so* hard growing up as the apple of their eye."

"Look, it's not my fault I was objectively the cutest," he says. "Being the youngest just means you get caught in a different kind of spotlight. Everyone else already had their lives figured out—and then there was me, scribbling poems on napkins and saying I wanted to write books for a living."

"Scandalous," I say, though my voice is quieter now, less playful. There's something in the way he phrases it—a flicker of self-deprecation, maybe—that makes me want to tread carefully.

"Tell me about it," he says with a wry smile. "They didn't exactly throw parades for the idea. Except Aoife, of course. She was the only one who didn't look at me like I'd lost the plot."

"Your sister?" I ask, tilting my head.

"Yeah." His gaze shifts to the trail ahead, his jaw tightening almost imperceptibly. "She... she just got it, you know? The whole needing-to-create thing. She was always the one pushing me to go bigger, dream louder. She made me believe I could actually do it."

"Sounds like she was your biggest fan," I say softly.

"She was," he says, his voice nearly a whisper now. "Still is, I think. Even if she's not..." His words hang in the air like mist.

I don't push. I can sense the weight of whatever he's not saying, how carefully he's keeping it locked behind the easy charm and quick deflections. Instead, I let the silence stretch between us, offering what little space I could.

"Anyway," he says eventually, forcing a smile that doesn't quite reach his eyes. "Enough about me. Let's talk more about your leprechaun legs."

"You weren't complaining last night."

"And I'm not complaining now. Sure, aren't they the finest leprechaun legs in the whole of *Tír na nÓg*?"

"Piss off."

"Right so."

Apart from birdsong, the only sound is the crunch of boots

on damp leaves and the occasional rustle of wind through the canopy above. It's... peaceful. Almost disarmingly so. I don't trust it.

"Alright," he says suddenly, breaking the quiet. "Your turn."

"My turn for what?" I ask, even though I know exactly where this is going. He's been poking around the edges of my carefully guarded personal life all day, peeling back layers with a mix of charm and persistence.

"To share your origin story." He tilts his head toward me. "You've heard mine—baby of the family, black sheep, golden boy, yadda yadda. Now, I want to know how Lara Yates became the queen of red ink and biting feedback."

"Queen of red ink?" I snort. "That's a new one."

"Come on. Spill. When did you first realise you wanted to crush writers' dreams for a living?"

"Wow. You really have a way with words," I deadpan, but he's not letting this go.

"Fine," I say with a sigh, adjusting my glasses out of habit. "If you must know, I didn't start out wanting to be an editor. I wanted to write."

"Really?" He sounds genuinely surprised, which—okay, fair. I'm not exactly the poster child for whimsical, creative dreams. "What happened?"

"Reality happened," I say, keeping my tone deliberately breezy. "Turns out, writing is hard. And messy. And requires a level of vulnerability I wasn't particularly interested in culti-vating at the time. Editing on the other hand? That made sense to me. It was clean. Precise. I could take someone else's chaos and shape it into something coherent. Something... better."

He doesn't respond right away, and when I glance at him again, his expression is thoughtful, like he's turning my words over in his mind, examining them from every angle. It's unnerving.

"That's a very diplomatic answer," he says finally. "But it doesn't explain why you stopped writing altogether."

"Who said I stopped?" The lie comes out too quickly, too reflexively, and I immediately regret it. His eyebrows lift in silent challenge, and I sigh again, this time more heavily. "Okay, fine. I stopped. Happy?"

"Not particularly." His tone is mild, but there's an edge of something else beneath it. Curiosity, maybe. Or concern. "Why did you stop?"

"Because it wasn't good enough." The words hang in the air between us, piercing and raw and much too honest. I clear my throat, trying to regain some semblance of control. "I mean, I wasn't good enough. At least, not by my own standards. And if I couldn't meet those, then what was the point?"

"Ah." He nods slowly, as if that explains everything, which it absolutely does not. "The old perfectionist paradox. If it's not perfect, it's not worth doing."

"Something like that," I agree, kicking a loose rock off the trail. God, why did I let him drag me out here? Fresh air is overrated.

"That's ridiculous, you know," he says, his voice softer now. "No one starts out perfect. Hell, no one ends up perfect, either. Not even you, Queen of Red Ink."

"Thanks for the pep talk, Coach."

"Anytime," he says with a faint smile. But he doesn't press further, and for that, I'm absurdly grateful.

We round a bend in the trail, and suddenly the trees open up, revealing a wide, sloping clearing that overlooks the valley below. The view is staggering—rolling hills bathed in the soft, golden light of late afternoon, fading into a horizon that seems to stretch on forever. For a moment, neither of us speaks. There's nothing to say.

"Wow."

"Yeah," Rory says quietly, coming to stand beside me. He doesn't look at the valley, though. He looks at me.

The sky above us is shifting now, its pale blues deepening into richer shades of amber and rose. It's hard to believe that this is England. It feels like standing on the edge of something vast and unknowable, and for the first time in a long time, I don't feel the need to fill the silence.

The breeze picks up, threading its way through the clearing and brushing cool fingers against my neck. I shiver—just once, a quick, involuntary ripple. Of course, Rory notices. He doesn't miss anything.

"Someone walk over your grave?" he asks, already shrugging off his coat. His tone is casual, but there's something about the way he moves, deliberate but unassuming, that I adore.

"I'm fine," I say quickly, even though I'm not. The evening air has teeth now, cold and biting, and my jumper is laughably inadequate against it. But admitting that feels like losing some unspoken battle I can't quite name.

"Ah, come on," he says wryly, stepping closer. Before I can think of another excuse, his coat is draped around my shoulders, warm and heavy and smelling faintly of him. It's absurdly cliché—the gallant hero lending his coat to the damsel in distress—but instead of scoffing, I find myself gripping the lapels, tugging it tighter around me.

"Chivalry isn't dead after all," I say, mostly because sarcasm feels safer.

"Don't get used to it," he says with a smirk. "If the temperature drops another two or three degrees, I'll be prising it off your back without apology."

"Leaving me to die forgotten in a ditch of hypothermia?"

"Forgotten, no! You'll probably get a nod in the acknowledgements, along with my parents, my agent, and God. The finest of company."

I glance at him sideways, trying to read his expression

without being obvious about it. There's no teasing glint in his eyes now, no trace of his usual cocky charm. Instead, there's an openness—a quiet, steady kind of warmth—that disarms me completely.

"Anyway, I think we'll make it back to the cottage before we have to make any difficult decisions about who is going to eat who."

"Good to know."

We stand there in silence, the clearing stretching wide and empty around us, the horizon painted in soft, dusky hues. It should feel awkward, standing this close, saying nothing. But it doesn't. Instead, it feels... easy. Like we've somehow stumbled into a rhythm neither of us knew we were looking for.

"Do you ever..." I start, then stop, shaking my head.

"Do I ever what?" he prompts, his gaze steady on my profile.

"Nothing. Forget it." I wave a hand dismissively, but he doesn't let it go.

"No, go on. What?" he asks again, more gently this time.

"Do you ever just... wish you could turn off your brain? Stop second-guessing everything for five minutes and just *be*?" The words tumble out before I can stop them, raw and unpolished, and I immediately regret letting them escape.

"All the time," Rory says quietly, like it's the most obvious thing in the world. And somehow, that simple admission hits harder than any grand declaration ever could.

I turn to look at him, and for a moment, the rest of the world falls away. It's just him and me, standing on the edge of something I don't have a name for yet. Something that feels terrifying and inevitable all at once.

"Guess we're both a bit of a mess, huh?" I say, attempting a weak smile.

"Speak for yourself. I'm a delight," he shoots back, his smirk returning, but his eyes stay soft.

And just like that, the tension eases, slipping into something lighter, easier. But it doesn't disappear entirely. It lingers, humming just beneath the surface, a quiet reminder of everything we're not saying.

Rory steps in front of me, blocking the trail like a smug, six-foot roadblock. His arms cross over his chest, and there's a challenge written all over his face, clear as day.

"Alright then," he says, his voice laced with mischief. "How about we up the stakes? First one back to the cottage wins."

"Wins *what*, exactly?" I ask. It's an automatic response—stalling, really—because there's no way I'm agreeing to whatever nonsense he's cooking up.

"Bragging rights, obviously," he says, shrugging. Then, with a wink, he adds, "Unless you're scared, I'll leave you in the dust."

"Scared? Of you?" I gesture at him in exaggerated disbelief. "You write romance novels for a living, Rory. Let's not pretend you moonlight as an Irish Olympian."

"Big talk from someone who probably hasn't run since secondary school." As I say it, I'm already shifting my weight, sizing up the uneven trail ahead of us. There are roots everywhere, patches of mud, and I'm not entirely convinced I won't twist an ankle within the first ten seconds.

"Fine," I add after a beat, because apparently, I have zero self-preservation instincts when it comes to competitive banter. "But don't cry when you lose."

"Don't worry, Yates. I'll be gracious in victory." And before I can respond, he's gone—bolting down the path like a man possessed, all long legs and reckless confidence.

"Cheater!" I shout after him, already scrambling into motion. The trail blurs underfoot as I take off, the snap of twigs and the rush of cool air filling my ears. Somewhere ahead, Rory's carefree laugh carries back to me.

"Watch out for the mud!" he calls over his shoulder.

I don't even care that I'm panting as I yell back, "*You* watch out for the mud!"

And just like that, the tension between us breaks wide open, replaced by a wild, breathless energy that feels a lot like freedom.

FOURTEEN

It's our final day at the cottage, and the soft tapping of rain against the windowpane is oddly soothing as I stare at Rory's latest chapters. There's a rhythm to his words now, a depth that wasn't there before. It's like watching someone finally find the right piece to complete a puzzle they've been fumbling with for ages.

"About time," I say under my breath, enjoying reading the story for the first time. Not that I'd ever admit it to him, but he's made real progress. The pacing is tighter, the dialogue sharper. And the emotional beats—God, the man can write longing in a way that makes me feel like I'm intruding on something private.

Fiona was right about this trip. As much as I grumbled about being dragged out to the middle of nowhere with one of our star authors—one who, let's be honest, has an ego the size of London—she knew what she was doing. Rory needed focus, and apparently, I needed... well, whatever this is. A change of scenery? A reminder that editing isn't just triage but sometimes involves actual collaboration? Whatever it is, it's working. For both of us.

The door swings open behind me, and a gust of damp air announces Rory's return. I glance up as he strides in, enormous supermarket bags-for-life dangling from both shoulders, looking far too chipper for someone who has written about forty-thousand words in a week. His hair is damp, curling slightly at the edges, and there's a smattering of raindrops on his jacket that he shrugs off with a casual shake.

"I stocked up," he declares, his voice bright and annoyingly self-assured. He drops the bags onto the counter and starts unpacking without so much as a glance my way. "I've had enough of microwave meals and carry-outs. We're having a home-cooked dinner for our last night."

"Really? Shame, there's two microwave lasagnes in the fridge that are going to go to waste now."

"Take them home with you if you want, but tonight, Yates, we shall dine like gods. My treat."

"By all means, knock yourself out. I hope whatever you've got planned is edible."

"Not just edible." He pulls out a bundle of fresh herbs and sets it down with a dramatic flourish. "Memorable. You're going to tell your friends you've never eaten better in your life."

"High bar," I warn. Though, truth be told, my curiosity is piqued.

Rory doesn't strike me as someone who spends much time in the kitchen—too busy brooding over love stories and charming the members of online book clubs. But there's a confidence in the way he moves now, pulling ingredients from the bags with a practised ease that's almost... unsettling.

"Don't look so sceptical," he says without turning around, as if he can hear the raised eyebrow in my silence. "I've got this."

"Famous last words." I stand, stretching and feeling the ache in my shoulders from sitting hunched over my laptop for hours. Crossing the room, I lean against the doorway to the kitchen, arms folded. "What exactly is 'this,' anyway?"

"Patience, Yates." He flashes me a grin over his shoulder, the kind that probably makes half the women in Britain swoon. "You'll see soon enough."

"Terrifying," I say, but I stay where I am, watching as he unpacks a carton of cherry tomatoes, a bulb of garlic, and a loaf of freshly baked bread. There's a flow to his movements I wasn't expecting, something almost rhythmic as he rinses the vegetables and lines up the ingredients on the counter. He's already shrugged off his jacket and rolled up his sleeves, revealing those forearms that are far too distracting for someone who claims to make a living from words.

"You're oddly confident about this," I note, quirking an eyebrow. "Should I be concerned?"

"Only if you have something against good food," he quips, pulling out a block of Parmesan and setting it down with a flourish. "Trust me, I've got this."

"You're building this up now. Expectations are being set." I tilt my head, watching him as he pulls out a bottle of virgin olive oil. "You do realise I've survived this long without trusting anyone who says, 'trust me' unironically, right?"

"Ah, but I'm not just anyone," Rory says, not missing a beat. His hands work quickly, retrieving a knife from the drawer and setting it down beside a cutting board. "I'm the man whose manuscript *you* said had potential. That has to count for something."

"Potential is a relative term. I tend to use it for all new authors regardless of ability," I tease.

"See? That's practically a glowing endorsement from you," he says, smirking as he cuts off the woody stalks from a bunch of asparagus. "Maybe you're softening."

"Not likely," I reply, though I don't move from the doorway. There's something oddly compelling about watching him like this—so at ease, so... purposeful.

Rory moves around the tiny kitchen like he's been the executive chef here for years. The knife in his hand flashes as he chops an onion with a precision I didn't think possible for someone who referred to smashed avocado on toast our second morning here as "his signature dish."

The rhythmic sound of blade meeting wooden cutting board fills the space, and I begin to feel a little self-conscious that I'm not doing anything to help.

He tosses the chopped onion into a waiting pan with a practised flick of his wrist, then reaches for a red pepper.

"Did you learn to cook, take classes, or—?"

"Mum taught me."

"Smart woman."

"She is," he says, slicing into the pepper with the same swift precision. "It was more of an ultimatum, really. I decided I wanted to go vegetarian when I was fifteen—figured it'd make me edgy or something. She took one look at me and said, 'Fine, but I'm not making two dinners every night.'" He grins, clearly amused by the memory. "So, it was either learn to cook, or survive on carrot sticks and hummus forever."

"Let me guess," I say, arching an eyebrow. "You went through a phase where everything you made involved tofu."

"How'd you know?" He laughs, gently laying two salmon steaks into the pan with a satisfying sizzle. "It was all stir-fries and sad lentil stews for a while. But then I got hooked on cooking shows and started experimenting. Turns out, it's kind of fun when you realise that a recipe is just a prompt, a suggestion, and the magic happens when you find the confidence to just chuck stuff in."

"Fun," I scoff. "I'll take your word for it."

"Come on. You've never cooked something just for the hell

of it?" His expression caught somewhere between teasing and genuine curiosity.

"Does microwaving popcorn count?"

"You're a tragic woman, Lara Yates," he says, shaking his head. "We need to work on that."

"Hard pass, thanks."

"Anyway," he continues, stirring the contents of the pan as the scent of garlic and onions fills the air, "my mum always said, knowing how to cook would be useful if I ever wanted to impress someone."

"Is that what this is?" I ask, gesturing toward the stove. "An elaborate attempt to dazzle me with your culinary prowess?"

"Who says I need to impress you?" His eyes meet mine, dark and mischievous. Then he shrugs, utterly casual. "But if I can, why not?"

"Confident, aren't we?"

"Confident enough." He sprinkles something green and fragrant over the pan—parsley, maybe. Coriander?—and gives it a final stir. "You'll see. Dinner's almost ready, and I promise it'll be better than instant noodles."

The cottage smells incredible. It's the kind of smell that makes your stomach forget it was ever full—fragrant pepper, earthy herbs blooming in the heat, and something rich and tangy I can't quite place.

"Alright, moment of truth," he announces, breaking my train of thought.

He turns, holding two plates dressed to perfection. To accompany the salmon, there is roasted asparagus and garlic green beans. It's vibrant and fresh, flecks of red chilli flakes popping against caramelised green asparagus spears. It's almost too pretty to eat.

"Don't let the presentation fool you," he warns. "There's about ten seconds' grace between salmon being under or overdone."

"It looks amazing," I say as I lean over the plate to take in the wonderful aromas.

"It does, doesn't it? I won't take it personally when you beg for seconds."

"There are always those lasagnes in the fridge if we need a Plan B." I pick up my fork, aiming for some asparagus with deliberate slowness while he watches, arms crossed, the picture of confidence.

Fine. Here goes nothing.

The first bite hits me like a revelation. The flavours are bright and layered—the sweetness of roasted tomatoes, the zing of lemon, the subtle kick of chilli lingering on the back of my tongue. It's the kind of meal that demands savouring, but I just want to be left alone to wolf it down.

"Well?" he prompts, cutting his salmon. He's waiting, really waiting, and for a second, I forget how to speak.

"Okay," I manage finally, swallowing. "It's... edible."

"Edible?" He raises an eyebrow, but I see the relief in his eyes, the way his shoulders loosen just a fraction.

"Fine," I admit, setting my fork down with exaggerated reluctance. "It's incredible. Absolutely delicious."

"Ha! And here I thought you'd be harder to win over."

"Win over?" I scoff. "Let's not get ahead of ourselves. It's just salmon."

"Yeah," he says softly, his gaze locking onto mine for just a beat too long. "Just salmon."

Rory twirls his fork, scooping up some beans. "You know," he starts, a mischievous glint in his eye that immediately puts me on alert, "this is probably the first time I haven't completely botched dinner with someone."

"I find that hard to believe after seeing you in action tonight."

"Hard to believe or not, it's true." He reaches over with the wine bottle and tops up my glass. "There was this one time—

first date, very fancy, or at least I thought it was at the time. I decided to make this... What did I call it? Oh! 'Rustic Mediterranean Feast.'"

"That sounds ambitious."

"Ambitious doesn't begin to cover it." He gestures animatedly, nearly knocking over his wineglass in the process. "Picture it: a feast of undercooked aubergine, burnt couscous, and hummus so garlicky it could've warded off vampires for miles."

"Wow," I say, setting my fork down to give him my full attention. "And how did your date react to this culinary masterpiece?"

"She tried to be polite at first," he says, sighing dramatically. "But then she just... couldn't do it anymore. She spat out a mouthful of couscous mid-sentence. It sort of sprayed everywhere."

"Everywhere?"

"Everywhere," he confirms, gesturing vaguely around the room like he's still haunted by the memory. "The table. The floor. My shirt. Honestly, I think some of it got in her bag. It was carnage."

"Was there a second date?"

"Sadly not."

Rory leans back in his chair, a lazy grin tugging at his lips as he licks the edge of his fork. It's nothing—just an absentminded gesture—but for some inexplicable reason, it lands like a jolt to my system. My gaze flicks to his mouth, and I feel the air between us shift, subtle but charged, like the seconds before a summer storm.

"You're staring," he says, his voice low and teasing. The words are light, but his eyes—they're locked onto mine now, dark and intent, and suddenly I can't breathe.

"Am not."

"Are too." His grin widens, smug and infuriating, and I

want to wipe it off his face. Or maybe... do something else entirely.

"Fine," I say, pushing back my chair with more force than necessary. "You've got some olive oil or something on your chin."

"Nice try." He swipes at his jaw with the back of his hand, still watching me, amused. "But there's nothing there, is there?"

"Not anymore," I confirm, standing abruptly. My pulse is racing, my thoughts a jumble, and honestly, I need space. Distance. Perspective. But instead of walking away like a sane person, I take exactly one step toward him.

And then I kiss him.

It's not planned. Not even remotely. One second I'm glaring at that stupidly self-satisfied face, and the next, my hands are gripping the front of his shirt, yanking him forward as my lips crash against his.

For a heartbeat, he freezes. Just long enough for panic to creep in—*Oh God, what am I doing?*—and then his hands are on me, firm and insistent, pulling me closer. The kiss deepens, slow at first but quickly spiralling into something hot and urgent and completely out of control.

His fingers tangle in my hair, tilting my head back, and I gasp against his mouth. He takes advantage of the opening, his tongue brushing against mine, and the sensation sends a shiver down my spine. This is madness. Pure, unfiltered madness. But his grip is steady, anchoring me, and I find myself leaning into it, into him.

"Bloody hell, Lara, I didn't even serve dessert," he says. There's a flicker of hesitation, just enough to let me pull back if I want to.

I don't.

"Shut up, Keane," I whisper, dragging him down again.

The chair scrapes loudly as he stands, lifting me effortlessly. My arms wrap around his neck instinctively, and before I know it, we're stumbling toward the sofa, bumping into furniture along the way. He lowers me onto the cushions, his weight pressing me down, solid and warm and utterly overwhelming.

"Wait," I manage, my voice barely audible over the pounding in my ears. "What about—"

"Later," he says firmly, cutting me off with another kiss. His hands slide down my sides, finding the hem of my jumper, and suddenly it's gone, flung somewhere behind us. I should object—this is reckless, impulsive, absolutely not what I came here for—but when his lips trail down my neck, any coherent thought evaporates.

"God, you're impossible," I say, though it comes out more like a moan.

"Complaining?" He smirks, his fingers deftly working the clasps of my bra.

"Don't get cocky," I shoot back, though the words lack bite. Especially when his hand slips beneath the fabric, skimming over bare skin, and I arch into him reflexively.

"Too late."

His mouth finds mine again, and the rest is a blur of heat and motion—his shirt joining my clothes on the floor, his hands mapping every inch of me, my leg hitching over his hip as he settles between us. It's frantic and messy and so unlike me, but God, it feels right. Like everything else has been gray-scale until now, and this—*this*—is technicolour.

Rory's chest rises and falls beneath my cheek, his skin still warm and slick from the chaos we just unleashed. My breath hasn't quite caught up yet either, coming in shallow drags as I focus on the wooden ceiling beams above us. One of them is crooked, I notice, because apparently now is the time for architectural critiques.

"Well," Rory says, voice low and raspier than usual, breaking the quiet. He shifts slightly beneath me, adjusting so one of my legs—bare, tangled with his—doesn't dangle awkwardly off the sofa. "If that's how you react to my cooking, I'm almost afraid to see what happens when I really impress you."

A laugh bubbles out of me before I can stop it. It's not fair how easily he does this—knocks me off balance, then acts like it was never a big deal to begin with. I prop myself up on one elbow, narrowing my eyes at him even as my lips twitch.

"Don't let it go to your head. I'll need a follow-up meal to check you're not a one-trick-pony."

I shift slightly, pulling away just enough to sit up, dragging the throw blanket from the back of the couch around my shoulders like armour. My glasses are somewhere across the room, flung aside in the heat of the moment, and the world looks softer without them—blurry edges and muted colours. Fitting, somehow, given the state of my thoughts.

"Hey." Rory props himself up, his dark hair deliciously rumpled and his gaze fixed firmly on me. There's no smirk now, no easy banter to hide behind. Just him—open and unguarded in a way I wasn't expecting. "You alright?"

"Yeah," I say quickly, too quickly. I don't meet his eyes; instead, I busy myself smoothing the blanket over my lap, pretending there's some invisible wrinkle that urgently needs addressing. "Just... thinking."

"Thinking," he repeats, his tone unreadable. He doesn't push, though. Doesn't press for elaboration or try to lighten the mood with a joke. Instead, he sits up fully, his knee brushing mine, and waits. Patient. Steady.

The problem is, I *can't* stop thinking. About the way he looked at me earlier, like I was something he'd been searching for without realising it. About how much I've enjoyed this week, his company, our arrangement—to lose control, to want him, to take him. About how much worse it's going to hurt when this inevitably falls apart.

Because it will. It has to. This was supposed to be a bit of fun. A mutually beneficial arrangement. Casual. It wasn't supposed to be *this*. Him. Us.

"Do you regret it?" Rory's voice cuts through my spiral, soft but firm, pulling me back to the present. There's no accusation in it—just curiosity. Like he's bracing himself for an answer he doesn't want to hear.

"Honestly?" I force myself to look at him, taking in the faint crease of his brow, the cautious hope lingering in his expression. My chest tightens painfully, and I hate it—how much I care, how much I wish I didn't. "I don't know."

It's not a lie. I don't regret it—not the way his hands felt on me, or the way he made me feel alive in a way I haven't in years. But I do regret how dangerously close I'm skirting the edge of something I might not survive intact. Something deeper, messier, more real than I ever intended to let it get.

"Fair enough," he says after a beat, settling back against the cushions, his gaze never leaving mine. There's no disappointment in his voice, no judgment—just quiet acceptance, like he understands more than I'm willing to admit out loud.

And maybe that's what scares me most of all.

He reaches for the blanket, tugging it gently until I relent and let him pull me back against him. His arms wrap around me, solid and warm, and for a brief, fleeting moment, I let myself lean into it. Into him. Into the impossible, terrifying idea that maybe, just maybe, I don't have to face everything alone.

But even as my eyes drift shut, my mind refuses to quiet. Because if tonight proved anything, it's that I'm already in deeper than I ever meant to go—and there's no telling how—or *if*—I'll find my way back out.

FIFTEEN

The quirky falafel restaurant that had somehow become a monthly pilgrimage comes into view just as I round the corner, my heels clicking against the pavement in a staccato rhythm that mirrors my heartbeat. Late. Again. My usual punctuality has been sabotaged by an endless morning of back-to-back meetings, an inbox overflowing with manuscripts, and—oh, let's not forget—the utterly charming tube delay that left me wedged between a man who bathes once a month and a teenager chewing gum like it owed her money.

I spot Danny immediately. Of course, he's already here, lounging at our usual table at the back like he owns the place. He's holding a fork in one hand and his drink in the other, apologising that he's gone ahead and ordered.

"Look who decided to put in an appearance," he calls out before I even reach the table, his grin wide and insufferable. "Fashionably late or just regular late? Don't answer, I already know."

"Hi, Danny, I'm so sorry," I huff, sliding into the seat across from him and setting my bag down with more force than necessary. I tug off my jacket—it was a good idea this morning at seven, not so much now—and drape it over the back of my chair. "Nice to see you, too."

"What was it this time? Conference call from hell? Editor emergency? Or..."—his tone shifts, mock conspiratorial now—"Should I be congratulating you on finally having a life?"

"Work," I reply curtly, waving a hand as if swatting away a fly. "You know how it is. Deadlines, authors, words on a page. All very glamorous."

"Right. Because that totally explains why you're glowing like someone just got serenaded under a balcony by a shirtless poet."

"Excuse me?" My voice pitches higher than intended, but I grab the menu in front of me and bury my face in it, pretending I don't know its contents by heart. Anything to avoid his gaze—and that knowing smile.

I pick up the glass of mint tea Danny ordered for me— bless him, he at least knows my priorities—and take a long sip. Or I try to. The second the rim touches my lips, his voice drifts over, dripping with that trademark sarcasm.

"Ah, there it is," Danny says, leaning back in his chair with an air of theatrical satisfaction. He folds his arms across his chest like some all-knowing oracle. "The unmistakable glow of someone who's been thoroughly... appreciated."

The sip I was planning? Abandoned. Instead, I inhale suddenly, and the tea decides it would rather make its grand debut through my windpipe than my stomach. I cough violently, nearly slamming the glass down on the table as I try to catch my breath.

"Jesus, Danny!" My voice comes out strangled, eyes watering from both the assault on my throat and the mortification clawing at me. "Could you not?"

"Sorry," he drawls, not looking sorry in the slightest. In fact, he's grinning wider now, clearly delighted by my near-death experience. "But you walked right into this one.

Glowing skin, extra sparkle in your eye, showing up late? If that's not post-good-sex vibes, then I don't know what is."

"You're insufferable," I sputter, grabbing a napkin to dab at the tea I managed to spill on my hand.

"Admit it," he presses, tilting his head and studying me like I'm some kind of curious art piece he's trying to decipher. "Someone's putting a little spring in your step these days. Who is he? Or she? Or they? Spill, woman."

"There's no one," I say firmly, finally regaining enough composure to glare at him. It's a weak glare, though—it's hard to summon proper indignation when you're caught in a lie.

"Mm-hmm." His eyebrows lift, and he gestures vaguely toward me with one hand. "Then explain the blush, darling. And don't give me that 'it's warm in here' nonsense. It's England, and it's permanently cold and wet."

"You're imagining things," I say, lifting my chin in what I hope looks like casual disinterest, but probably just makes me look constipated. "It's called makeup, Danny. I know you're unfamiliar with the concept, but sometimes women wear it."

"Nice try," he shoots back immediately. "But unless Boots started selling 'Just Rolled Out of Bed After a Night of Passion' bronzer, I'm sticking with my original theory."

"You're ridiculous." I fill my glass from the silver teapot, determined to salvage some shred of dignity, but my hand betrays me when it trembles ever so slightly. Of course, Danny notices. Because of course he does.

"Ridiculous? Maybe," he says, his tone light. "But also right."

"Fine. You win. Are you happy?"

"Ecstatic," he replies smoothly. "But don't stop there. Go on, who's the lucky scamp?"

"Rory," I say, cutting him off before he can start listing names. The word lands between us like a wayward grenade, and I brace for impact.

For a second, Danny just stares at me, blinking once, twice, like maybe I've spoken in tongues. Then his eyebrows shoot up so high they practically disappear into his hairline. "Rory *Keane*?" His voice pitches higher, incredulous, and I know I'll never hear the end of this. "As in Mr. 'International Romance Heartthrob'? That Rory?"

"Do you know another one?"

"Well, no," Danny admits. "But I didn't exactly have *him* pegged as your type. What happened? Did he seduce you with tragic metaphors and whispered sonnets?"

"Nothing... dramatic. It just... happened. Naturally."

"Right. Because nothing says, 'natural progression' like jumping into bed with a man whose book covers should come with a warning label for spontaneous swooning."

"Will you stop being so—" I search for the right word but come up empty. "So *you* about this?"

"Never," he says cheerfully, but then his grin softens into something quieter, more thoughtful. "So, let me get this straight. You're sleeping with Rory Keane. *Your client.*" His emphasis on "client" is subtle but pointed, like a gentle nudge with a pointy stick.

"Not *my* client," I correct, tapping the rim of my glass. "Scott & Drake's client. There's a difference."

"Sure. Okay." Danny waves his hand vaguely, but his frown deepens. "And what? This is just some casual, no-strings-attached fling? A bit of fun?"

"Exactly." My voice comes out firm, confident, like I've rehearsed this line in front of a mirror. Which, to be fair, I might have.

"Uh-huh." Danny doesn't look convinced. In fact, he looks downright sceptical now, his lips pressing into a thin line. "Lara, you do know who we're talking about here, right? Rory Keane? The guy whose reputation could fill an entire Google search page—and not all of it flattering?"

"Yes, I'm aware," I say. "I know all about his reputation, thank you very much."

"Then explain to me why you thought mixing business with pleasure was a good idea," he says, his voice tinged with exasperation now. "Because as your friend—and someone who has witnessed your reaction to even minor workplace drama—I'm struggling to see how this ends well."

"God, you sound like an HR manual."

"Maybe," he says, shrugging. "But I also sound like someone who knows you better than you think, Lara. And I'm telling you—you're playing with fire here. Rory Keane isn't exactly known for his... stability."

"Neither am I," I quip, trying to lighten the mood, but Danny's expression doesn't budge. He's serious now, his concern etched plainly across his face. It unsettles me more than I want to admit.

"Look," he says quietly, folding his hands on the table. "I'm not saying you can't handle yourself. God knows you're smart. But this? Him? Just... be careful, okay?"

"Always am," I reply breezily, forcing a smile that feels a little too tight.

Danny doesn't answer right away. Instead, he watches me for a long moment, his gaze heavy with something I can't quite name. Finally, he exhales and runs a hand through his already messy hair.

"Alright," he says eventually, his tone lighter but still carrying an undercurrent of worry. "But don't come crying to me when this blows up in your face."

"I won't," I say. "Let me spell this out for you so we can all move on with our lives, yeah?"

Danny raises one eyebrow, tilting his head like a bemused golden retriever. "Oh, this should be good."

"Rory and I—" I pause briefly, refusing to let the flicker of amusement in his expression throw me off. "We're two consenting adults who happen to work together and... occasionally enjoy each other's company in a very casual way. That's it. No strings. No complications. No emotional investment."

"Right," Danny drawls. "Because *you* are such a bastion of emotional detachment. Tell me more about your newfound ability to compartmentalise feelings, because I must've missed that memo."

"Oh, come on, Danny. It's not rocket science."

He snorts. "No, but it's *you*. You're not exactly the 'no-strings-attached' poster child. I mean, you're the same woman who cried when she accidentally killed her Sims character."

"That was different!" I snap, jabbing my fork in his general direction. "Mortimer Goth deserved better, and you know it!"

"You're not wired for casual hookups. Believe me, I'd know —I've been your sounding board through every single relationship since university. And let's just say, none of them screamed 'chill fling vibes.'"

"Well, maybe I've changed," I counter. "People evolve, Danny. Not everyone gets stuck in their ways like you, with your decade-old Spotify playlists and your refusal to try oat milk."

"Oat milk tastes like regret," he says seriously, but his eyes don't leave mine. "You might think you've got this under control, Lara, but I'm telling you—you're playing a dangerous game here. Rory Keane isn't some harmless experiment. He's... complicated. And you? You're not nearly as detached as you think you are."

"Thanks for the vote of confidence, *bestie*."

"I'm not trying to piss on your chips or whatever, okay? I just... I know you. And I don't want to see you get hurt because you're too busy convincing yourself it's all fun and no feelings. You're already halfway there, even if you won't admit it."

"Okay. Thanks for the concern. Look, we're having fun. That's it. Fun. Full stop. End of story."

"Riiight." Danny raises an eyebrow. "It's cute how you think saying 'fun' twelve times in one sentence makes it true."

I laugh then, mostly because if I don't, I might scream—or worse, actually *consider* his point. "Oh, my God, Danny. Your concern is noted and filed under 'Unnecessary.' Can we move on now?"

"Fine, thus ends my sermon for today," he shoots back, grinning now. "Will you be ordering the sweet potato fries, by any chance?"

"Are you asking because you want to steal them?"

"Maybe."

"This is why no one trusts project managers. Always taking liberties."

"No. They just taste better when they're off someone else's plate. It doesn't make sense, but it's undeniably true, and I'll die on this hill."

We order the fries and a fresh pot of mint tea, and I sit back in my chair, determined to enjoy what's left of my lunch break. Whatever happens next—whatever mess I might be walking into with Rory—I know Danny will still be there. Smirking. Stealing fries. Calling me out on my nonsense.

And honestly? That's enough. For now, anyway.

SIXTEEN

We've been back in London for nearly a week before I suggest to Rory that we meet up again in person. The moment we step off the bustling pavement and into the second-hand bookshop, it's like someone hit a mute button on London. The city's chaos dissolves behind us, replaced by the quiet hum of fluorescent lights buzzing faintly overhead and the soft rustle of pages being turned somewhere in the back. The air smells like old paper, wood polish, and just a hint of dust—like stepping into a memory you didn't know you had. My chest tightens, but not unpleasantly; it feels like coming home.

"Wow," Rory exhales beside me, his voice dropping to a reverent whisper, as if he's walked into a church instead of a cramped bookshop sandwiched between a café and a dry cleaner's. "This is... something."

"Something good?" I glance at him, noting how his usually cocky smile has softened into something quieter. Genuine. It throws me for a second before I recover with a shrug. "I mean, it's not Foyles, but it does the job."

"Are you kidding? This place looks like the kind of spot

where books come alive after closing time." He grins like a schoolboy.

"Careful," I say dryly, heading toward the nearest aisle. "If you romanticise this place too much, I might think you're one of those people who buys books for the aesthetic and never reads them."

"Who says I don't?" He follows me, close enough that I can feel his presence without having to look, which is... distracting.

"Well, I'll know soon enough," I counter, letting my fingers trail lightly along the spines of hardcovers. "If you start misquoting Austen or calling Hemingway 'underrated,' I'm leaving you here to fend for yourself."

"I'll take that on board," Rory promises, but there's laughter under his breath.

We weave through the narrow aisles, past leaning towers of fiction and precariously balanced piles of memoirs. I stop abruptly at a shelf near the back, tilting my head to examine a familiar title.

"This one," I say, pulling out a worn paperback and holding it up for him to see. The cover is faded, the corners dog-eared. "*Rebecca.* First read it when I was fourteen. Stayed up all night because I couldn't put it down."

"Du Maurier," Rory says immediately. "The creepy house, obsessive jealousy, sinister undertones. Sounds about right for fourteen-year-old you."

"Excuse me?" I raise an eyebrow, though I'm secretly pleased he knows it. "Are you implying I was a moody teenager?"

"Implying? No. Stating outright? Absolutely."

"Fine," I admit, sliding the book back onto the shelf. "Maybe I did have some... angsty tendencies. But I also appreciated the craftsmanship. The pacing, the tension, the way she builds dread without spelling everything out. That was the first time I realised stories could do that."

"That makes sense," he says, his tone softer now. "You edit like someone who learned from authors like her—precise, unrelenting, but... elegant."

I blink at him, caught off guard by the compliment. It leaves me flustered enough that I quickly move on, leading him to another section.

"Over here," I say briskly, gesturing toward a collection of poetry anthologies. "My favourite escape route when novels felt too big. Poetry always felt... manageable. Like a single scene distilled into its purest form."

"Let me guess," Rory says, scanning the spines. "Sylvia Plath for the darker days, Mary Oliver for the lighter ones?"

"Not bad. Though, if you must know, I went through a serious Pablo Neruda phase, too. Something about yearning in Spanish just hits harder."

"Yearning, huh?" His voice dips, teasing. "So, you *do* have a soft side."

"Don't get used to it,"

"Too late."

Rory falls into step beside me. His arm brushes mine briefly, a light touch that lingers in my mind longer than it should.

It's fine. Everything's fine. Just two colleagues browsing books together. Nothing earth-shattering about that.

Except, of course, that it feels like a lot more than that.

The garden is tucked behind the shop, hidden in plain sight. A narrow iron gate creaks as I push it open, its hinges protesting against years of disregard. The scent of blooming jasmine and damp earth greets us like an old friend, softening the edges of the cool evening air. It's quieter here, the distant hum of London traffic reduced to a faint whisper on the breeze. For a moment, it's as if we've stepped into some alternate reality—one where the city doesn't press down on your chest quite so hard.

"Did you know this was back here?" Rory asks, his voice low, almost reverent. He trails a hand along the ivy-covered brick wall, his fingers brushing leaves like he's afraid they might crumble under his touch.

"Of course," I say, leading him further in. "It's not exactly a secret, but most people don't bother looking for quiet when noise is so readily available."

"Sounds like something you'd write in one of your editor's notes. 'Find the quiet. Let the story breathe.'" He glances at me, but there's no malice in it—just recognition.

"Careful, Keane," I shoot back, narrowing my eyes. "Remember my note about bad metaphors."

He smirks, but for once, there's no pithy reply.

I point to a weathered bench beneath a tree in the corner, its wood bleached grey by time and rain. "Let's sit before you start composing poetry about the 'hidden oasis' or whatever nonsense is brewing in that head of yours."

"Don't tempt me," he says, following me as I sink onto the bench. The wood creaks beneath us, groaning under the weight of two people.

We sit in silence for a beat, the kind that doesn't demand filling. My shoulders relax despite myself, and I let my gaze wander over the flickering tea lights strung haphazardly through the branches. It's... peaceful. And annoyingly intimate in a way I hadn't prepared for.

"Alright then," Rory breaks it first, leaning back and stretching an arm along the top of the bench. Casual, like we're just two friends enjoying the afternoon and not whatever complicated thing we actually are. "Favourite author. Go."

"That's impossibly reductive," I scoff. "You can't just distil a lifetime of reading into one name."

"Sure, you can. Watch." Without missing a beat, he says, "Toni Morrison. Done."

"Show-off." But I can't help the smile tugging at my lips. "Fine. Virginia Woolf. Happy?"

"Admittedly impressed," he says, tilting his head toward me. "Why Woolf?"

"Her prose feels alive. Fluid. Like she's writing the space between things instead of the things themselves." I shrug, suddenly self-conscious. "Plus, she wasn't afraid of imperfection. Her drafts were messy, chaotic even, but somehow that chaos turned into brilliance."

"Ah." He nods slowly, his expression shifting to something softer, more thoughtful. "Chaos into brilliance. Sounds like a good mantra for life."

"Or what it's like editing your manuscripts,"

"Fair enough," he concedes. "And for the record, you're not wrong about Woolf. But if we're talking fluid prose, Baldwin gives her a run for her money."

"James Baldwin?" I ask, needing to confirm we're talking about the same author. "Interesting choice for someone who writes steamy contemporary romance."

"Why? Because he doesn't do happy endings. He doesn't sugarcoat things. He digs into the mess of it all—love, pain, identity—and still makes it beautiful. That's what I aim for. Or try to, anyway."

"Messy but beautiful," I repeat softly, more to myself than to him. My instinct is to deflect, to slap on another layer of sarcasm to keep the conversation safely superficial. But... I don't.

"Okay, your turn," he says, his voice breaking through the knot in my thoughts. "What's your guilty pleasure read? And don't tell me you don't have one. Everyone does."

"Fine," I admit with a dramatic sigh. "Mass-market Regency romances. The more ridiculous the titles, the better."

"'The Duke Who Dared'?" he guesses, grinning. "'Her Scandalous Earl'?"

"Try 'The Viscount's Secret Vow,'" I say, and he laughs again, the sound warm and easy in the cool night air.

"Now that I'd pay to see. Lara Yates curled up with a bodice-ripper. Glasses askew, furiously annotating margins with red ink."

"Don't be absurd," I counter, fighting a smile. "I would never annotate a paperback. That's sacrilege."

"Glad to see you have limits," he teases, nudging my shoulder lightly with his own.

"Someone has to." I glance at him, the words slipping out before I can stop them. "Lord knows you don't."

"Ow!" His grin tilts crooked, his gaze holding mine for just a second too long.

"Anyway," I say briskly, straightening my glasses and looking away. "We should get moving. This garden's nice, but it's not exactly insulated. I'm freezing."

"Right," Rory says, standing and offering me a hand. I hesitate just a fraction before taking it, his grip warm against my chilled fingers. "Wouldn't want you catching a cold, Yates. Can't have my editor out of commission."

"Exactly," I say, but the excuse feels flimsy even to me. As we step back through the gate into the hum of the city, I risk a glance at him. His expression is unreadable, but there's a quiet intensity to it that lingers in the back of my mind long after the moment passes.

This is fine. Everything's fine.

Except, of course, it doesn't feel fine at all.

The lift dings and Rory strides out first, holding the door with a casual flick of his wrist as I follow. Typical. Always just enough charm to make it look effortless. The rooftop bar is already buzzing softly, though it's far from crowded. Glass railings encircle the space, offering a breathtaking view of London's patchwork skyline.

It's the kind of scenic moment that would make a lesser person sigh wistfully—or worse, pull out their phone for an Instagram post tagged *#blessed*. But I just stand there, arms crossed, trying not to give Rory the satisfaction of knowing it's beautiful... and, I have to admit, romantic.

"Nice, isn't it?" he says from somewhere behind me, his voice low and unhurried. There's no trace of smugness in it, which is irritating because I was fully prepared to roll my eyes at him.

"Acceptable," I say instead.

"Coming from someone who edits romance novels for a living," he counters, stepping closer—close enough that I can feel the faint heat of him even before his shoulder touches mine, "that almost sounds like a compliment."

We stand there for a beat, watching the lights flicker on in the distance like stars waking up. It's so annoyingly romantic.

"So, what should we drink to mark the occasion? Something pretentious with a sprig of rosemary in it?"

"Leave it to me." He tosses the words over his shoulder as he heads to the bar. I'm left standing there, hands shoved into my coat pockets, trying not to feel self-conscious.

It's not long before he's back, two glasses in hand. He sets one in front of me with a flourish, the amber liquid reflecting the warm glow of the string lights overhead.

"Old Fashioned," he says simply, sliding into the seat across from me. "No rosemary, no-nonsense. Just how you like it."

I blink, surprised. "How do you—"

"Don't look so shocked, Yates." He leans back, the corner of his mouth quirking up. "You mentioned it on your Instagram. At that dreadful industry event, remember? You made some snarky comment about the trend of deconstructed cocktails."

"That was... months ago." My voice falters slightly. "You've read through all of my social media?"

"Of course. When Fiona called to say you were my new editor, I had to know who I was getting into bed with, so to speak." His tone is light, but there's something underneath it.

"Well," I say, grasping the glass and taking a deliberate sip to cover my reaction. The drink burns smooth and sweet, just the way I like it. "Good to know you're capable of basic character research."

"I'd argue my research efforts are nothing if not thorough," he says with a wink.

"Cheers," I say, clinking his glass lightly. The city stretches out below us, alive and glittering, and for a moment, I let myself sink into the quiet hum of it. But then I feel his gaze on me, steady and unflinching, and it pulls me back like gravity.

"Alright, Yates," he says. "If you had to choose one book—one single book—to read for the rest of your life, what would it be?"

"That's an impossible question," I say immediately, taking another sip of my drink. "No serious reader would answer that. It's like asking me to pick a favourite child."

"Do you have children?" he asks, brow quirking.

"Obviously not." I roll my eyes. "It's hypothetical."

"Fine," he concedes, grinning like a schoolboy. "I'll narrow it down. You're stuck on a desert island—"

"Why am I always stranded in these scenarios?" I cut in, unable to help myself. "Am I shipwrecked? Plane crash? Did I anger Poseidon?"

"Focus, Yates," he says, smirking. "One book. What is it?"

"Something practical. *How to Build a Raft with Minimal Resources*," I offer, and his laugh is sudden and bright.

"Of course you'd pick a survival guide," he says. "You'd probably edit it while you're at it."

"Only if it needed it. Alright, your turn," I say, setting my empty glass down with a soft thud. "Desert island. One book."

"Easy," he says without hesitation. "*Pride and Prejudice.*"

"Seriously?" I'm genuinely surprised. "Mr. Darcy over here?"

"Don't knock it," he says, leaning closer, elbows resting on the table. "It's a masterpiece. Timeless. Plus, I figure if I'm stuck on an island, I could use the inspiration to brood properly."

"Naturally," I say, lips twitching. "Would you spend your days walking out of the water in your breeches?"

"Now you're getting it," he says, laughing, and I force myself to join him, even as the air between us shifts subtly, almost imperceptibly. His laughter fades, leaving behind a noticeable silence.

"Rory—" I start, but the words tangle in my throat because suddenly, he's closer. Not much, but enough. Enough that I can see the faint trace of stubble along his jaw, the way his gaze flickers to my lips for half a second before meeting mine again. My breath catches, and for once, I can't think of a single cutting remark to deflect with.

"Can I—" he begins, voice low, but he doesn't finish. He just shifts over, closing the remaining distance with a quiet certainty that steals the ground out from under me.

The kiss is warm, soft, and I want it to go on forever. I lean in, just a fraction, and everything else falls away.

The air between us feels brittle, like one wrong move might shatter it completely. My heart is pounding so loudly I'm sure it's echoing off the rooftop tiles, but Rory doesn't say a word. Neither do I. We sit there, suspended in this strange, humming stillness, and I stare at his profile as he looks out over the city, his jaw tight, his fingers drumming against his knee.

"Look, Rory..." I trail off, unsure what I really want to say. "Spending the day with you has been... nice,"

"Right," he says quickly. "*Nice.*"

"Okay, it was much nicer than nice, but I'm going home alone tonight."

I reach into my bag and pull out the flash drive I've been carrying all day, the one I had to scramble around the flat to find, loaded with his latest manuscript edits. Handing it over feels strangely transactional after everything that's just passed between us, but it also feels safe. Like I'm slamming the lid on a box that should never have been opened.

"Here. Your notes. I figured you'd want them sooner rather than later."

"Work," he says, taking the flash drive with a small, humourless laugh. "Always back to work with you, huh?"

"Someone has to keep you in line. We've got three weeks, Rory. You've got to hit that deadline. It's as simple as that. We're not meeting up again until you've made these changes."

"Right," he says again, slipping the drive into his jacket pocket. For a second, it looks like he wants to say more. Instead, he just stands and offers me a hand. "C'mon. I'll walk you down."

"Thanks," I say, letting him pull me to my feet. The warmth of his hand lingers long after he lets go.

We descend the lift in silence, the night abruptly over. Outside, the city hums with its own rhythm, but it feels oddly distant, like I'm watching it through glass. I stop at the curb, turning to face him.

"Goodnight, Rory," I say softly, adjusting my glasses out of habit.

"Night, Lara," he replies, his voice equally muted. He hesitates for a moment, then gives me a small wave before walking away, his figure disappearing into the crowd.

I stay rooted in place for another moment, the ghost of that kiss still lingering on my skin. Then I shake my head, square my shoulders, and remind myself to breathe.

It was just a kiss, I tell myself firmly, *no different from the many we've shared before*. But as I start toward the tube station, I can't help feeling like something fundamental has shifted and I've just stepped onto uncharted terrain, and there's no map to guide me back.

SEVENTEEN

The train shudders as it comes to a stop, and I step onto the platform, the air thick with that cloying mix of diesel fumes and damp concrete. It's strange how even the smell feels like a judgment. Welcome home, Lara Yates, where you're always too much or not enough.

I adjust the strap of my laptop bag on my shoulder, its weight pulling me slightly off balance. The station looks the same as it did when I left for university fourteen years ago, right down to the "OUT OF ORDER" sign sellotaped to the vending machine. Nostalgia doesn't hit—it creeps, slow and insidious, curling around me like ivy through cracks in old stone.

The cab ride from the station to my parents' house is uneventful, which is to say, suffocatingly familiar. Rows of identical brick houses blur outside the window, each one indistinguishable from the next, save for the occasional brazen display of individualism in the form of cement render. By the time I pull up next to the house, my chest feels tight, like I've been holding my breath since stepping off the train.

The front door swings open before I can even unbuckle

my seatbelt, and there she is—Mum. Still peering out at the world with that particular mix of concern and mild disapproval she's always worn like armour, her arms folded tightly across her chest. Her hair is shorter than I remember, dyed a shade too dark to look natural. She doesn't wave, just stands there, framed in the doorway like she's bracing herself for whatever version of me has shown up this time.

"Well, you made it," she says as I lug my suitcase up the steps. No hello, no hug. Just those four words, delivered in that tone that somehow manages to sound both relieved and disappointed.

"Yep." I force a smile that feels more like a grimace. "Still capable of navigating public transport."

"Just about," she replies, eyeing my shoes as if they offend her. They're sensible flats, but apparently not *sensible enough.*

Inside, the house smells like lemon polish and something faintly burnt—a combination as persistent as it is uninviting.

Dad appears in the doorway of the living room, his reading glasses perched at the end of his nose. He glances up from his crossword long enough to muster a half-hearted, "Hi, love," before retreating into the safety of his armchair fortress.

"Hi, Dad," I reply, though he's already disappeared behind the rustle of newspaper pages. Classic.

"Did you eat on the train?" Mum asks, her eyes darting toward my laptop bag. Not because she cares if I ate, of course, but because she's dying to ask if I was working the whole journey.

"Yes," I lie, because explaining that I spent two hours reading about a fictional duke ravishing a countess would only lead to questions I'm not prepared to answer.

"Good," she says, the word clipped and efficient. "You look tired."

"Thanks," I beam. "Exactly what every woman wants to hear."

She doesn't laugh, just purses her lips in a way that makes me feel about ten years old.

"Well, don't just stand there," she says briskly, already turning toward the kitchen. "Dinner's in an hour, and your cousin Emma's coming over."

Of course she is. Because nothing says "welcome home" like being reminded of all the ways you're falling short compared to someone else.

"...and then we're thinking of a spring wedding," Emma chirps, her voice as bright and sugary as the lemonade Mum insists on serving to house guests. "You know, cherry blossoms, soft pastel aesthetic, maybe an outdoor ceremony—if the weather cooperates, of course."

"Of course," I echo absently, swirling my fork through the mushed broccoli on my plate. It's been steamed to death, which feels fitting, given my current emotional state.

Emma doesn't seem to notice—or care—that my enthusiasm is about as genuine as Mum's compliments. She barrels ahead, waving one manicured hand in the air like she's already tossing a bouquet. "We just didn't want anything too fussy, you know? Tim and I are all about *simplicity*."

"Mm," I say noncommittally, glancing at my parents across the table. Dad is focused on his roast chicken like it holds the answers to life's great mysteries, while Mum nods along to Emma's monologue, her expression somewhere between polite interest and smug satisfaction.

"That sounds... nice," I add, because someone has to say something, and apparently that someone is me.

"Doesn't it?" Emma beams, radiant in a way only people with flawless skin and boundless self-confidence can be. "I mean, I know it's not for everyone"—her eyes flick toward me, just briefly enough to sting—"but Tim and I just feel so ready, you know? Like, why wait?"

"Why, indeed," I mutter under my breath. Emma doesn't hear me, but Mum does. Her pointed inhale is almost theatrical.

"Emma, darling," Mum says, steering the conversation like a pro. "Have you decided on bridesmaids yet?"

"Not officially," Emma giggles, though it's obvious she knows exactly who will—and won't—be standing beside her on her big day. Spoiler alert: It's not me.

"Well, you'll have plenty of time to figure that out," Mum assures her, before turning her attention to me. And here it comes—the pivot. "Speaking of time, Lara, how is work? Still keeping you busy, I imagine."

"Always," I reply, forcing a tight smile. "You know how it is."

"Do I?" she counters, tilting her head in that way that makes me want to scream into a pillow. "I mean, you're always working, aren't you? Even on weekends?"

"Publishing isn't exactly like teaching, Mum," I say, keeping my tone light despite the tension building in my chest. "We don't have a bell that rings and we can all go home. Deadlines don't take days off."

"Mm," she says, her lips pursing ever so slightly. "But surely you could find time to—"

"To what, Mum?" I cut in. "To plan a wedding? Because unless you've got a groom stashed in the pantry, I think I'm good."

The words hang there, awkward and heavy, until Emma clears her throat, clearly uncomfortable. "I think weddings are, um, overrated for some people," she offers, her voice faltering just enough to make me regret snapping.

"Sorry," I say, dropping my gaze to my plate. The broccoli florets glare back at me, unhelpfully.

"All I meant," Mum continues, ignoring the tension like a true professional, "is that it wouldn't hurt to take a break now and then. You work so hard, Lara—too hard, really. You shouldn't be on your own. Not at your age."

"Thanks, Mum, exactly what I needed to hear."

"Well, I'm only saying it because I care," she says, her tone just shy of defensive. "And because, honestly, I worry about you sometimes. You put so much energy into your career, but…"

"But what?" I prompt, my voice quieter now. Smaller.

"Nothing," she says quickly, brushing imaginary crumbs from the tablecloth. "Forget I said anything."

"Done," I reply, though the annoyance is beginning to boil.

Emma shifts in her seat, clearly desperate to change the subject. "So, uh, anyway, about the cake…"

Her words fade into background noise as I focus on cutting my chicken into precise, even pieces, pretending the table isn't closing in around me. My mother's words echo in my head, louder with each repetition: *You work too hard. You look tired. I worry about you.*

Translation: *You're not enough. You've never been enough.*

"Excuse me," I say abruptly, pushing my chair back from the table. "I need the loo."

No one stops me as I slip upstairs to my childhood bedroom. I lean against the back of the closed door, staring at the faint Blu Tack marks still mapping out where my posters once took pride of place, willing myself to breathe. To let it go.

But the knot remains, tangled and stubborn, refusing to loosen.

The muffled sounds of conversation downstairs—Emma's laugh, my mum's voice, piercing even when she's trying to be kind—fade slightly, but not enough. Never enough.

The room is smaller than I remember. Or maybe I've just grown too big for it, like an old cardigan I keep in the back of the closet out of misguided sentimentality.

The shelves are stuffed with books, their spines lined up in uneven rows, some leaning precariously as if they're exhausted from holding themselves upright all these years. Titles I devoured in hours, worlds I escaped into when this house felt too stifling. It's overwhelming and comforting all at once, like being wrapped in a blanket that smells faintly of dust and sorrow.

I kneel by the bed, pulling up the floral quilt that has remained since my mum bought it on sale at Marks & Spencer when I was twelve. My fingers fumble blindly until they hit cardboard. The box is heavier than I expect, or maybe I'm just out of practice lifting the weight of my teenage self.

I drag it out and sit cross-legged on the floor. The lid resists for a moment before giving way, revealing its chaotic contents: notebooks, loose papers, and a few crumpled envelopes. A time capsule of angst and ambition.

The first journal I pick up has a glittery purple cover. Of course it does. I flip it open and am immediately greeted by my own handwriting—big, loopy letters scrawled across the page with the urgency of someone who thought every word mattered.

My first and only attempt at keeping a diary. I began the first entry on January 1st and only made it to February 5th. Oh God. No. I slam it shut, face burning like someone might walk in and see. As if anyone cares what my fourteen-year-old self thought about... I glance again at the page. "...*whether Ben noticed my new haircut today.*" Jesus Christ.

"Moving on," I say under my breath, digging deeper into the box. Another notebook catches my eye, this one black and spiral-bound, edges frayed from being shoved into too many backpacks. When I open it, the pages are filled with half-written stories, fragments of dialogue, ideas jotted down in frantic shorthand.

One catches my attention—a scene between two characters whose names I don't recognise anymore, arguing over something dramatic and life-altering. The dialogue is clearly influenced by Brontë and Hugo, who I was reading at the time, dripping with melodrama, but there's something raw about it. Honest. I can almost feel the version of myself who wrote this, curled up on this very floor, pouring everything I had into these words because I didn't know where else to put it.

I flip through more pages, faster now. There are beginnings of stories—so many beginnings—but none of them are finished. Every single one cut off mid-sentence, mid-thought, like they were abandoned the second they demanded more than I was willing to give.

"Classic," I whisper, leaning back against the bed frame. The familiar knot tightens in my chest, the same one I've been carrying since dinner. Since forever.

Because here it is, laid bare in front of me: proof that I've always been good at starting things and terrible at finishing them. Proof that even then—even before deadlines and editorial meetings and the constant pressure to fix other people's work—I doubted whether I was good enough to create anything worth keeping.

I let the notebook fall closed in my lap, staring at the ceiling. The glow-in-the-dark star stickers are still up there, faded and peeling. I used to lie here at night, imagining they were real, wondering what it would feel like to reach for something so far away and actually hold on.

"Pathetic," I say aloud, though my voice cracks on the word. I swipe at my cheek before I realise the tears are even there.

I shove the notebook back into the box and slide it under the bed with my foot, like that'll somehow bury the mess of emotions clawing their way up my throat. Out of sight, out of mind—or at least, that's what I tell myself. Except the weight doesn't go away. It just sits there, heavy and unwelcome, pressing against my chest like one of those weighted blankets people swear are supposed to calm you down. Spoiler: it's not working.

"Fixing," I say aloud. My voice bounces off the walls, startling me. I scrub a hand over my face and try again, softer this time. "I'm good at fixing things."

That much is true. Give me a manuscript riddled with plot holes and flat characters, and I'll whip it into shape. Tighten the prose, rearrange the scenes, supercharge the stakes—it's practically second nature now. I've spent years honing that skill, carving out a little corner of the publishing world where I'm the fixer. The surgeon. The person who makes other people's stories better.

But creating something from scratch? That's... different. It's terrifying.

The last time I tried—really tried—was eight years ago, when I had just joined Scott & Drake as an editorial assistant, typing furiously every evening like my life depended on it. And maybe it did, in some small, melodramatic way. I wanted so badly to be good at it. To write something that wasn't just decent but great. Something that mattered.

And when I couldn't? When the words on the page didn't match the ones in my head? I quit. Just like I always do.

"God." I drag a pillow over my face like that'll muffle the thoughts spiralling out of control. "What am I even doing?"

It's not just about writing. It's about everything. My job, my life, my endless string of carefully curated routines that make it look like I have my shit together when, really, I feel like I'm running on autopilot most of the time. Editing is safe. Comfortable. I know what's expected of me, and I meet those expectations with ruthless efficiency, because that's what I do. That's who I am.

Isn't it?

Beneath the pillow, I exhale, slow and shaky. The truth—the ugly, inconvenient truth—is that I don't know anymore. I don't know what I'm working toward or why. I don't know if I want to climb higher in the publishing world or if I've already hit the ceiling. I don't even know if editing is enough. Not when the idea of writing still lingers in the back of my mind, persistent and painful, like an old wound that never quite healed.

My phone is in my hand before I realise I've reached for it. It's instinctive now, this endless cycle of distraction. Instagram, email, something, anything to keep my brain from spiralling too far inward. Except the Wi-Fi here is as bad as it was on the train, and the signal barely exists. Still, I swipe aimlessly, watching the little loading wheel spin like it might eventually unlock the secrets of the universe—or at least give me a meme that's funny enough to make tonight feel like it was worth the trip.

The screen glitches, freezes, then kicks me back to my home screen. Perfect. I let out a breath that sounds more like a growl and drop the phone on my stomach. It bounces once before settling there, mocking me with its blank, unhelpful face.

I close my eyes, but that only makes things worse. With nothing else to occupy the space between my ears, my mind wanders. And where does it go? Straight to Rory Keane, like it always does when I'm not paying attention.

It's stupid, really. He's just this... guy. A ridiculously charming, annoyingly talented guy who somehow made me agree to whatever this is. Friends. Lovers. Friends who some-times sleep together, but definitely don't talk about feelings, because that would ruin the whole casual vibe. Yeah, that's us. Casual. Totally normal.

And yet, here we are. Or rather, here I am, lying on a single bed in my childhood bedroom, staring at glow-in-the-dark stars that have long since lost their glow, wondering if Rory's even thought about me today.

"God," I groan, shoving the pillow over my face. "You're pathetic."

But it doesn't stop the questions. Has he thought about me? Does he care that I'm here, marooned in suburbia, slowly losing my mind? Or is he perfectly fine, living his perfectly fine life, completely unaware of the fact that I'm over-analysing every detail of our previous conversations?

Casual. Like saying it enough times in my head will make it true. Because that's what we agreed on. No attachments. No complications. Just two people who happen to enjoy each other's company—and occasionally each other's beds.

Except it's not that simple, is it? It never is.

Without thinking, I grab my phone again. My thumb hovers over the screen, and before I can stop myself, I'm scrolling through my contacts. Past coworkers, old friends, numbers I should've deleted years ago. And then there he is.

Rory.

His name sits there, glowing faintly in the dim light of the room, as if it's daring me to press it. To call. To text. To do *something.*

But what would I even say? *Hi, just checking in to see if you're still unbearably attractive and emotionally unavailable. Cool, great, talk soon.*

Yeah, no thanks. I lock the screen and toss the phone beside me, face down, as though hiding it will also hide the mess inside my head. But the weight of it lingers, heavy and insistent, pulling my thoughts back to him, no matter how hard I try to steer them elsewhere.

We're fine, I tell myself. We're exactly what we said we'd be. Nothing more, nothing less.

I lie back on the bed, staring up at the ceiling like it holds some kind of answer. It's just beige paint and a faint crack that looks vaguely like Italy if you squint hard enough. The same ceiling I used to stare at when I was sixteen, dreaming about things like college or leaving this town or, God help me, marrying Jake Gyllenhaal. And yet here I am, thirty-two years old, lying in the exact same spot, no closer to figuring out what I want than I was back then.

Except now, instead of daydreaming about Jake in his US Marines uniform, I'm thinking about Rory Keane and his stupidly perfect jawline. Not exactly progress.

The truth, the one I've been tap-dancing around for weeks, sneaks past the cracks I've tried so carefully to plaster over. I like him. Not in the casual, "you're fun to hang out with" way. In the dangerous, heart-thudding, why-hasn't-he-texted-me-back way. The kind of way that wants more. More time. More nights. More... everything.

But admitting that out loud? Even just to myself? Feels like stepping onto thin ice and hearing it creak beneath me.

Because what happens if I say it—if I acknowledge that I've already broken the only rule we set, and he hasn't? What if this whole thing really is as simple for him as we promised it would be? What if he is just fine keeping things light, while I'm over here mentally rewriting our meet-cute into something Nicholas Sparks-level tragic?

I sit up abruptly, tossing the pillow aside. My phone is still there, face down on the mattress, practically humming with accusation. Calling me a coward without even lighting up.

Okay, I think. *Let's say I text him. Let's say I tell him I'm feeling things I shouldn't be feeling. What's the worst that could happen?*

He'd hesitate. He wouldn't reject me outright—not Rory—

but there'd be a pause, a beat too long before he answered. And in that silence, I'd hear everything I already know but have been too stupid to accept. *Oh, Lara,* he would begin, not wanting to let me down, probably holding my hand earnestly. And then he'd remind me—gently, always gently—that this isn't what we agreed to. This was to help him write the best book possible. Nothing more, nothing less.

And he'd be right.

I flop back onto the bed, exhaling hard. *You're being ridiculous,* I tell myself, but the words don't land the way they should.

Because the truth is, Rory hasn't done anything to make me think he feels the same way. If anything, he's been consistent. Affectionate, yes. Attentive. But never more than what we set out to be. Never anything that suggests *this*—whatever *this* is—could exist outside of our temporary editor/author relationship, beyond the pages of his manuscript.

And the real kicker? I knew what I was signing up for. I agreed to this. I knew what the dangers were. So why am I lying here, dissecting every look, every touch, every lingering pause, as if any of it actually means something?

It doesn't.

The book is what matters. That's the priority. That's why I'm doing this. And if I have even an ounce of self-respect left, I'll get it together and focus.

I close my eyes, forcing the tension from my body. There's no point entertaining this anymore, no point indulging in foolish fantasies. I have a job to do. I won't be the editor who gets too close, who complicates things for no reason. I won't be the reason this book doesn't get finished.

So, whatever I think I'm feeling? It doesn't matter.

I take a deep breath, then another. I'll bury it. Lock it away.

The book comes first. It has to.

EIGHTEEN

All weekend, I resist the urge to call, text, or in any way contact Rory before our agreed-upon editorial catch-up tomorrow. I want to give him the space to write and he—well, he hasn't called me either—which proves my point.

So, when the text comes in, just as I'm settling onto the couch with a cup of tea and my latest guilty pleasure—an absurdly dramatic historical romance that has both bodice-ripping and pirates—I'm genuinely not expecting it. My phone buzzes against the armrest, and my immediate reaction is annoyance.

> Drinks tonight? Let's talk book. Rory x

Curiosity gnaws at me; if his most recent draft was anything to go by, then I'm genuinely excited to read the latest iteration to see how he's incorporated my notes and made the story his own. My thumb hovers over the keyboard. On one hand, it's probably nothing—just Rory being Rory, all charm and spontaneity. On the other hand... No, there is no other hand.

Still, I hesitate. But the truth is, I haven't been able to stop thinking about his book. Over the past weeks, it's transformed from mediocre to good, which is no small feat given where we started. Although it's still a long way from being the finished article, it also feels rawer than his usual polished fare, like he's peeled back some hidden part of himself and he's really trying to grow as a writer.

Fine.

I request the details before I can second-guess myself.

Where and when?

The response is immediate, as if he'd been waiting for me to cave.

8 PM. Flanaghan's, Piccadilly. First round's on me.

By the time I push open the heavy wooden door of Flanaghan's, I'm already regretting this. The bar is dimly lit, all dark wood and warm amber lights, with the low hum of voices and clinking glasses filling the air. It's cosy but crowded, the kind of place where people come to unwind after long days at jobs they secretly hate.

My editor brain kicks in almost instantly, scanning all the little details. The framed vintage posters on the walls. The worn leather booths that look like they've been there for decades. The bartender expertly pouring a cascade of blue liquid into a glass without spilling a drop.

And then I see him. Rory. Sitting at a small corner table, half-hidden by the shadow of a hanging Edison bulb. My traitorous stomach flips at the sight of him, but I push that feeling aside, forcing my hormones to obey.

I weave through the crowd, dodging a man gesturing wildly with his pint glass and a couple arguing softly but intensely. The closer I get to Rory's table, the more apparent it becomes that he's... dressed up. Not in an over-the-top way, but enough to make me hesitate mid-step.

He's wearing a dark shirt, sleeves rolled to the elbows just so. The top two buttons are undone, leaving just enough room to imply casual effortlessness while still looking annoyingly put together. His hair—always slightly tousled in that "oh, I did this by accident" kind of way—is suspiciously perfect tonight, like he might've actually spent time on it.

"Really?" I ask as I approach. "Just a casual drink?"

I tell myself it's just who Rory Keane is. This isn't about me. He's definitely not trying to impress me.

...Right?

"Well," I say as I slide into the seat across from him, setting my bag down deliberately, "don't you look like you just walked off the set of some GQ photo shoot?" I let my gaze flick pointedly from his shirt to his neatly cuffed sleeves. "Did I miss the memo? Was there a dress code for tonight?"

Rory's lips twitch into a grin, one corner pulling higher than the other. It's maddeningly self-assured, like he knows exactly what he's doing. Because of course he does.

"Can't a fella put in a little effort?" He leans back in his chair, fingers brushing the side of his glass. "Besides, everything else is in the laundry basket."

"Mm." I cross my arms, tilting my head. "And what, pray tell, would you have done if this were an actual manuscript discussion? Brought a velvet smoking jacket? A monocle?"

"Tempting," he says smoothly, eyes sparkling under the

dim lighting. "But I figured it'd be hard to take notes squinting."

"Ah, practicality wins out,"

"Always." He lifts his glass to take a sip. Then, lowering it just enough to meet my gaze, he adds, "Though, I'll admit, it's nice to see I caught your attention."

"I'm an editor. Observing details is literally my job."

"Is that what we're calling it?"

Whatever game he's playing, I'm determined not to let him win. Even if part of me—a very small, very stupid part—wonders if maybe, just maybe, he *is* trying to impress me after all.

"Alright," I say, taking the glass of stout that Rory promises is the best outside of Ireland. My fingers brush against the condensation on my glass as I eye him with what I hope passes for detached professionalism. "Please tell me you've made the changes."

"Straight to business," he says. "Not even going to ask how my day was? Maybe ease me into it with some light conversation?"

"Your day is irrelevant to whether or not we'll be ready to send something to the proofreaders."

"You'll hopefully find the changes to your satisfaction. It's waiting for you in your inbox. Sent it across before I left, ready for you to rip it apart.

"I don't rip apart," I correct as I check my phone and see that there is indeed an email from Rory, with an attachment. "More like... gently dismantle it in the name of improvement."

"Ah." He leans forward, resting his forearms on the table. The movement draws my attention—unfortunately—to the way his rolled-up sleeves reveal just enough forearm to be distracting. "Gentle dismantling. That's what you call the fifty-three comments you left on the first two chapters alone?"

"Fifty-two," I shoot back, levelling him with a pointed look. "One of those wasn't a comment. It was a question."

"Right. My mistake."

I should look away. I don't. Instead, my eyes catch on the tiny dimple that appears at the edge of his smile—a trait I've noticed exactly twice before but refuse to admit I find charming. My grip tightens around my glass, and I force myself to focus on something, *anything* else.

The lighting in the bar shifts without fanfare, a quiet dimming that softens the edges of everything. The overhead fixtures, so bright and clinical just an hour ago, now glow with a warm amber hue, like someone draped the room in honey. Even the chatter around us seems to have dialled down, the once boisterous hum reduced to low murmurs and occasional bursts of laughter from distant corners. It's as if the universe itself has decided to conspire against me, wrapping Rory and me in this unintentional cocoon of intimacy.

"Everything alright? You're awfully quiet all of a sudden," Rory says, his voice breaking through my thoughts. "Not running out of notes for me already, are you?"

"Hardly," I shoot back, swirling the last bit of dark liquid in my glass for something to do. "Just trying to decide which flaw to eviscerate next. There are so many options."

His laugh is low and rich, the sound curling in the small space between us like smoke.

"You wound me, Yates. Truly."

"Good. Keep bleeding—it builds character." I lift my glass as if to toast him.

"Admit it," he says, his voice low enough that it dips beneath the hum of conversations around us. "This could pass for a date."

"Could it?" I counter, arching a brow. My tone is breezy—practised—but the question lands heavier than I intended. The word *date* lingers in the air between us, weightier than it should be.

"Well, let's see." He tilts his head, his grin edging toward wolfish. "There's a bar, drinks, questionable lighting. All classic markers, wouldn't you say?"

"Missing one key element," I point out, forcing myself to sound unaffected.

"Which is?" His gaze is direct—too direct—and I have to look away before I drown in it.

"Romance," I say flatly.

"You're right. Not an ounce of the stuff. Not a smidgen." His denial only reinforces the fact that Rory Keane—a man who gets paid to write about grand gestures and stolen kisses— is sitting next to me, looking at me like *I'm* the plot twist he didn't see coming. And worse? I don't hate it.

"Okay," he says after a moment, turning slightly so he's facing me more fully. There's something different in his expression now—a shift I can't quite place. "Can I ask you something?"

"Since when do you ask permission?"

"Fair point," he admits. "But this one's important."

"Go on, then," I say, bracing myself for... What, exactly? I'm not sure. A question about edits, maybe. Or a thinly veiled attempt to say something salacious. What I *don't* expect is—

"Why don't you write your own books?"

I blink. "What?"

"You heard me."

"Rory..." I laugh nervously, setting my drink down. "Where is this coming from?"

"From the manuscript on the pen drive you gave me." His voice is calm, steady, like he hasn't just detonated a bomb in the middle of our conversation. "The one you probably forgot was still saved on there."

My stomach drops. "What are you talking about?"

"An old file," he says, watching me carefully now, like he's gauging whether I'm about to bolt. "It wasn't labelled or anything. Well, it was called doc.doc, so I almost didn't open it. But curiosity got the better of me, and... well..." He shrugs, as if the rest of the sentence isn't monumental. "Let's just say I didn't stop reading."

I stare at him, words failing me for the first time tonight. Maybe for the first time ever.

"Page one," he continues softly, leaning closer. "That's all it took. You hooked me from page one, Lara. And by the time I finished, I couldn't believe it. I couldn't believe you'd been hiding *that* talent all this time."

"Rory," I manage, though my voice comes out quieter than I intend. "You weren't supposed to see that. It's—it's nothing. Just an old draft I played around with ages ago."

"Nothing?" His brows pull together, incredulous. "Lara, it's *brilliant*. The characters, the pacing, the dialogue—it's all there. It's raw, sure, but it's real. And it's good. So good."

"Stop," I say quickly, shaking my head. My palms feel clammy, and the room seems smaller somehow, like the walls are inching closer. "It doesn't matter. It's not—"

"Not what?" he presses gently. "Not ready? Not perfect? Because news flash: no book ever is. You know that better than anyone."

"Rory—" I start, but he cuts me off.

"Do you know how many writers would kill for your instincts? For your voice? You've spent your career making other people's stories better, hiding behind your red pen, but Lara..." He pauses, his gaze locking onto mine. "You deserve to be seen, too."

I can't breathe. Or think. Or speak. All I can do is sit here, reeling, as his words sink in—deeper than they have any right to.

My fingers curl tightly around the edge of the table,

anchoring me as the weight of Rory's words settle on my chest. *You deserve to be seen, too.* They echo in my head, uninvited and relentless, like a song I didn't ask to hear but can't seem to forget.

"Rory," I say finally, my voice steadier than I expected. "It's not what you think. That manuscript... It wasn't meant for anyone else to see. Ever."

His head tilts with curiosity, those dark eyes still locked on me like he's trying to figure out how I work.

"Why not?"

"Because it's old." My laugh comes out brittle and unconvincing. "And messy. And unfinished. And—" I take a breath, adjusting my glasses even though they don't need it. "*Personal.*"

"Exactly." He says it like it's the most obvious thing in the world, like he's just declared the sky is blue or water is wet. "That's why it's so good."

"Rory." His name escapes me like a sigh. "You don't understand. I wrote that—" I pause, searching for the right words, but all I come up with are ones that feel too exposing. "It was a long time ago. I was just messing around. It's not—"

"Not worth sharing?" he finishes for me, his tone soft but probing. "Trust me when I say, you're better than half of the authors on Scott & Drake's list."

"Please stop," I snap. It's easier to sound irritated than to admit the truth—that his words are hitting something inside me I've kept buried for years. Something fragile and foolish and entirely too hopeful.

"I'm being honest." His mouth curves into a small, knowing smile, but there's nothing smug about it. If anything, it's disarming. Damn him. "You're hiding in plain sight, Lara. Editing other people's work when you should be publishing your own. You've got the talent. The voice. The guts—"

"Stop," I interrupt. "I don't have the—" My voice falters. *Courage? Confidence? Stupidity? All of the above?*

"Yes, you do," he counters firmly, cutting through my hesitation like it's nothing. "You just don't want to admit it."

"Why are you doing this?" The question slips out before I can stop it. "Why do you even care?"

"Because I know what it's like." His answer is immediate. "To doubt yourself. To second-guess every word you put on the page, wondering if it's good enough. But it is, Lara. *You are.*"

The air between us feels impossibly thick now, heavy with things unsaid and things I'm not sure I'm ready to hear. I glance away, focusing on the flickering candle at the centre of the table. Its soft glow seems to mock me, romanticising a moment that shouldn't feel as significant as it does.

"Look," Rory says after a beat, his tone forthright. "If you won't believe me, maybe you'll believe the fact that I couldn't put it down. I stayed up until three in the morning reading it—then I read it again the next day—and you're saying that's a rough draft? Imagine what it could be if you actually finished it."

"Rory..." I don't even know what I'm trying to say anymore. My thoughts are a tangled mess, each one bumping into the next before I can grab hold of it. All I know is that I feel exposed, like he's seeing a part of me I didn't even realise I was guarding so fiercely.

"Just think about it," he says gently. "That's all I'm saying."

"I'm not good enough."

"That's bullshit," he says flatly.

I blink again. Did he just—?

"Excuse me?"

"That's. Bullshit." Each word lands with its own little punch, and somehow, it feels less like an insult and more like he's handing me a mirror I don't want to look into. "You're not fooling anyone, least of all me. I think you're just scared."

"Scared?" My laugh is humourless. "Please. I *edit* writers, remember? I'm perfectly happy staying where I belong—behind the scenes. Not everyone wants to be thrust into the spotlight, Keane. Some of us prefer to avoid the inevitable crash-and-burn."

"Yeah, sure," he says, his tone dripping with sarcasm. "Because avoiding failure is totally the same thing as avoiding success."

"Not everyone needs success either," I counter, though the words taste bitter even as they leave my mouth.

"Keep telling yourself that," Rory says.

"Not everyone *needs* to be seen. Some of us are perfectly fine letting other people hog the spotlight while we do the heavy lifting behind the scenes. You know, the stuff that *actually* matters."

"Right." He doesn't even blink, doesn't flinch at the barbed tone I've perfected in editorial meetings. No, Rory Keane just sits there, calm as a monk, like he's been waiting for this exact moment. "Because you're so selfless, right? Just a humble editor making sure the rest of us get our gold stars."

Rory pinches his nose and sighs. "Let's cut the crap, Lara. It's not about the spotlight, is it? It's about what happens if someone looks too close. If they really see you."

"That's ridiculous," I say quickly, but it sounds weak even to my own ears. "Not everything is some deep psychological—"

"Isn't it? I think you're scared, Lara. And I get it. Putting yourself out there? Letting people judge your work? It's terrifying. But don't sit here and tell me you'd rather stay invisible when the truth is, you're just afraid of being seen."

"Stop." I'm done. Done with this conversation. Done with him. I need to get out of here.

The realisation hits me like a slap, cold and jarring, and

suddenly I'm moving before I've fully decided to. My chair scrapes loudly against the floor as I stand, the sound cutting through the charged silence like a knife. My hands fumble for my bag, clumsy and uncoordinated in a way that pisses me off because it's proof—undeniable proof—that he's gotten under my skin.

"Lara? Where are you going?" His voice is calm, but there's an edge to it, a note of disbelief that almost makes me stop. Almost.

"Home," I hear myself say, even though I'm not entirely sure I mean it. My heart is pounding so hard it might break through my ribcage any second now, and I can feel the sting of tears welling up behind my eyes. No. Not here. Not in front of him.

"Don't," he starts, but I'm already halfway to the door, my grip on my bag strap white-knuckled. My vision tunnels, locking onto the exit like it's the only thing keeping me afloat. I don't trust myself to look back. If I do, I might unravel completely, and I can't afford that—not here, not now, and definitely not in front of Rory Keane.

I'm halfway to the door when his voice cuts through the air behind me, direct and unrelenting.

"Don't walk away from this, Lara."

It's not loud, but it's enough to stop me cold. There's something in his tone—frustration, sure, but also concern, like he thinks I'm about to do something irreversible. Like leaving this room is some kind of line I can't uncross.

My fingers tighten on the strap of my bag, the leather biting into my palm. My back is to him, but I feel his gaze like a weight pressing between my shoulder blades. For a second— a fraction of a second—I consider turning around. Saying something. Anything. But what would I even say? That he's wrong, that he doesn't get it, that I'm not whatever it is he seems so hell-bent on believing I am?

Instead, I stand there, frozen in place, my breath shallow and uneven. The silence stretches, heavy and expectant, daring me to break it. And for one terrifying moment, I almost do. My lips part, but no sound comes out.

"Of course," Rory says softly, filling the void I leave behind. "You'd rather run than risk being seen."

The words land like a blow, precise and devastating. I feel them settle inside me, hot and unwelcome, and every nerve in my body screams at me to fight back. To turn around and tell him exactly where he can shove his amateur psychoanalysis. But then what? Prove him right by losing it?

No. Not here. Not with him.

"Just finish your own damn book, and stop worrying about mine." I shake my head and march towards the door.

The air outside is cooler, the street quieter, but it does nothing to steady the storm raging inside me. My heart is racing, my chest tight, and my thoughts are a chaotic mess of anger, humiliation, and—God help me—something dangerously close to hope.

Hope for what, exactly? That he's right? That I shouldn't be afraid? That maybe, just maybe, he sees something in me worth fighting for?

NINETEEN

It's been years since the last crisis meeting was called at Scott & Drake. I was a junior editor at the time, relatively new to publishing. It was a brutal affair that saw the entire production team in the dock for switching the printer prior to a major book release without completing robust due diligence—or informing Fiona and the rest of the board. The new printer delivered a sub-par product, which had to be pulped. It cost the publisher a significant headache and tens of thousands to reprint. It cost the head of production and two senior managers their jobs.

I'd hoped I would never have to witness one again. But to be the subject—or at the very least, a major contributor—to this one? It's the single most embarrassing moment of my professional career. I push the heavy glass door open, and every head turns to me for a split second before snapping back to their laptops. Every head, that is, except Rory's, whose gaze follows me across the room and lingers long after I settle into my seat. The tension is palpable, hanging in the air like a storm cloud that's been threatening to burst all week.

They're all aware that Rory's latest manuscript is a mess.

After all, that's why the meeting has been convened. Most of them probably haven't read it, not in its entirety, but the faults have certainly been shared among the wider team, and they're worried. Rightfully so.

I'm at a loss to explain what's gone wrong because it's not the story we were working on in the cottage, or similar to the drafts he's written since. What we have now, is something completely different. Rory didn't just throw the baby out along with the bathwater, he also tossed the bathtub out the window, and then chucked a grenade in the bathroom for good measure.

My hands are steady, thank God, though I can feel the heat creeping up my neck. *Professional. Cool. Detached.* That's what I tell myself as I settle in, unzipping the leather portfolio in front of me with slow precision. My pen is poised, in a convincing bid to hide the chaos inside my head.

"Don't look at him," I remind myself, because if I do, I'm afraid of what I might say to him. A bestselling romance author who can't seem to finish his book, and also the man who has managed to turn my already complicated life into one giant editorial migraine. There's no room for personal feelings here—not with this much on the line. Not when we're staring down deadlines tighter than Fiona's tailored jacket.

"All right." Fiona's voice slices through the chitchat and tapping keys, commanding immediate silence. She doesn't raise her voice; she never needs to. Authority radiates off her in waves, from the deliberate cadence of her words to the resounding click of her pen as she caps it. "Let's get straight to business. We've got eight days to get this manuscript to the printers—or we don't have a book at all."

The room stiffens collectively, the weight of her words settling over us like lead. I glance at her out of the corner of my eye as she leans forward slightly, palms flat on the table. Fiona Scott in no-nonsense professional mode is a sight to behold:

poised, implacable, and just intimidating enough to keep everyone on edge.

"This isn't just about hitting a deadline," she continues, her tone clipped, each word landing like a perfectly aimed dart. "This is about credibility. Our reputation. Rory, your last two books topped every chart imaginable. If we fumble this one, we look incompetent. You look incompetent. And incompetence, ladies and gentlemen, does not sell books."

I nod faintly, pretending to jot something down while my stomach twists itself into increasingly creative knots. No pressure, then. Just the future of our most profitable author and the publishing house dangling precariously over a cliff. Perfect.

"Now," Fiona says, her gaze narrowing, "we need solutions. Not excuses, not delays—solutions. This manuscript is slipping through our fingers, and if someone doesn't grab hold of it soon, we'll lose it entirely." She lets the words hang there for a moment.

"Questions? Comments?" Her eyes sweep the room again, daring anyone to speak. I keep my mouth shut, but my mind is racing. Solutions. What Fiona really means is that we need to figure out how to fix Rory's mess without stepping on his ego— or mine, apparently, since I'm the editor responsible for shepherding this disaster to publication. No big deal. Just another Thursday at Scott & Drake.

Rory, with his arms crossed tightly over his chest—the picture of a man who doesn't want to be here and is certainly not used to being spoken about, rather than to. His jaw is set, and he's glaring at the manuscript in front of him like it insulted his mother. I can't tell if he's about to argue with her or spontaneously combust, but either option feels likely.

"Well," he finally says, voice clipped, "I'm glad we've gathered here today to dissect my soul in front of a live studio audience."

"Your soul?" I counter, arching an eyebrow. "Funny, I

didn't realise your soul came with a subplot that still goes absolutely nowhere."

His eyes snap up to meet mine. Oh, good. We're doing this now.

"Taking some time out to reassess is essential for Sophie," he fires back. "It ties into the main theme—"

"Of what? Overindulgent navel-gazing?" I interrupt, keeping my tone even, professional. Mostly. "Rory, when I suggested replacing the car chase with something a bit more grounded, I was talking about the setting. The narrative structure still requires the same emotional drive, just not in a vehicle. Now Oliver's just wallowing in self-pity for three chapters straight. We've been over this, time and again."

"Forgive me for writing characters with depth," he snaps, his frustration curling around each syllable. "Not everyone wants cardboard cutouts, Lara. Some of us aim for nuance."

"*Nuance*," I repeat, letting the word hang between us, tasting its bitter edge. "Rory, there's a difference between nuance and indecision. This draft feels like a step backwards. Now Oliver spends an inordinate amount of time staring out of windows and brooding about his past mistakes. That's not depth—it's filler."

"Right, because God forbid a romance novel has actual emotional complexity," he shoots back, his voice rising just enough to draw side-eyes from the unlucky bystanders at the table.

Fiona doesn't flinch, which only makes her presence feel more ominous. Like a lion waiting to pounce.

"Emotional complexity isn't the issue," I say, keeping my voice low and controlled. "But readers need to care about what happens next. And right now? They won't, because nothing is happening apart from some witty banter. The pacing is still off after the midpoint, Rory. If you don't tighten it, they'll put the book down halfway through."

"Maybe they'll notice the pacing issues because the editor didn't do her job," he says under his breath, but loud enough that I hear it. Loud enough that everyone hears it.

The room goes still. My cheeks burn, but I keep my composure—or at least, I hope I do. I steal a glance at Fiona, who's watching us both with the kind of practised neutrality that could double as a death glare. Great.

"Excuse me?" I say, my voice deceptively calm, though my grip on the pen tightens like it's the only thing tethering me to sanity.

"You heard me." Rory leans back in his chair, arms still crossed, his expression daring me to challenge him.

"Last I checked," I say, sitting up straighter, "it's not my job to rewrite your book. It's my job to make sure your book is worth reading. If you're unhappy with my notes, maybe you should focus on fixing the manuscript instead of blaming me for pointing out the flaws."

"Flaws," he echoes. "You mean the parts of the story you just don't like? Admit it, Lara. This isn't about the book—it's about you wanting everything to fit your neat little boxes."

"Boxes?" The word tastes acidic coming out of my mouth. "Oh, please. You think I don't want this book to succeed? That I don't want *you* to succeed? Forgive me if I care about putting out something that doesn't read like one long therapy session disguised as a plot."

"Maybe if you loosened up once in a while, you'd understand," he bites back, his words laced with something darker, something personal. Too personal.

"Loosened up?" My voice shakes, more from anger than anything else. "Are you seriously—"

"Enough!" Fiona's voice cuts through the tension like a whip, silencing us both instantly. Her expression is unreadable, but her patience is clearly hanging by a thread.

I break eye contact with Rory, focusing instead on the

scrawled notes in my notebook that suddenly seem blurry. My heart is pounding, my thoughts racing. I don't look at him again, but I can feel his gaze, heavy and unrelenting, burning into me like an accusation I don't know how to defend against.

"I can only work with the material put in front of me, I can't—"

"I said, that's enough." Fiona's voice slices through the room with all the grace of a guillotine. The air seems to shudder under its weight, and I nearly flinch. Nearly.

Across from me, Rory leans back in his chair, arms crossed, jaw tight. His defiance radiates like heat off tarmac, but he stays silent for now. Smart.

"Do I have to remind you both what's at stake here?" Fiona asks, her tone slow and deliberate—like she's speaking to particularly dense children. She rests her hands flat on the table, her manicured nails clicking against the polished wood, and fixes us both with a stare. "This isn't just about one book. This is about *your* reputation, Rory. And about Scott & Drake's reputation as a publisher that delivers quality work every single time. We're not in the business of half-baked narratives or personal grudges masquerading as creative differences."

"Personal—" I start, but the look she fires my way freezes the words in my throat.

"Let me finish," she snaps, her clipped vowels landing like a gavel. "I don't care what unresolved... whatever this is"—she gestures vaguely between Rory and me—"you two have brought into this room. What I care about is delivering a manuscript that reflects the level of excellence we're known for. Your little sparring match"—her gaze narrows—"isn't helping anyone. Least of all yourselves."

I catch the faintest twitch of Rory's mouth, like he's fighting a smirk.

Oh no, sunshine, we're not doing that right now. I glare at him, daring him to say something stupid, but he thankfully opts for silence. For once.

"Here's how this works," Fiona continues, her voice like a drumbeat of finality. "You're going to resolve this. Today. I don't care how you do it, but you will find common ground, and you will do so without wasting any more of my time. Am I clear?"

"Crystal," Rory says smoothly, though there's an edge to his voice, a tautness that suggests he's biting back what he really wants to say.

Of course he sounds charming even when he's barely holding it together.

Must be nice.

"Good." Fiona straightens, smoothing the front of her jacket with brisk efficiency. She glances at me, then at Rory, and sighs, the kind of sigh that carries years of dealing with difficult people. "Because if this book goes out looking anything less than perfect, it won't just be your heads on the chopping block—it'll be mine. And I don't intend to let that happen." With that, she picks up her notebook and strides toward the door without a glance back. The rest of the marketing and publishing team immediately stand, every one of them looking at their phones as they follow her out.

The last one to leave has the presence of mind to shut the door behind her, and the silence left behind is almost suffocating. I tap my pen against my notebook, staring at the messy scrawl of notes that might as well be written in Sanskrit for all the sense they make now. My chest feels tight, but I force myself to breathe evenly, to channel all of my frustration into the rhythmic click-click-click of the pen. It's fine. Everything's fine. I'm a professional. I can handle this.

"Well, that was fun," Rory says, breaking the silence. There's a bitterness in his voice that's new—less playful, more jagged. "You okay over there? You look like you're plotting my murder."

"I'm fine," I say dryly, though my hands grip the pen a little tighter than necessary. I keep my gaze firmly on the page in front of me, refusing to meet his eyes, because I know—I *know*—that if I do, I'll see that damnable mix of arrogance and vulnerability that always makes me feel like I'm standing on a ledge. "I thought we were getting somewhere, but that last draft—"

"Right. It's Lara's way or the highway, isn't it? A box-checking exercise."

"For fuck's sake, Rory." My frustration comes out harsher than I intended, and I regret it instantly. But before he can respond, I push back from the table, the legs of my chair scraping loudly against the floor. My skin feels too tight, my thoughts too loud, and I need... space. Air. Something to untangle the knot of emotions twisting inside me.

As I gather my things, I try to focus on Fiona's words, on the stakes she hammered home. The future of the book, the publishing house, our careers—all of it hangs in the balance. That's what matters. That's the only thing that matters, I tell myself firmly. And yet, no matter how many times I repeat it like some desperate mantra, I can't quite shake the lingering weight of Rory's gaze or the way his words burrow under my skin like splinters.

Focus, there's still time to fix this. I gather my things and head to the door. There's nothing more to be said. Professionalism. Poise. Distance. Those are my pillars. Not... whatever this mess of feelings is. Definitely not that.

I'm halfway down the corridor before I realise I've left my favourite pen on the table. But going back isn't an option.

"Let him deal with it," I say out loud as I storm toward my office. My pulse is a thunderstorm I can't silence, rattling through me with every step. And yet, here I am, fleeing the battlefield like an intern who accidentally hit "Reply All" on their first day.

The Uber drives off, leaving me standing on the pavement outside Rory's house. It felt like a little win to storm off earlier, but I know it was petty and self-sabotaging. Rory's on a deadline, which means *we're* on a deadline. Thanks to my strop, we've lost an afternoon and an evening we could have used to try and fix this mess.

I knock on his door, only now thinking it might have been wise to check first that he was still awake, and more importantly, home.

The door swings open so fast that I jolt back, my fist still half-raised in the air. Rory's standing there, barefoot, wearing a wrinkled t-shirt and jeans. His hair is a mess, all dark waves pushed in every wrong direction, like he's been running his hands through it—or tearing it out. He blinks at me, confusion giving way to something darker.

"Lara," he says, my name a low rasp that feels like it's scraping against the edges of my resolve. "What—"

"I needed to talk." The words come out too fast, clipped and shaky, like they might shatter if I try to hold them in any longer. My throat is dry, and my heart is pounding so hard I'm sure he can hear it.

He leans one arm against the doorframe, his eyes narrowing as he studies me. "It's almost midnight. Couldn't this wait until morning?"

"Probably," I say, forcing out a laugh that sounds brittle. "But I wanted to apologise."

His mouth makes a perfect circle of surprise, but he steps aside. "Oh, then you'd better come in."

I don't move. Not right away. Instead, I just stand there, staring at him, at the way his t-shirt clings to his shoulders, at the faint shadow of stubble on his jawline, at the flicker of exhaustion and exasperation in his eyes. And for a second, I hate him—for being here, for looking at me like that, for changing his book so drastically without giving me a heads up.

But mostly, I hate myself. For how I behaved. For caring. For coming. For needing him in ways I can't even begin to unpack without risking everything I've built around me.

"Lara," he says again, quieter this time, and something in his tone snaps whatever fragile thread was holding me back.

I step inside, and before I can second-guess it, before I can give him—or myself—a chance to ask questions or put up walls, I grab the front of his shirt and push him back against the wall by the door. His breath hitches, and his hands instinctively come up to steady himself—or maybe to steady me—but I don't stop. I don't think. I just kiss him.

Hard.

It's not graceful or elegant or even particularly coordinated. It's desperate, messy, all teeth and heat and frustration bleeding out of me in one reckless, irreversible motion. His lips are warm, soft but firm against mine, and for one terrifyingly perfect moment, he doesn't move. He just lets me take, lets me pour every ounce of anger and longing and confusion into him.

And then he kisses me back.

It's like striking a match on petrol. His hands slide to my waist, pulling me closer, anchoring me even as everything else —the room, the world, my carefully constructed sense of self-control—falls away. One hand tangles in my hair, tilting my head just enough to deepen the kiss, while the other presses against the small of my back, pinning me against him with a force that makes my knees threaten to buckle.

I dig my fingers into his shoulders, my nails catching on the fabric of his shirt as I press harder, needing to feel something solid, something real, even as everything inside me unravels. There's no space between us now, no room for air or doubt or logic. Just the intense, electric pull of him, of this, of the maddening, undeniable truth I've spent months trying to bury.

When we finally break apart, gasping, my forehead rests against his, and for the first time in what feels like forever, I let myself breathe. Really breathe.

"Okay," Rory says, his voice rough and uneven, his fingers still fisted in my hair. "So... we're doing this now?"

"Apparently," I manage to say, though my voice is barely more than a whisper. My lips are still tingling, my heart is still racing, and I can't bring myself to look at him directly because I know—God, I *know*—that if I do, I'll see exactly what I'm feeling reflected at me.

And then I'll have no choice but to face it.

Rory's shirt hits the floor. My hands are everywhere, dragging over the hard planes of his chest, the curve of his shoulder blades, like I'm trying to memorise him through touch alone. His skin is warm under my palms, impossibly so, and for one dizzying moment, I wonder if I'll catch fire from being this close to him.

"You're sure about this?" Rory asks, the words ghosting across my skin and sending a shiver down my spine.

"Don't talk," I snap, tugging at the waistband of his jeans with more force than necessary. My fingers fumble with the button, shaking, impatient. "Just—" I say, swallowing hard as my breath catches. "Just... don't."

Because if he talks, it will become real, and if it's real, then I'll have to deal with everything that comes after. The fallout, the mess, the unbearable truth of what I've been denying these past weeks. And right now, I can't afford to think. I can't afford to feel anything but this—the heat of his body, the press of his mouth against mine, the raw, aching pull that makes it impossible to stop.

"Okay," he says softly, his tone threaded with something I don't want to name. He doesn't push, doesn't argue, just lets me take the lead even as his hands find my waist, steadying me, grounding me in a way I desperately need and hate all at once.

My jacket slides from my shoulders, pooling at my feet, followed quickly by my blouse. His fingers skim over the bare skin of my back as he unhooks my bra with practised ease, and I breathe in, my whole body tightening in response. It's too much and not enough all at once, and God help me, I think I might actually come apart right here in his arms.

"Just—" I bite my lip, frustrated by how unsteady I sound. "Just let me do this."

"Let you?" His lips quirk into a half-smile, but there's no humour in it, only a soft, biting sadness I try very hard not to notice. "You're not exactly giving me much choice here."

"Good," I reply, forcing a smirk I don't feel. "Maybe for once, you'll listen."

He huffs out a short laugh, but doesn't say anything else. Instead, his hands slide lower, gripping my hips as he guides me backwards until my legs hit the edge of the sofa. Before I can overthink it, I pull him down with me, drawing him closer, needing to erase every inch of space between us.

This is fine. This is good. Physical. Simple. A solution, not a problem.

But even as I convince myself of that, there's a crack somewhere deep inside me, a fine fissure spreading wider with every touch, every kiss, every whispered sigh that escapes my lips before I can catch it. Because this isn't simple, and it never was, not with him. Not with us.

As my skirt joins the growing pile of clothes on the floor, I squeeze my eyes shut, hoping the darkness will drown out the voice in my head screaming at me to stop. To pull back. But it doesn't work. If anything, the darkness only amplifies the weight of his hands on my skin, the way he whispers my name like it's some kind of prayer, like I'm something worth worshipping.

"Not that I'm complaining," he says, voice lazy and amused, "but I have to admit... this wasn't exactly how I pictured our next conversation going."

We're lying naked on the sofa. His sofa. And it feels good. "Oh, shut up."

He laughs. "Seriously, though. I had this whole speech planned. Thought I'd have to grovel. I was dreading it, to be honest. Instead, you just turned up, ravished me, and—"

I throw a cushion at him. He dodges, still smirking. "For the record, this does not mean all is forgiven."

He rubs my shoulder, fingers sliding over my skin in a way that is far too distracting for a man who still owes me an entire book. "Oh, I'm very aware," he says, tugging me just a little closer. "But you did just storm in here and have your wicked way with me, so forgive me if I'm struggling to take your outrage seriously."

I wrench my shoulder away, shaking my head, determined not to let him sidetrack me. "This is why I'm here, actually. To talk about the book. Not to provide you with an ego boost."

His brows lift. "You came here to talk about the book? Can I say that I wholeheartedly approve of this new editorial approach? Unorthodox, certainly. But you make your points loud and clear."

"Stop it. We need to agree on the direction of the story and stick to it."

His grin falters just a little, enough that I know he sees I'm serious. He exhales and scrubs a hand through his hair.

"Alright. What's the plan?"

I cross my arms, bracing myself. "First off, no more surprises. No more impulsive structural changes because you feel like it. We need to be pushing in the same direction or it's game over."

His eyes scan my face, like he's searching for something, then he nods. "Okay."

"Okay?" I blink. "That's it?"

He spreads his hands. "You're right. I'm sorry I blindsided you. I'll revert to the last draft."

I have his agreement and I know I should leave it there. But I don't. I can't.

"What happened? Why the drastic shift?"

Rory takes a deep breath. His whole chest rises and then he exhales. "I felt like I was writing a biography rather than a novel. Whether it was your suggestions or my subconscious, it wasn't Sophie and Oliver's story anymore. It was Lara and Rory's."

I shake my head immediately. "I don't think that's true—"

"Oh, come on." His gaze lifts to meet mine, serious but not unkind. "It was. The dialogue, the setting, the conflict—it was us. Every scene started feeling like something pulled from my own life. From *us*. And I—I can't write *that*. Not yet."

His words land like a punch I didn't see coming. I stare at him, my pulse picking up, not knowing what to say.

"So, what?" I manage, my voice too tight. "You panicked and reverted to type?"

Rory exhales, raking a hand through his hair. "I did what I always do when something gets too close—I pulled away. I stripped it back to something safe, familiar. Something I *know* works."

"Formulaic," I say before I can stop myself.

His mouth twitches. "Exactly."

"And you think what you submitted is the better version? The one you actually want published?"

A beat of silence. Then—

"No." His jaw tightens. "But it's the one I could finish."

The words settle between us, heavy, unspoken truths pressing in at the edges.

I want to push him, tell him he should have fought through it, that he should have written the real version, the messy, unpredictable one—but maybe I don't have the right. Maybe I should be grateful he pulled back. Because if Rory isn't ready to write *that* story... maybe I'm not ready to read it.

"Anyway, for the record, I'm nothing like Sophie."

"Oh really. Why don't you believe in happy-ever-afters then?" Rory asks, his voice low, almost tentative, like he's testing the waters and fully prepared for me to bite.

My stomach drops. Not because of the question itself—I've been asked it before, though never so directly—but because of the way he's looking at me now.

"I don't recall ever saying I don't believe in happy-ever-afters."

"Didn't have to," he counters, tilting his head slightly, his gaze narrowing like he's dissecting my every word, every movement. "It's all over your edits. The way you cut through sentimentality like it's mould growing on perfectly good bread. The way you strip every romantic scene down to its bare bones, like you're afraid of letting the characters feel too much."

"That's called tightening prose," I shoot back. "And if you look again at all my comments, instead of cherry-picking what supports your theory, you'd see I left plenty of room for emotional depth. Frankly, if anything, I'm saving you from drowning your readers in overwrought clichés."

He doesn't look away. Doesn't let me off the hook.

"Look, Rory, we're not here to discuss my views on... whatever this is. We're here to make sure we get this book finished. That's the job. That's all that matters right now."

"Do you think love is real?" he asks, his words careful, deliberate. "Not in books or movies or... whatever. Just—real."

I freeze. For once, I don't have a clever retort, or even a deflection. All I have is the truth, which feels like the last thing I want to share with him right now.

"Sometimes," I say finally, my voice barely audible. "But not for everyone."

"Why not for you?" His gaze holds mine, steady and patient, like he's willing to sit here all night waiting for an answer.

"Because..." I hesitate, the word catching in my throat. *Because it's easier not to hope. Because disappointment is far less painful than the alternative.* But I don't say any of that. I can't.

"Because I've seen what happens when it falls apart," I say instead, my tone clipped, distant. It's not a lie, but it's not the whole truth either. It's the version of the story I've rehearsed, the one that keeps people from asking more questions.

"Fair enough," Rory says after a beat, his voice neutral, though I can see the flicker of something deeper in his eyes. Disappointment? Understanding? Maybe both.

TWENTY

"Sixty's a big deal, isn't it?" Rory asks, not looking up from his laptop. His voice is casual, a throwaway comment as if he's asking me to pass the salt instead of inviting me to meet his *family*. "Mum's doing this whole thing tonight—cake, cousins, chaos. The world and his friend are all over from Ireland. You should come, meet the lot of them in one fell swoop."

I freeze mid-reach for my mug of tea, my fingers tightening around the ceramic handle. I glance at him over my glasses, trying to gauge how serious he is. His tone might be flippant, but I know Rory. He hides real things in offhand remarks, like slipping a secret into a joke and hoping no one notices.

"Come... to your mum's birthday party?" I repeat slowly, as though the syllables are alien on my tongue. *"With you?"*

"That's usually how these things work, yeah." He leans back in his chair, stretching until his shirt pulls taut against his chest. The picture of nonchalance. "She'd love you. And you've already survived me, so the rest of the Keane clan will be easy."

"Rory—" I start, but I have no idea where that sentence is going. My mind is stuck on *she'd love you* and the way he said it so effortlessly, like it's a fact carved into stone. Like the thought of introducing me to his family isn't sending me into full cardiac arrest.

"Look," he interrupts, flashing me that disarming grin that's gotten him out of more trouble than it should. "You can think of it as research. Authors and their tragic backstories. I'm giving you material here, Yates."

"Research," I echo, hating how weak my voice sounds. Meeting his *mum?* That isn't casual. That's... significant.

"Don't overthink it," he adds, like he knows exactly what I'm doing. His eyes flicker to mine, softening just a fraction. "It's just a party. No pressure."

No pressure. Right. Like there's no weight behind this invitation. Like stepping into his world won't mean something bigger than either of us is ready to admit. But all I can manage is an awkward nod before saying something about not having anything to wear, while my heart is thudding too loud in my ears.

The car hums steadily beneath us as we leave the urban sprawl of London and everything seems a lot more green and lush, the skyline shrinking in the rearview mirror. Rory taps the steering wheel in time to a song playing faintly on the radio—a folksy melody I don't recognise. He looks so at ease, one hand draped lazily over the wheel, like we're just heading to the grocery store instead of the lion's den masquerading as his childhood home.

Meanwhile, I'm clutching my handbag like it contains state secrets, staring out the passenger window as if the darkness beyond has answers to the questions I can't stop asking myself. *What does this mean? Why now? Are we... something?*

"You're unusually quiet," Rory says, glancing sideways at me. "If I didn't know better, I'd say you were nervous."

"Who, me? Nervous?" I scoff, though I suspect it comes out less convincing than I'd intended. "Just mentally preparing myself for whatever familial circus you're about to drop me into."

"Ah, the Keane clan's not so bad." He grins, his voice warm, teasing. "A bit loud, maybe. But you'll manage. You're tougher than you look."

"Right. Because nothing screams 'tough' like pencil skirts and colour-coded calendars," I deadpan, earning a low chuckle from him. It's unfair how good that sound is at diffusing tension.

"Don't sell yourself short. You've got claws under all that polish."

"Claws or not, I don't do well with crowds. Or small talk. Or..." I catch myself. Admitting that meeting his family feels impossibly intimate—that it scares me—isn't something I'm ready to say out loud. Not yet.

"Relax," Rory says, his voice softer now. "I told you already, they're going to love you."

"Love me? Based on what, exactly?"

"Based on the fact that I do," he replies easily, then immediately winces, like the words slipped out without permission. He clears his throat, focusing a little too intently on the road ahead. "I mean—they'll love you because you're... uh, great. Obviously."

My heart stumbles over itself, tripping on the implications. *He loves me?* No, surely not. He couldn't have meant it like *that*. Could he?

"Obviously," I say, staring straight ahead, my pulse racing. The silence that follows is thick, charged with everything we're not saying.

And suddenly, the drive feels far longer than it is.

The car rolls to a stop in front of a white pebble-dashed semi-detached house that practically radiates warmth. Fairy lights are strung along the porch railing, flickering cheerfully against the twilight, and the muffled sound of laughter spills out through an open window somewhere above. There's already a cluster of parked cars, many with Irish registration plates, lining the driveway and spilling onto the street, hinting at the number of people crammed inside.

"Here we are," Rory announces, like we've just pulled up to a branch of Pizza Express instead of the epicentre of my social anxiety for the evening.

He cuts the engine, leaning back in his seat with easy confidence. Meanwhile, I'm frozen, gripping my bag like it's a life jacket.

"Great." My voice is flat, betraying none of the chaos currently rioting in my chest. "Looks... lively."

"Don't worry," he says, glancing over at me with a grin so disarming it should come with a warning label. "They don't bite. Often."

"Good to know," I say, only half-joking as I look at the house again. The distant clink of dishes and bursts of conversation carry on the breeze, underscored by what sounds suspiciously like someone belting out a tune slightly off-key. "Unless the singing counts as assault."

"That would be Uncle Declan," Rory says with a chuckle, already stepping out of the car. "And it absolutely does."

By the time I manage to unclench my fingers from my bag and climb out, he's waiting for me by the passenger side, one hand extended. I hesitate—because apparently, chivalry still throws me off—but eventually I take it. His palm is warm, grounding me, as he leads me up the path toward the house.

"Relax," he whispers, his thumb brushing lightly over mine before letting go. "You're going to be fine."

A set of keys have been left in the door and before I can turn and flee, he's already letting himself in.

The noise hits me first—a cacophony of voices, laughter, and music all jumbled together. Then comes the smell: roasted meat, garlic, something sweet and cinnamony in the mix. It's the kind of aroma that belongs to a home, not a house, and it tugs at something buried deep in my chest. Something I'd prefer stayed buried.

"Rory!" A woman's voice calls from somewhere in the swarm of people gathered in the living room. A blur of faces turns toward us, and suddenly, I feel like I've walked into the middle of a stage play without knowing my lines.

"Hey, Ma! Happy birthday," Rory replies, slipping effortlessly into the room like he's done this a thousand times. Which, of course, he has. His hand slides to the small of my back, a subtle pressure urging me forward. It anchors me and sends my heart galloping in equal measure.

"Everyone, this is Lara," he announces, his tone casual yet deliberate. "Lara, meet... well, everyone."

"Hi," I manage, my voice coming out a touch too high. I adjust my glasses reflexively.

"Ah, so *this* is Lara," says a man who must be Uncle Declan, judging by the pint in one hand and the mischievous twinkle in his eyes. "Rory's been very—"

"Declan," Rory interrupts smoothly, his smile tight but his grip on my back steady. "Maybe save the stories for later, yeah?"

"Fine, fine." Declan winks at me. "But don't think you're off the hook, Lara."

"Wouldn't dream of it," I reply, my tone dry enough to earn a surprised laugh. Good. Sarcasm is safer than sincerity right now.

"Come sit, love," Rory's mum says, bustling over and enveloping him in a quick hug before turning her attention to me. She's short, round-faced, and exudes an energy that could probably fuel a small city. Her smile is warm, genuine, and entirely overwhelming. "It's lovely to finally meet you! I'm Rory's mammy, Evelyn. He's told us so much about you."

"Has he?" I shoot Rory a look, but he just shrugs, unapologetic.

"Only good things, I promise," she insists, taking my hands in hers briefly before pulling me further into the chaos. "Now, let's get you something to eat. Have you tried Declan's infamous sausage rolls? Oh, and there's trifle—or pavlova, if you prefer. Or both!"

"Both sounds great," I say meekly, not sure how else to respond.

Rory follows close behind, his hand never leaving its place on my back, as if he can sense the exact moment I might bolt.

"And there might be a little sliver of apple pie left if you're lucky. Oh, and if none of those float your boat, I've a tub of Ben & Jerry's in the chest freezer—"

"*Mum.* We'll figure it out. Don't you be fussing now, it's your birthday. Relax."

"I can't relax, I've cocktail sausages in the oven that need turning and I've sent Shiv to the corner shop to get some more mayo for the Thousand Island sauce. Lara, I'll get you a drink in the meantime, you must be parched."

Evelyn heads down the hall towards the kitchen, clearly on a mission to ensure I'm well-fed and watered.

"See?" he whispers, low enough for only me to hear. "Told you she'd love you."

"Debatable," I reply, earning another laugh from him. But when I catch the way his mum turns and beams at him—and at me—I wonder if he might actually be right. Well, mostly.

The living room hums with overlapping conversations, bursts of laughter punctuating the air like a melody I can't quite follow. Every corner is occupied—cousins of all ages sprawled on the floor, flipping through old photo albums, aunts perched on armrests with glasses of wine in hand, and Rory smack in the middle of it all, completely at ease. His laughter booms across the room as one of his uncles claps him on the shoulder, and I feel a pang of something sharp and unfamiliar. Envy? Maybe. Or just the sheer alienness of watching someone so thoroughly belong.

I sit on the edge of the couch, legs crossed at the ankles, trying to fold myself into the furniture as much as possible. My glass of wine is practically full because sipping it feels like committing to a level of relaxation I'm not sure I'll reach tonight. Every now and then, someone glances my way—a polite smile here, a passing question there—but mostly, I'm an observer. Slightly overwhelmed by the frenetic energy in the house.

"Comfortable?" Rory's voice rumbles above me, low and warm, as he leans down to speak near my ear. His hand brushes my shoulder, casual but grounding.

"Like a giraffe in a tea shop," I answer, earning that crooked grin of his. He looks entirely too pleased with himself, the traitor.

"You're doing great," he says softly, straightening up. "They're already obsessed with you."

"Obsessed with whether I'll implode, maybe."

"That too." He winks before being pulled back into another conversation, this time with a cousin of a similar age. I watch him move through the room, effortlessly charming, the centre of gravity around which everyone orbits. It's maddeningly endearing.

I take a deep breath and try to focus on something tangible —the framed photographs lining the mantelpiece, the mismatched cushions strewn about, the faint scent of roasted lamb and rosemary wafting from the kitchen. But it's impossible to ignore the undercurrent of energy in the air, the sense that something—or someone—is missing. Just as I think I might be imagining it, the front door creaks open, and a gust of cool evening air spills into the room.

"Is that...?" someone starts, their words swallowed by a collective gasp. Heads swivel toward the doorway, and suddenly the atmosphere shifts, charged with a new kind of excitement.

"AOIFE!" Rory's mum cries out, her voice a mix of shock and unabashed joy. The room erupts into chaos—chairs scraping, people standing, voices overlapping in a cacophony of names and greetings.

Rory freezes mid-laugh, his expression flickering between disbelief and delight. "No bloody way," he says under his breath, already moving toward the door.

I follow his gaze, and there she is—a striking whirlwind of black curls and a bright green coat, sliding an enormous rucksack off her shoulder. She grins as she steps inside, cheeks flushed from the cold, and the entire room seems to tilt toward her, magnetised.

"Surprise!" she announces, her voice lilting and musical, as if her very presence isn't enough of one.

"Jesus Christ, Aoife," Rory exclaims, reaching her in three long strides. "I thought you were still in Thailand." He pulls her into a bear hug that lifts her off the floor, and she laughs, the sound light and bubbling over. It's the kind of laugh that makes you want to join in, even if you don't know the joke.

"Put me down, you great big oaf," she chides, though her tone is nothing but affectionate. As soon as her feet hit the ground, she swats his arm playfully before turning to greet the rest of the family, who are clamouring for her attention. Aoife saves the biggest hug of all for her mum. Evelyn wipes the tears from her cheeks, as she tries to reel off all the food options available, at the same time as asking how her time away has been.

I stay rooted to my spot, watching the scene unfold with a strange mix of fascination and unease. There's something disarming about Aoife—an effortless charisma that draws people in, much like Rory, but softer, less polished. She moves through the room like she belongs in every part of it, hugging and laughing and somehow making each person feel like they've been waiting all night just to see her.

My gaze snaps back to Aoife and Rory—brother and sister —standing close, their heads bent together as they talk. There's an ease between them, a shorthand born of years and shared history, that makes me suddenly, acutely aware of how little I really know about Rory.

"Aoife's fierce craic. Voice like Celine Dion," Declan continues, his tone filled with unmistakable pride. "Always off gallivanting, but when she shows up, it's like Christmas has come early."

"Seems like it," I confirm, unable to look away. Rory's face is lit up in a way I haven't seen before, open and unguarded, and Aoife matches him beat for beat, her hands gesturing animatedly as she speaks. Whatever tension was hanging in the air before has shifted entirely, replaced by something warmer, more intimate. And for reasons I can't quite explain, it sets my nerves jangling all over again.

"Well, well," Aoife says, her voice carrying across the room like sunlight breaking through clouds. "So this is the famous Lara."

I straighten instinctively, caught off guard by the sheer warmth radiating from her as she crosses the room toward me.

Her handshake is firm but unpretentious, and her smile— wide, bright, devastatingly genuine—makes me feel both seen and immediately scrutinised.

"Famous?" I manage, my tone far cooler than what's swirling beneath the surface. My heart's pounding out an uneven tattoo. "That's a bit of an overstatement."

"Not at all," Aoife says, eyes sparkling with something between mischief and admiration. "You're all he messages about these days. Well, you and work. But mostly you."

"Mostly work," Rory cuts in smoothly, appearing at my side with an easy grin. His hand hovers near my back again, just barely brushing against the fabric of my dress, and I can't tell if it's meant to steady me or himself. Maybe both.

"Sure, sure," Aoife teases, her Irish lilt thickening with her amusement. "Work. Which, incidentally, you owe entirely to me. Or have you conveniently forgotten who gave you your start?"

"Start?" The word slips out before I can stop it. Both of them glance at me—Rory quickly, warily; Aoife with a breezy sort of curiosity, like she's just noticed I might be paying attention.

"Ah, so," she says, laughing lightly. "The dirty little secret of the Keane family empire." She waggles her fingers dramatically, as though unveiling some grand conspiracy. "Rory writes the words, but I polish the diamonds in the rough."

"Polish," Rory echoes, though there's a tightness to his jaw now that wasn't there moments ago. "That's one way of putting it."

"Don't let him fool you," Aoife says, leaning toward me conspiratorially, her curls bouncing as she moves. "He's brilliant, of course. But sometimes a brother just needs a sister to tell him when his leading lady is acting like a total eejit or when his love scenes are more cringe than swoon."

"Right," I say faintly, my lips curving into a polite smile that feels plastered on. My mind is already spinning, trying to piece together what I've just heard. Rory's books—the multi-million copy bestsellers, the Scott & Drake cash cow—have been... what? A group project?

"She's exaggerating," Rory interjects, his voice pitched low and careful. "It's not—"

"Exaggerating?" Aoife interrupts, raising an eyebrow in mock offence. "What, you don't remember the nights we stayed up until dawn reworking that god-awful ending for *Lakewood Hearts*? Or when I had to rewrite half of *Falling for April* because your hero sounded like he'd swallowed a thesaurus? How did you fare this time on your own, without my genius to fix everything, huh? You had your work cut out for you there, Lara, I've no doubt."

"Enough, Aoife," Rory says, his smile faltering entirely now. There's an edge to his voice that only makes her laugh harder, oblivious—or maybe indifferent—to the tension thickening between us.

"Anyway," she continues, undeterred, turning back to me with a wink. "You know how he gets—he's all big ideas and no patience. Someone's gotta make sure those grand gestures on the page actually land, right?"

"Aoife, please."

"Don't worry, Lara. He's still the genius everyone thinks he is. I'm just the invisible MVP behind the curtain."

Invisible. The word lands like a stone in my chest, heavy and cold. My gaze flickers to Rory, searching for some kind of denial, some reassurance, that this is all just a sibling's playful exaggeration. But his expression—tight-lipped, guilty, defensive—tells me everything I need to know.

"Interesting," I say, though my voice comes out thinner than I'd like. My throat feels dry and scratchy, like it's closing in on itself.

"Isn't it?" Aoife beams, clearly pleased with herself. "And here I thought *you'd* be the intimidating one, being a big-deal editor and all. But look at you—" She gestures toward me, her tone warm but distinctly patronising. "Perfectly normal. Lovely, even."

"Thanks," I say, though my stomach is knotting tighter by the second. Normal. Lovely. Invisible.

I force a sip of the wine Rory handed me earlier, but it tastes bitter now, like vinegar on my tongue. Across the room, Rory's mum laughs at something another guest has said, the sound ringing out cheerfully, obliviously. The air feels stifling, the warmth of the house pressing against my skin like a weight I can't shake.

"Excuse me for a moment," I say, setting my glass down on a nearby table with careful precision. My voice sounds detached even to my own ears, but I can't bring myself to care.

"Everything alright?" Rory asks, his brow furrowing, but I don't look at him as I step past.

"Fine," I lie, my heels clicking against the hardwood floor as I make my way out of the front room towards the hall.

Because I need space. Air. Something to hold on to while the ground shifts out from under me.

Co-writing. Polishing. Whatever they want to call it. The details hardly matter now. What matters is that the man I've spent weeks believing in—the man I've... God, the man I've started to fall for—isn't who I thought he was.

And that, somehow, feels worse than any of the lies themselves.

My lungs forget how to work.

I stand just inside the doorway of the living room, gripping the frame like it might stop the world from spinning. My chest feels tight, my heartbeat a frantic battery that drowns out the hum of conversation around me. The heat that prickles at the back of my neck has nothing to do with the crowded house or the wine I'd barely touched. Across the room, Rory is laughing at something his cousin said, his head tilted back in that easy, careless way he does, like the universe itself bends to make him comfortable.

Co-writing, Aoife had said, her voice lilting and amused, as if she hadn't just detonated a bomb right in front of me.

I swallow hard, the sound loud in my own ears. My fingers

twitch against the doorframe. My skin feels too tight, like the betrayal has seeped into my very cells, and now I'm stuck wearing it. Carrying it.

"Hey."

Rory's voice cuts through the haze, sudden and far too close. I blink and realise he's standing in front of me, his smile faltering when he sees whatever must be written across my face. He looks confused for half a second, but then something shifts. His eyes widen, and his expression—God, it's like watching the mask slip off a magician mid-trick.

"Is it true?" My voice slices through the layers of noise filtering from the front room. I don't even care who hears. My hands are trembling now, so I shove them into fists at my sides. "What Aoife said? About your books?"

His jaw tightens. It's the same look he gets when he's about to bluff his way through a plot hole during one of our editorial meetings. Except this time, there's no manuscript between us. No professional distance to cushion the blow.

"Lara—" His voice is softer now, almost pleading, but it only makes my stomach lurch harder.

"Don't." I take a step back, holding up a hand like it might physically stop him from coming any closer. "Just—don't."

His shoulders sag, and for the first time since I've met him, Rory Keane looks utterly lost. Vulnerable in a way that doesn't suit him and maybe never will. The charm, the bravado—it's all gone. Replaced by a boy who looks like he got caught with his hand in the biscuit tin. But I can't focus on that, not when my breath is coming in shallow bursts and my brain won't stop screaming at me to *fix this,* even though I don't know how.

"Let me explain," he says, his voice low and urgent now. "It's not—"

"Not what it sounds like?" My laugh is bitter. "Don't insult both of us by pretending this isn't exactly what it sounds like, Rory."

His mouth opens, but no words come out. And for once, his silence speaks louder than anything else could.

I don't wait for him to try again. My feet move before my brain can catch up, carrying me toward the front door like it's the only lifeboat on a sinking ship. The house is suddenly too loud and too quiet all at once—the muted hum of conversations dying, the clink of glasses halting mid-toast. It's a cacophony of stunned silences that chase me as I go.

"Where are you—" Rory's voice cuts through, hoarse and desperate, but I don't turn around. If I look at him now—at his stupidly earnest face, at those pleading eyes—I might crumble. And I can't afford that. Not here. Not in front of his entire family.

My heels click-clack with every step, a hammer driving nails into the coffin of whatever this... thing between us was supposed to be. I make it to the front door, my hand fumbling for the latch. The air feels thick, like I'm wading through syrup, and my fingers won't cooperate. Of course. Of course, even the door is conspiring against me now.

"Let me help—" Rory again. Closer this time. Too close.

"Don't you dare." I finally get the door open, cold night air slapping me in the face like some cosmic attempt at resuscitation, and I step outside without glancing back, letting the door swing shut with a satisfying *thunk* behind me.

TWENTY-ONE

The crisp evening air bites at my cheeks as I storm down the drive. Betrayal sits heavy in my stomach, twisting and churning like something alive.

"How did you fare this time on your own, without my genius to fix everything, huh?" Her exact words. It all suddenly makes sense. All this time, every draft, every late-night call about plot twists and pacing issues. Aoife. His sister. His secret muse.

How could I not see it? The hints were there, scattered like breadcrumbs—his vague answers when I asked where he got his ideas, the way he always changed the subject when I pressed why this book was so different from the others. And Aoife... She slipped into the evening like she belonged there, like she was the missing piece I hadn't realised I was looking for.

All this time... My throat tightens, and I blink hard against the sting threatening to spill over. No. Not now. Not here. I refuse to let Rory Keane—or anyone, for that matter—see me fall apart like this.

"Dammit, Lara, wait!" Rory's voice cuts through the quiet night, but I don't turn.

Of course, he follows me. He always has to have the last word, doesn't he? I pick up my pace, the gravel path giving way to flagstones. Each step feels like an exclamation point to the thoughts racing through my head: *How dare he? How* dare *he?*

"Just—" His footsteps crunch behind me, faster now, closer. "Lara, will you just stop for one second?"

"Why?" I throw the word over my shoulder, not slowing down. My voice is biting, bordering on the hysterical. Good. Let him hear the edge of it. Let him choke on it. "So you can spin another story? Or maybe workshop a new ending, Rory? Something more... satisfying for your audience?"

"Can we just talk about this? Please?"

"Talk?" I whirl around without warning, forcing him to skid to a halt a few feet away. The sudden movement sends my glasses sliding down my nose, and I shove them back into place with more force than necessary. "Talk about what, exactly, Rory? Because I think we've already said plenty."

He looks at me then, really looks at me. There's something raw in his expression—something almost boyish in the way his dark hair falls messily across his forehead, his breathing uneven from chasing after me. But I'm not falling for it. Not this time.

"Look," he starts, running a hand through his hair like he's trying to buy himself time. "I didn't—"

"Don't." I hold up a hand, cutting him off. "Don't you dare try to explain this away. You don't get to smooth this over with your charming little speeches or whatever it is you do to make people forget you're full of—"

"Stop it," he snaps, stepping closer. His voice is louder now, angrier, and it startles me enough to cut me off mid-sentence.

For a second, we just stand there, the tension between us

crackling in the cold night air. His eyes search mine, desperate, wild, like he's trying to find something there he knows he's already lost.

"Please," he says again, softer this time. His voice cracks on the word, and something inside me twists painfully.

Damn him. Damn his stupid sincerity, his stupid earnestness, his stupid everything.

"Tell me then," I say, my voice low but lethal. "How does Aoife fit into all this?"

He freezes. Just for a second, but long enough for me to notice. Long enough for the tiny, foolish part of me holding onto hope to shrivel up and die. His mouth opens, but no words come. It's like watching a learner driver stall out at a green light, and I think: *Oh God, this is it, isn't it?*

"Rory." My voice cracks, but I press on. "You wanted me to believe in you. To trust you. And now you can't even look me in the eye and tell me the truth?"

He finally meets my gaze. He swallows hard. Hesitates. Again.

My voice rises, fuelled by the sheer audacity of his silence. "Say something! Anything! Or am I just supposed to connect the dots myself? Because let me tell you, Rory, the picture isn't looking great from where I'm standing."

Still nothing. His throat works like he's trying to push the words out, but they're stuck somewhere between his ego and whatever shred of decency he has left. The longer he stays quiet, the louder everything else becomes—the rustling leaves, the distant hum of traffic, the roaring in my ears.

"Unbelievable," I say, taking a step back. My chest feels tight, like all the air's been vacuumed out of the world. "So this is it. This is who you really are."

"Wait," he says finally, his voice rough and hesitant, like he knows it's too little, too late. "Lara, it's not—"

"Don't." I cut him off, shaking my head. My anger starts to

falter, cracking at the edges, making room for something deeper. Something heavier. "You don't even realise what you've done, do you?"

And there it is—that flicker of guilt in his expression. A spark of regret that only makes me angrier because it's not enough. It'll never be enough.

I throw my hands in the air, a sudden gesture that cuts through the charged silence between us. "You know what's funny, Rory? I was actually starting to believe you." My voice comes out louder than I meant it to, but I don't care. The words are trembling on the edge of fury, like they've been waiting for this moment to burst free. "All that talk about writer's block and finding your inspiration again— God, I was such an idiot."

His eyes widen, his mouth parting as if he's about to interrupt, but I barrel forward, steamrolling any attempt by him to speak.

"Do you have *any* idea how humiliating it feels to find out the hard way that I was just... What? A convenient replacement for your sister? A shortcut around your supposed creative dry spell?"

"That's not—"

I cut him off with a laugh that tastes bitter in my throat.

"Don't even try it, Rory. Don't." I jab a finger at him, my hand shaking slightly, though I hope he can't see it. "You sat there, day after day, feeding me line after line about how stuck you were. How much you needed me. And the whole time, Aoife—" her name burns like acid on my tongue "—was doing what, exactly? Filling in the blanks for you while you played tortured genius?"

He steps closer, his hands raised as though he's warding off a blow. "Lara, stop. Just—just let me explain."

"Oh, please do," I snap, crossing my arms over my chest.

"I'd love to hear the explanation for why you lied to me. Why you used me."

"I wasn't using you!" He runs a hand through his hair, the gesture so frantic it almost looks like he's trying to rip it out. "I swear, Lara, it wasn't like that. I just—Aoife wasn't involved in this book at all. On my mother's life, not one word of it."

"That seems unlikely, given her little admission in there."

"She went travelling before I came up with the premise of *Fully, Forever*. She was supposed to be gone for a month, but ended up falling for someone out there and told me she wasn't coming back and that I was on my own for this one."

"Oh, come on. There's email and video chat and—"

"I wrote the first draft entirely myself. I had to. She was on the other side of the world, and wanted no part of it."

He takes a step closer and I match it with a step back.

"Once I realised she was serious, I started writing. I wanted to prove I could do it myself."

"Well, congratulations," I say, throwing my arms wide in mock celebration. "You proved something, all right. You proved you're a liar."

His face crumples slightly, and for half a second, I think I might've hit some kind of nerve. But then he speaks, and the words tumble out in a rush, each one more desperate than the last.

"I wasn't lying. Not about the block, not about... not about needing you. God, Lara, you have to understand." His voice cracks, and he presses his palms together, like he's praying for me to believe him. "The pressure—the expectations—it's like this weight crushing me every second. Everyone expects me to be brilliant, to deliver another bestseller, and I just— I couldn't do it on my own. I froze."

"So you thought, 'Hey, I'll just drag Lara into the mess,'" I shoot back. "Because clearly, she has nothing better to do than rescue Rory Keane from himself."

"No!" he says quickly, too quickly. "I didn't plan for this to happen. I just... I thought maybe if I had someone who understood, someone who believed in the work itself—" His voice falters, and he lets out a frustrated breath. "I didn't mean to hurt you."

I stare at him, my arms still crossed, my nails digging into my forearms.

"Well, congratulations again, because you managed to do it anyway."

He flinches, and for a brief moment, I see it—his mask slipping. The charming, confident Rory Keane is falling away to reveal something raw and unpolished beneath. Something that almost—almost—makes me want to soften. But then I remember the silence earlier, the hesitation that screamed louder than any apology ever could, and the flicker of sympathy snuffs out.

"You don't get it," I say quietly, my voice dangerously calm now. "You didn't just lie to me. You made me believe in something. In you." My chest tightens, and I hate the wobble I feel threatening to creep into my voice. "And then you ripped it away like it meant nothing."

"It meant *everything*," he says, his voice breaking on the word. "You mean everything, Lara. I just... I fucked up, okay? I made a mistake."

I shake my head slowly, my jaw tightening as I force down the lump in my throat. *Mistake.* The word feels so small compared to the gaping hole he's left in my heart. "A mistake is forgetting someone's coffee order, Rory. What you did? That's not a mistake. That's a choice."

"Lara, please—"

"No." The word slices out of me before I can stop it, like one of my editorial redlines. "No more excuses. No more half-truths. Just answer me this..." My voice shakes, not with weakness but with a fury so potent it feels like it might burn me alive. "Was any of it real? Or was I just another plot device to you?"

He flinches, like the question physically knocks the air out of him.

Good. Let him squirm.

"That's not fair," he says, his voice low and strained. "You know it was real."

"Do I?" My laugh is hollow, bitter, and so unlike me, I barely recognise it. "Because right now, it kind of looks like all of this"—I gesture between us, my hand trembling despite myself—"was just a convenient way for you to play tortured artist while I cleaned up your messes. Did you need *me*, Rory? Or did you need a co-writer who made good coffee and didn't charge overtime?"

"Stop it," he pleads, his eyes searching mine desperately, like he thinks he can find the right lever to pull to undo everything collapsing between us. "You're twisting this into something it wasn't. You think I planned this? That I sat down and thought, 'Oh, you know what would really help with my writer's block? I'll find a replacement for Aoife.' You think I could've orchestrated *this*?"

"Why not?" I counter, my words quick and biting. "You managed to fool everyone else. The publishers. The readers. Hell, you even had me convinced. So tell me why I shouldn't believe you were just using me to write your book for you."

"Because I—" he stumbles, visibly choking on whatever excuse he wants to spit out. If this were one of his books, this would be the part where the hero makes some grand declaration, something sweeping and poetic that fixes everything in a neat bow. But without Aoife's guiding hand to write that scene for him, he just looks... lost.

"Because I wouldn't do that to you," he finally says, his voice cracking under the weight of it. "I couldn't."

"Couldn't or wouldn't?" I press, leaning into the silence that follows. "Big difference, Rory."

His hands drop helplessly to his sides, fingers twitching like they want to reach for me but don't dare.

"It was real," he says, and there's something raw in his voice now as he gulps for breath. "All of it. Every single moment. You have to believe me, Lara."

"Do I?" I whisper, hating the tremor in my voice, hating the tears pricking at the edges of my eyes.

"Yes!" He takes another step forward, almost close enough to touch, but he stops himself—and somehow that restraint hurts worse than if he'd grabbed me. "You weren't just someone I leaned on when things got hard. You *are* the thing, Lara. The only thing that made any of it worth it." His words rush out, desperate and unpolished, each one like a plea. "You made me want to be better. For you. For us."

"Us," I echo bitterly, the word foreign and jagged on my tongue. "That's rich coming from someone who spent weeks lying to my face."

"I wasn't trying to hurt you," he says, his voice breaking again. "I swear, I thought—I thought if I could just finish the book by listening to your guidance, then maybe I'd be... enough."

"Enough for who?" I demand, anger flaring hot again. "For me? Because news flash, Rory—I never asked you to prove anything. I never needed you to be perfect. I just needed you to be honest."

"Well, I failed at that, didn't I?" he replies bitterly, "but don't you dare stand there and act like what we had wasn't real. I know you felt it, too. Tell me I'm wrong, Lara. Look me in the eye and tell me you didn't feel it."

I meet his gaze, the weight of his words settling heavily in the pit of my stomach. But then I remember the lies, the betrayal, and I force myself to hold steady.

"Maybe I did," I say quietly, my voice cold and clipped. "But that doesn't change the fact that you ruined it."

I shake my head, the motion clear and final, like a door slamming shut. My arms cross over my chest, as if that can somehow hold me together, keep the fractures from spreading any further.

"God, you really don't get it, do you? You didn't just lie to me, Rory. You *used* me. Like one of your damn outlines or character sketches—just another tool to get your story where you wanted it."

"Lara—"

"Don't," I snap, holding up a hand to stop him in his tracks. "Don't stand there and try to rewrite this, Rory. I'm an editor, remember? I know a plot device when I see one."

He flinches, and for a fleeting second, I almost feel bad. Almost. But then I remember the weeks I spent poring over his manuscript, improving it, believing that every word, every moment we shared, was building toward something real. Not this. Not... nothing.

"Do you have any idea how humiliating this is?" I continue, my voice rising despite the lump forming in my throat. "To think that while I was falling for you, you were just —" I gesture vaguely, angrily, as if the words might appear in the air between us. "*What?* Taking notes? Gathering material?"

"I care about you—I *love* you. This wasn't some game to me. I screwed up, okay? I made mistakes, but everything I felt for you—that was real. It still is."

"Well, good for you," I say, the sarcasm dripping from my words like venom. "But here's the thing, Rory: love isn't enough. Not without trust. And you? You've obliterated that. I'm done, Rory."

I walk away from him and I don't look back. If I do, I might crumble entirely—and I can't afford that. Not now. Not ever again.

I yank my phone out of my bag, my fingers trembling as I unlock the screen. The cool night air bites at my skin, but it's nothing compared to the frost spreading in my chest. My thumb hovers over the Uber app for a split second before I press it, because God forbid I hesitate long enough for Rory to think I'm reconsidering.

"Let me drive you home," he says from behind me, his voice low, ragged, desperate.

"Not a chance," I snap, not even bothering to look back at him. If I do, I'll see that face—those stupidly earnest eyes, that unshaven jawline that somehow makes him more irritatingly attractive—and I might... no. No. I'm not doing this. Not again.

The app loads slowly, mocking me, and I tighten my grip on the phone like I could physically will it to move faster. A message pops up: "Searching for drivers in your area." Great. Just great. I tap my foot, each beat against the ground a reminder to keep it together. Left foot, right foot. Breathe in, out. Stop crying. Not here. Not in front of him.

"Lara..." His voice cracks.

"Go back inside, Rory. Your sister's back, go finish your book. Should be easy now."

Finally, a driver accepts the request, and I exhale shakily, relief and dread tangling in my throat. Seven minutes. I can survive seven more minutes of this.

"Goodbye, Rory," I manage, the words catching slightly in my throat. I don't wait for his response. I don't even know if he has one. Instead, I cross the road and wait at the edge of the curb, staring down the empty street like it holds some kind of salvation.

TWENTY-TWO

I've spent the last three months pretending Rory Keane doesn't exist. It's been easier than I expected. Routine is a reliable thing, and mine has swallowed me whole—morning coffee, new author manuscripts to work on, meetings that blur into each other. I've buried myself in other people's words, fixing, refining, perfecting stories that aren't his. It's what I do best.

After completing the final copy edit of his book, after signing my name on the last page and sending it to the proof-readers, I told myself that was it. Done. Over. A closed chapter —one that never should've been written in the first place.

And yet, it lingers. Not in the obvious ways. I don't Google his name or check for industry buzz. I don't wonder where he is, what he's doing. I certainly don't think about how it felt to work alongside him, argue with him, want him. But every now and then, I'll catch a passing comment in the office, a casual mention of his book, or the upcoming launch. And it hits like a paper cut—small, sharp, invisible until it stings.

I shove the thought away as I take my seat in the weekly acquisitions meeting. Rory Keane is old news. Right now, my job is to focus on what comes next. And whatever that is, it has nothing to do with him.

"...What we're really looking at here is the market's saturation with billionaire redemption arcs," Claire says, her voice zipping across the conference room like a well-aimed dart.

I nod, my pen poised over my notebook like I might actually write something down. Billionaires finding their hearts in unlikely places—a dog park, a cupcake shop, a goat yoga retreat. It's all very *been there, edited that.* Normally, I'd be contributing to this meeting with precision insight and a touch of sardonic flair because, let's face it, nothing screams "engaged" like a clever quip about the improbability of a Wall Street tycoon knowing how to bake scones. But today, my brain feels like it's buffering.

"Thoughts, Lara?" Fiona's tone is neutral, but her raised eyebrow—not so much.

"Uh, yes," I say, straightening in my chair. I flick through the bullet points on the literary agent's submission letter, trying to conjure something coherent. "I think... if we're going to move forward with stories in this vein, we need to focus on unique settings or stakes that feel fresh."

"Such as?" Fiona wants more. Like a dog with a bone, she isn't going to let up. She leans back in her chair, arms crossed, waiting for me to deliver.

"Well..." I hesitate—just for a second, but long enough to feel a prickle of heat crawl up my neck. *Think, Lara. Think.* "We could request the author sets her book in a... less conventional industry. Maybe a tech billionaire who left it all behind to run a vineyard?"

"Interesting," Fiona says, though her expression remains inscrutable. The kind of inscrutable that makes you want to question every decision you've ever made, starting with your career choice.

"Or," Claire, one of the editorial assistants, chimes in,

mercifully redirecting the spotlight, "we lean into nostalgia. A billionaire who buys his hometown library to save it from being turned into a block of flats."

The room hums with agreement, and I manage a small, professional smile. Crisis averted. For now. But the gnawing frustration at myself lingers.

I shouldn't have hesitated. I shouldn't have needed Claire to swoop in. I'm supposed to be the one who's unshakable, who always has the smartest take in the room. That's my thing. Except, apparently, my thing is currently on holiday somewhere far away from this conference room—I'm a mess and I can't seem to snap out of it.

"Walk with me," Fiona says as soon as the meeting adjourns, her clipped tone leaving no room for argument.

"Of course," I reply, falling into step beside her as she strides down the hallway.

"You did a good job on Rory's book. You should be proud of yourself."

"Thanks. I am."

An actual compliment from Fiona. If I was a betting woman, then there's likely to be a follow-up—

"So, how do you think that meeting went?" she asks, not looking at me.

"Fine," I say, careful to keep my voice steady. "We've chosen some strong titles, and I think our offers are compelling."

"Did we?" Fiona stops abruptly, turning to face me. "Because what I saw was Claire making the bold choices and you just going along for the ride."

Ouch. Direct hit. I resist the urge to adjust my glasses—a

tell Fiona knows too well—and force myself to meet her eyes. "I'll admit I wasn't at my best just now."

"Not just today," Fiona says, her voice softening just enough to make the words land harder. "Lara, you helped Rory Keane deliver his strongest manuscript yet. It was genuinely unputdownable. You're one of the most talented editors I've ever worked with. But for the last couple of months, since he submitted in fact, you've seemed... distracted. Uncharacteristically so."

"I've had a lot on my plate," I say, the excuse tasting hollow even as I offer it.

"Everyone has a lot on their plate," Fiona counters. "That's the nature of this job. And while juggling plates, we also have to make sure none of them shatter. I need you on your A-game every day, especially with our mid-list authors who depend on us to elevate their work. Not every client is a Rory Keane, but they all deserve the same level of attention."

There it is again. His name dropped like a grenade between us. My stomach knots, but I keep my expression neutral.

"Understood," I say crisply, even though the word feels like swallowing glass.

"Good," Fiona says, her tone brisk again. "Because I don't want to have this conversation twice. You're better than this, Lara. Don't prove me wrong."

With that, she turns and walks away, leaving me standing in the hallway, the weight of her words pressing down on me like a boulder. Better than this. Am I? Or have I been fooling everyone—including myself—all along?

Fiona's words echo in my head as I push open the door to my office and step inside, closing it firmly behind me like I'm trying to keep her voice—and the gnawing doubt—on the other side. The familiarity of my office normally soothes me, but it feels stale, like someone else's life. Not mine.

I drop into my chair, the leather creaking under my weight, and stare at the stack of manuscripts on my desk. They're neatly arranged, the way I always insist, spines aligned like soldiers awaiting orders. Normally, this would be satisfying—a tangible sign of control in a chaotic industry. Today? I just see clutter. Pages upon pages of other people's stories that I'm supposed to polish, perfect, elevate.

"Be better," Fiona had said. As if it were that simple. As if all I need to do is snap my fingers and become some editorial wizard again, untouchable and unshakable. But there's no snapping happening here. Only the sound of my breath—shallow and uneven—as I sit frozen, hands limp in my lap.

"Pull it together, Yates," I say under my breath, glancing at the manuscript on top of the pile. A romance. God help me. The title, *Windswept Desires*, is splayed across the cover page in swirly font. I pick it up, flipping through the first few pages. Tropes everywhere—star-crossed lovers, forbidden passion, a stormy night where everything changes. Ordinarily, I'd be ruthless, tearing through clichés with my red pen and relishing the process.

Today, I can't even muster the energy to find it funny.

Instead, Rory's face flashes in my mind—his crooked smile, his stupid dimples, his absurd confidence that somehow made vulnerability look easy. And then, worse, his voice: *You're so quick to fix everyone else's work, Lara. Ever thought about why you don't take a chance on your own?*

"Stop it," I hiss, slamming the manuscript down. The sound reverberates off the walls, startling me. My hand trembles as I pull it back.

The thing is... he wasn't wrong. That's what burns the most. Beneath the charm and the half-truths and the ability to see too much too quickly, he saw me. And I hated it. Still hate it.

Dammit. The room still feels too small, the walls hemmed

in too close, the weight of expectation pressing down on my chest.

This job used to thrill me. Used to make me feel alive. Now, all I feel is stuck—like I'm running in circles, chasing deadlines, avoiding mistakes, fixing things for everyone else but myself. Maybe Fiona's right. Maybe I'm not cut out for this anymore.

No. No. I refuse to spiral.

I press my palms to my temples, willing the doubt away. Outside, I hear muffled laughter from a neighbouring office. Someone else is thriving—probably closing a deal or delivering brilliant feedback or whatever it is that "better" editors do.

I glance at *Windswept Desires* again. Then at the rest of the submission pile—every manuscript represents an author's dreams, their ambitions, their souls. Each one represents months and possibly years of the writer's life. It's my job to work through them and decide if they're good enough for Scott & Drake. My stomach churns. I want to care. God, I *need* to care. But right now, all I feel is the heavy, aching distance between who I am and who I used to be.

Okay, one thing at a time. Just one.

My pen tumbles from my fingers, clattering against the desk. I don't pick it up.

Instead, I shove my chair back and stand, pacing the tight length of my office. Three steps to the window. Three steps back to the door. I can't concentrate on anything. Not now. Not with *his* voice looping in my head like it's got some kind of all-access pass to haunt me.

You're afraid of being seen, Lara.

I snort under my breath, crossing my arms tightly over my chest. The nerve. The absolute audacity of Rory Keane to call me out like he's some kind of oracle of personal truths. Like he knows me better than I know myself.

What does that even mean?

But the truth is, I know exactly what he meant. And worse —I know he wasn't wrong.

I stop pacing, leaning back against the edge of my desk. My hands grip the cool wood like it might steady me. A highlight reel of every moment I've chosen safety over risk, invisibility over vulnerability.

University. It started there, didn't it? When my creative writing lecturer suggested I submit my short story to *The London Magazine*. I'd smiled politely, thanked him for his 'kind' words, and then buried the manuscript in a drawer so deep it might as well have been a grave. Too risky. Too exposed. What if they hated it? What if they loved it? Either way, I couldn't handle it.

Better to stay in the background, I've always thought. It's comfortable. It's familiar. *It's safer there.*

And oh, how I leaned into that safety. Editing other people's work, fixing their mistakes, *shaping their stories*. Never mine. Always theirs. Because shaping someone else's story doesn't require you to be vulnerable. Doesn't require validation from someone else. Doesn't demand you put your heart on the page and risk watching it get shredded to pieces.

"God," I groan, pinching the bridge of my nose beneath my glasses. "When did I become such a cliché?"

Rory's face flashes in my mind—the way his jaw tightened when he said those words, like he was daring me to argue but already knew I wouldn't. He saw right through me. Through the crisply ironed blouses and the cutting critiques and the air of unflappable professionalism, I've spent years perfecting.

You're afraid of being seen.

He'd said it like a challenge. Like he was trying to provoke me. And damn him, it's working.

I squeeze my eyes shut, but the memories keep coming. The way his voice had softened when he added, "You're hiding, Lara. And it's a shame. Because you have more talent in you than you realise."

My throat tightens, heat prickling at the corners of my eyes. I hate this. Hate that he got to me. Hate that his words hit home, forcing me to confront things I've kept neatly boxed up for years.

Because the truth is, I've always doubted myself. Always assumed that whatever I had to say wasn't good enough, smart enough, important enough. It's why I stayed quiet in meetings unless I was absolutely sure I was right. Why I edited manuscripts with surgical precision, terrified of missing something and proving Fiona—or anyone—wrong about trusting me.

And it's why I never told Rory the truth. About how much I admired his final submission. About how much I wanted to believe in his story, even when my doubts screamed louder. About how much I—

No. I shake my head, cutting off the thought before it can take root. I won't go there. Not now. Maybe not ever.

But one thing is clear: Rory saw something in me that I've spent my entire life convincing myself didn't exist. And no matter how much I want to dismiss him, to write him off as a liar and a fraud and a self-important narcissist, I can't ignore the truth beneath his words.

"More talent than I realise," I say, testing the phrase on my tongue. It feels foreign. Uncomfortable. But there's something there—a flicker of possibility, small and fragile but undeniably alive.

"Maybe he's right," I admit quietly. The words hang in the air, heavy with the weight of everything they imply.

Maybe it's time to stop hiding.

I look down at my satchel.

I take a deep breath, reach into the zip pocket, take the memory stick out, and insert it into my laptop. For a moment, nothing happens. Then a little green light begins to blink.

There are only two files: an early draft of Rory's story, with hundreds of track changes, before I'd convinced him to lose the car chase and explosive mid-point, and my manuscript. *My story*. Not someone else's for once.

I stare at the filename of a document that I haven't opened in eight years.

Doc.doc

Eight years. Long enough for my hair to grow out and for me to convince myself this particular failure was better off stuffed inside a digital coffin.

"Just open it," I whisper under my breath, as if talking to myself will somehow make this less pathetic. My fingers hover over the trackpad. They don't move. God, even my hands are staging a rebellion now.

But my heart is pounding like I've run a marathon, each beat screaming at me to eject it. Take it out. Walk away. Go back to editing other people's work, picking apart their sentences while mine sit here, untouched, untested, unseen.

"Okay. Fine." I try to purge the self-doubt, and double-click the file. The screen flickers, and there it is: *The Longing Between Us, by Lara Yates*, written in an obnoxiously hopeful font I now regret choosing. It feels like looking at a younger, more naïve version of myself who thought she might actually pull this off. Poor thing. I still can't believe Rory read it.

The first sentence stares back at me, a line I once agonised over for weeks. I start reading. At first, it's like opening an old wound—tender and familiar, but not entirely unbearable. Then, somewhere around page two, the ache sets in.

My protagonist, Ashley, a no-nonsense junior editor navigating her own messy love life, feels unnervingly close to home now. Too close. Did I really write this? Or did my subconscious just take notes on my future and decide to leave breadcrumbs?

The parallels are stark. The male protagonist, Matthew, a

grumpy-yet-irresistible tree surgeon with the smirk and the baggage... Yeah, he might as well have Rory's name tattooed across his forehead. Ashley's habit of overthinking every inter-action while simultaneously pretending she doesn't care? Check. The way she keeps pushing people away because it's easier than admitting she might actually want something—or someone? Double check.

"Jesus Christ,"

But instead of closing the file and dragging it to my trash folder where it belongs, I keep going. Page after page, scene after scene, I'm dragged deeper into this world I created, and the emotions bubbling beneath it. It's raw, clunky in places, but there's something true at its core, something I didn't see before. Back then, I was too busy trying to make it perfect, sanding down the edges until it felt sterile. Now, I can see that it's structurally sound; it just needs tweaking to improve the pacing.

Buried under the awkwardness, something glimmers. A turn of phrase here, an unexpected observation there. Tiny sparks of something powerful, unpolished but alive. It's like rummaging through a dusty attic and finding an old box of forgotten treasures—half of it junk, sure, but the other half? The other half is intriguing.

"Okay, not terrible," I admit grudgingly. "Definitely salvageable."

My hands find the keyboard almost without thinking. It starts with small fixes—tightening up the prose, cutting the fluff, swapping out clichés for more specific imagery. Then, before I realise it, I'm rewriting entire chunks, weaving in details and introspection I never would've dared to include back then. Things I've seen, felt, lived through since. A side-ways jab about the weight of expectations. An awkward, too-honest confession in the middle of an argument. A moment of silence that says more than words ever could.

The more I work, the less it feels like editing and the more it feels like exhaling after holding my breath for years. I let myself write messy and imperfect, not caring if it's polished or marketable or any of the things I'd demand from one of my authors. For once, I'm not worrying about who's going to read it—I'm just writing for me.

"She didn't fall gracefully," I type, deleting the original, cringe-worthy opening line without ceremony. "She fell like a tree struck by lightning—suddenly, violently, and impossible to ignore."

I pause, rereading the sentence. Is it perfect? No. But it's honest and intriguing. And right now, that feels like enough.

When I reach the midpoint—a charged argument between Ashley and Matthew that ends in a kiss neither of them admits they wanted—I have to stop reading. My heart's pounding, my head spinning. It's so obvious what needs fixing. The dialogue is stiff, the tension diluted. I didn't let them feel enough, didn't let *myself* feel enough when I wrote it. If I were to add a few extra chapters at the end of Act One, it would better explain the emotional wound Ashley carries, and that would provide a bigger payoff later in the novel.

Just some comments, I try to convince myself as I switch the document into review mode. My fingers begin to type out new comments almost automatically, capturing ideas, writing snippets of dialogue that can be input later. The words fill the right margin like a stream of consciousness, faster than I can organise them, but I don't stop. If I stop, the doubt will creep in again, whispering that I'm wasting my time. That I'll never measure up to real professional writers, like Rory, who seem to bleed brilliance onto every page.

Rory. His name alone tightens something in my chest. I shake it off, focusing on the notes in front of me. This isn't about him. Not completely, anyway. But as much as I hate to admit it, meeting him—the arguments, the intimacy, the way he seems to just *get* me—has changed something in me. And maybe, just maybe, that's exactly what I needed to finally get this story right.

I highlight sections of prose, add more and more comments, and delete entire scenes as if I'm trying to outrun my own second-guessing.

"Ashley wouldn't *say* that." I highlight a passage of dialogue in bright yellow. *She'd... she'd deflect. Make some sarcastic comment instead of admitting what she's feeling.*

I type out a new conversation. The first act is coming together piece by jagged piece, pacier now, more alive. I add a comment to come back to later: *More tension here. Let her want him, but fight it harder.*

A small smile tugs at the corner of my mouth as I keep going, shaping the story into something that feels closer to mine. Rory's stupid voice drifts into my head again—*You're afraid of being seen.*

"Yeah, well," I say, my fingers flying over the keys, "maybe I'm ready to be seen."

The cursor blinks at me, expectant and unrelenting. My fingers ache faintly from typing—I don't even know how long I've been sitting here, hunched over my keyboard like some kind of caffeinated gremlin. The mug beside me is empty, a smudge of lipstick dried on the rim. There are probably coffee grounds in my teeth. Glamorous.

I lean back against my chair, stretching my arms over my head until my spine cracks in protest. A breath escapes me— long, deep, shaky in a way that feels too personal for an empty office. My gaze falls to the screen. Words. *My* words. Pages of them. Some polished, some rougher than Rory's five o'clock shadow, but they're there. Real. Mine.

A nervous laugh bubbles out before I can stop it, tinged with disbelief. It's not perfect—not even close—but for once, that doesn't feel like failure. It feels... honest. Like I've pulled back some protective layer I didn't even know I was wearing and let something raw slip through.

"Well," I whisper, adjusting my glasses as if that'll somehow make me see straighter, clearer. "There you are, you messy little thing."

The manuscript stares back at me, unapologetic, daring me to keep going. I should be terrified. And I am. A little. But beneath that fear is something else, something warmer, stronger: resolve.

For years, I've been the quiet one—the fixer, the polisher, the invisible scaffolding propping up someone else's master-piece. I've told myself I'm fine with that, that being in the background suits me. But sitting here now, staring at these imperfect, fiercely alive sentences, I feel the lie collapsing. Maybe Rory was right. Maybe I've spent so much time hiding behind other people's stories that I forgot I had one of my own.

And maybe—just maybe—it's time to change that.

I hover the mouse over the save icon, my hand trembling slightly. It's ridiculous, really. Saving a Word document shouldn't feel this monumental, but it does. It feels like choosing something—like choosing *me*. I click.

The screen blinks once, confirming the file is safe. There's more to edit, of course. I haven't even revisited the last one hundred pages yet. There are pacing issues, especially in the midsection, and I might yet change the female best friend into a male best friend to play more on the male protagonist's jealous streak. But there's a clear path. A way forward.

My heartbeat slows. I sit back again, hands resting uselessly in my lap as a strange, unfamiliar calm settles over me. Not the absence of nerves—I still have plenty of those buzzing around—but a quiet certainty underneath them. I'm doing this. For better or worse, I'm finally working on my manuscript after an eight-year hiatus. To what end? I'm not quite sure yet, but it just feels good to be back in the weeds.

As I glance toward the window, the late afternoon sunlight cuts through the blinds, painting stripes of gold across my desk. Outside, the city hums along, indifferent to this tiny revolution happening in the corner office of Scott & Drake Publishing. But I feel it—a flicker of hope, stubborn and new, taking root inside me.

"Okay," I whisper to no one in particular, the word soft but steady, a promise to myself. "Let's see."

TWENTY-THREE

The boardroom is so pristine it makes me itch. The steel and glass desk between us could double as a catwalk—if catwalks were designed to intimidate. I shift slightly in my chair, smoothing my skirt, which suddenly feels too tight, too confining. Across from me, Vanessa Scott—co-founder of Scott & Drake Publishing and all-around destroyer of egos—leans forward with laser focus. Her manicured nails tap rhythmically against an open folder. My name is printed neatly at the top.

"Well, Lara," she says, "you've outdone yourself this time."

I force a smile. *Outdone myself?* That implies that my work isn't usually up to this standard—not sure if there's a barb in the compliment or not. I nod, because what else do you do when your boss's boss looks at you like you're a magic trick she hasn't quite figured out yet?

"Rory's pre-sale numbers have officially broken two hundred thousand, and there's still a week until launch," Vanessa continues, her lips curving into a rare but calculated smile. "You took a good writer and made him exceptional. The team is buzzing about it. This kind of success doesn't just happen." She pauses, letting the compliment hang in the air like bait.

"Thank you," I say, adjusting my glasses even though they don't need adjusting. My throat feels dry, so I swallow and immediately regret it when the sound seems unnaturally loud in the silence. "It was... a team effort."

"Don't be modest," Vanessa replies, waving off my deflection. "Writers like Rory don't come along every day, but let's not pretend his latest success isn't directly tied to your editorial brilliance. Fiona had eyes on an early draft and said it left a lot to be desired." Her eyes narrow slightly, calculating. "Which brings me to why I called you in today."

Here it comes. The ambush. I sit up straighter, trying to look composed—or at least less likely to bolt.

"Given your track record," Vanessa says, "we'd like to offer you an editorial directorship. Effective immediately." She says it so casually, as if she's asking if I'd like milk in my coffee.

My heart stutters. Editorial director. The words should make me feel triumphant—validated. But instead, there's this slithering unease curling low in my stomach. Director. As in responsible. As in visible.

"Wow," I manage, my voice calm, steady. Inside, chaos reigns. "That's... an incredible offer."

"Yes, it is," Vanessa agrees, with the kind of confidence that suggests it's not up for debate. "We need someone who can spot hidden gems, nurture them, and take risks." Her gaze pins me in place, daring me to flinch. "You've proven you have the instincts—and the tenacity—to do just that. Rory's book is proof of concept."

I nod again, my head moving like it's detached from the rest of me. My thoughts are a tangled mess of pride and panic. Pride because, well, *hello*, career milestone. Panic because I can already hear the whispers: *She got lucky.*

"Of course," Vanessa continues, oblivious to the imposter

syndrome party raging in my brain, "this role will require a certain level of boldness. Championing debut authors means taking chances—on them, and on yourself. Are you ready for that?"

Am I? My chest tightens. I should say yes. Yes, I'm ready to mould raw talent into bestseller gold. Yes, I'll rise to the challenge. Yes, of course, I belong here. But the truth is, I don't know if I am. Because what if I fail? What if Rory's book was a fluke, and I'm just a fraud with a red pen and a knack for faking it?

"Absolutely," I say instead, because apparently my mouth has no regard for my existential crisis.

"Good." Vanessa smiles again, wider this time, but no less intimidating. "We'll announce it officially at Friday's staff meeting. In the meantime, start thinking about who your first project will be. I want someone unexpected. Someone with potential only you can see."

"Got it," I say, though my brain is screaming, *Abort! Abort!* The idea of handpicking fresh talent is exhilarating—and utterly terrifying. What if I pick the wrong person? What if I ruin their career before it even begins?

"Congratulations, Lara," Vanessa says, standing up and extending her hand. "This is well-deserved."

"Thank you," I reply, matching her movement and shaking her hand with what I hope is professional composure and not sheer desperation.

As I leave the boardroom, my legs feel like they're moving on autopilot.

"Congratulations, Lara!" someone chirps as I pass by the break room, their voice barely cutting through the rush of blood pounding in my ears. I manage a tight smile and lift a hand in some vague approximation of a wave, but my pace doesn't falter. If I stop, I might crumble into a thousand pieces of self-doubt right here in the middle of Scott & Drake's very shiny, very public corridors.

The place is alive with motion—assistants hustling past with precarious stacks of manuscripts, editors huddled in door-ways debating cover designs, the hum of printers spitting out contracts that will probably change someone's life. It's all so familiar, yet today it feels like I'm walking through it wearing the wrong skin, like an imposter trying to blend into a world she accidentally stumbled into.

"Editorial director," I try out the new title as I sidestep a group of interns clustered around the coffee machine. The words sound foreign, absurd even, like they belong to someone else entirely. Someone who isn't secretly terrified of being exposed as a fraud.

By the time I reach reception, my thoughts are a jumbled mess of *What ifs* and *How the hells.*

How the hell did I get myself into this? What if Vanessa made a mistake? What if I can't live up to her expectations?

The cool breeze hits me as soon as I step outside onto the street, chasing away the suffocating stillness of the office air. I pause on the pavement, letting the noise of London wash over me. It's chaotic, but oddly grounding—like the city itself is reminding me to inhale, exhale, repeat.

I glance up at the sky, grey and heavy with clouds, then down at the polished toes of my shoes. My hands find my hips, and I close my eyes for a moment, trying to drown out the storm raging in my head.

Get a grip, Yates. But the words don't stick. Instead, my mind drifts to Rory—his usual confidence cracking like old paint, his quiet confession over late-night wine about how he wasn't sure his new book was "enough." How he wasn't sure *he* was enough.

And now, standing here on the crowded pavement, I get it. God, do I get it.

Because as much as I reassured him back then, told him he didn't have to prove anything, the truth is I'm not sure I'd believe those words if someone said them to me. Not when every part of me feels like I've been thrown into the deep end of a pool without knowing how to swim.

The weight of it presses down on me—this fear that maybe we're both just faking it, waiting for someone to notice. But then I think about how Rory dragged himself out of that spiral, how he poured every ounce of doubt and insecurity into something real, something tangible. And maybe... maybe I can do the same.

"Alright," I whisper, straightening my jacket and squaring my shoulders. The city surges around me, but somehow that feels comforting. Like it doesn't matter if I fail or succeed; the world will keep moving either way.

I take a deep breath and step forward, merging into the flow of pedestrians. Doubt still ticks at the edges of my mind, but there's determination there too, stubborn and unrelenting. Because if Rory can fight his demons, maybe—just maybe—I can fight mine.

TWENTY-FOUR

The manuscript sits on my coffee table. Three hundred and eighty pages of single-sided, double-spaced A4. I've reworked, polished, tweaked and altered practically every word on screen, but this is the first time I've worked off of a paper copy. My final backstop before I confidently say it is finished.

Probably.

Maybe.

Depends how this read goes.

With a deep breath, I reach out and flip the title page over. My hand shakes slightly, but I ignore it. The first page stares back at me: Chapter One.

Here we go.

I start reading, expecting the worst. Bracing for clichés and clunky metaphors and stiff dialogue, but I find that it's quite the opposite. Tight, clever prose that flows so naturally I almost don't recognise it as mine. For a second, I wonder if I plagiarised it.

Well, that's... unexpected.

And then I keep going. My editor brain takes the wheel,

dissecting every word, every comma, every beat. I can't help it —this is what I do. But instead of finding a mess, I find a story. Pacing that works. Characters that breathe. And then the newer chapters hit—the ones I wrote after Rory bulldozed into my life like some kind of overconfident tornado.

Those chapters? They're alive.

I can see him in them, in the charming wit of my hero, in the messy vulnerability of my heroine. His fingerprints are everywhere, and not because he gave me notes or feedback or anything like that. It's more subtle than that. He's woven into the fabric of the story itself. Little moments, little truths, borrowed straight from conversations we didn't realise were important at the time.

The irony isn't lost on me. Rory turned our story into fiction first, shaping and twisting pieces of us into something palatable for readers, something aspirational. And now, here I am, doing the exact same thing.

Except... it's different.

Because this isn't a performance. I'm not sculpting some glossy, perfectly structured romance out of us. There's no neat three-act resolution, no grand declaration on cue. This isn't about turning pain into a perfectly marketable love story. It's about understanding it. Understanding him. Understanding myself.

"Of course you'd show up here too," I scoff, shaking my head as I turn the page. "You just can't help yourself, can you?"

But even as I roll my eyes, there's no denying the warmth blooming in my chest. Because somewhere along the way, this stopped feeling like an exercise in self-flagellation and started feeling like... hope.

I flip another page, my fingers smudging the ink slightly. The words blur for a moment, and I blink hard, forcing them back into focus. I've been at this for hours now—or maybe minutes; time feels elastic when you're trying to decide whether you're brilliant or completely delusional. Either way, one thing is clear: Rory might have taken pieces of me and spun them into fiction, but he only ever borrowed. I took pieces of him and understood.

And that's why, this time, it's different.

The scene I'm reading is one of the newer ones—one of Rory's unwitting cameos. My heroine is pacing her flat, arguing with the hero over the phone. Their banter is on point but layered with something heavier, something unsaid. It's good. *Really* good. The kind of dialogue that makes you lean in, makes you feel like you're eavesdropping on something real.

"Okay," I say aloud, because apparently, I've reached the stage where I talk back to my own manuscript. "That wasn't half bad."

Not half bad quickly becomes *actually pretty great* as I keep going, each page tugging me deeper into this world I built, piece by painstaking piece. Of course, it needs a third party, another editor to spot the flaws. But what's working is... kind of everything. There's voice here, rhythm. Characters who feel like people, not puppets. There's heart.

By the time I reach the end of the chapter, I'm sitting up straighter, my editor brain uncharacteristically quiet. For once, it's not dissecting or second-guessing. Instead, something else entirely has crept in—a sensation I've spent years running from. Pride.

That's when it hits me: *this isn't just good. It's* worthy.

And that thought? That single spark of validation? It's both exhilarating and terrifying. Because if it's worthy—if *I'm* worthy—then I don't have an excuse anymore. No shield to hide behind, no self-deprecating jokes about how I'm "just" an editor who dabbles. If I believe in this story—even a little—I might actually have to do something about it.

I put the pages down, standing abruptly. My heartbeat is loud, too loud, like the sound alone could shatter this fragile realisation. The manuscript sits there, quietly accusing, while I pace the length of my living room. One step, two steps, pivot. Rinse, repeat.

"Submit it?" I mutter under my breath. "Sure. Why not? Let's just rip open my chest and hand someone my still-beating heart while we're at it."

Because that's what this would be, wouldn't it? Submitting this manuscript means inviting someone else to see everything —all of me—the parts I've kept hidden for so long that I almost forgot they existed. It means risk. Vulnerability. Potentially catastrophic humiliation.

And yet... I can't stop thinking about Rory. He's the one who told me months ago, between drafts of his own book, "It's the fear that means you're onto something. No one's scared of mediocrity." At the time, I'd rolled my eyes so hard I thought I'd sprained something, but now? Now, it feels like he was talking directly to me, like he somehow knew this moment would come.

Rory gets it. He knows what it's like to chase something that feels too big and too personal and too impossible all at once. He knows what it's like to put yourself out there, even when every instinct screams at you to stay small, stay safe. And he does it anyway. Every time.

"Must be nice," I grumble, though there's no heat behind it. Just a faint, reluctant admiration.

And maybe a little envy, too. Because the truth is, I want that courage. I want to be the person who takes the leap, who believes in herself enough to risk the fall. Or, at the very least, I want to know that if I crash and burn, it won't be because I never even tried.

I glance back at the manuscript, sitting patiently on the coffee table, its pages slightly raised on the corners and the unmistakable weight of possibility. My stomach twists, half dread, half hope.

So. What's it gonna be?

The question hangs in the air, unanswered but alive, daring me to find out.

It's ready. Or at least, as ready as it's ever going to be. I've spent weeks tweaking, second-guessing, convincing myself it needs just one more pass. But the truth is, I'm not afraid of the edits—I'm afraid of what comes next. Submitting. Being judged. Failing publicly.

That's exactly why I can't send it to anyone at Scott & Drake. If they rejected it, I'd have to walk into work every day knowing my colleagues—*the people who see me as the editor, the one who fixes stories, not writes them*—know I wasn't good enough. And if they did accept it? I'd never know if it was because the book deserved it or if they just felt obligated.

So I'm sending it to a literary agent instead. A fresh set of eyes. Someone who doesn't know me, doesn't care about office politics—just the work. Because if this book has a chance, I want it to stand on its own. And if it doesn't? I need to be the only one who knows.

The cursor blinks at me like it's taunting me, daring me to chicken out. My hands hover over the keyboard, trembling slightly—not from caffeine this time, but from something heavier, something rawer. Fear, maybe. Or hope. They feel the same when they're this close together.

The first step is easy enough: opening the submission portal. The website loads slowly, each spinning wheel another opportunity for doubt to creep in. But I don't let it. Not this time. Instead, I focus on the mechanics—the click of the mouse, the tap of keys—as if breaking it into smaller tasks will keep me from noticing the magnitude of what I'm about to do.

I type the book's title into the box. My fingers falter for half a second before I force them to keep going. *Author. That's me, I guess.*

"File upload," I read, dragging the file with the first three chapters into the glowing blue box. My chest tightens as the progress bar inches forward, the seconds stretching impossibly long. Lastly, I paste in my query letter. This is it. The point of no return.

Before I can think too hard about it, I press submit.

There's a tiny whoosh sound as the file disappears into cyberspace, and for a moment, everything goes still. Quiet. Like the universe itself is holding its breath alongside me.

And then it hits—a rush of adrenaline so fierce it leaves me dizzy. I lean back in my chair, exhaling shakily as the enormity of what I've just done sinks in. It's gone. Out there. Irretrievable. My work, my heart, my risk—it's all in someone else's hands now.

A laugh bubbles up unexpectedly, startling me with its brightness. It's not relief, exactly, or even triumph. It's something closer to freedom, unspooling inside me like a ribbon finally released from its knot. For the first time in years, I feel... weightless.

I glance out the window, where the city lights flicker against the night sky like tiny points of possibility. Somewhere out there, someone might be reading my words soon, judging them. Hopefully liking them.

I stand, stretching out the tension that's wound tight in my shoulders like coiled springs. My chair creaks in protest behind me as I push it back. It's quiet in here—too quiet—the kind of quiet that makes you hyperaware of your own breathing, your own thoughts. The hum of the refrigerator in the kitchen is suddenly deafening.

The journey isn't over. Hell, it might be just the beginning. But standing here, barefoot in my living room, staring at the confirmation message on my screen, I finally feel ready for it— for all of it. Whatever happens next, I think I'll be okay.

TWENTY-FIVE

The Southbank hums with life, a chaotic symphony of buskers, chatter, and the occasional shriek from an overzealous toddler. I try to focus on Danny's voice as he weaves through the crowd beside me, hands shoved casually into his jacket pockets.

"Is it just me," he says, dodging an errant skateboarder with the grace of someone used to city chaos, "or does this place always feel like everyone decided collectively to forget the concept of personal space?"

"That's London for you," I reply, sidestepping a couple taking selfies with a living statue. "A masterclass in proximity management."

"Proximity mismanagement, more like."

We walk a few more paces before Danny's head swivels toward something ahead. His expression lights up like a kid spotting Santa Claus, which immediately puts me on edge. That look means trouble.

"Ah, now *that's* what I'm talking about," he announces, steering slightly to the right without waiting for my response. My gaze follows his, landing on—of course—an ice cream stand. Never mind that we just had lunch barely twenty minutes ago.

"Don't even think about it," I warn, though my tone lacks any real bite. He's already scanning the menu board like it's the Rosetta Stone.

"Come on, Lara," he says, dragging my name out in that melodramatic way he knows will irritate me. "Life's too short to walk past soft-serve without acknowledging its existence."

I raise an eyebrow. "We literally just ate. Like, *just.*"

"Details," he waves me off, stepping closer to inspect the options. "Besides, dessert isn't about hunger. It's about spirit. And my spirit says I need a double scoop of salted caramel with sprinkles."

"Sprinkles?" I repeat, incredulous, because of course *he'd* be the kind of person who orders sprinkles like he's eight years old. "You do realise you're a grown man, right?"

"Sure," he says breezily, glancing back at me over his shoulder. "But what's the point of being a grown man if you can't occasionally act like a child? You should try it sometime. Might loosen you up."

"Thanks, I'll pass." There's something almost contagious about his enthusiasm, even when it's aimed at something as ridiculous as ice cream.

"Suit yourself," he replies with an exaggerated shrug. "But don't come crying to me later when you're struck with dessert envy. You're not having a lick."

"Yeah, I'll survive," I say, crossing my arms as I watch him step up to place his order. The vendor hands him a cone piled precariously high with golden swirls and—yep—an absurd amount of rainbow sprinkles and raspberry sauce. Danny takes one triumphant bite, then turns back to me with the kind of satisfied expression that belongs in a commercial.

"See? Happiness in edible form." He holds the cone out

toward me in offering. "One bite. Just one. I promise it won't compromise your stern editor facade."

"Hard pass," I say. He knows me too well to take anything I say at face value, and the truth is, I'm not really annoyed. Amused, maybe. Begrudgingly charmed, definitely.

"Your loss," he singsongs, strolling back to my side like a man with nowhere to be and all the time in the world. The sun catches in his wavy hair, the breeze ruffling his jacket as he licks another dollop of caramel off the top of his cone. He looks so utterly at ease, so completely unbothered by the frenetic energy buzzing around us, that I almost envy him. Almost.

"Okay, but hypothetical question," I say as we fall back into step together. "What happens if you drop that thing? Do I have to pretend I don't know you?"

"Bold of you to assume I'd ever let such a tragedy occur," he retorts, holding the cone aloft like it's some sacred artefact. "This is a bond forged in trust, Lara. A man and his ice cream."

"Right," I say, rolling my eyes. "And here I thought you reserved your loyalty for humans."

"Humans are overrated," he states, then flashes me a quick grin. "Present company excluded, obviously."

Danny veers suddenly to the left, nearly colliding with a man holding an entire bouquet of sunflowers. I halt mid-step, watching as he zeroes in on one of the second-hand bookstalls like it's some hidden treasure chest. His ice cream cone—miraculously intact—dangles precariously from his hand, but his other is already reaching for a worn paperback propped up at an angle.

"Ah," he says, turning the book over dramatically as though inspecting the Holy Grail. "Here it is. The crown jewel I've been searching for: Rory Keane's Definitive Guide to Pretentious Literary Fame." He flashes me a devilish grin, tapping the dusty cover with his index finger.

"Very funny," I say, stepping closer despite myself. The

book isn't even Rory's—it's some ancient self-help manual—but Danny's performance has drawn a small smirk out of me before I can stop it. He notices, of course. He always notices.

"Come on, admit it," he says, waving the book at me like it's proof of my guilt. "You're secretly hoping I'll find a bootleg copy of his next big hit before the official launch. Maybe something titled *How Not To Be A Knob*."

"First of all, that would require Rory actually finishing his drafts without me holding his hand," I shoot back, though my stomach twists uncomfortably at the mention of the launch. I glance down at the spines of books lined neatly on the stall, feigning interest in a battered Agatha Christie. "Second of all, you're not funny."

"Really?" Danny arches a brow and leans in conspiratorially. "Because that little groan-slash-eye-roll combo just now felt like a laugh trying to escape. Don't fight it, Lara, give in to the laughter. Free the titters."

"Trust me, it's not laughter. It's despair." I know what's coming next. I can feel it brewing in the way Danny looks at me, his teasing shifting gears into something far more deliberate.

"Despair? About the book launch, you mean?" His tone is deceptively casual, but there's no mistaking the intent behind his words. He slots the random book back onto the shelf without looking, his full attention landing squarely on me. "You've been avoiding talking about it all day. Thought I wouldn't notice?"

"Maybe I just don't want to bore you with publishing drama."

"Nice try." Danny steps closer, blocking my view of the books entirely. Not that I was really reading them. "But we both know that's not it. So what's the deal? Scared of the spotlight? Or is it just Rory himself that's making you want to fake your own death and flee the country?"

"Neither," I lie, my voice too quick, too defensive. "I'm totally fine. It's just... not my scene, that's all."

"Uh-huh. Sure. And I guess the fact that you're practically vibrating now I've mentioned it is just... What? A fun new quirk?"

"Drop it, Danny," I warn, but my attempt at firmness lands about as well as a soggy paper aeroplane. He doesn't budge, his expression softening but still insistent.

"Look, I get it," he says, his voice lowering just enough to make me stop in my tracks. "Big events, schmoozy people, the whole 'hey, everyone look at me' vibe—it's not exactly Lara Yates' idea of a good time. But avoiding it isn't going to fix whatever's rattling around in that overanalytical brain of yours. It's your night too."

I turn away as if the view over the river might offer some escape from his line of questioning.

"It's not the launch itself, okay? It's... everything around it. Rory, the book, the fact that I—" I swallow hard. My throat feels tight, and my voice dips lower. "The fact that I basically had to drag that book out of him kicking and screaming. And now I have to stand there and act like I'm proud of it. Of him."

"Wait," Danny says, pulling up short. He steps slightly ahead, forcing me to slow down too. "You had to drag it out of him? What does that even mean?"

"Exactly what it sounds like," I reply, waving a hand vaguely. "Do you have any idea how much of that book came from *me*? Structuring scenes, fixing dialogue, detailed notes on what needed to be changed..."

"But, correct me if I'm wrong, isn't that what an editor does?"

"Yes, but somehow, through all the changes and the rewrites, he sort of injected me into the book, injected us. Turned us into the characters and the characters into us."

"And the result is a great story. You said it yourself."

"It is. Hands down, it's the best thing he's ever written."

Danny side-eyes me, genuinely confused. "Sorry, and that's a problem because?"

"Because I don't want to be a character in someone else's story. I don't want others reading snippets of what I say when I'm happy, or sleepy, or infuriated."

"Don't all writers borrow from real life?"

"Maybe they do, but—" I hesitate, the words sticking briefly. "But then there's the other part. The part where I know things about Rory that no one else does. Things that make all this success feel... hollow. Like I helped build a house knowing the foundation was cracked."

"Okay, stop." Danny's voice snaps back at me, and suddenly, he's in front of me, blocking my path entirely. I nearly crash into him, stumbling back a step.

"Seriously?" I say, glaring up at him. "What are you doing?"

"Making a point." His tone is light, but his expression isn't. He plants himself firmly, arms crossed over his chest like he's daring me to try and get past him. "You're doing that thing again."

"What thing?"

"That thing where you convince yourself you're the villain of everyone else's story. Like you're some kind of editorial puppet master pulling the strings, and poor Rory Keane is just your unwitting marionette." He shakes his head, exasperated. "Lara, come on. You know that's not true."

"Do I?" I snap back, crossing my arms to mirror him. "Because it sure feels like I crossed a line somewhere. If people knew how much of that book was my—"

"Stop," he says again, firmer this time. His eyes meet mine, steady and unflinching. "You didn't cross a line. You did your job. Hell, you went above and beyond, like you always do. And yeah, maybe Rory leaned on you more than most authors would, but that's not on you. That's on him."

I open my mouth to argue, but he holds up a hand to cut me off. "Nope. Don't even start. You're not at fault, you're not undermining anyone, and you're definitely not responsible for whatever existential crisis Rory Keane might be having about his creative process. You're allowed"—he emphasises the word like it's a foreign concept—"to take pride in what you contributed without feeling guilty about it. Because guess what? Without you, that book wouldn't be half as good as it is."

"That's a pretty low bar," I reply, staring down at the pavement.

"Don't do that," Danny says gently, stepping closer. His voice softens, but his stance doesn't budge. "Don't downplay it. You're brilliant, Lara. And you deserve to be recognised for everything you bring to the table—even if it makes you uncomfortable, even if it scares the hell out of you. Because hiding behind the scenes forever? That's not brilliance. That's fear."

I cross my arms tightly against my chest, the universal signal for: *I'm done with this conversation.*

But Danny doesn't relent. "Rory Keane owes you his soul —okay, maybe half his soul. And this book launch? It's not about showing up to stroke Rory's ego; it's about showing up for something you helped make happen. Big difference."

"Not to me," I grumble, my gaze darting down to the river. The water ripples against the banks, and for a second, I wish I could dissolve into it. Just sink into the current and let it carry me somewhere far away. Somewhere where neither Rory Keane nor his stupid, over-hyped literary masterpiece exists— and neither does this conversation.

Danny sighs, the sound exaggerated but not unkind. "How about this: you don't have to stick around for the whole thing. Turn up, nod sagely during his reading, do the polite mingling thing for twenty minutes tops, then sneak out the back when they start queuing to get their books signed. Hell, I'll even help you plan the escape route. We'll time it perfectly so you can disappear while everyone's distracted by the hors d'oeuvres."

I glance up at him, narrowing my eyes suspiciously. "You're bribing me with an early exit strategy?"

"Yes," he replies without missing a beat. "And snacks. Because I know you—you'll be too stressed to eat beforehand, so we'll swing by somewhere after and get celebratory dumplings or something. Your pick."

My arms loosen just a fraction, but I keep my tone frosty. "You're really determined to make me go to this thing, huh?"

"Make you? No." He grins, leaning in slightly as if sharing a secret. "Strongly encourage with charm, persuasion, and unwavering logic? Absolutely."

TWENTY-SIX

I step into the main hall of the Natural History Museum and immediately feel like I've wandered onto the set of someone else's movie. Tonight, the majestic Victorian architecture is bathed in warm, carefully placed uplighting, casting shadows that dance across marble pillars and vaulted ceilings. The museum's grandeur is striking on its own, but paired with the meticulous efforts of our marketing team, the space feels downright magical.

Above me, the massive skeleton of a blue whale—Hope, as the museum calls her—is suspended from the ceiling, her colossal frame frozen in an eternal dive. The bones, reflecting blue and pink thanks to our event lighting, stretch the length of the hall, casting elongated shadows onto the walls.

Further back, a prehistoric giant looms—a dinosaur's ribcage arcing overhead like the remnants of a shipwreck, its vertebrae a jagged, ancient spine against the glass panels and gilded stone.

The bones are suspended by near-invisible cables, giving the eerie illusion that the creatures are mid-flight, desperate to get their own front-row seat at the book launch.

I glance around, looking for a way to help—a way to edit—but everything is complete. The tables are dressed flawlessly, linen crisp, centrepieces subtle but elegant. Projection screens loom gracefully above, cycling through vivid images of the book jacket, interspersed with carefully chosen quotes from glowing early reviews. In the centre of it all is a glossy, over-sized display of freshly printed hardbacks, arranged as precisely as sculptures in a gallery. And there, larger-than-life beside them, is Rory's author portrait, captured in black and white—his easy confidence radiating from the canvas like a beacon.

There's absolutely nothing left for me to do. My editorial fingerprints are invisible here, hidden neatly behind marketing gloss and moody lighting. The book exists beyond me now, and apparently, so does Rory.

I should walk away. I *want* to walk away. My heels are already pivoting toward the exit when, for some inexplicable reason, I freeze. Damn it.

I glance back at the display, and the author portrait beside it.

"Don't do this," I mutter under my breath, adjusting my glasses as if they might somehow shield me from the pull of curiosity clawing at my resolve.

Rory Keane, bestselling author and resident pain-in-my-professional-neck. Also, the man I decided to have a friends-with-benefits relationship with, that neither of us was able to handle. Forget the fact that I practically bled over every draft of this damn book, coaxing it out of him when he found himself without his usual co-writer. Forget the fact that I helped him find the heart of the story he's now promoting to the world. Nope. He walked away smelling of roses, leaving me with nothing but a bruised ego, keen disappointment, and a lingering sense of unfinished business.

You're better than this, I tell myself, gripping the strap of my bag tighter. "You don't need closure. You don't need to see him. You certainly don't need to stand in a crowd of swooning fans while he basks in the glow of his own brilliance."

Still, my feet remain planted. I stare at the glossy poster again, at Rory's name in big block letters. Rory Keane. The man who could never quite decide what he wanted—from his plotlines, from his career, from *me*. And yet, against all logic, he got everything anyway.

Of course he's thriving. Why wouldn't he be?

My phone buzzes in my bag, jolting me back to reality. I fish it out, half hoping for a distraction, but it's just an email reminder about a meeting tomorrow. Nothing urgent. No excuses to leave just yet. And I am looking for excuses.

But am I? Because the truth—the ugly, uncomfortable truth—is that part of me *wants* to be here. Not because I miss Rory (I absolutely do *not* miss Rory) but because there's a small, petty satisfaction in knowing I had a hand in his success. I was the one who pushed him to dig deeper, to write something real. If he's going to stand up there and read from *our* book, shouldn't I at least get to see it?

And there it is, the crux of the problem. If I stay, I have to face him. If I don't, I'll spend the evening wondering what he said, how the audience reacted to the reading, whether he noticed I wasn't there. Either way, I lose.

My fingers tighten around the strap, knuckles white. I take a deep breath, trying to steady the riot of emotions swirling inside me. Hurt. Anger. Curiosity that tastes suspiciously like hope. None of it makes sense. All of it feels like too much.

Make up some excuse and just walk away.

The voice is of someone who refuses to let a charming man with pretty words derail her life any further.

But my feet? Again, they refuse to move.

I drift towards the book display, drawn to it like a moth drawn to a flame.

His name gleams in embossed gold lettering across the glossy covers, practically screaming *bestseller*. Because it is. It's obnoxious, really.

My heart skips, then stumbles into an uneven rhythm. Of course, it does. Because nothing says "you're completely over someone" like your cardiovascular system staging a coup at the sight of their name.

The book is heavier than I expect, solid in my hands. Clearly, no expense was spared on this first print run. I glance around, irrationally certain someone is watching, judging me for this moment of weakness. No one is, of course. The universe isn't that cruel. Just... cruel enough to let our orbits collide in the first place.

My thumb brushes the edge of the cover, and before I can talk myself out of it, I flip it open. Straight to the dedication page. Like a fool. Like someone who doesn't know better.

The words hit me like a sledgehammer:

To L.Y.—
FOR TEACHING ME WHAT IT MEANS TO WRITE WITH MY WHOLE HEART.
FOR SEEING ME WHEN I COULDN'T SEE MYSELF.
FOR EVERYTHING. ALWAYS.

My breath catches, as if the air's been knocked out of me. For a second, I just stand there, staring at the page, the letters blurring together until they don't make sense anymore. And yet, they make *too much* sense. Every word feels like a carefully aimed dart, hitting its mark with precision.

"Always," I whisper under my breath, trying out the word like it's new, unfamiliar. My throat tightens as something warm and unbearable blooms in my chest. Anger? Sadness? Hope? God, I don't even know anymore. It's all tangled up, a knotted mess of emotions I have no idea how to unravel.

"Seriously?" I hiss, glaring at the page like it might glare back. "He gets to do this? He gets to… dedicate a book and just —" I snap the cover shut, holding the novel against my chest like it might escape. My eyes burn, and for a terrifying moment, I think I might actually cry. But no. Not here. Not now.

I clutch the book tighter, my nails digging into the dust jacket. This is exactly why I didn't want to come here. Why I told myself I wasn't going to care. Because Rory Keane never does anything in half measures. Not his writing. Not his charm. And apparently, not his ability to rip my carefully constructed walls to shreds with a single damn paragraph.

"You're such an idiot," I whisper to myself, but the words lack bite. They sound hollow, even to my own ears. My reflection stares back at me from the glossy cover, distorted and warped, and I hate how small I look. How vulnerable.

Always.

If I think about it enough, it'll lose its power. But of course, it lingers, wrapping itself around me like smoke, refusing to let go. Damn him. Damn his stupid talent and his stupid words and—

My fingers tremble as I set the book back on the stack, careful not to disturb the others. But it doesn't matter. The damage is already done. Those words are burned into my brain now, tattooed on the inside of my eyelids.

"Walk away," I whisper, my voice shaky but determined. "Just walk away." And this time, my feet listen. Sort of. One step, then another. But the weight in my chest doesn't lighten. If anything, it grows heavier, pulling me down, tethering me to something I thought I'd left behind.

Always.

The word clinging to me like a shadow as I head towards the exit.

The book stares back at me from the pile, exactly where I

left it. Its spine is glossy and unassuming, but it might as well be screaming my name. I hate how it's there, just sitting innocently like it doesn't hold a grenade of emotions with my name engraved on the pin.

Always.

The word echoes in my mind, curling under my ribs like a hook, pulling me backwards—or maybe forward. Toward him.

I cross my arms tightly over my chest, ignoring the way my pulse insists on picking up speed. The dedication—it wasn't just a string of poetic nonsense wrapped in Rory's usual charm. No, this was intentional. Calculated. An invitation disguised as a goodbye. I can almost hear his voice weaving through the words, low and steady, daring me to do something about it.

I can't attend the launch now. What would that even look like? Would I linger near the back, pretending I'm just another face in the crowd? Or would I be stupid enough to march straight up to Rory and demand an explanation? No. No, it's better to pretend I'm sick and go home. Logical. Professional. Safe. That's what I'm good at, right?

I push through the side exit, the cold night air hitting my skin like a slap. The streets outside are quiet, save for the occasional cab blaring its horn and the hum of conversation from groups heading towards more exciting Friday night plans. I take a deep breath, pressing my fingers against my temples. I've made the right choice. Leaving was the only option. There is absolutely no reason to subject myself to the circus inside.

I'm already halfway down the pavement when I hear my name.

"Lara!"

I turn to find Danny striding towards me, looking equal parts relieved and exasperated. He's slightly out of breath, his navy suit jacket askew, and his hair ruffled like he's been in a fight with the wind.

"Are you—" He stops short, taking me in. "Hang on. Where the hell have you been? I've been calling you. You were supposed to meet me at the station."

I wince, realising I'd put my phone on silent hours ago. "Oh. Right. Yeah, sorry about that."

Danny squints at me, then looks at the grand museum entrance behind me.

"Wait, were you inside?"

"No." I cross my arms. "I mean, technically, yes. But now I'm not."

He exhales sharply. "Lara, what the hell?"

"It's complicated," I mutter, already hating the way this conversation is going.

"Oh, I bet it is." He folds his arms, studying me. "And by complicated, do you mean 'completely avoidable but requiring an intervention because you're catastrophically overthinking everything again?'"

"Danny—"

"Because," he barrels on, ignoring me, "you've done the hard bit. You made it here."

I stare at him. "That's... not true."

He smirks. "Lara, I know you."

"Okay, fine. Yes. I left." I sigh, running a hand through my hair. "It felt—wrong. Being in there. Like I was complicit in this whole thing. In supporting him."

Danny tilts his head. "Or was it more that you felt something, and you didn't like that?"

I shoot him a sharp look. "I felt nothing."

"Right." He exhales. "Okay, then let's get practical. You're an editor. You worked your arse off on this book. You said yourself it's already looking like a bestseller. That's your success too. You don't have to talk to Rory if you don't want to, but you should be in there. You should own this."

I hesitate, my fingers twitching at my sides. He's right, of course. I hate that he's right.

"And," he continues, "we had a deal. I came all this way on the promise of expensive wine and the vague possibility of celebrity gossip. You cannot leave me to fend for myself in a room full of publishing types. I'll get adopted by some high-brow literary agent who only reads 600-page experimental novels about grief and capitalism."

I exhale sharply. "So this is about your suffering, is it?"

"Obviously." He grins. "But also, it's about you. Look, I get why you're freaking out, but what's done is done. You worked on the book. It's out in the world now. You might as well celebrate the fact that you did a damn good job."

I glance back at the grand museum entrance.

Danny nudges me. "Come on, Lara. Do it for me. Do it for the wine. Do it because, deep down, you know you'd rather regret going than regret not going."

I exhale slowly, my resolve faltering.

"Fine," I mutter.

Danny throws his hands up in victory. "There she is."

"Shut up and walk before I change my mind."

He grins, looping his arm through mine as we turn back towards the museum. "Oh, I'm walking. Straight to the bar, for my suffering."

I roll my eyes, but as I glance at my watch, I pause. "Wait. The event doesn't even start for another hour."

Danny stops mid-stride, scandalised. "You mean to tell me I rushed over here, full of concern and righteous indignation, only to learn we have an entire sixty minutes to kill?" He tuts dramatically, shaking his head. "Not to worry, dear Lara, for I have a solution."

"Oh, God."

He straightens, adopting his most grandiose tone. "We shall head to The Queen's Arms, and she will embrace us with the finest of stouts, ales, and wines until merriment commences."

I exhale, amused despite myself. "You just want a pre-drink."

"Absolutely," he says. "And, ideally, some chips. I can't endure a literary event on an empty stomach."

I hesitate, but he gives me a gentle tug, guiding me away from the museum steps.

"Come on. A drink will help. Fortify the spirit. Drown the doubt. Plus, you get to bask in my delightful company for just a little longer."

I shake my head, finally relenting. "Fine. But if I'm drinking before an industry event, you're buying."

Danny presses a hand to his heart. "It will be my honour."

And with that, we veer towards the pub, my stomach still knotted but my resolve a little steadier.

TWENTY-SEVEN

By the time we make it back to the museum, the event space hums with energy, a kind of buzzing anticipation that makes my skin prickle. As we step inside, I instantly regret everything. Every *single* choice that led me here. From the black heels pinching my toes to the jacket I grabbed in some misguided effort to protect myself against whatever tonight might bring. None of it works. I still feel exposed. Naked, almost.

Danny nudges my arm with his elbow, a silent reminder that I'm not alone in this circus.

"Breathe," he murmurs, like he's talking to a skittish horse. "Or at least pretend to."

He reaches out to hold my hand as we navigate past the cloakroom and into the main hall.

"Nice turnout," someone says behind me, their tone casual, like we're talking about the weather instead of the book signing of the year. I dodge to the side, letting them pass, and pull Danny over to the corner of the room, trying to disappear.

"Love what you've done with our vantage point. If we crouch slightly, we might pass for decorative plants."

I shoot him a look. "You didn't have to come, you know."

"And miss this?" He gestures at the opulence around them. "Please. It's the most fun I've had in years."

Trying to hide doesn't help. The space is alive—people chattering, laughing, sipping champagne from delicate flutes—and even though no one's looking at me, I feel seen. Too seen.

Why am I here again? Maybe it's professional curiosity. Maybe it's masochism. Probably both.

My eyes scan the room despite my better judgment, searching for him. For Rory. Of course they are. Because apparently, self-control is optional now. My throat feels tight, and not just because the air smells of expensive perfume and anxiety. This isn't my world. Not really. And yet, here I am, standing in the middle of it, heart pounding like I'm waiting for something.

Correction: someone.

"Glass of fizz?" Danny offers, as he takes two from the table. I shake my head, and he shrugs. "Oh, well. I've touched it now, would be rude not to drink it."

The lights dim just slightly, and the hum of conversation dampens down as Rory steps onto the small stage. He looks... *good*. Of course, he does. Tall, poised, wearing that annoyingly perfect combination of casual confidence and tailored charm— a navy jacket over a white shirt, the sleeves rolled up like he's about to get his hands dirty with something creative and profound. His dark hair is artfully tousled, which I know for a fact takes him at least five minutes in front of a mirror, pretending it's effortless.

"Good evening," he says, his voice cutting through the silence like warm honey, smooth and impossibly steady.

The crowd leans in—literally. Danny claps excitedly. Even I feel myself swaying forward slightly, like some magnetic pull I can't fight. Great. Just great. My plan to blend into the wallpaper is going swimmingly.

"Thank you all for being here tonight to celebrate the publication of *Fully, Forever*." His gaze sweeps across the room, not landing on me—thank God—but my chest tightens anyway, an involuntary reaction I didn't sign off on. "This book is... Well, it's special to me. For a lot of reasons."

I stiffen. My palms are clammy against the cool stem of the champagne glass that I'm clutching like a life raft. Don't do this, Rory. Stick to your script. Talk about how long it took to write, or how much caffeine was consumed during revisions. Make a joke about deadlines. Anything but what I think you're about to say.

He doesn't open the book yet. It rests on the podium like a secret waiting to be told, its cover gleaming under the soft spotlight.

"Writing is always personal," he continues, his tone shifting, softer now, almost introspective. "But this one... this one challenged me in ways I didn't expect."

My heart thuds harder at that, because I know exactly what he means. I was there for it. Every late-night brainstorming session. Every rewrite. Every argument where his stubbornness collided headfirst with my perfectionism. Every touch, every feeling, every desire...

"Sometimes," Rory says, his hands gripping the edges of the podium now, "you need help finding your way. A muse, you might call it. An inspiration. Someone who sees you—even when you're not sure what they're looking at. Even when you're not sure you want them to see the true you." His voice catches just slightly, a crack no one else might notice, but I do. God, I feel it in my chest. I feel it in my hand too as Danny squeezes it hard—he's as caught up in the speech as everyone else.

Rory pauses. There's a shift in the room, a collective breath held, and I realise mine's caught somewhere between my throat and my ribcage. He's deviating. I can tell. The Scott

& Drake PR team, sitting at one of the tables closest to the stage, can tell too, and their faces are now displaying fifty shades of panic. This isn't rehearsed. The Rory I know—the professional, polished author who can charm any audience—is stepping aside for someone else. Someone raw. Vulnerable.

"Before I read from the book," he says, meeting the eyes of the crowd but somehow, impossibly, making it feel like he's only talking to me, "there's something I need to say. Something I should've said a long time ago."

No. No, no, no. My pulse spikes, panic flaring hot behind my sternum. *Rory, don't you dare—*

The room is utterly silent, save for the faint rustle of someone shifting in their seat. My grip tightens on Danny's hand, my nails pressing crescents into his palm, but he doesn't withdraw. All I can do is stare at him—at Rory—and try to reconcile this moment with the man I thought I knew.

A hush settles over the grand hall, the kind of expectant silence that only comes when an audience knows they're about to hear something important. Rory stands at the podium, microphone in hand, the oversized cover of *Fully, Forever* glowing on the screens behind him. His usual confidence is there, but there's something else, too—something heavier.

I know that look. I've seen it before, when he's standing at the edge of an idea, unsure whether to take the leap.

He exhales, scanning the crowd, then leans slightly into the mic. "I had a speech prepared for tonight. Something polished and charming and full of the usual thanks to my incredible team at Scott & Drake, my agent, Samantha, and of course the Big Man upstairs. And they do deserve that. More than I can say." His eyes flicker toward the crowd at the back—toward me—before moving on.

"But there's something I need to say first."

A ripple of curiosity runs through the audience. I grip Danny's hand a little too tightly and this time he squeaks in pain and I let go. "It's okay," he whispers. "Squeeze all you want, I've got a spare."

Rory takes the microphone from the stand and begins to pace.

"For years, I've been lucky enough to stand on stages like this, accepting praise for my books. Bestsellers. Adaptations. Awards. A career most writers would kill for." He pauses. "But the truth is... I never did it alone."

Whispers ripple through the room.

Danny leans in, whispering, "I swear, if this turns into one of those grand 'stop the wedding' moments, I'm filming it."

I shoot him a glare.

He grins. "Too soon?"

Rory takes a deep breath, then continues, voice steady. "Every book with my name on the cover—the ones you've read, loved, recommended to your friends—they weren't just mine. From the very beginning, I had a co-writer. Someone who poured just as much heart into these stories as I did, if not more. Someone who never asked for credit, never demanded the spotlight."

He turns slightly, as if searching for her. "My sister, Aoife, deserves every bit of recognition I've ever received. More, probably. She is the best writer I know, the best partner I could have asked for, and the best sister anyone could ever wish for." His voice softens. "And I should have said this a long time ago."

The room is dead silent. A second stretches. Then another.

He shifts, gripping the edges of the podium. "Does this change anything about the books? Does this change how you view me?" He lets the questions hang, scanning the faces in front of him. "Maybe. Maybe not. You'll have to be the judge of that."

A beat. Then, a smattering of applause.

"Thank you, Aoife," he says, his voice steady but thick with emotion. "For everything."

I can't clap. My hands are frozen, my mind racing. Because if Rory can stand there, under the glare of a hundred watchful eyes, and lay himself bare like that... What excuse do I have for hiding?

The applause stutters awkwardly, like the crowd isn't sure if it should commit. Hushed voices collide in an undercurrent of surprise and confusion. Someone near me gasps softly—possibly dramatic, possibly genuine—and I swear I hear the word 'scandalous' whispered from somewhere behind my left shoulder. Danny hands me a flute of prosecco and instinctively I accept.

I can feel it—the energy shifting, crackling, filling the air like static before a storm. People are leaning toward each other, their excitement palpable, and yet I'm rooted to the spot, my heart pounding like a drumline gone rogue. My head is spinning, trying to keep up with what just happened. Rory Keane —*perfect Rory Keane*, whose public persona is as attractive as his book covers—just tore open his chest and handed the audience his bloody, beating truth.

Aoife. He said her name. Admitted it. Out loud. To everyone.

My fingers tighten around my glass, the cool condensation slipping against my palm. I want to be angry at him—for something, anything—but the emotion doesn't quite land. Instead, there's this terrible, all-consuming ache blooming beneath my ribs as my brain scrambles for footing.

Danny must notice because he gently pries the glass from my fingers before I snap the stem clean off. "Let's not add 'glass-related injury' to tonight's drama, yeah?"

Rory, owning his shortcomings? Rory, standing under these blistering lights and stripping himself bare? This isn't a man who's playing it safe anymore. This is... something else entirely. And damn him for making me feel it.

"That's not all," Rory says, his voice cutting cleanly through the growing noise.

The crowd is well and truly primed at this point. And that's when it happens.

His eyes find mine.

It's not immediate; he sweeps the room first, as if searching, as if needing permission. But then those green eyes lock onto mine like they're tethered by an invisible string, and suddenly everything else—the low hum of chatter, the shuffling of feet, even the too-sweet scent of perfume wafting from the woman beside me—fades into static.

Danny, never missing a beat, quips, "If you bolt now, I'll fake a fainting spell to cause a diversion."

"One more person deserves my thanks tonight," Rory says, and there's this tiny quake in his voice, so small most people wouldn't notice. But I do. Of course, I do.

"Someone who has challenged me, frustrated me, and pushed me in ways I never thought possible."

Oh no. Oh, absolutely not.

"She's the reason this particular book exists," Rory continues, holding a copy of *Fully, Forever* aloft, his gaze still pinned on me, unwavering and relentless. His voice lowers, softens, but somehow carries even further. "Not only did she rewrite most of this book, for which she deserves my eternal thanks. She reminded me of what honesty looks like. What bravery feels like. She reminded me how to be vulnerable, even when it terrifies you."

My lungs seize. I can't breathe. I think I might actually pass out right here in the middle of this infernal museum, surrounded by twenty-something Bookstagrammers and some guy wearing red braces over a white shirt.

He shifts slightly, and for the first time all evening, his

posture isn't easy confidence—it's something rawer, stripped of performance.

"The truth is," he says, voice steady despite the flicker of uncertainty in his expression, "I was stuck."

Members of the audience sit up a little straighter, really paying attention now.

"I don't mean writer's block. I mean stuck. Because for the first time in my career, I had to do this alone. I had to prove to myself that I could write something without my sister by my side, without the person who helped shape every book that came before. But I wasn't ready. I didn't know how." He swallows. "Because the truth is, I'd spent my entire career writing about love, but I had no idea what it really was. Not until her."

The words settle like an avalanche in my chest.

The room is utterly silent now. No one moves. No one dares.

"I built my success on the idea of perfect love," Rory continues, his fingers gripping the podium a little tighter now. "Love that follows a neat formula, love that always lands on its feet. The kind that makes sense in a three-act structure. But that's not what Lara Yates taught me."

Oh God.

"She taught me about messy love. The kind that challenges you. That forces you to grow, to be better. The kind that isn't neat or predictable, the kind that can't be packaged into tropes and happy endings on demand. The kind that terrifies you." He exhales shakily, like he's forcing himself to keep going, despite the weight pressing on his chest. "She ripped apart my pages and called out every lie, every lazy shortcut, every time I leaned on clichés instead of truth. She didn't just make this book better. She made *me* better."

My throat is tight. Too tight.

Rory shifts, then looks directly at me again.

"And, Lara," he says, my name dropping from his mouth like a stone into a still pond. "I need you to know something."

No. Please don't.

"Working with you changed my life." His voice dips, barely more than a breath. Then, quieter—not for the audience, not for anyone but me.

"Loving you..." His voice cracks, just slightly, but enough to make my hands clench. "Loving you has been the greatest risk I've ever taken. And the best thing I'll ever do."

The silence that follows is deafening, the weight of his words hanging heavy in the air.

I'm dimly aware of the crowd's reaction—soft gasps, a few audible exclamations—but it's all background noise to the roaring in my ears. Because this isn't real. It can't be real. Rory Keane, bestselling author and professional heartbreaker, is not standing on a stage in front of dozens of strangers and admitting that he loves me.

I can feel them looking, their gazes heavy and intrusive, but I can't move. Can't speak. All I can do is stand there, exposed, while Rory waits—hope and determination etched into every line of his face. Danny doesn't pressure me, doesn't speak. He just squeezes my arm gently, like he's wordlessly saying, *I've got you.*

The air feels too thick, like I'm trying to breathe through a wool sweater. My legs are rooted to the spot, even though every instinct in my body is screaming at me to *move*. Forward, backwards, anywhere but here. Rory's words are still ricocheting around in my skull—*"Loving you has been the greatest risk"*—like some cruel echo designed to short-circuit my brain.

This cannot be happening.

A part of me wants to laugh. A hysterical, borderline-manic laugh that would probably get me escorted out by security. Because this—this grand, sweeping declaration of love in front of an audience—is the stuff of romance novels. *His* romance novels, specifically. The ones I spend months editing, rolling my eyes at all the overblown speeches and "I'll die without you" proclamations. And now, somehow, I'm *living* one.

The irony is not lost on me. At least he's on brand.

"Just go," I whisper under my breath, willing my feet to turn toward the door. Leave. Run. Do *anything* but stand here like a deer in headlights while Rory Keane bares his soul for everyone to see. For *me* to see.

But I don't move. My traitorous body stays frozen, my hands clutching the strap of my bag so tightly my knuckles ache. Because as much as I want to bolt, there's another part of me—a quieter, more dangerous part—that doesn't want to run. That wants to stay. That wants to believe him.

This isn't real. It's... a publicity stunt. A gimmick. The rationalisations tumble in my mind, weak and hollow.

He's still looking at me—straight at me—with an intensity I didn't know he was capable of. His expression is raw, unguarded, and so achingly vulnerable I can't look away.

"Goddamn you, Rory." He wasn't supposed to do this. He wasn't supposed to make *me* the story.

My pulse is a drumbeat in my ears. The crowd's attention feels suffocating, their whispers like static pressing against my skin. And yet... and yet, beneath all the fear, all the doubt, there's something else. Something warm and insistent, tugging at the edges of my resolve.

Hope.

Don't be stupid. Hope is dangerous. Hope gets you hurt. But Rory's words keep replaying in my mind, stubborn and relentless: *Loving you, has been the best thing I'll ever do.*

Danny leans in, voice low and sure. "Go." One word, firm and unrelenting. When I hesitate, he adds, "You'll regret it if you don't. And trust me, I don't have the patience to listen to you analyse this for the next decade."

My throat tightens, and before I can talk myself out of it, I take a step forward.

Then another.

And another.

Each movement feels monumental, like wading through quicksand, but I keep going. The crowd parts around me slowly, faces blurring into a haze of colour and sound. I focus on the ground at first—shiny shoes, scuffed heels, chair legs, the edge of someone's handbag. Anything but Rory. But as I get closer, my gaze lifts, drawn to him like a magnet.

He hasn't taken his eyes off me. Not once.

I reach the edge of the stage. My palms are damp, and my stomach is a storm of nerves, but there's no turning back now. Whatever happens next, I'm here. I'm *choosing* to be here.

For him. For us. For whatever this might be.

He's standing there, tall and steady, microphone in one hand, his other hanging awkwardly by his side as if he doesn't know what to do with it. His eyes are locked on me, wide and unguarded, and for the first time since I've known him, he looks... nervous. Rory Keane, the man who could charm a room full of literary critics into loving a poorly written shopping list, is nervous. Because of me.

"Hi," I manage, my voice barely above a whisper. It's absurd, really, because I'm pretty sure half this crowd has stopped breathing just to hear what happens next.

"Hi," he says back, soft and certain. His lips twitch, like he wants to smile, but doesn't quite trust himself. And God help me, I think I love him even more for that.

There's a pause—no, a *moment*. One of those cinematic beats where the world seems to collectively hold its breath. I can feel the weight of everyone's eyes, the heat of their curiosity pressing down on me.

"Rory..." I start, but my voice catches. Damn it. Why

couldn't I have rehearsed this? Oh right, because I never planned to be here in the first place!

"Don't," he cuts in gently, stepping closer. The mic drops to his side, forgotten, and now it's just us. "You don't have to say anything right now."

"That's good," I admit. "Because I have no idea what to say."

His laugh is short, breathless, but there's a flicker of relief in it. "You showed up. That's enough."

Enough. The word sits heavy in my chest, cracking something open inside me. For years, nothing I did ever felt like enough—not in work, not in life, not even in the quiet moments when I dared to dream about something more. But Rory... he's looking at me like I hung the moon, and I think, maybe, just maybe, he's right. Maybe showing up *is* enough.

"Do you always sabotage your own book launches with dramatic public confessions?"

"Only when the person I love most in the world is involved," he counters, quick as ever. His voice dips lower, quieter, and suddenly it's just for me. "And only when I'm absolutely terrified of losing her."

Damn him. Damn his stupid, beautiful sincerity. I take another step closer, close enough now to see the faint stubble on his jaw, the way his pulse flutters at his neck. He's vulnerable too, I realise, and somehow that makes this whole thing both easier and infinitely harder.

"Rory," I try again, softer this time. I'm not sure what I'm about to say, but it doesn't matter, because in the next second, he closes the distance between us.

The kiss is— Well, it's everything. Soft and urgent, tentative and consuming, like a thousand unsaid words spilling out in a single breath. His hand cups my face, fingers threading into my hair, and I melt into him before I can overthink it. There's no room for doubt or fear, just the overwhelming certainty that this, right here, is exactly where I'm supposed to be.

The crowd erupts. Applause, cheers, someone wolf-whistling from the back—I'm pretty sure it's Danny—but it barely registers. Rory pulls back just enough to rest his forehead against mine, his breath warm and unsteady. His eyes search mine, and I swear there's an entire galaxy of emotions swirling in them: hope, relief, love, and something else I can't quite name.

"Hi," he says again, grinning like an idiot.

"Hi," I reply, breathless and smiling despite myself. And for the first time in a very, very long time, I feel like I might actually be okay.

"That was... dramatic."

"Had to make sure I had your attention. You know I have a thing for big romantic gestures. And for the record, it would have been even better during a car chase."

"Congratulations," I say wryly, letting my hand drop back to my side. "You've officially made a spectacle of both of us. Hope you're happy."

"I am," he replies, his gaze holding mine. "Are *you* happy?"

Happy. The word lands softly, but is heavy, like a stone skipping over water before sinking into the depths. I blink up at him, my mind scrambling for an answer that won't betray how entirely undone I feel right now. Happy? Who has time to process happiness when they've just been publicly kissed by their ex-collaborator-turned-muse-turned—

"Ask me again in five minutes," I manage to say, my voice steadier than I expected.

"Okay," Rory says, his eyes not leaving mine. "But for the record, I'm going to keep asking until the answer's yes."

I don't know whether to laugh, cry, or slap him. Instead, I just shake my head, biting back the smile threatening to break through.

The crowd is still buzzing—clapping, cheering, someone probably live-streaming this whole thing—and it's starting to dawn on me that we're standing here on a stage, under very bright lights, being incredibly... visible. My cheeks flush hot as reality crashes back in.

"Rory," I hiss, leaning closer, my voice low enough that only he can hear. "People are staring."

"Let them." His tone is impossibly easy, like he hasn't just detonated my carefully constructed life in front of half the publishing industry. "They'll get over it."

"Will they?" I shoot back, arching a brow. "Because I'm pretty sure we'll be trending on BookTok."

"Good." He smirks, and for a second, I want to hate him for how insufferably confident he looks. "I've always wanted to go viral on social media."

I roll my eyes so hard it's a miracle they don't fall out of my skull. But then his fingers brush against mine—just the lightest, briefest touch—and all my snark evaporates like mist under the sun.

"Rory..." I start, but my voice falters. There's too much to say, too much I'm not ready to say, and the words knot themselves up in my throat. He seems to understand anyway, because his expression softens, the smirk giving way to something quieter, something real.

"Hey," he says gently, his voice dipping low enough that it grounds me. "It's okay. We'll figure it out."

"Figure what out?" I ask, though I already know the answer.

"Everything. You and me. Us. Whatever this is."

My heart does this ridiculous little flip, and I suddenly feel like I'm standing on the edge of a cliff, wind whipping through my hair, the ground miles below. Terrifying, exhilarating, inevitable.

"Bold of you to assume there's an 'us,'" I say, aiming for dry, but landing closer to breathless.

"Bold's kind of my thing," he shoots back.

"Rory," I say again, softer this time, and I don't even know what I'm about to follow it with. Maybe nothing. Maybe everything.

"Yeah?"

"Don't screw this up," I say, half-teasing, half-serious. Because if anyone has the power to ruin this—whatever this is—it's him. Or maybe it's me. Probably both of us, if I'm being honest.

"Wouldn't dream of it," he promises, and for the first time, I think I might actually believe him.

We pull back then, just enough to look at each other fully, and the weight of what's happened—what's *happening*—settles between us like a fragile, precious thing. His eyes meet mine, steady and searching, and in that moment, it feels like we're standing on the cusp of something vast and unknowable. Something terrifying. Something wonderful.

And maybe, just maybe, that's enough.

TWENTY-EIGHT

EIGHTEEN MONTHS LATER...

My fingers trace the edges of the proof copy on the table in front of me—my proof copy. The cover is smooth, the paper sturdy, heavier than I expected. It feels... real. Too real.

I flip through the pages for what must be the hundredth time, my thumb catching slightly on the corner of chapter one. There it is. My name. In bold, serif font, glaring up at me like it's mocking my audacity.

Lara Yates. *Author.*

"Ridiculous," I say, shoving my glasses higher up on my nose. It earns me a curious glance from the barista behind the counter, but I ignore her. Instead, I stare down at the book. My book.

My chest tightens. *Excitement? Terror? Both. Definitely both.*

A shadow moves across the table, and before I can look up, someone slides into the chair opposite me with the kind of effortless confidence I'll never understand.

"So this is it?"

Rory Keane. Of course. He's wearing that lazy grin that should come with a warning label, his dark hair falling just enough over his forehead to give him an air of "I woke up like this" charm. His shirt is hanging loose, jacket slung casually over one shoulder, because Rory Keane doesn't just enter a room—he saunters into it like he owns the place. If he notices how tightly I'm gripping the proof copy, he doesn't say anything.

"Congratulations, Lara," he says softly. Not teasing. Just… sincere.

Rory doesn't ask. Of course, he doesn't ask.

Before I can blink, his hand darts across the table, long fingers brushing mine as he plucks the proof copy right out of my hands like it's some casual trinket and not, you know, *the culmination of my entire existence.*

"Ah, ah," I say, narrowing my eyes at him. "That is classified material."

"Good thing I love secrets." His smirk is maddening, the kind that drips with enough mischief to make a saint reconsider their vows. He leans back in his chair, flipping open the front cover with an exaggerated air of nonchalance. "Let's see what we've got here."

"Rory," I warn, but it's weak—embarrassingly so. My voice does that wobbly thing, half stern, half secretly thrilled, because there's something completely absurd about watching him—*The Sunday Times* bestselling author, the undisputed king of romance, professional heartstring-puller—reading the first sentence of *my* book.

He clears his throat dramatically, squinting at the page like he's preparing for a public reading. "'In the margins of his life, she had only ever been an editor—until the day he wrote himself into hers.'" He lowers the book slightly, raising one dark eyebrow at me. "Oof. You're really coming for my gig, huh?"

"Give it back." I reach forward, but he holds it just out of range, his grin widening. The audacity of this man.

"Not yet," he says, tilting his head as if considering something deeply profound. "You might actually be better than me. Should I be worried?"

"Yes. Now return the stolen goods before I call security."

"Security?" His laugh is low, warm, and entirely too contagious. I feel it curl around the edges of my resolve like smoke. "Lara, please. You'd miss me if they dragged me away."

"Debatable."

"Admit it," he continues, tapping the edge of the proof playfully against the table. "This is good. Like, really good. You should be proud."

"I am. Very."

I can't seem to stop looking at the book. It's mine—every word, every comma, over ten years in the making, if you count the time from when I began to when it's published. And now here it is, sitting in the middle of a sticky café table next to a half-empty latte cup. Somehow, it's more terrifying than exhilarating.

"Hey," Rory says, breaking through the static in my head. He stands and approaches my side of the table. He holds a hand out, palm up, stopping just short of touching mine. I reach up and take it; he waits until I meet his gaze again. "It's real, Lara. You did this."

"Yeah," I whisper, barely audible. "I did."

Something shifts then, subtle and impossible to pinpoint, but I feel it anyway. I stand and Rory closes the space between us. His forehead brushes against mine, warm and steady, and my breath catches in surprise.

"See?" he says. "Not so scary, right?"

I don't respond, not with words, anyway. Instead, I let my eyes drift shut, leaning ever so slightly into him—into this moment, fleeting and fragile but undeniably real.

And for the first time, maybe ever, I believe him.

Rory pulls back just enough to meet my eyes, his forehead still so close I can feel the faint trace of warmth lingering there. His gaze is steady, searching, and—of course—just a little smug, like he knows exactly what kind of chaos he's causing.

"Alright, Yates," he says. "So, what happens next?"

I blink at him, thrown for a second by the question, though I shouldn't be. That's Rory for you—always diving straight into the deep end without checking if I've had time to put on a life jacket.

"Next?" I echo, stalling because, well, I'm not sure I trust myself to answer without sounding like an idiot. My brain feels like it's been rewired entirely in static since he leaned in.

"Yeah, next," he repeats, drawing the word out like it's obvious. "Because now you're a big, famous author and all. I guess... I need to know you're still happy slumming it with this big lummox."

It hits me then, how much weight those words are carrying, despite the lightness in his delivery. For all his bravado and cheeky grins, Rory doesn't say things like this lightly. Not when it matters. And this? This definitely matters.

"Rory," I start, but my voice catches halfway through his name, and I have to clear my throat to try again. "You're ridiculous, you know that?"

"That I am,"

I glance down at the book again, its crisp pages marked with the fingerprints of every doubt that got me here. The culmination of years spent behind the scenes, convincing myself that stepping into the spotlight wasn't for people like me. And now? Now I'm sitting across from the person who never stopped pushing me to believe otherwise, the one who saw through every excuse and stayed anyway.

"Always," I say finally, the word slipping out before I can overthink it. I look up as I say it, meeting his gaze head-on, and this time, my voice doesn't falter. "You're always part of what's next."

The smile that spreads across his face is slow, deliberate—like he's savouring it—and it feels like the sun breaking through clouds I didn't realise were still there.

Rory leans forward first.

Not all at once, not in some grand cinematic sweep. No, it's smaller than that—intentional, deliberate, like he knows exactly what he's doing to me. And of course, he does. His hand comes up, pausing just shy of my face, like he's waiting for me to stop him. But I don't. God help me, I don't.

Always, I'd said, and now there's no taking it back.

"Say something," he begs, his voice low enough to send a shiver down my spine. His breath is warm, close enough to skim my cheek. "Anything. Tell me to stop, tell me to keep going—tell me I'm an idiot, I don't care."

"You're an idiot."

"Thanks a bunch," he says. His eyes flicker over my face, searching, analysing, waiting.

And then he kisses me.

It's tentative at first, almost hesitant, like he's testing the waters, gauging whether I'll pull away. But I don't. Instead, I lean in—just slightly, just enough—and that's all it takes. The world tilts. Or maybe it's just me. Either way, everything narrows to this one moment: the soft press of his lips against mine, the faint scrape of stubble brushing my skin. It's... grounding. Disarming. Terrifying.

Perfect.

I don't realise I've closed my eyes until the rest of the café disappears—the clink of cups, the hum of conversations. All that's left is him. Him, and the steady warmth of his hand now cupping my jaw, as though I might disappear if he lets go.

I tilt my head slightly, deepening the kiss, and a soft sound escapes him—surprise or relief or something else entirely, I don't know. I barely register it before his other hand finds its way to my face, anchoring me to the moment. There's a heat to it now, a quiet insistence, but it's never rushed. Never careless. Every movement feels measured, intentional, like he's aware of every barrier we've crossed to get here.

When we finally break apart, it's not because either of us wants to—it's because we have to. Oxygen is apparently non-negotiable.

"You know what?" he says. "We should write a book together."

"We already did."

"I mean one with both of our names on the front cover.

"Collaborations are risky."

"Sure," he agrees easily. "But sometimes they're magic."

God, he's infuriating. And brilliant. And possibly right.

"Fine," I say, exhaling a laugh as I lean forward. "Magic it is."

"Magic it is," he echoes, and then his hand finds mine on the table, his fingers threading through mine like it's the most natural thing in the world.

For once, I don't overthink it. I don't analyse or dissect or search for hidden meanings. I just let myself feel it—the warmth of his hand, the steady thrum of possibility between us, the quiet certainty that whatever comes next, we'll face it together.

"Ready?" he asks, his voice low and brimming with something that feels suspiciously like hope.

"Always," I say, the word slipping from my lips without hesitation.

And when he leans in for another kiss, I know—I *know*—that this is the beginning of something bigger than either of us. Something worth every risk.

ABOUT THE AUTHOR

Alia Smith writes heart-warming romantic comedies filled with wit, charm, and just the right amount of chaos.

When she's not crafting love stories, she can usually be found curled up with a book, getting emotionally invested in reality TV, or attempting to keep Galaxy—her cat and chief muse—from sitting on her keyboard.

She lives in a cosy Oxfordshire home, where she firmly believes that every great romance starts with a good cup of tea.

www.aliasmithbooks.com

instagram.com/aliasmithbooks

amazon.com/author/aliasmith

The
Maine
Event
When love collides
with ambition,
sparks fly.
alia smith

THE MAINE EVENT

Rachel Holmes is a high-powered PR exec with a laser focus on success. Her life revolves around landing the next big deal.

Dan Rhodes used to be a soap opera star. Now, he's a single dad living a quiet life, far from the limelight.

When a travel mix-up leaves Rachel stranded on the wrong side of the country, her plans for a career-defining pitch go up in smoke. Instead, she finds herself navigating an unexpected connection with the charming—but stubborn—Dan, and his daughter, Chloe.

Rachel doesn't do detours, but between getting tangled up in Dan's world and uncovering a softer side to her own ambitions, she's facing a crossroads she never saw coming.

Her future was always clear... until now.

A swoon-worthy, opposites-attract romance about love, family, and the unexpected journeys that lead us home.

ONE

I take a deep breath and stride into the conference room, my heels clicking sharply against the polished floor. The air is thick with the scent of expensive coffee and barely concealed skepticism. A dozen fast food executives sit around the sleek glass table, their arms crossed, their gazes expectant. They don't think I can sell them on this. That's adorable.

I flash my best boardroom smile and place my portfolio on the table with a crisp *thud*.

"Gentlemen. Imagine a plant-based burger that not only tastes amazing, but also aligns perfectly with your brand's commitment to sustainability," I say, my voice clear and strong. "Our campaign will position your new offering as the go-to choice for health-conscious and environmentally aware consumers."

A pause. One executive raises an eyebrow, as if I've just suggested they start serving kale milkshakes.

I hold their gaze and continue. "It's not just another burger —it's the burger that changes the conversation."

As I delve into the details of the proposed marketing strategy for their new healthy choice menu item, I can see the executives nodding along, any objections they had planned to raise melting away. I highlight the key selling points—the burger's delicious flavor, its nutritional benefits, and its potential to attract a new demographic of customers. You get a sixth sense about whether your pitch is landing right with an audience and, not to toot my own horn too hard... seven minutes in, I have everyone in the room eating out of my hand.

"By partnering with influencers in the wellness space and leveraging social media, we'll generate buzz and drive demand for your plant-based option," I explain, gesturing to the colorful slides projected behind me. "This is an opportunity to establish your brand as a leader in the fast food industry's shift toward healthier, more sustainable offerings. In a nutshell, my team and I will position your product as a burger that's good for you, good for the planet, and good for business."

The lead executive, a silver-haired man with a perpetual frown, clears his throat. "That's... impressive."

Damn right, it is.

The polite applause tells me I've nailed it. I field questions with ease, keeping my responses tight and strategic.

This is my playground, and I own it.

Just as we're wrapping up, a man I hadn't paid much attention to—a tall, dark-haired exec with the confident ease of someone used to getting what he wants—steps forward, smiling.

"Great presentation." He offers his hand. "Lyle."

I shake it, firm but brief. "Rachel Holmes."

"You clearly know your stuff. I'd love to discuss it further. Maybe over dinner?" His smile is smooth, like he already knows the answer.

I return it, but mine is professional, unwavering. "I make it a policy not to mix business with pleasure."

His expression falters for a split second before he recovers.

"Well, that's a pity." He hands me his card. "But either way, I look forward to working with you."

I tuck the card into my portfolio, already moving on. As I stride down the hallway, the familiar rush of success hums in my veins. One step closer to landing this account. One step closer to making partner. My personal life might be a barren wasteland, but my career? *On fire.*

The truth is, I've always been better at managing brands than people. Crafting narratives and selling ideas come as naturally to me as breathing, but building relationships? That's where things get messy. At work, everything follows a strategy —objectives, deliverables, measurable outcomes. If a pitch doesn't land, I can pinpoint why, learn from it, and try again. But in my personal life? There's no tidy PowerPoint presentation to guide me through the chaos of human connection.

I've spent years perfecting my professional image—the competent, confident, always-prepared woman who can sell anything to anyone. I know how to make an impression, how to leave a room buzzing with ideas and possibilities. But after hours, when the office lights dim and I'm alone in my immaculate, lonely apartment, I feel the weight of that polished veneer crushing me.

I think of my old friends, the ones who slowly drifted away while I was climbing the corporate ladder. Birthday texts that went unanswered, dinner invites declined because of deadlines and meetings. Now, even if I wanted to rekindle those friendships, I wouldn't know where to start. I've wrapped myself in my ambition like a safety blanket, convinced that I don't need anyone.

But sometimes—just sometimes—I catch myself scrolling through social media, pausing on photos of people I used to know. Laughing in crowded bars, holding hands on beach vacations, watching their kids take their first steps—living their best life. And it hits me, sharp and unexpected: I've built a life so perfectly curated that I don't really fit into it anymore.

I shove the thought away, focusing instead on the rush of victory from the pitch. There's no room for self-pity today. I won them over, and that's what matters. I'll celebrate later—maybe with a glass of something expensive and a quiet toast to myself. After all, who else will?

As I stride down the hallway, still riding the high of the successful presentation, I catch sight of Helen through the glass walls of her office. My boss is the picture of effortless authority, well put together in a tailored navy suit, her manicured fingers laced together. But her expression is unreadable, and that—*that*—is unsettling.

"Rachel, sit down."

I lower myself into the chair opposite her desk, still riding the post-pitch high. "What's up? The meeting went well."

"It did," she agrees. "In fact, it went so well that I'm forcing you to take a vacation."

I blink. "I'm sorry. You're *what?*"

Helen leans back, studying me like a puzzle she's just figured out. "You haven't taken a single day off in eighteen months. You need a break before you break. Two weeks. No arguments."

"But—"

She holds up a hand. "Non-negotiable. Go read a book, reconnect with your family. Hell, get a hobby."

I open my mouth, then close it. Helen is one of the few people on earth who can out-stubborn me. I could fight this, but I'd lose. And the truth is, there's no one in my life demanding my time. No partner. No kids. Even my friendships have faded under the weight of work.

A convenient excuse not to face that reality.

"Fine." I exhale. "But I'm not happy about it."

Helen smirks. "I don't expect you to be. Now get out of my

office before I start to suspect you *like* being here. And who knows? Maybe you'll surprise yourself and actually enjoy yourself."

I let myself in with the key my sister Claire keeps hidden under a plastic rock that is, frankly, an insult to camouflage. Technically, it's Claire and Richard's house—a big, modern place they bought after Lily was born. They invited Mom to move in with them soon after. She'd been on her own for decades, still living in the little house we all grew up in, and they didn't like the idea of her rattling around in it alone. This place had the space, and the logic was simple: more help with childcare for them, more company for her.

Still, the moment I step inside, it smells like Mom's house —lavender and freshly baked cookies. A scent so deeply nostalgic it nearly knocks me sideways.

A familiar warmth wraps around me, tugging at memories I'd thought long buried. The layout's different, sure, but the feeling is the same. And Mom's touch is everywhere—the floral cushions, the knitted throw on the back of the couch, the armchair where she still reads the newspaper with her tea, just like she did back when we were kids.

Back then, I'd convinced myself that being the best—at school, at track, even at the annual science fair—was the only way to matter. Mom never pushed me to be perfect, but I craved the reassurance of straight As and trophies as proof that I was doing something right. Once, after winning the regional debate championship, Mom had hugged me so tight I thought I'd break, whispering how proud she was. But all I could think about was the kid who came second, the way his face fell when they called my name.

In my mind, there was no room for mistakes or second place. I thought that if I just worked hard enough, controlled every variable, I'd never have to feel that gnawing sense of inadequacy again. Even now, standing in this familiar hallway, it's hard to shake the compulsion to be the best—to outwork, outperform, and prove to everyone, including myself, that I'm worth the effort.

Maybe that's why I never stopped pushing—why I buried myself in work instead of forming lasting relationships, why success became synonymous with self-worth. If I let up, even for a second, it might all unravel. And that's a risk I've never been willing to take.

"Mom? Claire?" I call out.

Mom's voice cuts through my thoughts, bringing me back to the present. "Rachel? You okay?"

I force a smile, shaking off the remnants of old insecurities. "Yeah, Mom. Just... had some time to spare."

I find her in the living room, curled up in her armchair, eyes glued to the TV.

"Hey." I move some toys out of the way and plop onto the couch beside her.

"Oh! Perfect timing. You have *got* to see this show I'm watching."

I glance at the screen. A ruggedly handsome man with piercing blue eyes is engaged in a heated argument with an equally beautiful woman. *Malibu Lagoon*, the title graphic reads —I've never heard of it, but that doesn't mean much. I barely have time to switch on the television, so major zeitgeist shows pass me by all the time. A quick search on IMDb reveals that this telenovela-type soap opera ran for four seasons before being abruptly canceled eight years ago. It has a surprisingly high rating and judging from the comments, a legion of fans just like my mom.

I arch an eyebrow. "Really? A soap opera?"

Mom waves me off. "It's *very* well done. And the lead actor? *Ugh*, so talented."

I study the screen. The guy *is* striking, all brooding intensity and movie-star good looks. If I were casting a campaign, he'd be a marketing dream.

"Isn't he handsome?" Mom gushes, as if reading my thoughts. "So good."

I nod absentmindedly, my mind already drifting back to work. Instinctively, I reach for my phone to check my emails, but a breaking news alert catches my eye.

"Mount Spurr erupts again in Alaska," the headline reads, accompanied by a dramatic image of a massive ash cloud billowing from the volcano.

I feel a knot form in my stomach. I can't imagine living next to such a frightening force of nature that could erupt at any time. I'm not sure how those who do can possibly sleep at night.

"Rachel, are you even listening to me?" Mom's voice snaps me back to reality.

"Sorry, Mom. Just catching up on world events. I'm all ears, promise."

Mom sighs, shaking her head. "You're always glued to that thing. Even when you're supposed to be relaxing."

I feel a pang of guilt, knowing she's right. I've been so consumed by work lately that I've barely had time for anything else, including visiting my mother.

I sink back, allowing myself to relax for the first time in what feels like months. I haven't been to visit in ages, and it feels... strange. Almost like I don't belong here anymore.

I moved out of Mom's house as soon as I could, desperate to make something of myself. Even back in high school, I was the girl with the color-coded planner and the stack of textbooks bigger than my head. The girl who stayed up until midnight finishing extra credit assignments just to make sure no one could beat me to valedictorian.

God, I remember the feeling of opening that acceptance letter to Northwestern, my hands shaking so badly I almost ripped it in half. It wasn't even about leaving—no, I was ready for that. It was about proving I could do it. That I could be the best. That all the late nights and stress-induced migraines meant something.

Mom used to worry about me back then, always saying I was pushing myself too hard. Claire, on the other hand, just thought I was nuts. "You're like a hamster on an espresso drip," she once joked when I was cramming for finals. "Chill out, Rach. You're already a shoo-in."

But chilling out never felt like an option. Not for me. I couldn't let myself be just good enough. I had to be the best. I had to make something of myself—something big, something important.

Maybe Mom was right all those years ago. Maybe I have been pushing myself too hard. But the thought of slowing down, of stopping to take stock of my life, terrifies me. Because what if, when I stop, I realize that none of it is worth anything at all?

"I know, I know," I concede, putting my phone away. "I'll try to unplug more, I promise."

"You'd better. You're not too old for the flying slipper, you know."

To be fair, my mom's ability to nail someone with a slipper from across the room is legendary. When Claire and I were growing up, she could hit your arm or your leg, or whatever appendage was offending her, from thirty feet. It was never thrown with particular malice, but the accuracy was astounding.

"Still think you've got it, Mom? You're not in your thirties anymore, and I'm not eight."

"That's true, but *you* are in your thirties now, and luckily for me, you're a much bigger target. I like my chances."

Mom hovers a hand near an ankle, fingers twitching over her slipper like a gunslinger ready to draw.

"Okay. Okay." I concede and place my phone face down on the coffee table, out of sight, out of mind.

As soon as I do, Mom smiles and turns off the television. "So, what's going on?"

"Nothing's going on."

"It's four o'clock in the afternoon. Have you been fired?"

"No!" I squeak, horrified at the thought. "I'm... I'm on vacation."

"Since when?"

"About an hour ago."

I fill Mom in on my forced sabbatical and foolishly admit that I don't really know what to do with myself. But even as the words leave my mouth, I know it's a mistake.

With the lithe grace of a mountain cat, she's up and out of her armchair, dialing my sister's cell phone before I know what's happening.

Thirty minutes later, my life is ruined.

"Claire will pick you up at ten on Sunday," Mom announces, far too pleased with herself. "Pack warm."

I stare at her. "Mom. No."

"Oh, come on. A cabin on Lake Michigan! Fresh air! Family time! You *love* your nieces."

"I love them in small doses," I mutter. "Preferably when they're asleep."

Mom grins. "Then think of this as character-building."

"I *don't* need character. I need Wi-Fi and a coffee machine that doesn't require manual labor."

Mom pats my cheek. "You need to live a little, sweetheart."

"Thanks for the support."

"Don't mention it."

"I was being sarcastic."

"I know. Well, I think it's lovely you're all going away together," she says and turns back to her program.

I stare in disbelief at my mom's beaming grin of self-satisfaction. I don't like vacations. I certainly don't like camping. And I'm more of a "here's your birthday gift, now run along and play" kind of auntie, at least until they're potty trained and can string a sentence together.

Somehow, I'm now signed up to spend ten days cooped up with my sister, her husband, and their two rambunctious toddlers at their log cabin on Lake Michigan. It's not that I don't love my sister and her family, but the idea of being away from work, from the city, fills me with an unsettling sense of dread. Somehow, I'm signed up for a trip to the wilderness, hunting elk, and drinking from streams—or whatever it is people do when they're in the great outdoors.

I groan.

This is going to be a disaster.

Or, at the very least, deeply, *deeply* inconvenient.

Two weeks away from work? Away from my team, my clients, my *progress*? I've been working toward a partnership for years, and I can't impress the powers that be if I'm off roasting marshmallows and pretending to enjoy nature.

They say out of sight, out of mind. What if someone else steps in and wows them in my absence? What if I come back to find that all my hard work has been quietly shuffled onto someone else's plate?

I'll make it work. I *have* to. Because the last thing I can afford is to be forgotten.

TWO

"Woohoo, we made it to Wisconsin!" Richard cheers as we pass the sign announcing the state border. Claire, sitting shotgun, grins and gives him a high five.

The road trip to the cabin is already an exercise in patience and we've only been on the road for ninety minutes. I'm crammed into the back between two car seats, my nieces babbling and giggling on either side of me. The air is thick with the scent of strawberry yogurt and baby wipes, and I can already feel a headache forming behind my eyes.

"Rach, Rach, look!" My older niece, Lily, thrusts a sticky handful of chips towards my face. "I'm sharing with you!"

"Oh, um, thanks, Lily," I manage, gingerly accepting a soggy chip and trying not to grimace. "That's very nice of you."

Claire catches my eye in the rearview mirror and grins. "Isn't this fun, Rach? Just like old times, hitting the road for a family adventure."

"Sure, if by 'old times' you mean 'never,' since we definitely didn't take many road trips growing up," I mutter, shifting uncomfortably as Lily's baby sister, Anna, lets out a piercing shriek.

"Oh, come on, where's your sense of adventure?" Claire teases. "This is going to be great, you'll see. Quality family bonding time!"

I open my mouth to retort, but suddenly there's a clatter and a splat, and I look down to see a blob of purple yogurt dripping down my blouse. *Versace. Ruined.*

"Oopsie!" Lily giggles, waving her now-empty yogurt cup. "Auntie Rachel is wearing my snack!"

I close my eyes and count to three, reminding myself that this is just temporary, that I can handle a little mess and noise for the sake of my family. But as I feel the cold yogurt seeping through to my skin, I can't help but wonder what the hell I've gotten myself into.

This is a mistake, a voice warns in my head. *You should be back in Chicago, focusing on your career, not playing babysitter in some backwoods cabin.*

But then I remember my promise to Mom, and the wistful look in her eyes as she urged me to find something more than just work. And I think of Claire, who's always been there for me even when I've been too busy to return the favor.

No, I tell myself firmly. *This isn't a mistake. This is an opportunity. A chance to reconnect with what really matters, to figure out who I am beyond just my job title.*

I open my eyes and smile at Lily, who's now happily smearing yogurt on her own face. "You know what, Lil? I think purple might just be my color after all."

Claire laughs from the front seat, and I feel a flicker of warmth in my chest. Maybe this trip won't be so bad after all.

"Okay girls, what should we do first when we wake up at the lake house tomorrow?" Richard asks Lily and Anna.

"Make s'mores!" Lily exclaims.

"Go swimming!" Anna counters.

They chatter on excitedly, while I try to tune it out. I clear my throat.

"So, um, Lily... how's kindergarten going?" I ask, attempting to make conversation with my five-year-old niece.

She turns and blinks at me. "I don't like it." An awkward pause. "They make us do work. Writing letters and numbers. Boring."

"Oh, uh, wow. That sounds... fun." I force a smile.

I'm saved from further small talk when my cell phone rings. I frown at the caller ID—it's Helen, my boss. This can't be good.

"Sorry, I have to take this. Work emergency," I say, relieved at the interruption. "Helen, what's up?"

"Rachel, I have huge news," Helen says breathlessly. "Guess who was just on the phone inviting us to pitch?"

"Don't do this to me. Who?" I knew immediately if Helen was playing coy, it was big news. "Who?!"

"You've been trying to poach them for months?"

My pulse quickens. "GreenShoots?"

"Yep. They're looking to go in a new direction. But here's the rub—they've put the account up for tender. Four agencies, including us."

A thrill runs through me, followed by steely determination. I've worked too hard on landing GreenShoots to lose them now. Nearly eighteen months of subtle but constant engagement, and it's finally paid off.

"A pitch is fine; I can handle the competition. When do they need the proposal by?"

Helen exhales. "That's the kicker. They want pitches tomorrow."

"Tomorrow?!" The word explodes out of me, making Richard glance back in concern. I wave him off.

"I know, I know. They're doing it on purpose, to see how we react to pressure. They want fresh ideas, not a polished dog and pony show," Helen explains.

My mind races, already envisioning the key messages,

tactics, case studies I'll need to wow them, jetlag be damned. I'm their woman and they need to know it.

"Okay, I'll make it work," I say firmly. "Text me all the pitch details, I'll start strategizing. Tell GreenShoots they'll have the most persuasive damn proposal they've ever seen, even on short notice."

"That's my star closer," Helen says proudly. "I knew I could count on you."

I hang up, adrenaline surging through my veins. This pitch could make my career. I have to win it. I have to get to Portland, fast.

But as I look up, I suddenly remember where I am—wedged in my brother-in-law's SUV, zooming farther away from the airport with each passing mile. My stomach sinks.

What the hell am I going to do now?

I steel myself for the conversation I'm about to have. "Richard, I need you to turn the car around. I have to get to the airport."

"What?" Claire twists around in her seat to face me, her eyebrows knitted together. "You can't be serious! We're literally going on vacation."

"I know, I know." I hold up my hands placatingly. "But this is a huge opportunity. I've been trying to land a huge client for over a year, and the pitch is tomorrow. I have to be there."

"Unbelievable." Claire shakes her head, her lips pressed into a thin line. "You're really choosing work over family? Again?"

I wince at the accusation, but I don't back down. "If I win this client, I'm a shoo-in for partner. It's everything I've been working towards. I promise, once I close this deal, we can take a proper vacation, my treat."

Claire scoffs and turns away, her arms crossed tightly over her chest. The girls have gone silent in the back, their earlier excitement fizzled out. They have no idea what we're talking about, but they can sense it's not good.

"Richard, please." I lean forward, my voice urgent. "I wouldn't ask if it wasn't important."

Richard meets my gaze in the rearview mirror, his expression conflicted. After a long moment, he sighs. "Alright, Rach."

Relief floods through me, followed quickly by a pang of guilt as the girls start to whine.

"But Mom, that means it'll take even longer to get to the lake!"

"I don't want to spend more time in the car!"

I tune out their complaints, my mind already whirring with ideas for the pitch. This is my chance to prove myself, to show everyone at Channing Gabriel that I have what it takes to be a partner.

As Richard navigates the car through the traffic, heading back towards Chicago, I pull out my phone and start typing furiously. I have a presentation to plan, and I'll be damned if I let this opportunity slip through my fingers.

The airport bustles with activity as I hurry through the sliding doors. I spot my assistant, Emily, near the check-in counters, her red hair a beacon amidst the crowd.

"Emily!" I call out, waving to catch her attention.

"Rachel, there you are!" She rushes over, handing me my ticket, a small carry-on, and a garment bag. "I picked out the blue suit, hope that's ok. You're going to crush this pitch."

I take the items gratefully, a smile tugging at my lips. "You're a lifesaver, Em. Truly."

We navigate the throngs of travelers, making our way to security. As we wait in line, Emily fills me in on the latest office gossip, but my mind is already on the pitch, running through key points and anticipating potential questions. Em waves me off as I show my ticket to the TSA agent.

Once in the air, I pull out my laptop and immerse myself

in the presentation, refining slides and practicing my delivery. The hours slip by, and as the plane touches down in Portland, I feel a surge of confidence. I've got this.

Disembarking, I reach for my suitcase in the overhead bin, my mind still running through the opening lines of my pitch. As I step onto the airbridge, a deep, mellifluous voice breaks through my thoughts.

"Excuse me, miss? I think you might have my suitcase."

I turn to find a striking man with chiseled features and a charming smile. There are jawlines... and there's him. He gestures to the bag in my hand, and I glance down, noticing a small red ribbon tied to the handle. Heat rises to my cheeks as I realize my mistake.

"Oh my gosh, I'm so sorry!" I hand him the suitcase, flustered, and he hands me mine.

His eyes sparkle with amusement. "No worries, it happens to the best of us. I take it you're here on business?"

We fall into step, chatting easily about the trials and tribulations of corporate life. There's an undeniable spark, and I find myself drawn to his wit and warmth.

But as we exit the airbridge, a beautiful woman with flowing blonde hair rushes up to him, pulling him into a tight embrace. "Honey, I missed you so much!"

Reality comes crashing down, and I laugh inwardly at my foolishness. Of course, a man like him would be taken. I offer a polite nod and turn to head towards the exit, my focus shifting back to the task at hand.

And that's when I see it. The sign that stops me dead in my tracks.

"Vacationland, welcome to the State of Maine."

No!

This.

Is.

Not.

Happening?

My heart plummets as the realization hits me. I'm not in Portland, Oregon. I'm on the wrong side of the country.

No. No, no, no. That can't be right. I blink hard, as if willing the sign to change. I dig into my bag, nearly ripping the zipper off as I yank out my ticket and unfold it with trembling hands. My eyes scan the fine print—Portland International Jetport (PWM).

Oh my God. PWM. Not PDX.

My heart thunders so loudly in my ears that I barely hear the chatter of the other passengers around me. I stare at the letters, trying to force them to rearrange themselves, to magically morph into the correct airport code. But they don't. Because they can't.

I clutch the ticket like a lifeline, my brain scrambling to piece together what the hell had just happened. How did I not notice this? How did I let this happen? I'm always so meticulous, so organized—I double-check everything, triple-check, even.

I feel lightheaded. I look around, as if someone might pop up and tell me it's all a joke, that I haven't just flown to the wrong damn side of the country—it's just a hidden camera, YouTube prank channel. But there's no one to laugh with me, no friendly face to reassure me it's not as catastrophic as it seems.

Frantically, I pull out my phone and scroll to the confirmation email from Emily. There it is, plain as day—Portland, ME. My stomach lurches. How did I miss that? How did neither of us catch it? I thumb through the flight information again, as if somehow the words will change, but they're still the same damning coordinates pointing to Vacationland instead of the West Coast.

My knees go weak, and I stumble toward a bench, collapsing onto it. The gravity of my mistake hits me like a freight train. I'm in Maine. I'm supposed to be in Oregon. I'm supposed to be pitching to one of the biggest potential clients of my career tomorrow morning.

I can't breathe. I press my palm to my forehead, trying to calm down, but it's no use. The reality is suffocating me, stealing the oxygen from my lungs.

"Oh, my good God." The words escape my lips, disbelief and panic rising simultaneously in my chest. "What have I done?"

Frantically, I rush to the airline's service desk, my mind reeling with the gravity of my mistake. The line seems to stretch on forever, and every passing second feels like an eternity. I tap my foot impatiently, my eyes darting to the departure boards, hoping against hope that there's a flight that can get me to Oregon in time.

As I wait, the TVs above the desk flash with breaking news. The anchor's grave tone fills the air. "The ash cloud from the eruption of the Alaskan volcano is rapidly spreading across Canada and the Northern United States, causing unprecedented disruptions to air travel. Experts predict massive delays and cancellations in the coming hours."

My stomach churns as I watch the departure board flicker, the word "DELAYED" morphing into "CANCELED" next to flight after flight. The reality of the situation crashes over me like a tidal wave. I'm stranded, and there's no way I'll be flying to the pitch.

With shaking hands, I pull out my phone and start searching for alternative routes. Train schedules, bus timetables, anything that could get me to Portland, Oregon. But deep down, I know it's futile. The distance is too vast, the time too short.

I step out of the line, my legs feeling like lead. The bustling airport seems to fade away as the weight of my failure settles on my shoulders. I find a quiet corner and sink into a chair, burying my face in my hands.

"Think, Rachel, think," I mutter to myself, desperately trying to come up with a solution. But the more I rack my brain, the more apparent it becomes that there's no way out of this mess.

The disappointment is a bitter pill to swallow, but I know I have to accept the reality of the situation. The pitch, the partnership, the future I've worked so hard for—it's all slipping through my fingers, and there's nothing I can do to stop it.

With a heavy heart, I pull out my phone again, my fingers hovering over Helen's number. I hesitate, dreading the conversation that's about to unfold. But I know I can't put it off any longer.

As the call connects, I steel myself for the inevitable fallout. "Helen, it's Rachel. I have some bad news..."

While I explain I'm in Maine, she mostly remains calm, although it would be fair to say her choice of language is zesty. However, the magical solution I was hoping she could conjure from thin air isn't forthcoming.

"TSA is shutting down all flights. There's no way you're getting to Oregon."

My heart sinks. "But the pitch—"

"Don't worry about it. Given the circumstances, Zoe will handle the presentation instead. She can drive from Seattle."

"Zoe?" I feel a surge of frustration. "But I've been working on this for months, Helen. GreenShoots is *my* client."

"Not yet, they're not, Rachel. I don't have a choice. The pitch is happening tomorrow, we have to be in the room."

I pace, my mind racing. "What if I use my influence with GreenShoots to change the pitch day? I'm sure they'll understand, given the situation."

"No, Rachel," Helen says firmly. "They've set the date, and we have to comply. We're sending Zoe."

"But Zoe doesn't have my *green* credentials," I argue, desperation creeping into my voice. "She primarily works on Big Oil accounts, for God's sake. And she drives a 5-liter Mustang GT. Wouldn't it be better to Zoom into the meeting, to reduce our carbon footprint?"

My arguments fall on deaf ears. "Rachel, this is not up for discussion," Helen says, her tone leaving no room for debate. "Zoe is the next-best closer in the company, and GreenShoots is a must-win client for Channing Gabriel."

I feel my anger rising, but I try to keep it in check. "So, if Zoe closes the deal, does that mean she'll get the partnership?"

There's a pause on the other end of the line. "Rachel, I suggest you enjoy your two-week vacation in Maine and forget about work for a while."

"But Helen—"

"That's an order, Rachel. Send your presentation and notes to Zoe. Now."

The line goes dead, and I'm left staring at my phone, seething with frustration. I can't believe this is happening. I've worked so hard, and now Zoe is swooping in to steal my thunder.

I want to scream, to throw my phone across the airport, but I force myself to calm down. Losing my cool won't solve anything.

I glance out the window, watching planes that were supposed to be departing return to the terminal to offload their passengers. None of us are going anywhere.

Two weeks in Vacationland. You'll have to forgive me if I'm not jumping for joy.

The taxi swerves through the crowded streets of Portland, and I lean forward, scanning the buildings for any sign of a hotel vacancy. I try looking again at the multitude of travel apps I have on my phone, but everything is grayed out, mocking me with a 'sold out' banner. The driver glances at me in the rearview mirror, his eyes sympathetic.

"Tough luck with all these flight cancellations, huh?" he says, shaking his head. "Seems like everyone's stranded."

I nod, my attention still focused on the passing storefronts. "You wouldn't happen to know of any hotels with available rooms, would you?"

He chuckles. "Wish I could help, but I've been driving folks around all day, and every place is booked solid."

I slump back against the seat, my mind racing. I can't spend the night wandering the streets of Portland. I need a plan.

As if on cue, my phone rings. It's my mother. I hesitate for a moment before answering, bracing myself for the inevitable barrage of questions.

"Rachel, honey, are you alright? Your sister told me what happened with your flight."

I sigh, rubbing my temple. "I'm fine, Mom. Just trying to find a place to stay for the night."

"Oh, sweetheart, don't be like Mary and Joseph and end up in a manger. Why not just rent a car and come join us at Lake Michigan? We'd love to have you."

I'm not sure Mom fully comprehends just how far I am away from Wisconsin. "Mom, it would take me days to drive back to... Hang on? You're with Claire?"

"Yes, when they dropped you off at the airport, Richard drove over and asked if I'd like to take your spot. So here I am. Between you and me, I think they just wanted a babysitter, but I'll not look a gift horse in the mouth. Come on, join us."

The thought of spending the rest of my vacation with my

family is tempting, given that the alternative is spending it alone in a strange city. I'm about to give Mom's suggestion some serious consideration when the taxi passes a massive industrial complex, the sign reading "Harcourt Foods" in bold letters.

Suddenly, an idea takes root in my mind. Harcourt Foods is one of the largest frozen food manufacturers in the country. If I could land them as a client...

"Rachel? Are you still there?"

I snap back to the present. "Yeah, Mom, I'm here. Listen, I appreciate the offer, but I think I'm going to stay in Portland for a bit. There's something I need to take care of."

"Are you sure, honey? We'd really love to see you."

"I know, and I promise I'll make it up to you. But this is important."

There's a pause, and I can almost hear the wheels turning in her head. "Well, alright then. I can't say I understand you at all. Promise you'll call if you need anything?"

"I will. Thanks, Mom. Love you."

As I hang up, I lean forward, tapping the driver on the shoulder. "Actually, could you take me to the nearest car rental place?"

He nods, merging into the turning lane. I sit back, my mind already formulating a plan. Partnership or not, I'm not leaving Maine empty-handed.

Harcourt Foods, here I come.

The car rental place is a hive of activity, with frazzled travelers scrambling to secure vehicles. I join the line, tapping my foot impatiently as I scroll through my phone, gathering as much intel on Harcourt Foods as I can. Their CEO, Jonathan Harcourt, has something of a reputation as a die-hard traditionalist. Referred to as 'Old Man Harcourt' by friend and foe alike, he's certainly not known for his commitment to innovation and sustainability. A poultry industry stalwart, it's going to be a hard sell to convince him to diversify from the frozen chicken nuggets that built his empire.

But... thanks to my market research for GreenShoots and IncrediBurger, I have data. Lots of it. Compelling, detailed facts and figures that show a shift in eating habits and a growing demand for plant-based alternatives. If I can pitch CGPR as the agency to revamp their public image and convince him that plant means profit, it could be a game-changer.

Lost in thought, I startle when the clerk calls, "Next!"

I step up to the counter, flashing my most charming smile. "Hi there. I need to rent a car, preferably something electric, compact, and efficient."

The clerk, a young man with a name tag reading "Ethan," looks at me apologetically. "I'm sorry, ma'am, but we're pretty much out of everything due to the flight cancellations. The only vehicle we have left is a pickup."

I blink, processing this information. A pickup truck? That's about as far from my sleek, urban, green lifestyle as it gets. But beggars can't be choosers, right?

"I'll take it," I say, handing over my credit card.

Minutes later, I'm staring at a behemoth of a truck, its red paint gleaming under the lot lights. I clamber into the driver's seat, adjusting it to accommodate my shorter stature. The engine roars to life, and, truth be told, I can't help but grin. There's something empowering about being behind the wheel of this beast. It pains me to think it, but maybe, just maybe, I can understand why Zoe chooses to drive her Mustang despite the societal pressure to drive electric.

As I navigate the unfamiliar streets of Portland, my mind races with ideas for a potential Harcourt Foods pitch. I'll emphasize CGPR's track record with green initiatives, our innovative social media strategies, and our ability to connect with younger, eco-conscious consumers. Driving almost on instinct, I've left the city and find myself in the quieter suburbs.

Signs for Biddeford start to appear and as I'm approaching the city limits, I find a quaint motel on the outskirts of town, its neon 'vacancy' sign a beacon of hope after a very trying few hours. The owner, a gentleman in his early forties, introduces himself as James, insists on carrying my carry-on case to my room, and hands me a key with a knowing smile.

"Just call down to the front desk if you need anything," he says kindly.

I nod gratefully, suddenly feeling the weight of the day catching up with me.

"Thank you. I will."

BINGE THE SERIES

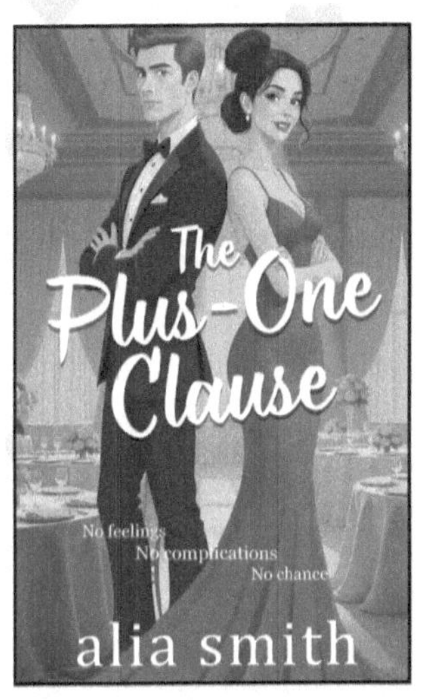

SUBSCRIBE TO ALIA'S MAILING LIST
&
RECEIVE YOUR FREE NOVELLA

www.aliasmithbooks.com

AUTHOR'S NOTE

Hi,

Thanks so much for reading *Bookish with Benefits*!

It was a lot of fun to write. I truly hope it was an entertaining read.

If you enjoyed the book, I would be incredibly grateful if you'd be so kind as to leave a review.

Reviews really help authors for a number of reasons, not least, providing feedback on what readers like and improving visibility of the book on online retail sites.

Thanks in advance and I look forward to reading your thoughts.

Alia xx

www.ingramcontent.com/pod-product-compliance
Lightning Source LLC
Chambersburg PA
CBHW030535190726
48283CB00006B/1932